The Mermaid's Song

"A lyrically woven tale that glows with romance, pulses with suspense, and shimmers with magic."

—Nora Roberts

"It is impossible to resist the lure of THE MERMAID'S SONG. From beginning to end, this love story, entwined with passion, intrigue, and mystical charms, held me in its spell."

—Julie Garwood

"In the grand tradition of Victoria Holt, Phyllis Whitney, Daphne du Maurier, and Madeleine Brent, Marianne Willman brings together the tangled thread of suspense, the mystical, and pure romance."

—*Romantic Times*

"A dynamic read . . . tantalizing . . . will thrill fans."

—*Affaire de Coeur*

The Enchanted Mirror

MARIANNE WILLMAN

St. Martin's Paperbacks

THE ENCHANTED MIRROR

Copyright © 1999 by Marianne Willman.

ISBN: 0-312-97080-3

Printed in the United States of America

St. Martin's Paperbacks edition/August 1999

St. Martin's Paperbacks are published by St. Martin's Press, 175 Fifth Avenue, New York, N.Y. 10010.

10 9 8 7 6 5 4 3 2 1

FOR PAT CARROLL
COUNSELOR, FRIEND AND GUARDIAN ANGEL
WITH LOVE

Prologue

ENGLAND, 1890

Crystals tinkled in the great chandelier overhead as Tess, the young Countess of Claybourne, came softly down the grand staircase. She and her new husband had only come up from the country two weeks earlier, and she was still overwhelmed by the splendor of his palatial London mansion.

As she passed the great arched window on the landing, the reflection from her wedding ring temporarily dazzled her. Diamonds caught the September sun in a sparkling web of light, while the exquisite, deep red-orange gem they circled burned ember-bright against her skin.

The *padparadschah* sapphire came from Ceylon, and had been in the Claybourne family for over a hundred years. Like everything else in the mansion, the exquisite sunset-hued gem bespoke exquisite taste, elegance, and immense wealth.

I am, Tess thought with a pang, *the only imitation here.*

Despite her fashionably coiffed black hair, her pearl and topaz earrings, and morning gown of cream-colored silk, she was out of her element. A pretender, playing the role of great lady, while inside she was still Miss Mallory, the eldest daughter at tumbledown Swanfield Manor, wearing made-over, hand-me-down clothes. Her sole ambition then had been to marry Roman McKendrick and live happily ever after with him in a rose-covered cottage.

Instead she was a countess, mistress of a London mansion, a grand country manor, and the owner of more gowns and jewels than she had ever imagined.

Had Cinderella felt this way? she wondered. *Did she ever look about her splendid castle and wonder how on earth she'd come to be there? Or what her life would have been, had she never met her prince?* In the old storybooks, they never told what happened to the heroine after the happy ending.

"If she had any sense," Tess told herself sternly, "she hid her qualms and was exceedingly grateful!"

As she descended the stairs to the glittering foyer, the butler stood at one of the twin ormolu-mounted consoles, sorting the afternoon post. She saw with a sinking heart that there were a quantity of gilt-edged invitations addressed to her. Or rather, to the new Countess of Claybourne.

Tess was no fool: except for Pippa Drake, the wife of a rising young diplomat, she had made no real friends among the society matrons who sought her patronage.

She thought that she recognized the writing on one envelope, but the stamps were Austrian, and her husband was in Scotland. "Is there a letter come for me from Lord Claybourne, Desmond?"

The butler gave an uncharacteristic start. It was apparent he hadn't heard her quiet footfalls. He tucked the envelope in question into another pile.

"No, my lady. But there is one from Miss Mallory, and another from Miss Minerva."

Tess's face lit up. She missed her sisters dearly. "I cannot wait until the school term is over and they join us for the Christmas holiday."

Desmond smiled. "Indeed, the presence of the young

ladies does liven up the house. Shall I take these to the desk in the drawing room, my lady?"

"Yes, if you please."

She followed him into Claybourne House's famous White Drawing Room, where the only colors were the mellow wood of the furnishings and the white, green, and gold of the figured carpet. Over the past few weeks she had been thinking of smuggling a few pieces of the Chinese rose-patterned china past the vigilant housekeeper. *I should not feel like an intruder in my own drawing room,* she thought with a wry smile.

When the letters were placed on the rosewood desk by the window, the butler bowed and silently withdrew. Tess stared at the growing stack of invitations in dismay. "There must be twenty new ones, at the least!"

Sighing, she picked up the old silver dagger that served as her letter opener. Once again, the splendid Claybourne wedding ring flared like a miniature sun, sending scintillating rainbow lights dancing across the rosewood desk, the gilt and crystal inkwell, and the neat stacks of vellum envelopes.

The Titian-hued gem was mesmerizingly beautiful, but she wished it were smaller. Less freighted with tradition and other women's memories. Five other Claybourne brides had worn the heirloom jewel in decades past—and, of course, all of them were dead now. A tiny shiver danced along her spine, as if someone were standing behind her.

Glancing in alarm at the carved mirror over the desk, Tess saw only herself—a delicate dark-haired woman with emerald-green eyes; but her skin prickled and she felt as if there were shadows materializing behind her, an endless procession of Claybourne women, watching her take over the reins that their ghostly hands had once held. Weighing her. Judging her.

Finding her wanting.

Untrained as she was for the great estate to which marriage had elevated her, Tess knew her duty to her title, and to the Claybourne line. She intended to do all in her power to fulfill the role required of her.

Her chin lifted with determination and she spoke to the restless shades that seemed to fill the room: "You may rest in peace," she murmured. "I shall not fail you."

Despite her brave words the unsettled air lingered in the room, as if it were filled with a chorus of ghostly sighs.

Tess gave herself a mental shake. She had no time for such nonsense. The invitations must be dealt with, and there were letters to write. It was only Leland's absence and her own jitters at facing society without her husband's support that had her nerves so suddenly on edge. She would be glad to have him home again at month's end.

Setting aside the envelope from Judith, the older of her two sisters away at school—and sure to be filled with manifold complaints—she took up the other. She was always delighted to hear Minnie's latest adventures, and she slipped the tip of the silver dagger beneath the sealed wafer eagerly.

Tess was unaware of the cloud passing over the sun, changing the color of the jewel in her wedding ring to a rich crimson color—or of the way the dagger's polished surface caught its glow, giving the illusion that the thin, sharp blade dripped red with blood.

EGYPT

Roman McKendrick shaded his eyes against the molten Egyptian sun. There it was again, that blaze of brightness overhead, among the distant jumble of stones and rubble.

His skin was burned as brown as those of the workmen clearing fallen stone from the ancient ramp, but those dark-lashed eyes were the same faience-blue as the sky.

Another burst of light. He tried to pinpoint its exact location, but the harsh sun had bleached all color from the cliffs and wadis of the desert valley. Distance and perspective were distorted by the lack of shadows and the shimmering veils of heat.

The rush of excitement made his blood tingle; it might be nothing, or it might be everything—perhaps a vital clue to a new tomb, or the ancient temple of Isis he sought among the crags and folds of rock.

Instinct told him it was something very special. He called to his foreman directing the work below.

"Jamil, do you see that ray of light? Halfway up the wadi?"

The foreman shrugged and shook his head. "I see nothing, effendi."

Roman tilted his dark head back. Wiping his face with his handkerchief, he squinted against the glare, then cursed beneath his breath.

"It's gone."

Gone again. He was the only one who had ever seen it, yet he didn't doubt that something was there. *Something significant, damn it!*

He could feel it in his bones.

But *what*?

There was no way that Roman could have spotted the object that so intrigued him. From the valley floor the mirror lay near the top of the rugged wadi, hidden from view by the split tomb wall in front of it, and the jutting ledge above. Yet once a day, when the chariot of the sun raced across the burning blue sky, the life-giving rays struck the highly polished metal surface in a mute explosion of scintillating light.

While its reaction was spectacular, the mirror itself was rather plain: a wide oval set between stylized lotus blossoms, whose twined stems formed the openwork handle. Already ancient when the pyramids were young, the artifact was still as smooth and unblemished as the day it was made. No film of desert dust, no veil of tarnish or corrosion, marred its perfect luster.

There were times, though, when the mirror's surface seemed to come alive. Images floated like dreams just behind the glinting, metallic sheen: pharaohs and queens, peasants and priestesses, slaves and scribes, gave way to soldiers in Egyptian headdress, the kepis of Napoleon's armies, the crested bronze helmets of Imperial Rome.

Yet most of the time the mirror dreamed its own secret dreams, and showed nothing but the weathered, sun-leached rock and Egypt's vast, fathomless blue sky.

At the present moment the polished oval darkened, rippling with sudden iridescence. Colors and shapes bloomed like enchanted flowers, flowed into one another and coalesced. Phantasms of the future sprang to life.

Scenes drifted on the surface, shifting rapidly: Roman McKendrick, sitting in the shadows of a lamplit room, watching a woman sleep. Through the partially opened wooden shutters at the windows, a silver moon shone over a shimmering desert landscape.

Another ripple, another sudden shift: the scene was unmistakably England, cool and green. This time the mirror showed the same woman—dark-haired, green-eyed—sitting at a rosewood writing desk in warm afternoon sunlight, examining the large gemstone on her hand. It burned like a flame against the whiteness of her skin.

Shadows chased across the mirror's surface, like clouds racing before a storm. New shapes formed: a darkened room, shuttered against the heat of noon; the rumpled sheets of a bed hung with swaths of mosquito netting, like a bride's airy veil. And Tess, Lady Claybourne, at a dressing table, unaware that she was no longer alone.

Then, a series of quick impressions, flowing and fading into one another behind the mirror's surface, like water clouded by spreading ink. A shadow falls across Tess as the secret watcher closes in. In eerie silence the mirror reflects a heavy paperweight shattering the looking glass on the dressing table into a crystal web . . . a spill of face powder across the carpet . . . fleeting glimpses of Tess's eyes, widening with astonishment, and then with fear.

Light bounces off a silver dagger . . . thin and sharp and bright with blood.

Another shiver of silvery light washes it away, leaving an image of Roman McKendrick's tortured face, filled with wild passion and a terrible anguish.

Suddenly the angle of sunlight altered, and the magical images vanished in a twinkling. The mirror was covered in lavender shadow again, a smooth oval of burnished metal, blank as a shuttered eye.

PART ONE

ENGLAND

1

Roman McKendrick looked out his hotel window at the street below. Despite the early-December cold, London was thronged and noisy—far more so than he remembered it. Ten years had passed since he'd last seen a winter snowfall. Or England, for that matter.

The people in the street all seemed to be laughing and smiling. Perhaps it was the coming Christmas holiday, or the first glittery sprinkle of snow that had the crowds in so merry a mood.

A snowflake landed against the latticed window, a perfect white hexagon with spear-shaped points. As he watched, the soot of London's chimneys turned the snowflake gray. It melted away into bittersweet memories of English winters past, replacing more recent images of mosaic domes and gilded minarets, with stone church walls pierced by jeweled stained-glass windows; the odors of sandalwood incense and sweat with the fragrance of roasted goose and warm plum pudding.

He followed memory's golden trail until it turned to lead: his last Christmas in England. Roman remembered trying to catch snowflakes for the girl he'd known all his life—the girl he loved, and who he thought had loved him in return—so that she might examine it through his enlarging glass. And when they were finally alone for a few stolen moments that evening, he'd given his sweetheart a small gold locket with a tiny pearl in the center, and pledged his heart and hand to her.

She'd returned his promise and his kisses eagerly, and he'd told her then of Mr. Moss's offer of excavating in Egypt that season. It meant that they could marry in the summer. Oh, but he'd spun marvelous plans and dreams, whispered them into her ear.

He cursed softly. *What a fool I was! Better not to think of her. Not yet. Not until the moment comes—if it does— when I have no other choice.*

Try as he might, Roman found himself incapable of doing so. The ghosts of old emotions stirred his blood. He'd been young and romantic and passionately in love with her, sure she was innocent and true to the depths of her soul. Instead she had proved false and shallow and worldly, and she'd shattered his romantic idealism to shards.

What surprised him now was that the pain still felt so raw and new. He had known many women in the past ten years, but there was not a single one whose perfumed embrace had eased his heart. Nor, since that time, had he let any woman come close enough to bruise it again.

As if it were only a few days earlier, he relived the agony of the moment when he'd read her note—a note, by God!—releasing him from his promise of marriage. Asking him to release her from hers. He had read and reread it so many times, that the words had etched themselves on his memory:

"After much soul-searching," she had written, *"I have come to the conclusion that we are too young to know our own hearts, and that I am far too green a girl to enter the estate of matrimony without first having some experience of the world. I have gone up to London on a prolonged visit to my aunt Helmsley, where I hope to enjoy the ben-*

efits of more cosmopolitan society than can be found in a small village such as Swanfield.''

He'd left England for Egypt shortly after, and thrown himself into learning everything he could about his chosen profession. Up at dawn, to bed at midnight, hoping to make a name for himself. Hoping to forget her face, forever.

Not that he ever had . . .

And now little Tess Mallory, who had so blithely broken his young heart, was Lady Claybourne, and a countess to boot.

Worse, he had an appointment to meet with her husband at Claybourne House this very day. Cursing the irony of fate, Roman checked his pocket watch again, and poured himself another glass of brandy.

Inside the lobby of the newly chartered Claybourne Foundling and Charity Hospital, Tess's voice carried clearly, as she gave her prepared speech. She held on to the garlanded podium to keep her balance: her knees were shaky. This was her first appearance in an active public role as Lady Claybourne, rather than as a dashing member of high society. Fashionable lords and ladies, members of parliament, prominent citizens—representatives of the *haut ton*—were her audience today.

Many of the well-dressed women were important matrons who had visited her with their giggling, hopeful daughters, and there were also several of the more fashionable gentlemen in the audience—would-be friends and admirers of Tess, Countess of Claybourne: *Not,* she thought wryly, *of Tess Mallory, the penniless eldest daughter of a poor country gentleman.*

Her origins, while genteel and certainly respectable enough, were no recommendation to members of the *haut monde.* They had expected the Earl of Claybourne to choose a wife from within the highest circles—from among their *own* kind. Lord Claybourne's sudden engagement and marriage to a plain Miss Mallory, of whom none had ever heard mention, had shocked many and disappointed more.

The red-orange sapphire on her ring finger flashed like a live coal. Tess would never forget the words she'd overheard Lady Ottily whisper at her wedding feast: *"And who is she, a mere nobody, to be elevated to the stature of countess, when my own dear daughters have so much more breeding and refinement to recommend them?"*

At the time Tess had wanted to sink into the ground. Six months of marriage to one of the first lords of the land had given her more backbone. She knew no fault could be found with her fashionable outfit of green faille trimmed with black military braiding, and a smart matching hat. *Odd, how the proper garments can give one a modicum of courage,* she thought, lifting her chin and smiling coolly at the haughty Duchess of Devonshire.

She had been sure she could pull it off without disgracing herself by forgetting her speech halfway through; thus far it had gone smoothly, but beneath the snugly fitted bodice, with its faceted jet buttons, her heart was hammering. The last time she'd given a speech it had been a stern instruction to her two sisters, Judith and Minnie, on how young ladies of quality conducted themselves—and it had been given in the privacy of her own bedchamber, not in public.

"It is the intention of the Claybourne Foundling and Charity Hospital Committee," she continued, "to use every scientific means of child-rearing and education to see that these children are healthy in body and in spirit. It is our most sincere hope that you will join with us in our endeavor to provide a haven of succor and safety for those unfortunate little ones who are orphaned or abandoned in the streets. To that effect, we ask that you continue your generous support and patronage . . .''

She waited as the polite applause swelled, indicating their willingness to continue their charitable contributions. Her husband caught her eye. Leland looked so proud that Tess felt herself blushing.

He was tall and fair, a gentle, kindly man some eight years older than she, and more enamored of his books and antiquities than sporting pursuits or gaming. He indulged her shamelessly. Tess hoped she would not disgrace him with some terrible gaffe today—and promptly lost her place. For a moment she went absolutely blank with panic.

Oh, dear God, where did I leave off?

Turning over a sheet of her notes to gain time, she kept her outward composure, a trait she'd fostered when she nursed her mother during her final illness. Over the years it had become ingrained: duty over emotion, others before self. It was only what was expected of any gentlewoman. She had learned the lesson at her mother's knee—and learned it well.

She must not think of herself, but of the foundlings who would be saved from a terrible fate in the streets of London, and of her sister-in-law's devotion to the cause: Alicia had worked long and hard to make this hospital possible.

Tess's mind cleared. *Ah, yes! The top of page three.* She found her place and went on. ''There are those who claim the poor should be left to fend for themselves; but a wealthy and civilized society cannot afford to harden its heart to those less fortunate . . .''

Almost finished now. *Only the conclusion and thank-you's to get through.* It took great effort of will to keep her voice from quivering with relief as she expressed her gratitude to the hospital's sponsors.

''. . . and last but certainly not least,'' she said, rushing a bit, ''our deepest gratitude to Lady Alicia Evershot and the Children and Foundlings Charity Committee, for their dedication to making this project become a reality.''

There was a burst of applause, and as she stepped back from the podium the Lord Mayor thrust a pair of gold shears in her hand. "But I am not to cut the ribbon," she whispered. "Lady Alicia . . ."

She looked over helplessly at her sister-in-law, but Alicia shook her head and smiled. There was nothing for Tess to do but snip the blue satin ribbon and officially open the charity hospital herself.

Afterward the Lord Mayor offered Tess his arm and escorted her down the length of the hall to the refreshment table. En route, she lost track of her husband and sister-in-law in the crowd. One moment Leland and Alicia had been at Tess's elbow, the next she was surrounded by various dignitaries offering their congratulations.

The Duchess of Devonshire was quite pleased with Tess's performance. "You did charmingly, Lady Claybourne. Quite charmingly!"

Someone put a glass of punch into Tess's hand and then a tall young man came up and presented her with an elegant bow. He had golden hair, thick-lashed dark eyes, and was dressed in the first stare of fashion. Indeed, Tess thought, he was the most elegant young man she had ever seen.

"My congratulations, Lady Claybourne," he said silkily. "No one could guess that you hadn't been opening fairs and making dedication speeches all your life."

The insult was subtle, but pointed. Tess felt her cheeks flaming. Her sister-in-law appeared beside the newcomer. Alicia sized up the situation instantly.

"Ah, Edgar. What a surprise! We are honored that you roused yourself so long before evening to attend this event."

He ignored the sting in her words. "*Dearest* Cousin

Alicia, how could I not? Since I haven't been invited to Claybourne House of late, it seemed the only way I could meet the newest addition to our . . . ah, cozy little family. Did my appearance wrest you from your brother's side?''

Alicia flushed unbecomingly. The scarcely veiled animosity between the two startled Tess, especially in a place where they might be easily overheard. The young man seemed to read her mind.

''Do not be alarmed, Lady Claybourne. All the world and his wife knows there is no love lost between the two branches of our family. Allow me to introduce myself. I am Brocklehurst.''

Tess gave him her hand reluctantly. ''How do you do, Mr. Brocklehurst.''

He kissed the air above her glove with exquisite panache, but made a moue of disappointment. ''I see that you have been remiss in your duties, Alicia.'' He turned his attention back to Tess.

''Brocklehurst is my title, Lady Claybourne. As in 'the Marquis of Brocklehurst.' '' His smile grew. ''I am—for the moment, at least—second in line to your husband's titles and estate.''

Sketching another bow, he stepped back and was soon lost in the crowd. ''What an extraordinary creature!'' Tess exclaimed in astonishment.

Alicia shrugged. ''His rudeness, like that of his father, is already legendary.''

People came up to congratulate Tess and Alicia and there was no further time to talk privately.

Time at last! Roman had been watching the hands of his watch creep by for the past hour. He took up his gloves and hat, wondering why he had been counting the minutes so impatiently. ''Unless it is the human wish to put an unpleasant situation behind one as soon as possible!''

Taking up a small leather case, he went down and hailed

a hackney in the street. He was completely unaware of the attention he attracted. It was as much his height and sun-bronzed skin that made him stand out from the pale Londoners, as the intangible air with which he carried himself.

The hackney driver, who'd served in the army, quickly sized up his new fare: *A gentleman, for all his skin is burnt brown as Bombay beggar.* One used to giving orders, not taking them. Not even the rashest footpad in Seven Dials would dare to accost him in a dark alley. *Looks like those blue eyes of his could see through steel, they do.*

He grinned cheekily. "Where to, your lordship?"

Roman laughed. "Save your flattery for someone who can afford a larger tip than I. I'm going to Claybourne House. Do you know it?"

"That I do, my lord. And if you're welcome to visit there, I'll not believe you to be a scaly nip-cheese like some of these riffraff clogging the streets."

Roman sat back against the worn leather seat, trying to relax. Depending on how his luck was running, this afternoon might be one of the best or one of the worst in his life to date.

It wasn't the vague implication that the Earl of Claybourne might be interested in funding his excavations that had lured him back to London, as much as Lord Claybourne's invitation to examine several papyrus scrolls he had acquired. Claybourne House had been the country seat of the earls for almost seventy years before London's increasing sprawl had surrounded it. It was renowned for its collection of antiquities.

Roman didn't want to give the earl's allusions to funding his work too much weight just yet. From experience he knew that hints and promises had a way of vanishing like English fog—but the Egyptian scrolls in Claybourne's possession were very real. He'd been trying to track their whereabouts himself, until they turned up in London. And, if what he knew of them was true, they might lead him closer to his goal: the earliest recorded temple of the goddess Isis.

He'd found mention of the temple on stone stelae, and the wall of a noblewoman's tomb. From his research he hoped that more definite information could be gleaned from the newest papyrus fragments residing in the Claybourne library. His hands, strong and tanned, flexed inside his gloves. He literally itched to get them on the ancient manuscripts. When he did, he would touch them with as much skill and tenderness as he would a lover.

Roman felt his throat go dry with anticipation. If only the hints of what the scrolls contained proved true! Then perhaps the cursed misery of his visit to Claybourne House could be turned to something good.

The hackney rounded a corner and Roman laughed in spite of himself. Ten years since he'd seen England, and he was so intent on the scrolls—on the possibility of seeing Tess once more—that he'd forgotten to look at his surroundings. New buildings had gone up in the past decade, and there was much to see.

He tried to turn away from his thoughts to the view. The attempt wasn't a success. As the vehicle turned from Picadilly Circus into Regent Street, it rumbled over a rough patch. He muttered a sharp oath beneath his breath.

"Sorry, guv'nor," the driver called out.

Roman's mouth flattened in a hard line. But it was not the sudden jolt that made him grimace; it was the bitterness of remembering. The anticipation of opening old wounds that still went deep. With every turn of the hackney's wheels, they became more painful.

Until today, opening that note from Tess had been the worst moment of his life. He anticipated that seeing her again, as the wife of his benefactor, would run a close second.

Roman leaned back against the seat, cursing Tess's long-ago cruelty. Cursing himself more, for still caring.

Tess's stomach was still jittery when the affair ended, and she and Alicia were alone in their carriage at last. The groom closed the door, then jumped on the back and the carriage started off. "But . . . where is Leland?"

"He asked me to make his excuses. He must stop by his club on an urgent matter of business."

As their carriage pulled away from the curb, they were suddenly cut off by a larger and more ornate vehicle, all done in lacquered black and gold. Lord Brocklehurst put his head out the window and waved his hat at them.

"Until we meet again, fair ladies!" He signaled the driver and his equipage took off at a speed more suited to an open road.

Tess eyed his departure in relief. "Insufferable! Is he indeed your cousin. And a marquis?"

"Oh, yes," Alicia said wryly. "Edgar has more titles than a lending library. But it is his father—the Duke of Audley—who is directly in line." She frowned. "*He* is even more arrogant than Brocklehurst! And his estates are so vast it galls me to think that he might one day add Leland's lands and titles to them."

She put a gloved hand to her mouth and made a small sound of distress. "Oh! I did not mean . . ."

"I understand you," Tess said quietly. "If I do not give Leland a son to inherit, everything will pass to the duke and his heir."

Alicia looked near tears. "My dear, it is early days yet. Scarcely six months since your wedding day."

"Yes." Tess laced her fingers and looked down. She would dearly love to have a child, but the way things were . . .

She sighed. There was still hope. "My mother was married almost five years before she bore me. Then she lost several children before producing the rest of the family.''

"Did she, indeed?" Alicia still looked upset. "Let us hope you are more fortunate, my dear."

Tess's skin flushed with delicate color. She would not dash Alicia's spirits for anything, but she greatly feared there might be no children at all from her marriage.

Her sister-in-law saw Tess's distress, and tried to make up for her gaffe. "Your father and mother both came from large families, I believe?"

"Yes. Mama had three older brothers—all killed in the service of the Queen in India. Papa was one of seven sons," Tess said. "His brothers emigrated to New Zealand well before I was born. It is strange to think there are likely dozens of cousins half a world away, whom I have never seen."

When they turned up Regent Street she turned the conversation from an uncomfortable subject. "My dear, I am awed at the way you have worked so long and diligently on setting up the foundling hospital. I was most dismayed when the Lord Mayor asked me cut the ribbon. That honor belonged to you, Alicia."

Her sister-in-law smiled. Although she was called "Lady Alicia," in a system where only the eldest male inherited, her title was merely an honorary one. Her brother was noble, while she was merely an aristocrat, and used the family last name of Evershot.

"Do not blame Sir Gerald, I beg of you. It was at my direction. It is far more important that you do the honors. As for myself, why, I am perfectly happy administering the foundation from behind the scenes."

"You are far too modest," Tess replied, but let the matter rest.

Alicia hated to be thrust into the public eye. Even her clothes seemed chosen to make her vanish into the woodwork, unflattering shades of fawn and brown and taupe. While Leland's sister could never be a beauty, she could look quite tolerable in warmer tones of peach or rose, but well-meaning suggestions were of no avail—the liveliest color Tess had ever seen Alicia wear had been an overly trimmed ballgown in a most unfortunate shade of puce.

"Shall Leland be long at his club?"

"I think not," his sister replied. "He is expecting a visitor. One of those fusty scholars with whom he corresponds is coming to examine and translate his newly acquired Egyptian papyrus. Leland may fund his further research."

Tess looked out the window at the busy London streets. People hurrying here and there, with purpose. Alicia had plans to meet with the directors of the Victoria and Albert Museum, while Leland intended to closet himself with yet another scholar of antiquities. Meanwhile, she would have the rest of the afternoon all to herself. Again.

Their carriage turned down a fashionable avenue, blocked by carriages disgorging their passengers, or pulled to while society matrons bowed and nodded to one another. It was a ritual that Tess had found exciting once upon a time, but now found boring.

As I do so very much these days!

She scolded herself. When she'd been acting as companion to her aunt Helmsley, with never a moment to rest, Tess had envied grand ladies their leisure. Things looked very different from this side of the proverbial fence. She had little in common with the matrons of the *haut monde,* not because of her birth or breeding, but because she had been used to occupying her days more diligently.

The problem was that at both Claybourne House and Claybourne Castle everything was done so efficiently, so competently, under Alicia's skilled hand, that Tess felt like an unused cog in a great, oiled machine. She needed something more than ballgowns and rides in the park to occupy her time. She was not cut out to be another ornament in her husband's drawing room.

The wives of politicians and policy makers, whose interest lay in furthering their husbands' careers, were far more interesting, but they tended to move in other circles, that touched hers only briefly. Most women at Tess's new level of society were interested in gowns and balls, in marrying off their sons and daughters advantageously, and in gossiping about one another. Her sister-in-law was the exception to the rule.

What a wickedly ungrateful creature I am! I should thank my lucky stars that Leland offered for me and made it possible for Judith and Minnie to have every advantage in life.

Alicia lifted an expressive eyebrow. "You sighed so soulfully. Are you tired? Or merely feeling a letdown now that the excitement is over?"

The ridiculousness of her discontent piqued Tess's ready sense of humor. Her lips curved in a small smile. "Neither. But if you should ever discover that I have taken up harp lessons, or you walk in upon me busily knotting a fringe, you shall know I am bored beyond hope of all salvation!"

Her sister-in-law laughed. "Your mind is too lively for that. And this afternoon there are so many things to do. Why, you must approve the menus for the coming week, and meet with Mrs. Pierce about arrangements for your sisters' arrival."

"Both mere formalities. The chef would be up in arms if I should try and tamper with his plans, and Mrs. Pierce has an eye like a camera, and can likely name the exact place that every item in the house belongs, to the inch. I expect to find that she has taken this opportunity to take all the Chinese vases from the White Drawing Room, where I had them moved and put back into their former places.''

''Jest if you like,'' Alicia chuckled, ''but your position is still one of great responsibility. You should go up to your room and rest a while. I would not wish you to over-exert yourself after today's excitement.''

That, Tess thought, *would take an act of Providence.* Leaning back against the velvet squabs, she resigned herself to just another quiet evening at Claybourne House.

''Mind your horses, man!''

Roman cursed. A horn blared. The hackney driver almost ran the vehicle up on the sidewalk as he was cut off by an elegant carriage, elaborately rigged with gold trim.

''It wasn't my fault, guv'nor,'' he exclaimed. ''That ham-handed sprig is the Marquis of Brocklehurst. Thinks he drives to an inch, that lad.''

Roman caught only a glimpse of a young man with curly fair hair and arrogant face, manhandling a pair of prime chestnuts. The aristocratic driver's curses mingled with the shrieks of pedestrians as men, women, and children raced to safety. The horses almost reared before he got them in control and went clattering down the street.

''The young ass!'' Roman said thunderously. ''Some-one should take a horsewhip to him.''

The driver chuckled. ''Sounds like you'd be willing to put your own hand to the task.''

''Only let me have the chance, by God!''

''Too much wealth and pleasure at too early an age. Ruins a man,'' the hackney driver said.

''Well, he'll be dead before he reaches the quarter-century mark, at the rate he's going.''

At least the near miss had taken Roman's mind off his destination for a few minutes. The farther the hackney got from the hotel, the more he regretted the decision that had brought him this far. For a moment he was sorely tempted to tell the driver to turn around and take him back to his hotel.

Instead he squared his shoulders. Too late now. And he was too close to making a major discovery to turn away because of old hurts and injured pride.

His discomfort grew as the driver left the busier areas and turned up quiet streets and secluded squares, where sleeping gardens in fenced enclosures were surrounded by elegant mansions.

The only sounds that filtered here were the clip-clop of the horses' hooves and the piercing warble of a female voice—young and exceedingly affected—from behind a closed window: *"Lu-huh-huh-huv's ta-roooo-hoo-hoo vow-ow-ows!"*

"Good God, the woman has lungs to rival a steam calliope!" Roman shuddered with sympathy for anyone beneath the same roof.

Too soon, the hackney pulled up at the front of a most imposing façade. "Here you are, guv'nor. Claybourne House." The driver grinned. "House, hah! Looks more like a palace to such as me."

Roman laughed without much conviction, then jumped down and tipped the driver handsomely. "Any man who can keep a hackney from being overturned, as you did, deserves it," he told the surprised driver.

The driver saluted him. "I knew you was a toff, guv'nor."

As the vehicle pulled away Roman glanced up at the sparkling windows and creamy limestone of Claybourne House. He wished he could find a hint of extravagant vulgarity in the stunning classical façade, but it was faultlessly elegant. He paused before ascending the flight of stairs.

Roman took a deep breath. *Ah, Tess!*

She had always reminded him of Briar Rose in the old

fairy tales—"Hair as black as night, lips red as blood, and skin as white as snow." He wondered if she had changed, if she were still as beautiful as he remembered.

Squaring his jaw, the man who had with dispatch faced down brigands and tomb robbers, cobras and scorpions and even a crocodile, mounted the curving stone staircase and steeled his nerves for the ordeal that might await him within: a face-to-face meeting with the only woman he had ever loved—and lost.

His muscles were knotted with tension. Inside he would find the end of one dream—but perhaps, if fortune favored him, the beginning of another.

Tess pressed her signet into a daub of hot wax on a folded piece of vellum. "Done at last!"

While most people used simple wafers to seal their letters nowadays, a lady of her status was expected to be more formal and conservative in official replies. *So many rules! So many things to learn—and unlearn.*

Waiting for the wax to harden, she straightened the stack of finished notes on her writing table, and smiled in relief. After changing out of the ensemble she'd worn earlier and slipping into an ivory silk-and-lace "at home" dress, she'd managed to keep busy.

She'd sent acceptances to five balls, several diplomatic receptions, a state dinner, the opera as guests of General Tate, and an "intimate" party to be given by Lady Warwick—which would likely draw everyone who was in town this early in the Season. Now she had only to take a nap or find a book to while away the hours until dinner.

In the five months since my marriage, I have spent more time accomplishing less than I ever thought possible!

Tess was startled from her thoughts when the tall drawing room doors were thrown open. Desmond stepped just inside.

"Mr. Roman McKendrick, my lady."

The butler's simple announcement had a profound effect on Tess. As she turned in her chair her jeweled wedding ring snagged the quill pen from the open inkwell. An arc of blue-black dots appeared like magic across her the skirt of her ivory dress. She covered them with her hand.

The butler bowed out and closed the doors, leaving Tess shaken and alone with the visitor.

"Roman?" The word was scarcely a whisper.

She rose without realizing she had gotten to her feet. Her heart pounded and all the air seemed gone from the room. Tess looked at him as if he were a phantom. The years rolled back. She was sixteen again. Her head filled with fairy tales and the romantic adventures of trembling heroines and dashing heroes, culled from the pages of the subscription library. A green girl, falling wildly in love with dashing Roman McKendrick and his stormy blue eyes.

She stared at him in disbelief. Time had fined down the handsome, gangling youth to a lean, weather-bronzed man with sharp cheekbones, sun lines radiating from the corners of his eyes, and deep grooves bracketing his firm, sensuous mouth.

But his eyes were still the same. Oh, yes! That burning blue gaze still had the power to rob her of breath.

He stood silently, watching her with an inscrutable expression on his face. He seemed to radiate antagonism. Surprise at finding him in her drawing room made Tess blurt out the first thing that came into her head.

"Why, Roman! You're the last person I would ever have expected to see here at Claybourne House."

"Am I?" His jaw hardened in the stubborn way she remembered so well. "Forgive me, *Lady Claybourne,* if I find that difficult to believe!"

His meaning baffled her. His anger was like a slap in

the face. She lifted her head and tried to keep her voice light. "I don't understand why you should. The last I heard, you were carousing in Cairo and trying to scare up funds to go searching for gold in the Sudan."

Roman's smile was bitter, but it still managed to make her blood pound. "That was ten years ago." He glanced around the room with its fabulous coffered ceiling, and famous paintings. "A far cry from Swanfield, isn't it? A lot has changed since then. Not you, of course: even then you aimed high."

His disdain lashed her like a scourge. Tess felt her color mount. "I see you are determined to dislike me."

"Not without reason."

Roman wished he hadn't come to London. Everything was going wrong. His instinct was to turn on his heel and leave. He'd known from the start that he might have to face Tess, and thought he'd been prepared for this moment. After all, he'd had the entire voyage back from Egypt to whip up the old anger. To plan out the cool and formal way he'd greet her if they met again. He'd been so sure he was free of her.

He'd been wrong.

He knew it the moment the drawing room door had opened and he saw her at the desk by the window. She was far more elegant and beautiful than he remembered. But still his Tess.

Then the ring she wore on her left hand caught the light in a blaze of orange fire, and the fact of her marriage was suddenly more than a few lines in a newspaper. It became cold reality.

No, by God, she is someone else's problem now!

His mind accepted it; his emotions couldn't.

The impact of seeing her was like a spear to the heart. He swore he could feel the piercing cold of the steel through the center of his chest. Even that couldn't compete with the swift rush of heat to his loins, the violent surge of longing. The need to protect, and to possess.

He felt a film of sweat along his brow. Roman's hands knotted at his sides as he fought for control. God help him—after all this time, after all the pain, he still wanted her! The urge to stride across the carpet and pull her roughly into his arms was almost overwhelming. To kiss her long and deep, until the past and present merged in a blur of need.

After ten long years, the magic was still there. She still had power over him, and he hated her for it.

Damn it to hell! I should never have left Cairo!

As always, Roman used anger as both shield and sword. He glanced about the White Drawing Room, sparked by glittering gilt and faceted crystal in the golden afternoon light. He willed his voice to be cool and remote.

"My congratulations, Tess. I see your plans to better yourself have exceeded even *your* high ambitions. You have snared yourself quite a prize. Whatever it took to lure Claybourne into your clutches was well worth the effort: You've landed in the proverbial cream pot."

The savagery of his words stunned her. Tess folded her hands to hide their shaking, unaware that the spreading ink stains on her skirt were staining her fingers black. "You have always misjudged me, Roman."

"Have I?"

Her lips trembled. "I never knew you to be cruel! It ill suits you."

Roman was almost ashamed. Suddenly he couldn't stand to watch the ink smear across white skin, like a contagion. He crossed the room and took her hand, dabbing at the smears of ink on it with his handkerchief. It was a test of his will power. The second their hands touched the old magic was there—at least for him. And the old conflict: he didn't know whether he wanted to take her shoulders and shake her, or pull her into his arms and kiss her until he was sated.

The jewels at her ears and throat reminded him—as if he needed any prompting—of the great gulf between them. Tess's fingers trembled in his, but whether from fury or some other emotion, he couldn't tell.

His own were unsteady. He couldn't believe she was real. She looked like a grown-up and even more beautiful version of the same Tess who had kissed him and pledged her love, who had promised to be his wife—and then taken it all back, in that goddamned note!

Tess was remembering the past, too. She'd thought that she'd put it all behind her, that what was done was done. Her emotions had been in such tight control for so long that she'd thought, when he'd first entered the drawing room, that she could pull it off. Let Roman think his surprise appearance had no effect upon her at all. Tess had had such a good deal of practice in hiding her passions, she'd almost convinced herself she had none at all.

But the touch of his strong, hard hand against her palm caught Tess in a tangle of conflicting feelings: heat and cold, joy and dismay, rejection and terrible yearning. The urgent impulse to flee the room—or conversely, to fling herself into his strong arms and pray to go back in time.

Roman dropped her hand, as if her confusion had passed to him. Tess took a small step backward.

"I wish you hadn't returned to England," she said quietly.

"No more than I."

He moved about the room, with the stride of a man more used to the outdoors. His restless, masculine energy filled the room, diminishing its size, making the heavily carved furnishings, the superb porcelain pieces, seem gaudy and frivolous in comparison. Tess stood quietly by the desk, a pool of studied calm, while inside her emotions were roiling.

"Why *have* you come?" she said abruptly.

He whirled about angrily. "Just how long do you mean to keep up the pretense? I was to meet Lord Claybourne here this afternoon, at his request. A command performance!"

"But . . . could he have forgotten? He went to his club earlier." *And left me here alone in this awkward predicament, without any warning.* But then, Leland never discussed business affairs with her.

"I didn't know that you and . . . and my husband were even acquainted."

"We've never met." His gaze held hers, his eyes dark and turbulent as a troubled sea. "Don't play games with me, Tess. This is all your doing!"

"This is *none* of my doing! " she snapped. "You insist on speaking in riddles, while I haven't the slightest notion of why you were invited here. Had I any inkling that you were in London, much less coming to Claybourne House, I would have taken myself off to the country!"

He was on his guard now. Tess had never been able to carry off a lie, even a well-intentioned one. Her face always gave her away. Either she'd become more skilled at it, or she was telling the truth. Perhaps it was all a coincidence. Roman changed his tactic.

"Then perhaps you can hazard a guess as to why your husband invited me to call upon him with promises of rare scrolls, and hints of funding my work in Egypt?"

"Did he, indeed?" Her too-pale skin suffused with delicate rose. "Oh, Roman, have you have found an untouched tomb?"

Tess's surprise and excitement echoed that in his own heart. "No. Not yet, but I'm closing in on something. I've found references . . . I can't say more just yet. But, oh,

Tess. I am very close to making an important discovery. I am sure of it!''

The glow in his eyes was just as she remembered. Time hadn't changed him. He still was as intense, as enthusiastic, as ever. She had fallen in love with him as a child, the first time they'd met. Not the silly crush of a young girl, but something far deeper.

The two of them would sit on the hill above the village with her sisters at play in the meadow, and he would tell her about the waves of invaders who had conquered Britain over the centuries, and left their mark on the land. About the legendary Egyptian empires, whose remnants he would uncover one day. And he had vowed to explore them, to reveal the secrets of the past, and bring the forgotten history of the ancients into the light of the present.

"I am happy for you, Roman. You have made your dreams come true.''

"Yes,'' he said wryly, "but I haven't had quite your success in doing so. Tell me, Tess, is it worth the price?''

"I don't pretend to understand your meaning,'' she said. But she wondered if he had heard of her husband's mistress.

Fannie Bonham had been an actress at the Haymarket in her prime—one of the Professional Beauties, like Lillie Langtry. Some claimed that she was still the most beautiful woman in all of England. It was whispered that Mrs. Bonham had been Leland's *cher amour* in his youth and that he had once published a book of sonnets in her praise.

Tess had been made aware of the former relationship between her husband and the older woman when she'd married him. Not, of course, in so many words. She had been gently given to understand, by Alicia, that Mrs. Bonham, who lived in one of the terraces in Bayswater, had been "a particular friend of Leland's in his youth.'' Someone else had hinted that Mrs. Bonham's son was actually Leland's bastard.

Whether or not he still visited Mrs. Bonham, she had no idea. In fact, if Tess were truthful, that had been one of the attractions of their arrangement: once a woman had provided her husband with an heir, his attentions at home were likely to slacken. A man who spent most of his time closeted with his precious books and artifacts, and another portion of it entertaining his mistress, was less likely to concentrate on pressing his marital claims at home.

A dull flush crept over her face. Thus far her plan had worked a little too perfectly.

Roman's hand curled over hers, a little too tightly. "What's the matter, Tess, did I cut too near the bone?"

"If you are bent on insulting me, I shall take my leave of you." She tried to wrench free, but he held her fast.

"Did you expect me to greet you with fond smiles for old times' saké, my dear? You turned down my honest proposal of marriage the moment your aunt Helmsley beckoned. You left me without so much as a good-bye, to fetch and carry for a venomous old woman, so that you would inherit her estate when she died. Evidently the life didn't suit you as well as had you had expected. Well, you have parlayed that small beginning into something grand!"

Tess was too angry and prideful to tell him her story. He didn't know, *couldn't* know, how hard it had been. She'd had nothing. Nothing but an aching heart, and a desperate determination.

"You forget that I was the eldest of three undowered sisters," she said heatedly. "Perhaps the situation is different in other countries. I have heard that in America a gentlewoman may have some sort of professional training, or run a business, and not lose her social status among her friends and townspeople. Her determination would be respected, her successes admired. But here in England, a woman who did so would fall so far beneath her place in society, that she would lose everything. You must see that!''

"I see that you have a need to defend yourself to me."

Her chin lifted proudly. "No, I do not! I did what had to be done. I owed it to my sisters to try and secure a future for *all* of us."

"Yes, and where are Judith and Minnie now, my fine titled lady? Not here with you at Claybourne House, I'm sure."

Fury shook Tess and tears of wrath stung her eyes. Over the years she had imagined a hundred times what her first meeting with Roman might be like, should their paths ever cross. Never, even in her wildest dreams, did she envision herself the object of such cruel scorn and contempt.

Roman smiled down at her grimly. "You have no answer for me?"

"None that you would care to hear!"

"Yes, I thought so. There is no place among your exalted company for two simply raised country misses. Just as there was no place for me among your ambitious plans. You use people, Tess, and discard them when you are done, as if they were empty walnut shells."

She wanted to slap the arrogance off his face. Her hand was half raised to do so, when the door suddenly opened. Unfortunately, it occurred at the exact moment that Roman had caught up both her hands in his, and yanked her closer.

They both gave a start when they heard the handle turn. Roman released her hands as if they'd scorched him, and Tess jumped back in alarm, glancing at the door.

Her husband stood just inside the drawing room, the light falling on his fair hair and aristocratic features.

"Ah, my dear," he said with exquisite politeness, "I see that you and Mr. McKendrick have made one another's acquaintance."

2

Tess pulled back at the same moment that Roman relinquished her hands. "Leland! I thought you were at your club!"

She colored, feeling the heat rise in her face as she imagined how it must look to her husband: returning home to discover his new wife holding hands with a virile and handsome man, both of them flushed and stained from the ink she'd smeared from her ruined gown.

And, to top it off, she had just blurted out what sounded like a line of dialogue from a drawing room farce.

Roman came to the rescue. "Lady Claybourne and I have been long acquainted, my lord. My grandfather's home was not far from Swanfield Manor, where her family resided."

"Indeed?" Leland smiled sweetly at Tess. "Indeed, you must have told me of it, my dear, and I have forgotten. My lamentable memory."

Roman shot her a quick, sardonic glance. He'd guessed from the start that she had had something to do with his being here, despite her earlier denials. Now her own husband seemed to confirm it.

Tess was intensely frustrated. *Leland's habitual vagueness makes me seem like a complete liar!*

She wished he could take back his words. She wished

herself anywhere but in the same room with the two men.

Most of all, she wished that her husband—the end product of generations of marriage in the same social circles—didn't look quite so tame and colorless beside Roman's hard-edged vigor. It was like comparing a purebred house cat to a Bengal tiger.

In her wildest fancies, she could not imagine her husband looking at her as if he wanted to throttle her, as Roman had a few minutes earlier. There was something dangerous and unpredictable about Roman; she could not imagine Leland doing anything more dangerous than venturing out on a chill morning without his muffler.

And even then, the butler would have to remind him to put it on!

Tess looked away, feeling ashamed for even thinking something so disloyal to Leland. And, unreasonably, she resented Roman for being the cause of it.

Leland was unaware of her turmoil. "I am certain now that my wife must have mentioned your earlier friendship." He favored Roman with a charming, self-deprecating smile. "I can recall dates of ancient kingdoms, yet frequently forget what day of the week it may be. My acquaintances accuse me of cutting them dead in the street, while I stroll along with my head in the clouds."

Lord Claybourne extended his hand to his guest, ignoring the smear of ink across Roman's left hand. "I must thank you, Mr. McKendrick, for coming all this way. I think you will not be sorry that you have done so."

It was the perfect cue for Tess to make her escape. "I shall leave you gentlemen to your business," she said. "I'm sure you have much to discuss, and I must change my gown."

"Very well, my dear. Before you are shown up to your suite, McKendrick, perhaps you would care to join me in a warming drink? It's getting quite cold outside." He strolled over to the decanters on the sideboard. "Brandy? Or would you prefer whisky?"

Tess stood frozen in place. Surely she couldn't have heard correctly.

Roman had the same reaction. "I believe there is a misunderstanding, Lord Claybourne. I am putting up at an hotel on the embankment, near Waterloo Bridge."

"Nonsense!" Leland shook his head. "I see in my haste to write you I did not make the matter clear, McKendrick. Of course you are to be my guest during your stay in England. I shall have Desmond send a groom to fetch your things immediately."

There was no polite way that Tess could protest her husband's invitation to house a guest beneath his own roof. Leland took Roman's stunned silence as acquiescence.

"There, that is settled. I shall show you my library. As I indicated, I have recently come into the possession of several papyrus fragments, which I am sure will interest you. This afternoon I have acquired another."

He gave his charming smile. "I am not an expert, of course, but it would seem to belong with the others."

The last comment swayed Roman's emotions from one extreme to another. He had been determined he would not spend another second beneath the same roof as Tess only moments ago. Now wild horses and a team of oxen couldn't have dragged him away.

Not, at least, until he'd examined the papyrus fragments.

The chance of adding to the knowledge of ancient Egypt was more than Roman could humanly refuse. "I accept your gracious offer, my lord."

It had taken an effort to get the words out. He'd forced himself to make it. There were unknown numbers of precious artifacts that could shed light on the past, locked away by wealthy collectors who didn't have a clue to their scholarly importance. Knowledge that could be lost forever.

God knows, the tomb looters have been carrying on their trade in Egypt since the first tombs were built. Greed is as old as mankind.

And, he thought with frustration, *there are always those willing to buy the stolen artifacts.* The only good thing was that nowadays, since the tomb robbers had become aware that the scrolls and ordinary items were as marketable as the gold and jewels, the precious manuscripts were being preserved instead of trampled underfoot or discarded.

"I shall look forward to viewing the papyruses, my lord."

As Leland poured out whisky, neat, into two crystal glasses, Tess realized she could finally make her escape with dignity. A word to Leland, a nod to Roman, and she exited the drawing room.

Once the doors were closed behind her by the footmen, she went quickly up the stairs and fled to the safety of her room. It was a grand chamber, with silk-covered walls in seafoam-green moiré, and a fabulous painted ceiling showing a rosy dawn sky. The suite was large, and she'd spent the first several nights alone in her huge, canopied bed, adrift in space like a castaway on a raft.

Now, knowing that Roman was beneath the same roof, the mansion felt a good deal smaller.

She was frankly amazed that her husband had been so calm at finding her in such a compromising state with Roman. Tess put a hand to her forehead. Other men might have thrown the visitor out of the house without waiting for an explanation. *Or their wife.*

Thank God Leland was a rational man. Or too well bred to bring the matter up. Aristocrats and noblemen had the most curious ways, she had discovered, taking umbrage at imagined slights to their high estate, yet pretending that some social embarrassments were completely invisible— until, presumably, they dealt with them later, behind closed doors. Perhaps that was it, the confrontation would come later.

She fumbled among her creams and lotions, looking for something that would get the ink stain off her hands. Her hands were shaking. *Roman, staying here! Seeing him at dinner every evening . . . I can't bear it!*

In her haste she knocked over a candlestick on her dressing table. Celeste, her dresser, came hurrying when she heard her mistress. She gave a loud gasp when she saw the ink stains on the ivory fabric.

"Oh, my lady! Your lovely dress, all ruined. I'm afraid I shall never be able to get the spots completely out."

Even if the gown could be restored to its former state, she knew that she could never bring herself to wear it again. "Don't even try. Get rid of it," Tess said.

"But it is one of my lady's favorites! A good deal of the silk is untouched. And the lace trim on the bodice could be saved."

Tess shivered. "If you can salvage anything of it for your own use, you are very welcome to it."

Celeste was delighted. Already she was planning to make a shirtwaist from the yards of precious silk, and detachable collar and cuffs to wear with her navy gown. Perhaps even line a short cape. How the other lady's maids would stare to see it!

"Oh, my lady! Thank you."

Tess smiled and nodded, but barely heard her maid's effusive thanks.

Celeste produced a bottle of a pungent liquid from the dressing room, and the ink stains came off Tess's hands fairly easily. "Shall I lay out your rose crêpe de chine with the velvet ribbons, my lady?"

"Yes. No!" She wanted to be alone. To think. "I believe I shall lie down a while, Celeste. Draw the curtains, if you please."

The maid hurried to comply. "Ah, my lady has the headache."

Yes, thought Tess, *a headache of epic proportions. And at the moment, he is downstairs in the drawing room, sharing a glass of whisky with my husband.*

"The library has been my life's work. It is my pride and joy," Lord Claybourne announced, as he led Roman down a wide corridor floored in white marble and edged in black.

As his host took him through the mansion, Roman sized up the man who had won Tess's hand in marriage. There was elegance in his every gesture, but he was no effete gentleman. He looked as if he could hold his own in a bout of fisticuffs, Roman judged.

The lucky devil has everything: wealth, privilege . . . Tess.

Long carpets in muted shades, specially commissioned for the mansion, muffled their footsteps. The busts of Roman emperors and gods watched their progress from deep wall niches set at intervals between the doors on one side. Priceless paintings of classical subjects hung on the walls between the tall windows on the other.

It was impressive for its design and architecture and the paintings and artifacts; but not quite as impressive to Roman as to most of Claybourne's visitors. He had stood at the base of the colossal columns of the Temple of Karnak, roamed Hatshepsut's elegant mortuary temple at Dier-el-Bahri, and climbed to the very top of Cheop's pyramid.

Whatever the accomplishments of the Claybournes might be, they paled in comparison to those remarkable achievements of the ancients. He was sure there was nothing here to awe him.

Except, perhaps, those papyrus scrolls which were the reason for his journey.

His host didn't stop until they reached a massive set of double doors at the far end. They were beautifully carved and inlaid with ornate bronze plates. "My great-grandfather brought these back from his travels."

Roman passed the unspoken test. "Wonderful work! Byzantine, third century, isn't it? I imagine they came from a Christian church in Constantinople before the Turks took over."

"You amaze me, McKendrick. I see why you were so highly recommended."

Claybourne opened one of the massive double doors to the library, and Roman's jaw finally dropped. Now *this* was an achievement of great merit. He had never seen such a collection outside of the British Museum. It was a treasure trove of knowledge and precious artifacts gathered from the ancient Egyptians, Greeks, and Romans. A life-sized statue of Athena regarded them gravely from a pedestal.

"You have created something wonderful here," Roman said sincerely. "I congratulate you, my lord."

Roman felt as if he'd stumbled into a scholar's wonderland. Two stories high, the magnificent walls of books rose up and up toward a domed glass skylight. An enormous gaslight chandelier hung from its center, providing light by day or night.

There were locked, grill-fronted cabinets, rows of drawers for holding maps, portfolios of drawings, and architectural renderings. Two massive globes stood in a window bay, one of the earth and the other of the heavens. A jeweled orrery, showing the rotation of the planets around the sun, rested on the pedestal beside them.

"You have an amazing collection here."

"Thirty thousand volumes, the work of three generations. My father did the bulk of the collecting, while I saw to augmenting it, and cataloging everything with Alicia's help. It was her idea to add this room on to house everything: she was sixteen at the time.''

"Your sister is surely a remarkable woman."

Leland smiled warmly. "Alicia is a retiring creature, and too bookish to capture the attention of men more interested in gaming, or racing and riding to hounds. She is a great comfort to me. And a great influence. I don't know what I should have done without her. We were orphaned quite young, and being three years older, she took on the role of mothering me. She routed several formidable governesses before our guardians agreed to let my sister interview the next applicants and choose from among them."

"Did she indeed?" A twinkle lit Roman's eyes. "I shall look forward to making her acquaintance."

"Excellent. You will meet her at dinner this evening. Meanwhile, I have business which I must attend to, unfortunately. After you've had a chance to settle in, you may make yourself free of the library's resources."

His host's generosity staggered Roman. "You are most kind, Lord Claybourne. The value of these books is beyond price. I notice you keep the key to the locked case on your person. You must tell me what is to remain off limits to me."

Leland raised his eyebrows. "Why, nothing at all, McKendrick. Make yourself free of the library's entire resources. I believe you will find the information that will help you pinpoint the tomb you seek. This entire section contains either originals, accurate copies, or translations of the works of ancient travelers—maps and descriptions from Herodotus and Josephus through the present day."

"It would take me a lifetime to search through them all, Lord Claybourne!"

"Ah, but it is not as daunting as you think. All the rare

books on ancient civilizations and their legends and religious beliefs are found here, in this locked case.''

Leland indicated a cabinet seven feet wide and as tall, tucked among the bookshelves. The leaded glass panels were adorned with bronze acorns and oak leaves. ''I purchased this from an antiquarian, said to have dabbled in alchemy in his younger days.''

He slipped the acorn-headed key into the lock and turned it. ''When he was blinded in the course of an experiment gone wrong, he put it all on the auction block.''

''A tragic story.'' Roman drank in the sight of the volumes, heady from the possibility that somewhere among them, he might find the clues to what he sought.

Leland handed him the little acorn key. ''Here you are, McKendrick. I sincerely hope my collection will prove of assistance to you. I have only one request: please take note if you should come across any references to Imhotep. The legendary genius who brought science and engineering to Egypt, and in a matter of years supposedly raised a primitive civilization to become the greatest empire of its time.''

''He is said to be buried secretly beneath the plateau at Giza.''

''I believe otherwise. I have a partial translation of an ancient scroll. It makes mention of Imhotep's tomb being in the Valley of the Kings . . . not far from your current excavation. Think of it, McKendrick! The legacy of Imhotep. A wealth of great knowledge in addition to the literal wealth that must reside in his tomb.''

Roman was intrigued, yet professional caution reared its head. ''Even if the tomb is there, it may have been plundered thousands of years ago. Or yesterday. The men of Gurneh have mined the valley as a source of income for generation upon generation.''

''No,'' his host said firmly. ''If it had been found, the

wonders it contained would be so great no one could hide them!''

Claybourne was so intense as he spoke that Roman eyed him narrowly. ''This is more than a passing interest in a long-dead sage. What is your interest in Imhotep?''

His host smiled dreamily. ''Some say his tomb contains marvels of science: clever machines that foretell the future; cures for disease; perhaps, the legends claim, even the secret of eternal life.''

''Ah,'' Roman said smoothly, ''but then he would not have needed a tomb at all.''

The Earl of Claybourne frowned down at his glass.

Candlelight glimmered on the silver candelabra, winked from dishes heavily encrusted in gold, and shot fire from the array of cut-crystal goblets. Instead of the cavernous formal dining chamber, dinner had been served in the cozy and intimate Rose Salon.

If, Tess thought silently, *eating in the presence of a discreetly hovering butler and two liveried footmen standing rigid as statues could be called that.*

Roman looked incredibly handsome in evening dress. Tess was aware that her low-cut gown of figured emerald satin set off her dark hair and creamy skin to equal effect. She feared that her smile, however, was as hard and brilliant as the circle of diamonds clasped round her throat.

The meal seemed interminable. She was so jumpy she'd almost overset her wine glass twice. The tension seemed to have affected her coordination—or perhaps it was the wine she'd taken too quickly. Her slender fingers curved around the smooth crystal stem of her empty wineglass and the butler hovered at her shoulder, ready to fill it once more.

She gave a tiny shake of her head and forced herself to

relinquish her hold on the glass. Desmond withdrew to wait near the sideboard.

Despite her nervousness, dinner had not been the ordeal that Tess had anticipated. In her upset over Roman's unexpected arrival, she'd almost forgotten that there would be other guests.

As the remains of the cheese and fruit were removed from the table, her husband summoned the butler. "Desmond, you must deliver my compliments to Monsieur LeFavre. The dinner was superb!"

"Indeed it was," Mr. Drake, a rising star in the diplomatic corps, joined in. "I doubt there is any finer dining in the land."

A pause ensued. Alicia sent Tess an encouraging smile. Belatedly Tess realized that the ladies were waiting for her signal to withdraw, and leave the men alone to indulge in their port and cigars. She rose and the gentlemen stood until they left the room.

With Alicia on one side, and Mrs. Drake on the other, Tess led the way. Every time she stepped into the drawing room by candlelight, she felt as if she had been transported to a fairyland, all soft shadows, golden auras, and flames like burning stars. The mirrors on opposite walls reflected one another, and gave the impression of mysterious corridors of wavering light, vanishing in either direction.

"My dear Lady Claybourne, what a pleasure it is to be at Claybourne House once more," Pippa Drake sighed happily as they entered the drawing room.

"No greater pleasure than it is to have you back from the Continent again," Tess replied earnestly.

Mrs. Drake was a particular favorite of both Tess and Alicia. She had wit, intelligence, and sophistication, combined with a warm and generous heart. And if she noticed any strain on the part of the hostess she made no comment. At Tess's and Alicia's urging, she told them all the tales and gossip she'd garnered in her four months abroad, and they chatted like old friends until the men joined them once more.

While Leland and Mr. Drake talked together, Roman leaned against the mantelpiece. He was incredibly vital and handsome, his ruggedness enhanced by the elegant setting. Tess had to force herself to look away.

"Now you must tell me all your news, Lady Claybourne." Mrs. Drake smiled at her hostess. "How are your charming sisters doing at Hazeldean? I have such fond memories of the place."

Tess's smile was rueful. "Judith loves Hazeldean, and is in raptures about all her new bosom friends; Minerva, however, has not taken well to life in boarding school."

From the corner of her eye she saw Roman glance their way in surprise. Hazeldean was one of the most exclusive academies for young ladies in all of England.

She gave him a quick look from beneath her lashes: *What did you think? That I left them to fend for themselves in Swanfield, when I rose in society?*

He gave a little shrug, stunned that they could still communicate across a room. *You were right. I did you an injustice.*

Her smile was a little brighter as she turned to face the other woman more fully. "The latest letter from the headmistress informs me that Minerva is capable of being at the head of her form, 'if only she would apply herself to her studies.' As to Minnie herself, I'm afraid she finds it all a dreadful bore. Which leads," Tess said with a smile, "to what the headmistress refers to as 'Miss Minerva's adventures.' "

"Yes," Alicia added. "Judith is a more social creature than Minnie. And I must say, as a doting aunt, that with her charm and beauty she is destined to make a brilliant marriage!"

"I believe it to be the sum of her ambitions," Tess laughed. "Minnie is more bookish. A veritable bluestocking, if truth be told."

Alicia nodded. "She would rather be here with us, poring through the books in the library completely on her own. I should not be surprised if she ended up a contented spinster, like myself."

"But you are not exactly at your last prayers!" Tess said, not at all happy at the prediction her sister-in-law had made for her favorite sister.

While Minnie was not a beauty like Judith, she was quite pretty when she chose to be presentable. Because she was retiring in company, people tended to assume she was shy. Tess knew better. At fifteen, Minnie was intelligent beyond her years and simply bored. Behind her quiet demeanor she was usually trying to calculate how quickly she could make her exit from a given situation, without appearing any ruder than possible.

"My dear Tess, I am older than Leland and have been out since I was sixteen. Not once in all that time did I meet a man for whom I would consider leaving Leland to rattle around his various homes, with nothing but his books for companions!"

Mrs. Drake touched Alicia's arm. "Your sentiment says much about your loyalty. But now that Tess is here to look after Lord Claybourne . . ." She cast a glance at Roman's stern profile. "You are entertaining more frequently and going about in company these days. Perhaps you will find someone worthy of your affections, after all."

Roman and Alicia? Tess was stunned at the notion. Fortunately, so was her sister-in-law, and neither of them noticed her reaction.

"Ah, no. I much prefer the role of doting aunt to that of wife and mother."

"Oh!" Mrs. Drake's face pinked with delight. "Would

I be presumptuous in taking that for an announcement?"

"No, no," Tess said hurriedly. "Disabuse yourself of that notion. I am not with . . . that is . . . Alicia is speaking of the possible *future*."

This time the other woman flushed with mortification. It was a terrible gaffe for the wife of a budding diplomat. "Please forgive my impertinence."

"There is nothing to forgive."

And, she mused sadly, *neither is there any reason to expect I will ever have a child.*

A shadow fell over her and she looked up to see Roman standing before them with a curious light in his eye. Tess was not the only one to feel her heart speed up a little.

"Lady Claybourne, will you sing for us? I recall that you used to sing rather charmingly."

"Oh, do! I shall accompany you," Mrs. Drake said.

Shaking her head, Tess demurred. "It is many years since I sang for anyone to hear."

Although Leland and Mr. Drake joined in, nothing anyone said could persuade her. It would remind her too much of Swanfield.

"If not music, then I shall ask Mr. McKendrick to tell you a story. It is one he told me he'd deciphered several months ago, from an Egyptian legend."

Alicia clapped her hands. "How exciting."

"There isn't that much to the tale," Roman explained. "The story is fairly recent—late Roman Empire—and rather incomplete."

"Do tell us!" Mrs. Drake cried out. Only Tess was silent.

He leaned an arm against the mantel frame and looked at them.

"It is the tale of an ancient marvel: an object of polished electrum created by ancient magic, so that it looked as new after hundreds of years—perhaps thousands—as it did the day it was made."

"Marvelous, indeed," Alicia said.

"Ah, but that is not all," her brother informed them.

Roman saw his audience was fairly caught. "The object is described as 'round as the moon and more glorious than the sun'—a sphere or disc, perhaps. It was the legacy of one Egyptian queen to the next. So precious was this artifact, that it was kept in a special shrine, the location of which is not given . . ."

He paused. The suspicion that the location was the tomb of a priestess of Isis had grown with every word he'd translated in Claybourne's library. He was almost certain of it.

Even Tess was intrigued. "What was so remarkable about this globe?"

He laughed, his eyes crinkling at the corners. "It foretells the future. At intervals it disappeared for decades, only to be found again. At such times as it was lost, disaster struck the land."

"Remarkable, indeed," Mrs. Drake murmured.

Leland could not resist joining in. "According to Mr. McKendrick, Cleopatra was the last queen of Egypt to possess the artifact—is that not so?"

Roman nodded. "Yes. And that when the doomed queen gazed into it, she saw Marc Antony dead, and herself dragged to Rome in chains, to be paraded before the populace and publicly disgraced. She flung it aside in horror."

He paused for drama. "And that is when she sent for the asp."

"But," Alicia protested, "Marc Antony was still alive. It was only upon learning that she died of the serpent's venom that he fell upon his sword!"

"That is what the papyrus chronicles." Roman turned his hands up. "You must not blame me, Lady Alicia. It is not *my* story."

*   *   *

"Well, the evening was a success," Leland said as he entered Tess's bedchamber.

Her throat was too dry to answer. *Not now! Not tonight!*

Every evening the ritual was the same. Tess would change into her combing gown and sit before the vanity in her boudoir. With the candlelight, the painted ceiling took on the look of a twilight sky, edged with the last faint traces of the setting sun. It always soothed her nerves.

Then Leland would come in to wish her good-night, while her maid brushed out her rippling black hair. A single kiss on the cheek from her husband meant she would sleep alone and undisturbed. A second kiss was the signal that he would return in an hour, via the communicating door.

How she dreaded that second kiss!

"I always enjoy the Drakes," her husband continued. "That young man will go far, and a great deal of his success will be due to his wife. Charming creature."

"Yes. I like them both very much."

"I shall sponsor him, then." He began to walk to and fro behind her in an excess of nervous energy. "And what do you think of Professor McKendrick?"

The question caught her off guard. What did he mean by that? "He has always been personable. He seemed to fit in quite well," she said quickly.

"Yes, yes. I thought so, too."

She watched his reflection in the mirror. Although her maid blocked part of the view, the three-sided mirror was large. Leland in triplicate made her more aware of the changes in him. He seemed to be both restless and stimulated, and his eyes were overbright.

"It was a very good idea to invite McKendrick here," he said, almost as if to himself. "If there is anything in those scrolls, he will find it." His pacing increased.

The maid finished brushing out Tess's long locks. She

recognized an eager husband when she saw one.

"Is there anything more, my lady?"

"No, that will be all. You may retire for the night. I shan't need you till morning."

The maid slipped away with a smile. *So romantic!* Such a beautiful lady, and such an elegant lord. Like something from a storybook, it was.

As she closed the door she saw the master lean down and kiss her mistress softly on the cheek.

Twice.

Tess lay in the darkness with a single, shielded candle burning on the mantelpiece. In the large, high-ceilinged room, it obscured more than it illuminated, filling the chamber with a dim glow that tricked the eye. By the ticking of the mantel clock, she knew there were exactly fifty-five more minutes before the connecting door opened and Leland joined her in the bed.

Fifty-five minutes to prepare herself, wondering how this night would end. Her stomach roiled.

The clock ticked loudly in the stillness, and she fought the urge to put the pillow over her head to block out the sound. Turning on her side, she got her legs tangled in the long lawn nightdress. All her fine silk and satin nightgowns were packed away in silver paper in the dressing room, unused.

This was the longest hour of her day. *The glaciers could advance and retreat with greater speed than the torturously slow movement of the hands on that china dial.* She willed herself to relax, and had almost succeeded in drifting away on daydreams, when the mantel clock whirred.

Exactly on the stroke of the chime, Tess heard the click of the connecting door to Leland's room. Her body went rigid. She tried to relax, to breathe slowly and evenly, and still the furious hammering of her heart.

Did he stand there, hand on handle, waiting for the chime to cover the sound of the door opening? She rather thought he did. The timing was too perfect.

There was no other sound until she felt his weight upon the mattress. She didn't speak, nor did he. On their wedding night he had told her he had only two requests: that she wear her nightshift with her silk stockings and garters beneath it, and that she remain silent unless he spoke to her first. Tess hadn't expected words of love, but she had hoped at least for some of reassurance.

She remembered that night with awful clarity: the sound of his blue silk foulard robe slithering to the floor. The dip of his weight upon the bed. The rustle of the sheets as he crept closer. Then the horrible, tense wait, while they lay side by side, with only the soft rasp of his breathing in the darkness.

After an eternity he rolled on his side, put out a hand, and slowly, ever so slowly, edged her nightgown up to the top of her stockings. Her legs trembled, and he leaned over unexpectedly and pressed his mouth to her breast through the fabric. Suckled like a greedy, starving child.

It was so intimate yet so impersonal that she wanted to shrink away—and yet . . . and yet . . . she could feel something strange happening in the center of her body. A dark warmth spreading through, a liquid tensing, a flutter of growing anticipation, of mounting eagerness for—what?

He lifted his mouth and stopped as abruptly as he had begun. Just when she wanted him to go on. Tess was frustrated. She moved her arm toward him, but instantly he pushed it away. She had broken one of the unspoken rules.

He waited a bit, and she thought he might leave. Instead he began stroking her thigh, just above the garter. His fingers moved higher and she found herself trembling until it affected her entire body. She wished he would embrace her, offer her gentle words. But bridegroom said nothing.

Then she felt him growing hard against her leg. He rolled over and his hands fumbled with her gown, pulling it up to her shoulders so that the cool air made her nipples tingle and harden. Her breath caught in her chest.

His hands clutched at her breasts as he knelt over her ... and then he rolled away, and beat his clenched fists against the pillow like an enraged child. Tess waited anxiously to see what would happen next. For a long while he lay beside her, breathing raggedly.

Afterward, as he had left the room, Tess had imagined that she heard him sobbing.

She remembered it so clearly now, because it was always the same since their wedding eve. Tonight was no different. His touch might be rougher, his mouth more frantic, but the end result would be the same.

This time Leland surprised her. After he rolled away from her, there was a change in the routine. He didn't pound his hands against the pillows, then toss the covers away and leave in silence. He lay beside her for a long time, taking in deep gulps of air, like a man who had run for a long distance.

She wanted to scream out of sheer nerves, when he finally broke the silence. His hand brushed her shoulder lightly.

"I am sorry, my dear. Infinitely sorry."

His voice was so soft, so forlorn, that Tess was suddenly afraid. She tried to answer but Leland pressed his fingers over her mouth firmly, so she would not speak. Tess felt the sharpness of her teeth against her bottom lip, and the hot salty taste of blood.

A moment later his weight shifted off the bed.

She heard the whisper of his dressing gown and then silence, followed by the sound of the connecting door closing softly behind him. Tess turned her face to the pillow and wept.

* * *

Alicia read by candlelight awhile. The book was amusing, but she was only turning the pages to pass the time. When the clock chimed once, at half past one, she rose and put on her robe.

Cinching the belt tightly, she went to the wall beside the wardrobe. The panels were painted in yellow, her favorite color, and the gilded wood bosses were picked out in gold. Alicia reached up and turned the largest one sharply. A muffled groan, a mesh of oiled gears, and a panel slid back to reveal a narrow passage. As a boy Leland had stumbled upon it while exploring the older section of the mansion, and had shown it to her one rainy afternoon. Until then, Alicia had never even guessed at its existence.

The main part of the passage, with only one high window, ran behind a blank wall to the dressing room of the master's suite. Her suite of rooms had once belonged to the young mistress of their paternal grandfather. The woman had been lady-in-waiting to his wife, and this was the discreet route that he had taken, to come to her of a night.

After the loss of their parents, so close upon one another's heels, she had put Leland up to insisting that he be moved to their grandfather's chambers, and herself into this suite. When frightened or upset, she and Leland had used it as a special route to reach one another. Two lonely children, seeking reassurance in a world turned upside down.

Often the two of them had played hide-and-seek between the rooms. Alicia smiled. On one memorable occasion, they had taken bread and cheese and a stone bottle of lemonade and spent the entire day there in the hidden passage, with pillows and a pile of books, playing at being marooned on a desert island. That escapade had led to the nervous collapse of one governess.

Miss Horricks had screamed that the young Lord Claybourne had been kidnapped for ransom, or murdered and flung down a well. She hadn't seemed to notice—or at least to care—that young Lady Alicia had also gone missing. If Miss Horricks hadn't been taken away, Leland would have insisted that she be dismissed for that transgression.

Looking through the peephole on the far side of the passage, Alicia saw that the dressing room was empty. Slipping inside, she opened the door to the bedchamber. The room was unchanged from their father's day, with darkly masculine furniture and wainscoting, and walls papered in stripes of taupe and brown.

Her candle made only a small circle of brightness in the huge chamber but she could see to make her way. Although the fire was banked to an ashy orange glow, a small night lamp was always kept burning in her brother's room these days. He didn't like the dark. He never had.

"Leland?"

There was no answer. Tiptoeing to the high bed, she saw he hadn't returned yet. She set her own candle down on the side table and stood on the step beside it. There had been a time when the mattress was too high for her to reach.

Alicia sat on the edge of the bed, and waited. The clock ticked and whirred and struck the hour and still Leland did not return. She lay back against the stacked pillows and pulled the quilt up for warmth. She was just dozing off in the firelight, when the door opened and her brother entered from the corridor.

"Alicia!" Leland stood frozen in the doorway.

"You certainly weren't expecting anyone else, were you?"

He gave a mirthless laugh. "No. Nor was I expecting you. It's been more months than I can remember since you used the old passageway. I miss your visits terribly, you know."

"As do I." Alicia sighed. Over the years they had become too dependent upon one another. "It has been difficult, I know, for both of us. But you are a married man now, Leland. I love you more than life, but I am only your sister. If you need comfort, you must seek out your wife."

He hurled a pillow across the room in sudden fury born of anguish. "There is no comfort anyone can give me tonight! Oh, my dear Alicia, what am I to do? I have failed again!"

The fit of temper vanished as quickly as it had come. Leland went to the bed and knelt beside it, placing his head in Alicia's lap. His body was wracked by dry sobs.

Leaning over, she held him and murmured in his ear, as if he were still a small, frightened boy. "It will be all right," she said, brushing his hair with her fingers. "It is early days still."

He didn't respond. She tried again. "I have been thinking . . . perhaps we should consult another physician. Dr. Pomeroy is getting on in years. There must surely be something . . . a new herbal remedy, or Continental technique that can be done to produce an heir. I have heard of a Belgian, newly come to London to set up practice. He is a foreigner, but his reputation is quite excellent."

Leland lifted his head. "Yes, that is very true. Monsieur Picard is highly thought of by those who seek his counsel. I will write personally for an appointment in the morning."

"Perhaps I should speak with Tess," Alicia added, more to herself than to him. "Explain the situation more clearly."

Her brother stared at her. "The whole truth, you mean?"

Alicia appeared to consider his suggestion. "No. I don't think that would be wise," she said finally. "Not yet. But, in time, I may have to tell her at least a *part* of it."

Tess's tears were long dry when she heard the clock strike three. Usually she fell into exhausted slumber after one of Leland's abortive visits. Tonight she couldn't sleep. The house itself seemed awake. Waiting.

Floors creaked and the wind sighed beyond the closed draperies while Tess stared into the darkness. What was wrong with her, that her husband avoided her bed? That when he finally came to her of a night, there was only silence and awkward fumbling, followed by mutual humiliation?

Five months ago she had stood beside Leland in church and vowed to be a good and dutiful wife. *It seems I am no good at promises,* she thought wistfully.

Throwing back the covers, she got up from the bed. As she turned, an image floated like an apparition on the other side of the room. After a second's fright, she recognized her own nightgowned figure in the vanity looking glass. Tess walked slowly toward it and watched her features materialize out of the darkness.

"I wish you could foretell my future, like the magical object in Roman's story." There was no change in the diamantine surface of the glass.

After a moment she turned and went to the window. Tess held the heavy draperies aside with one hand. The star-frosted gardens glowed like pearl beneath a diamond-studded sky. Remote and achingly cold.

Like myself.

Only now Tess knew that wasn't true. She'd thought she had buried her passionate nature and its wild urgings long ago. Buried them so deep they had surely died from lack of light. It had taken Roman's sudden appearance to disabuse her of that false notion.

Seeing him today had been a terrible shock. Discovering that his love had turned to hate was another. She was sure he would have forgiven her by now. But then, she had not forgotten him in the years since their parting.

The greatest shock of all had been learning that she was not a creature of ice and reason, but a live, passionate woman with all a woman's needs. For the first few months of her marriage, she had thought it was some inner coldness in herself that frustrated Leland. That he knew, or sensed, that her secret heart was not warm and red, but a pale, anemic thing incapable of more than sincere gratitude and mild affection.

"God in Heaven, how could I have been so wrong?" she murmured.

Tonight, when Leland had come to her and she'd felt her skin tremble beneath his touch, it had been Roman she imagined with her in the bed. Roman's hard, bronzed body stretched beside her and his mouth upon her breast. *His* fingers brushing against her inner thigh, urging her legs apart.

And she had felt those long-slumbering passions stir and awaken inside her. Uncoil from the pit of her stomach to send tendrils of heat and a sweet, languid heaviness through her blood.

Shame coursed through Tess, and with it despair: Leland's failure was not his alone. She was as much at fault. Perhaps more.

She still loved Roman. Had never, ever stopped loving him.

Stepping deeper into the window embrasure, she let the drapery close behind her. Perhaps the chill air close to the glass would cool her blood. She touched her breasts and felt the heat in them, the thudding of her heart against her ribs. She was on fire for Roman, and if she didn't quench it for good and all, she would be consumed.

Tess shivered. If he knocked upon her door now, at this very moment, she wouldn't have the strength to close it against him. Not that such an event was likely. He despised her. *But,* the thought whispered through her mind, *a man can separate love from passion.* And if he came to her . . .

The stars burned pure and cold as Tess stood at the window, her breath making little frost clouds against the chill pane. She pressed her fingertips against them and watched little ovals melt from the heat of her touch. Perhaps if she stayed here long enough, she could turn herself back to ice once more.

Better to be numb than in this agony of need and despair.

The clock struck the half-hour as she stood there, willing herself to feel nothing for Roman. She was shivering with cold but there was no relief for it. Its source was deep within.

She offered up a silent prayer: *Please, God, give me the courage to keep my distance from Roman. Give me the strength to hide my feelings for him, until he is safely abroad, and out of my life for good.*

Tess thought that she had done exactly that her sixteenth summer. That was the terrible year when she realized that she must follow duty's path—and had set Roman free, in the only way she knew, to find his own future.

As the eldest, she was responsible for her sisters. Tess had promised their mother, as she lay dying, that she would do everything in her power to see Judith and Minnie established. That promise had only crystallized what she had already known: she would have to be strong, for all their sakes.

Tess hadn't tried to explain her reasons in the note she left for him: Roman would never have understood. But how, when she loved him so desperately, could she have stood in the way of his career? His golden dreams of Egypt would not have survived the cold, hard light of reality.

No, she had acted for the best: A penniless wife with two younger sisters for him to support would have ended Roman's ambitions then and there . . . condemned him to a life of tutoring squirming boys more interested in chasing puppies and teasing girls. And condemned her dowerless sisters to lives of poverty, without hope of marriage or even the promise of a warm roof over their heads.

Judith and Minnie had deserved better than that.

And so had Roman.

Tess traced a jagged heart on the frosted glass. "I have kept my promise to you, Mama."

EGYPT

The Valley of the Kings was a fearsome place by night, filled with deep shadows and ancient sighs. The young boy Yusef followed closely on his uncle's heels. It was such a night that the afreets and demons snatched up the unwary. He murmured a prayer to ward off evil.

He knew the other men had wanted him to stay in the village. Even now they were still grumbling. This was their third trip to the tomb, but only his first. In the harsh land, the men of Gurneh had been mining the ancient tombs for their livelihood for generations. They did not want the boy's inexperience to end it.

Especially now, when they had broken through to such a rich store of treasures, with surely more to come. "This is far enough for your nephew," one suggested. "He can stand guard."

"I do not want such a callow youth watching my back," the oldest among them complained. "Better to have someone more experienced on lookout. Yusef can cause little harm inside with us.''

"He is clumsy," a tall man named Hussein agreed. "The boy trips over his own sandals."

"I will take them off," Yusef exclaimed, drawing down as much wrath for his ignorance as his volume. "I will be quiet."

"You must be more quiet than a mouse," Hussein told him, leaning close. "You must be silent as the *dead*."

Yusef swallowed. He feared "the dead" only slightly less than he did his uncle, who was headman of the village.

They slipped into the blackest shadows and, one by one, vanished into a hidden crevice. It was too dark inside to see anything at all, until his uncle lit the small candle he carried. The chamber sprang to light. They had broken through into an anteroom, with plain limestone walls and a door leading to an inner chamber. Space there was at a premium. After the small oil lamp they'd left there earlier was lit, the first man went inside, and came out carrying a small chest of painted camphorwood banded with brass and carnelian cabochons. "Very fine jewelry. The owner of this tomb had great wealth."

"And so shall we," Yusef's uncle chuckled. "Omar, see what you can carry."

Omar was the largest of them, and could bring out the heaviest pieces. He took his rope bags out of his robes. When he returned it was with a granite statuette of Isis, and an alabaster cosmetic kit. Smudges of crushed malachite and lapis lazuli stained his fingers.

Suddenly there was a low rumble and slither of falling rock. Yusef's throat was parched with fear. Hussein went in. He came back cursing, and covered with bits of plaster and limestone dust.

"The ceiling has caved in on the west side. We will

have to dig it out to reach the sarcophagus. There is hardly room to turn around."

The others groaned. They were on the scent of a big cache. Every instinct told them this. But now the most valuable of the treasures were under more rubble than before.

Finally it was decided that they would leave with what they had, and return another night. They started for the entrance. Yusef shifted his weight from one leg to another. He was small. He might be able to find something the other men could not reach.

"I am small. I can squeeze inside and I may find something more. I have come all this way . . ."

Hussein rolled his eyes, but Yusef's uncle handed him the candle. "A quick look only. It is dangerous."

The boy stepped inside and stopped in awe. The brilliant colors of the paint were stunning after the featureless outer chamber. To one side a painting of flute players and dancers looked as if it had been made that morning. He swore if he touched it the pigment would still be wet. On the ceiling he could make out Nuit, goddess of the night, arching across it. The tiny flame caught the gilded stars in her indigo dress.

Then something else glittered. He squeezed his way in deeper and crouched down. "I have found something," he called out.

It was difficult to breathe in the chamber, and his excitement made it worse. His brown fingers scrabbled along the edge of some fallen plaster, and he pulled out an amulet of malachite and another beside it of carved faience. There was something else . . .

There came the hiss of fine dust sliding across stone. He blinked his eyes against it. Minute pieces of plaster rained down on his head. Yusef dared not move until it stopped. As he waited, he saw a dull gleam just beyond his reach. Edging sidewise, he touched it. Metal. Gold, perhaps?

Sliding himself sideways, he caught a glimpse of starry sky beyond. There was a gap in the wall opening to the outside! Disappointment gave way to surprise. Strange, then, that the floor was not covered with bat and rodent droppings. *But there is something strange about this tomb itself.*

"Yusef! Do not touch anything. Back out with extreme care!"

The boy ignored Hussein's voice as his fingers touched metal. Yes! There was something wedged into the gap. Eagerly he worked it toward him, scarcely hearing the voices urging him to come out before he brought the entire ceiling down.

A shard of stone fell, zinging him on the end of his nose. *"Ow!"*

It burned like fire and he knew it was bleeding. But the object was almost loose from its rocky prison. He would not stop until it was his. Another rain of plaster and small rocks showered him. The others called to him.

"Get out of the chamber, accursed fool, before your meddling costs us all dearly!"

Yusef rubbed his aching nose. *If the tomb collapses upon me, they will not care, as long as they can still reach the treasures,* he thought sullenly.

Now he had the object freed. It was a round disk, with a handle of twisted metal in an openwork design. He had seen bronze mirrors before, and was elated. It should fetch a good price from old Ibrahim. His uncle would be pleased.

As he pulled it to him the light flickered, creating a strange illusion. He thought he saw a face looking out at him: a woman wearing the uraeus, the sacred cobra, upon her brow, and a wig of thin golden disks that moved as she tilted her head and flashed a blaze of light into his eyes.

For a moment the cramped space of the inner chamber was transformed. Yusef gasped. He imagined he saw a throne of gilded wood set in a peristyled hall, and the woman in the golden wig sat upon it. Supplicants bowed before her, seeking her rulings.

Then his uncle shouted for him to come out, the air was too bad to stay so long, and the illusion shattered. Yusef's head felt light and he knew he needed air. In panic, he scrabbled backward, working his way toward the outer chamber.

Since he had to use his hands, he tucked the mirror in the belted tunic beneath his outer robe. Then he gathered up the two amulets and several strings of beads threaded on wire that he'd uncovered in the debris.

As he emerged into the outer chamber with the beads dripping from his hands, the rock floor and walls trembled.

"Outside! Now!"

His uncle pushed him toward the opening and they all tumbled out of the stuffy tomb and into the cool, dry night air. Behind them there was a muffled rumble that grew into an angry roar. They leapt away, agile as goats. Somehow, in the rush to safety, Yusef's belt loosened. Rock and scree bounced down past them to the floor of the wadi below. The mirror fell with them.

The men filed sullenly away toward the village. No one spoke until they were safely back in Gurneh, inside Omar's home with the door barred.

The men laid out their finds, glancing at Hussein from time to time. He was furious. "I told you not to bring the boy. This is his fault."

"The walls were unstable," Omar pointed out.

"It is a curse of the old ones," another man mumbled.

Yusef's uncle folded his arms. "Enough! Let us see what we have."

They spread out the jewelry from the chest and examined the fine cosmetic kit and the alabaster vessels of unguents and kohl. A price and division of the goods was decided, before they were hidden in a secret niche below the floor.

"And where is this precious find of yours?" Hussein said to Yusef. The boy held out his amulets and the handful of wired glass beads. Hussein cursed again.

"Son of an afreet! Is it for such as *this* you brought down the walls of the tomb? I can buy better in the souk any day."

The boy flushed. All eyes were turned on him accusingly. He lowered his thick lashes to screen his eyes. He would say nothing to them of the mirror he had dropped along the way, except to his uncle.

And that could wait until morning.

3

On the third morning of Roman's stay at Claybourne
House, the fourth Earl of Claybourne entered his sister's
bedroom as Alicia finished her chocolate and toast. He
was dressed for riding and his aristocratic face was wind-
burned.

"I see you have been out already," Alicia said, nibbling
daintily on a crust.

"Yes, McKendrick and I went for an early ride. We ran
into Lord Wendell and his cronies. They invited us to dine
with them at their club later in the week."

Alicia signaled the maid to take away her tray, and dismissed her. "I have heard that Wendell's wife is pregnant
by her lover. Do you think she will successfully pass it off
as his?"

Leland tapped his riding whip against his boot. "I sense
some other meaning behind your words, but you are too
subtle for me."

"I think you understand me well enough. What are your
plans for the day?"

"I thought I might spend some time with McKendrick
in the library."

Alicia shook her head. "I am sure you have some pressing business in the city. How fortunate that Tess and Mr.

McKendrick are already acquainted. It makes everything so much easier.''

''They are both from Swanfield, you recall. Everyone there expected them to wed in time, until he hied himself off to Egypt.''

''Ah, yes. Poor Tess.''

''I suppose it is no wonder that she treats him so coolly. There must be some strain involved, although she is too much a lady to show it.''

''Not that being a countess, with jewels and houses and carriages at her disposal, is something to be sneezed at,'' Alicia said dryly. ''And she knows that her life and that of her sisters would not be so elegant and comfortable had she not married you. Tess is no fool.''

''No.'' Leland frowned down at his hands.

Alicia ran a stray strand of hair behind her ear. ''I wondered if you had noticed. It seems to me to be far more than mere coolness—there is almost a certain animosity between our distinguished houseguest and your wife. Something that goes far deeper than the normal pique of a young girl's disappointment, or the embarrassment of a former suitor finding himself a guest beneath her roof.''

''Speak plainly, Alicia. I'm in no mood for games.''

''Whether he admits it to himself I cannot tell—but I have observed him closely these past few days. I believe that Roman McKendrick is still very much in love with Tess.''

Leland stared at her. ''Are you certain?''

''Perhaps 'love' is not the correct word. Let us say that he is deeply, passionately attracted to her.''

''Are you implying that he intends to seduce her beneath my roof?''

Alicia took another bite of toast. ''He may desire her, but it would take great provocation for him to act upon it.

Mr. McKendrick is a man of intense passions—but he is a gentleman.''

Leland straddled a chair and digested this in silence. "What of Tess? Do you think she has tender feelings for him?''

"I cannot tell. She guards her emotions too well." Alicia cocked her head. "Are you picturing your wife luring our guest to her bed, and later foisting a bastard on the world as your heir?''

She saw from the look on his face that he had. "Put it out of your head, Leland. She is not like our sort. Tess has been raised with different values, different prejudices. The middle classes have far stricter morals than those in our circle.''

"Yes, that is so." He was lost in his own thoughts a while. "Then you do not think they will become lovers?''

"I am very sure that they will not." Alicia poured more chocolate into her bone china cup. "Unless they were thrown together. It would take more than ordinary temptation to cause Tess to throw over her principles. But sometimes old feelings can be re-awakened.''

"I see." Folding his arms along the back of the chair, Leland rested his chin and gave his sister a long, hard look.

"Do you know, there are times when I am completely astonished at the peculiar notions that you take into your pretty little head.''

"I believe this is my favorite room of all," Tess announced.

She and Alicia were in the airy parlor at the back of the house that had become their special sitting room, making lists of what they needed for the coming Christmas festivities at Claybourne House. Leland had decided that they would remain in London, and show Judith and Minnie the enjoyments of town life: there were plans to attend a pantomime and a play in Drury Lane, in addition to more educational trips to St. Paul's, the Victoria and Albert Museum, and the Royal Academy.

Despite Alicia's deficiencies regarding her own wardrobe, they had not affected her taste in decor. The figured wallpaper in soft yellow mocked the gray skies beyond the tall windows, and the touches of white, yellow, and Chinese blue made an elegant contrast.

"Should you like to have a fir tree for Christmas?" Alicia looked up brightly. "We usually do at the castle. We set it on a table in the great hall, and put candles on the tree and hang our gifts from the branches. Last year Leland brought me a lovely string of silvered glass beads."

"I think it would be so charming! We used to decorate our home with holly branches, but we never had a fir tree."

"Excellent! I shall send a note to the Castle to have the beads sent up, and the woodmen find us a fine tree. Perhaps Minnie and Judith would like to cut some snowflakes from silver paper to hang up as well. Leland and I used to do it every holiday season."

"They will be thrilled with all your plans for them! You are so very kind, Alicia."

"I dote on your dear sisters." She gave a wistful smile. "It is wonderful to feel like a real family. I cannot wait until they join us at the end of the term."

"Nor can they." Tess laughed. "My only fear is of trying to send them off again for the new term over their violent protests. Judith is still begging that she be allowed to put her hair up and join the adult parties. Minnie, of course, is sincerely hoping that we have no parties at all!"

Desmond entered with a silver tray piled high with envelopes for each lady. "The morning post, madame, Lady Alicia."

He withdrew as silently as he had come.

"So many!" Alicia exclaimed.

Tess eyed the great pile of invitations in dismay. "If there is so much going on already, I cannot imagine what it will be like after Easter Week, when the Season begins in earnest."

"Yes, we shall have to employ a secretary at this rate." Alicia began sorting her mail in several stacks, and Tess did the same.

She saw, with surprise, that there were letters from both her sisters, as well as another from the headmistress of Hazeldean. She hadn't expected them, as the term ended the coming week. It was due to Leland's generosity that they had been removed from the mean boarding school which was all Tess had been able to afford after their mother's meager estate was settled, and sent to such a fine place.

Opening Judith's letter first, she found it full of the usual details of her friendships with the Honorable Laetitia Ransome and Lady Sarah Barkindale, interspersed with requests for a new shawl, a pair of combs, and numerous complaints. The theme of the complaints was consistent throughout the missive:

> . . . and Minerva is such a complete hoyden, she continues
> to be a source of profound embarrassment and humiliation
> to me!
>
> Dear, *dear* Tess, I still do not see why you refuse to
> let me make my come-out this season, when so many of
> my friends will do so! It is horrid of you to treat me like
> a mere schoolgirl, when I am already seventeen and prac-
> tically on the shelf! If I become an old maid, like Lady
> Alicia, I shall never, never forgive you!!!
>
> > > Your loving and much put-upon sister,
> > > > Judith

Laughing at the three exclamation marks so unlike Judith, Tess still recognized the depths of her sister's dis-

content. It was difficult to be young and eager and have your heart's desire denied.

An image of Roman intruded into her mind, and she forced it away. Thank God he had gone out early with Leland. Tess feared that she would not have a moment of ease until he was gone for good. She picked up the second letter hastily.

Minnie's note was quite different, filled with ideas that Tess's younger sister had for their Christmas holidays. She had no interest in making her debut, although many girls her age had already put up their hair. Although her two sisters were opposites in most ways, they were alike in their emotional outpourings. Like Judith, Minnie had heavily underscored and punctuated the list with multiple exclamation points.

"Dearest Tess,
I hope this finds you well. Have you ever been to the Pool of Pearls? It is in a cavern not far from Claybourne Castle. They say *smugglers* used it in the time of Charles II. It is said to maintain the same temperature year round, so you need not worry that we will catch our death. Perhaps you might care to make up an expedition to see it one day, as I should like *excessively* to see such a marvel!

A long list of other proposed activities followed, all of which were based around local curiosities, and none of which involved fancy dress, balls, or friends from Hazeldean. Tess read on:

Did I say I have begun a book of poems? My own poetry, that is. I believe I shall become a poet and travel in Italy for my inspiration. I would prefer Greece or Egypt but they are rather too far from you, dear sister. Horrid Hazeldean is far enough!!!
There are no words adequate to describe how I *loathe*

Hazeldean and all the prissy misses trotting around with their airs and graces!!! (I do not mention *any names* here, as you see.) Please, please, dearest Tess, do let me come home to Claybourne. I shall be of no trouble at all, I vow.

        With love from your Most Affectionate sister,

                      Minnie

P.S. The incident with the chapel window was merely *a freak accident,* and not at all *intentional,* as the headmistress believes!''

"Good Heavens!"

Alicia looked up quickly. "Not bad news, I hope?"

Tess gave a rueful smile. "I am afraid to read the note from the head of Hazeldean, to discover what Minnie means when she writes that 'the incident with the chapel window' was 'accidental'!"

"Oh, dear." Alicia couldn't hide her laughter.

"A costly accident, I am sure! I doubt Leland will find it so humorous."

"Don't fret, my dear. My brother could buy the school a hundred chapel windows from his pin money. And you know how he dotes on dear Minnie!"

"Yes. Surprising, when she is always into such mischief."

"She is certainly a lively girl. Leland says she reminds him of me at the same age."

Tess stared. "You are pulling my leg. I cannot imagine you anything but demure and proper."

"I assure you I was a rare handful! Our guardians were delighted when Leland reached his majority and they could officially turn over the reins to him." Alicia chuckled. "He was the heir, but as our father lay dying, and knowing I was the bolder one, he charged me to look after Leland's welfare."

"And you have, dear Alicia. I'm so glad that you and

Leland are close," Tess said sincerely. "Minnie and Judith have been a great comfort to me! But it is a very odd thing—so many families seem like chance acquaintances, thrown together under the same roof."

"Like you and your sisters, we had no one else. Oh, there were trustees and cousins, but it is not the same. I think that is why you and I get along together so famously. We are used to taking care of others, and we both have had to make sacrifices for the sake of families."

The color rose in Tess's cheeks. For a horrible moment she thought that Alicia was referring to giving up Roman, and eventually marrying Leland. But the other woman continued on without a pause.

"I can imagine how devastated you were when your great-aunt failed to keep her promises and leave her estate in trust to you."

"It was not a pleasant time in our lives," Tess said quietly. "Being separated from Minnie and Judith for so long was the worst of it."

"And look how happily it all turned out," Alicia announced. "Nothing could be better!"

Well, there was one thing that would improve matters, Tess thought as she set her cup down. *Roman could go away and leave me to find my way in peace.*

"Never fear," her sister-in-law said. "We shall keep the girls busy while they are in town. I have many ideas for entertaining them."

"Thank heavens for that."

"Don't worry. We shall keep them occupied." Alicia set aside her mail and went back to her list. "You're doing an excellent job of keeping Professor McKendrick well entertained. Why, I don't believe we've sat down to dinner *en famille* in the week since he came to stay with us."

Tess flushed at the mention of Roman's name and looked up from her own list. "Leland's secretary gave me a list of people to invite to dine with us.'' Her eyes were wide with dismay. ''I didn't think . . . I should have asked your opinion. I hope that I have not presumed too much?''

Her sister-in-law was stricken. ''Oh, my dear! I meant no criticism.''

Rising, she went to Tess's side and took her hands in hers. ''*You* are Lady Claybourne, and mistress here! You may invite whomever you choose and no one can say a word against it!'' A discreet dimple peeked out at the corner of her mouth. ''Although I must say I would draw the line at opera dancers and highwaymen.''

Tess almost choked on her laughter. How like her sister-in-law to turn a heavy moment into something light, with her clever wit.

Alicia smiled. ''I know what you are thinking—a lady should have no knowledge of opera dancers! But I must admit I have always wanted to meet a highwayman. Your Professor McKendrick rather reminds me of one, with his dashing good looks.''

''He is not my Professor McKendrick,'' Tess said crisply. ''I have not seen him since we were young.''

''Was he as handsome then as now?''

''I suppose so,'' Tess replied evasively. Alicia's growing interest in Roman was a source of great discomfort to her. *Alicia deserves a wonderful man, who can value her as she deserves. But, dog-in-the-manger that I am, I do not want Roman as a brother-in-law! It would be unthinkable.*

''His presence has certainly enhanced our social life. I must tell you I am thoroughly enjoying having the house so full. Indeed, I didn't realize how much I missed it. My brother has been increasingly retiring over these past few years. Your marriage has had a very good influence upon him.''

''Th . . . thank you.'' Tess didn't know what to say in response, and they went back to making their lists.

She didn't want to discuss Roman. It had proved easier for her to stay out of his way than she'd dared to hope. She and Alicia always took their breakfast on trays in their rooms. Then there were letters to answer, shopping expeditions, carriage rides in the park. Later there were either calls to pay or visitors to receive, and finally preparations for dinner and the evening's festivities. The only difficult time was dinner, and she'd managed to have guests every evening.

Roman seems as intent as I to avoid another tête-à-tête. Only a few more weeks till he makes his departure.

On Boxing Day, Roman would be on his way back to Egypt, and the household at Claybourne would leave and return to Leland's country seat until the official London Season was in full swing. Then she could breathe easy again.

Tess was counting the days.

Roman *was* keeping his distance. If he wasn't closeted in the library, he was meeting with his associates or visiting the British Museum. Yesterday afternoon Lord Claybourne had taken him to visit his private club. It was a signal honor, but his host's easy sponsorship was a double-edged sword: Roman didn't know which was worse, to be under the same roof as Tess or out in the company of the man she had married.

Either way, there was no escape. If Tess wasn't in the same room with him, she was still in his thoughts. The only time he could ignore the curious predicament was when he was totally focused on his research. Nights were especially intolerable, lying awake. Thinking about Tess, warm in her bed. Wondering if she slept alone. It was sheer torture, and the less he saw of her, the easier it was.

At the present he was in the carriage with Lord Claybourne, who had kindly offered to drop him off at the museum. The sky was patchy blue ahead, peering through massing gray clouds. The temperature was dropping quickly. Warm inside the carriage, Roman was very aware of the ragged people glimpsed in alleyways and doorways along some of the side streets.

In Egypt he was used to seeing beggars and children blinded by parasitic eye disease. In so poor and struggling a country, dependent on the whims of the Nile, it was understandable. Here, in the heart of the Empire, it was shocking.

He heard a sudden commotion, and a beefy man came barreling out of a shop. Two urchins, mere children, raced away with a string of sausages, and lost themselves in the crowd. Before the carriage passed by he saw several men in pursuit, shouting outrage. They took the wrong turning.

Roman sat back. *At least the little beggars will eat tonight.*

" 'But the poor you shall always have with you,' " Claybourne murmured.

His apparent nonchalance angered Roman. "Yes, and hunger and thirst, as well! It is criminal to see women and children existing in such poverty."

"Most certainly," the earl responded. "Alicia's new foundling hospital will help only a few. A few grains of sand saved from the relentless pounding sea."

"A worthy cause," Roman replied. He was ashamed of his outburst.

He'd been guilty of the worst sort of prejudice, prejudging his host merely because of his rank and wealth. Claybourne might have been born with all the advantages, but he had a conscience: any hospital Lady Alicia sponsored must have her brother's financial backing.

The carriage slowed down as it neared the British Museum. "Ah, there is Audley just mounting his carriage at the corner. You will meet him at the Ellertons' ball,"

Claybourne said, as if he hadn't spoken. "The duke is my cousin. He has expressed some interest concerning you and your work."

Expressed interest in the treasures inside any unopened tombs more likely, Roman thought with increasing cynicism. He had met more than his share of such gentlemen in Claybourne's company.

It was far easier to get funding for excavating royal tombs, because the backers hoped for a wealth of golden statues and jewelry. Painted scrolls and alabaster jars were valued as a commodity to be bought and sold. His mouth thinned. The plain utensils of everyday living were discarded as useless, and more than one mummy had been torn apart or disintegrated as rough hands searched for precious amulets among the resin-hardened wrappings. It was becoming worse every year.

"The duke may be disappointed then. My quest is not for treasure, but for knowledge—specifically, a cache of ancient texts. I believe they are hidden among the ruins of an exceedingly old temple dedicated to the goddess Isis. If I am right, they will answer many mysteries about the Old Kingdom dynasties and their founding."

The carriage came to a halt. They'd reached Roman's destination, and he sprang down from the carriage with thanks to his host. "We shall see you at dinner this evening," Claybourne said.

Inside the British Museum, Roman busied himself examining the new exhibits, spent some time in the reading room with the latest published reports, looked up some colleagues, and finally let his restlessness get the best of him.

Muffled against the unaccustomed cold, he went for a long walk along the Embankment, past Waterloo Bridge, and finally took a bench in a quiet corner of the park. The snow was gone, melted into damp patches on the dormant grass. Wan December sun filtered through the thin clouds. He was as unused to seeing clouds as he was to the temperature. The wind ruffled his hair and sent a scattering of the last, dried leaves from the trees.

The truth was that he needed to get away from Claybourne House and its occupants. Since his arrival in London, Claybourne had expressed some interest in funding Roman's work, but the matter had never been explored in depth. It was just another source of frustration. The main one was Tess.

He was relieved that she kept herself away from him except at dinner, and at the same time furious. It was like being a schoolboy all over again, the way she made him feel. He spent half the time hoping he'd meet up with her, the other half praying he wouldn't. There must be a way to put it all behind him.

Two young ladies bustled out of a confectioner's shop, their fashionable gowns and velvet pelisses eclipsing the demure cape and hat of the maid trailing discreetly behind. "Do try a maple cream," one offered the other.

"No, but thank you. I so filled myself with them last week, that I declare I don't think I'll ever be able to touch another one. I've quite lost my taste for them."

After they passed by Roman laughed aloud and sprang to his feet. Sometimes the answer to a prayer came in strange ways. He'd been going about it all wrong. He shouldn't be avoiding Tess at all. What he needed to do was see as much of her as possible while he was in London.

It was the only way to get her out of his system.

Alicia had gone out with her maid and Tess decided to pass the time with a new novel. She had just come down from her sitting room, where she'd gone to fetch it from her night table, and was entering the drawing room when she heard a commotion in the entrance hall below.

Peering over the banister, she saw a flash of bright blond hair and a blue velvet cape. A high, slightly affected female voice drifted up toward her.

Judith? Heart thumping, she ran down the stairs.

The elder of her two sisters was at the foot of the stairs, talking to Desmond. Through the open door she saw leather trunks, valises, and bandboxes being unloaded from the carriage at the curb. The questions came tumbling out of Tess's mouth all in a rush.

"Judith! What is wrong? You weren't expected for another two weeks! Where is Minnie?"

Her sister turned, in a swirl of blue velvet that matched her thickly lashed eyes. Her lovely, china-doll face was pale and filled with distress. "Well, I hope you may be satisfied, Tess. The worst has happened!"

"What? For the love of God, tell me what has happened to Minnie!"

"Minnie, Minnie, *Minnie*!" Judith exclaimed. "I am sick to death of hearing her name!"

Tess grabbed her by the arms and gave her a little shake. "You're hysterical. Now sit down on this bench and tell me everything. Do not try to spare me."

To her dismay Judith burst into tears. Tess's stomach knotted painfully.

"Minnie has . . ."

"Yes, *yes*!"

"Minnie has caused us to be *sent down* from school!"

The urge to box her sister's ears was powerful, but Tess refrained. "Is that all? I thought something terrible had happened."

"I think it's quite wonderful," a laughing voice cried out from the open door. A brown-haired girl with light blue eyes threw off her red velvet traveling cloak.

"Minnie!" Tess rose and went to her younger sister,

gathering her in her arms before she could even set down the bandbox she carried.

She held her out at arm's length and examined her for signs of illness. Her sister's cheeks were rosy and her lithe figure had blossomed into the curves of young womanhood.

"You look the picture of robust health," Tess exclaimed. "My dear, you don't know what a fright I've just suffered."

"It couldn't be worse than driving back all the way from Hazeldean, with Judith alternating between lecturing me and being a watering pot."

Tess gave directions on where to put the luggage, ordered refreshments, and shooed her sisters into the drawing room like a hen with squabbling chicks. Head high, Judith took the most visible place in the room, on the small sofa, and arranged her skirts becomingly. Taking an embroidered handkerchief from her pocket, she dabbed daintily at her eyes, her face a mask of tragedy.

Minnie, not quite sixteen, snagged a sweetmeat from the Sèvres bowl on the console, and plopped herself down in one of the comfortable armchairs.

"Sit up like a lady, dear." Tess took a seat between them. "Now, tell me everything. What on earth is going on, and how did you get here?"

"Such fun! Miss Lillard sent us down in the school's traveling carriage, with one of the maids to chaperone. I slept all the way so I wouldn't have to listen to Judith's scolds and moans."

Judith turned her head away, the picture of injured innocence.

"There is nothing to tell," Minnie said. "One of the girls in our room fell ill, and there was some talk of bad drains, I believe. Miss Lillard decided to end the term early. She sent a telegram to Leland."

"Well, he did not receive it." Tess gave Judith a darkling look. "But what is the reason for all these histrionics? Surely you cannot blame Minnie for illness at Hazeldean."

Judith tilted her pointed chin. "The other girls are staying on till Saturday, while *we* were hustled out the door as if we were lepers."

"Only natural if the girl taken ill shared your room, darling."

"It was not *that*, it was Minnie taking the vicar's bicycle."

"I didn't *know* it was the vicar's," Minnie protested. "It was just *lying there* on the grass, if as someone had abandoned it! I merely took it for a ride and ended up in the hedge. The only harm was to my dress and my dignity."

"Yes," Judith said ominously. "You were not wearing bloomers."

Tess stared at her sisters in shock. Then leaned her head back against the chair and laughed in a most unladylike fashion. This was just what she needed to take her mind off Roman's awkward presence and her strange marriage.

"Oh, my dearest, darling sisters! I cannot tell you how good it is to have you home again!'

"Lady Claybourne is in the drawing room . . ." the butler responded to Roman's question as he took his hat and coat.

Before Desmond could finish, Roman was already striding across the polished marble tiles and up the stairs to the drawing room. He was eager to put his plan into action immediately.

Somewhere in his mind, there was an image of Tess stored away. Like all first, lost loves, time had glorified and gilded it. *The girl I "remember" may never have existed, except in my imagination.* The sooner he got to know the grown-up Tess, the sooner he would know all her foibles and flaws. Yes, that was the cure for the hold she had upon him.

Roman opened the door and stopped short just inside. Her beauty exceeded the image. Tess took his breath away in sapphire-blue silk with ruffles of white lace at her wrists and slender throat.

Afternoon sunlight brought out blue-black highlights in her shining hair. *It is a sin to keep hair like that bound up,* he thought. It should flow free as it used to, shimmering with her every movement and turn of the head.

"Good afternoon. We did not expect you back so early."

He gave a little start. He hadn't even realized that she wasn't alone; she had two elegantly clad young ladies were with her.

"My apologies, Lady Claybourne. I didn't realize you had visitors."

He started to withdraw but the brown-haired girl in the red dress launched herself out of the chair at him like a cannonball.

"Roman, is it really you?" Minnie threw her arms around him as she had when she was a child. "Tess said that you were here beneath this very roof, but I couldn't believe it!"

He tipped up her chin and flashed his dazzling grin. Was this the inquisitive little child who had climbed upon his knee and begged him to read her stories? Her face had rounded out with her figure, but there was no mistaking those mischievous, sky-blue eyes.

"Minerva Mallory, you have not changed one bit from the pretty hoyden I remember. Although when I first entered, I thought you were a fine society miss on the verge of making your debut."

"Phoo! I would rather go off to Egypt with you."

The blond lovely on the couch spoke in a cool voice

but her face was a little anxious. "And what of me, Ro . . . er, Mr. McKendrick? Do you find that *I* have changed?"

He looked over at her. She was already a little beauty. In another year she would rival Tess. But the same Judith he remembered was there, in the imperious voice that masked a world of insecurities. There was a twinkle in Roman's eye as he went to greet her, but he kept his face grave and respectful. He took the hand she extended, and favored her with his most formal bow.

"It is with great pleasure that I presume to renew our acquaintance, Miss Mallory."

Judith beamed, and dropped her assumed air of hauteur. "There! You see, Tess? Roman thinks I am out in society already."

Tess threw her hands up. "Now see what you have started, just as I was getting her calmed down again."

Minnie took Roman's arm and pulled him down on the larger sofa beside her. "Come sit by me and tell us all your most lurid adventures!"

"Minnie!" Judith cried out. She turned to Tess. "You see what I have had to endure at Hazeldean! She is incorrigible."

Minnie made a rude face. "Being an 'embarrassingly *farouche* schoolgirl,' as you called me earlier, has its benefits. I need not stand on ceremony with Roman."

"No, indeed." His glance went from her to Judith, then lingered on Tess. "None of you need do so. We are all old friends, together at last."

"Yes," Tess exclaimed. It was like being back at Swanfield in happier times. Minnie and Judith were so gay and animated it warmed her heart. It was the first time she hadn't wished Roman a hundred miles away.

"How comfortable it is, just to be the four of us again. Quite like old times." She smiled across at him. "I am glad that you came back early today, Roman."

"So am I, Tess." His eyes held hers just a fraction too long. Both looked away simultaneously.

Tess rang for more refreshments, and they spent the next hour catching up and reminiscing. Although Minnie wanted to pump Roman for his stories, it was he who kept turning the conversation back to them.

Judith, now out of her sulks, was filled with enthusiasm for London and all the wonderful friends she'd made at Hazeldean. Minnie's conversation was geared toward books she had read of late, her hopes for future travels, and teasing asides to her sister when Judith became too pretentious.

As for Tess—his plan wasn't working as yet. She said little about herself, but managed to draw both Roman and her sisters out. She guided the talk to safe subjects, and discussed plans for the girls' entertainment during their holiday.

All the while she watched her sisters lovingly, her face had a wonderful warm glow—she focused on them, as if they were her whole world.

It was not at all the way she looked at her husband.

But Roman remembered Tess's glowing face from days gone by, and felt a bitter pang. His jaw tightened.

Oh, Tess! Once you looked at me that way.

When Tess escorted her sisters up to their rooms, Roman closed himself away in the library. One of the linen-lined drawers in a map cabinet held fragments of various papyri, most with hieratic script rather than hieroglyphs. None of them were more than four inches on a side, and all were badly preserved.

All yesterday morning he had worked meticulously at unrolling them and enclosing each between pieces of glass. Today he meant to try and sort them out like puzzle pieces, seeing if any matched up with the others, or if some belonged to others he'd examined in Claybourne's collection.

One was an illegible scrap, ruined from careless handling and storage. A larger segment was from a student scribe's exercise in transcribing texts. *Not worth much for its expansion of knowledge,* Roman thought, *but priceless in the human sense.*

In Roman's mind the muted colors of the book-lined library shelves and the dark polished furniture were replaced by a partially roofed courtyard decorated in vibrant hues. The light was brilliant, the sky incredibly blue. A youthful Middle Kingdom student scribe sat cross-legged in the shade with his tight linen kilt forming a taut work surface. Roman imagined the young man anxiously grinding his colored inks, carefully preparing his stylus, and then copying the text his teacher had set out for his lesson.

He found himself wondering about the lad, his future achievements, his life and loves. Could he imagine that his simple practice text would be read by a foreigner thousands of miles away, and separated by so vast a gulf of centuries?

The mystique of archaeology, to him, was not just the knowledge or artifacts, but lay in that intangible reach of hands across the bridge of time. Roman gave himself a shake. He wouldn't accomplish much if he let himself become bemused by the unknown story behind each fragment.

Suddenly his heart gave a leap. *Yes, this small piece is a part of this other. And this belongs to the end of the large scroll I examined on my first day.*

Fitting the smaller sections next to one another, he could make out reference to the burial of an important priest named Amunoseh, whose task in life it had been to safeguard a temple and make offerings. Roman had already located the priest's tomb, buried beneath the rubble of other burials. What he needed was to know exactly which god of ancient Egypt was worshiped at that temple. Because if he was right . . .

Searching quickly through the glass-protected fragments, Roman came to the very last one. There it was. The same scribe had written it and the edges would match up almost perfectly.

Keeping his eagerness in check, he started to translate the flowing script. "Good God! Claybourne will be interested in this!"

There were two missing sections. He noted that the usual names and honorificies of the goddess were not listed, and the last part of the phrase was wording he'd never seen used before:

". . . offerings of wine and fruit and the burning of precious incense to honor the great goddess Isis. Beautiful Isis, golden Isis, who breathed life with . . . into the dead Good God Osiris, whose gilded sandals stand upon the jeweled pillars of the architect . . . Isis, mighty and wise, who protects the . . . and the secret knowledge of the gods for all eternity . . .

The hour with her sisters and Roman had flown by for Tess, as carefree and merry as the hours they'd spent together at Swanfield. She hadn't wanted it to end. Now she wished it had never occurred. *I should have taken the girls up to their rooms immediately. Then we could have avoided seeing Roman until dinner.*

But there was no way of avoiding him in her thoughts.

Her maid had spread a silk throw over the reclining couch in her mistress's bedroom. "Will my lady rest before dinner?"

"No, but I'll change into my wrapper now and read a while." An absorbing book would be a good cure for her unsettled mind. "You are free until it is time to change for dinner, Celeste."

"Thank you, madame."

Celeste saw that everything was settled properly and slipped away. She had seen Mr. Otten, the master's valet, going toward the cedar room to remove items from storage. Perhaps she would slip away to join him for a few stolen kisses.

Left alone, Tess stretched out on the couch with the shawl over her legs. Leland and Alicia were both still out, her sisters in their suites, resting from their travels, and Tess had absolutely nothing to do.

Where had she left that novel? It had been in her hand when she'd gone down earlier. She was about to ring for Celeste, when she remembered she'd given her a few hours off. No use trying to do up all those little buttons on her dress by herself. Tess was resigned to being alone with her thoughts.

Then she felt the quietness of the house seeping into her bones. This was the time of day when the women of the house retired, the men were out or occupied, and the servants vanished like djinns into their part of the house behind the green baize door. There was absolutely no reason she couldn't slip down the stairs, nip into the drawing room, and fetch the novel.

Putting on her velvet Chinese slippers, Tess fastened her wrapper securely and went downstairs. She didn't see a soul on her way to the drawing room, but neither did she find the book.

"Oh, yes! I went down to the blue parlor earlier. It must be there."

A separate ornate staircase led to that wing of the house, and Tess knew she could slip down it and back up quickly. The parlor was a quiet room near Leland's library, where the ladies sometimes retired on inclement days, to while away the hours with books or puzzles. A private, more comfortable space than the formal drawing room where they need not stand on ceremony.

She thought she heard a door close as she reached the foot of the stairs, but there was no one in sight. Had one of the parlormaids heard her coming down the stairs? The servants were trained to vanish discreetly when any of the family and their guests were about.

The first time she'd seen a parlormaid whisk behind an arch as she crossed a corridor, Tess had been startled. Now she was used to moving through a mansion seemingly run by an army of ghosts, or good fairies, who polished and scoured and swept the hearths, yet were rarely seen.

She'd almost reached her goal when Roman came around the intersecting corridor from the library. Tess hadn't known he'd returned. She bit her lip and put one hand up to hold the throat of her wrapper together.

"I thought you had gone out."

"Did you? Is that why you came down the side staircase in your dressing gown?"

A dark flush rose in his face as he realized how little there was beneath it. All his resolve to ignore the tension between them ignited and burnt to ashes in that instant. The heat of desire thrummed through his blood. Stepping into her path, he blocked the way.

"Please let me pass," Tess said angrily. "I only came down to fetch a book. I am not interested in your opinions of me, or your absurd and mistaken theories regarding my behavior."

"Yes, I suppose I deserved that. I implied on first coming here that you had abandoned or neglected your sisters," he said stiffly. "I was grossly in the wrong. For that, I owe you an apology . . ."

"Yes. I accept!"

She tried to push past him, but he opened the door of

the blue parlor and pulled her into the room. The thick damask draperies were drawn against the afternoon sun, creating a twilight dusk, filled with deep shadows.

His mouth firmed in that determined way she remembered. "At least let me have my say. I was unfair in what I said. It's apparent that you are doing everything humanly possible to secure their happiness."

She was forced to smile at that. "Fortunately for my reputation, you did not hear the conversation prior to your arrival: Judith is sure I am ruining all her hopes of an advantageous marriage by requiring her to stay at Hazeldean, while Minnie is equally certain I am blighting her young life by forcing her to go to a school so lacking in intellectual merit."

Roman tipped back his head and laughed, a rich and wonderful sound. Tess felt her heart give a leap. It was the first time he'd been himself with her since his arrival.

"I see your sisters have not changed a bit except for growing up so beautifully," he said. "Minnie was either up in a tree, or had her nose in a book; while Judith primped in the mirror with one eye, and checked out the likely lads with the other."

"Now you are painting a ridiculous picture," Tess protested. "My sister is definitely not walleyed!" But she was laughing, too. It was so long since she'd been unrestrained by decorum or her surroundings. She felt so free.

So young.

When had she stopped feeling that way?

Roman was startled at the abrupt change in her mood—one moment carefree, the other forlorn. Then, like a mask, she slipped on her calm, society face. It angered him out of all reason. This was the Tess who had turned her back on him in her quest for higher status. He wanted the other one back again.

He took her chin in his cupped hand and lifted her face

to his. A shiver ran over her skin, part fear and part something unnamed.

"You've changed, Tess. Until you laughed just then, I could barely recognize the open girl I knew in the stylish society matron you've become."

She wound her fingers around his wrist, but couldn't budge it. She was forced to look up into those turbulent blue eyes. "Let go of me, Roman," she said angrily. "I haven't changed at all. Only your perception of me has."

It was exactly the wrong thing to say, and she knew it the minute his face hardened. "Indeed? Let us put it to the test."

He shut the door and pushed her back against it. With his arms braced on either side she couldn't escape. His familiar scent surrounded her, stirring memories of warm summer days and stolen kisses by the weir. Although she was dizzy with his nearness, she fought to keep things from spiraling out of control.

"Let me go."

He moved in closer. Things had taken a turn he hadn't intended. Anger, and need, poured through him. Too late to go back now. Her eyes were wide, her mouth so soft, so tempting. He wanted her with an overwhelming desperation.

"How do you feel now, Tess?" he said dangerously. "*What* do you feel? Anticipation? Eagerness?" He paused, looking down at her. "Or is it merely contempt and loathing?"

She took a deep breath. "The last would be fairly close!"

He flushed darkly. "Ah, then you *have* changed, after all."

His mouth was inches from hers. "But I am a man of science. I always require proof."

His lips touched hers, not like a lover's but a conquerors's. Hard, insistent, and commanding. She struggled for just an instant, pushing at his chest with her hands. Then her body gave in to the sensations that overloaded her senses. Before she knew what she was doing, Tess was winding her arms around Roman's neck. Her breasts pressed against his muscled chest, and her mouth opened to his.

She went to his head like wine. Roman abandoned all caution. He took the kiss deep, as he never had before. Every atom of need and want were in it, heating his mouth against hers. The tender kisses they'd exchanged in her girlhood were nothing to this, mere candle flames compared to this blazing release of repressed passion.

Tess was completely unprepared. She trembled in his arms while he ravaged her mouth. Clinging to him for support, she lost herself in the kiss, in the desperate comfort of his strong embrace. Through the thin silk her lush body molded to his.

Roman was insane with wanting her. Drunk with knowing that she wanted him with equal ferocity. He wanted her with a fierce hunger, a naked desire that was almost overwhelming. Another moment and he couldn't vouch for what he'd do next. The thought of taking her down to the floor and making love to her right then and there was mad. Yet he knew that was on the verge of losing his precarious hold on sanity.

He fought it with all his self-control, with every bit of remembered anger. It was the one thing, the only thing strong enough to keep them from ruining their lives. He was the first to pull away, shaking his head.

"Oh, Tess, you calculating little witch! Is this how you snagged yourself a lord?"

His harsh words snapped her out of her dazed reaction. *To be kissed so resoundingly, and then treated like a woman of easy virtue!* Tears sprang to her eyes and Tess wiped her mouth with the back of her hand.

"How *dare* you!"

To see those unshed tears and know he was the cause made Roman feel like an utter knave. The only shield he had was forged of pride and anger.

"Don't act the affronted virgin with me. If that wasn't an invitation I saw in your eyes, I don't know what it was."

"You arrogant fool!"

She was still shaken by the kiss, by the way her body had turned traitor to her will the moment his mouth had captured hers. The need had almost ripped her apart. Passion turned to fury. She drew her arm back and slapped him stingingly.

"Stay away from me, Roman!"

The words were torn from him: "I wish to God I could!"

Tess grabbed the door handle and whirled out of the room, holding back a sob. She had scarcely gone ten feet when she heard footsteps from the opposite direction, and ducked into the music room. Her hands were shaking and she held her breath as the butler walked past the open door and proceeded on down the corridor in his usual dignified progress.

Dabbing at her eyes, Tess went to the door and closed it softly. She took a chair in a quiet corner and blew her nose. Her nerves were badly shaken by what had occurred between herself and Roman. It had caught her unprepared, and left her vulnerable and afraid. She was a woman of strong moral fiber—or so she thought. To realize her weakness and the depths of her great loneliness was devastating.

I should have stayed in Swanfield and married Roman. We could have managed somehow! In her heart of hearts she knew that wasn't true. Judith and Minnie would have been condemned to a meager existence, growing old and bitter in time. And Roman would have suffered terribly, as well. She could not have let his bold dreams die a whimpering ignoble death.

Soft footfalls sounded outside the door from the opposite direction that the butler had taken. Tess's body jerked in reaction. She held her breath, praying they went past. Whoever it was hesitated outside the music room, then went briskly on.

Tess dried her eyes and tried to compose herself. *Oh, if only I could weep my heart out! In this mansion of so many rooms, is there no place I can be alone?*

After Tess fled, Roman stayed in the dusky blue gloom of the parlor, cursing beneath his breath.

She is right. I am a bloody fool. A villain of the worst sort!

He was filled with self-loathing. He'd violated every rule of gentlemanly conduct by forcing his attentions on her—and had compounded it by doing so when he was a guest beneath her husband's roof, violating every rule of hospitality.

The only honorable course was for him to make some excuse and remove himself from this house immediately. And from London, as soon as possible.

No, from England entirely!

He wouldn't be easy in his mind until the sea separated him from Tess, and the spell she cast had on him so many years ago. He'd thought he was long over her, and he'd been hopelessly wrong.

He raked his hands through his disordered hair and left the room.

Quiet reigned in the blue parlor and the corridor beyond. When the clock struck the quarter hour, the door to a room farther down opened quietly.

With a quick glance around, the person who had been watching in fascination as Tess ran out of the parlor, disheveled and in tears, hurried away well pleased. Roman McKendrick was certainly stirring things up! Matters were progressing satisfactorily. Indeed, much more quickly than expected.

EGYPT

"It was somewhere by that rock," the headman of the village told the buyer he knew only as "Mr. Smith." He pointed to a rock vaguely shaped like the head of a lion. "Just at the fork of the two wadis. My nephew stepped on a loose pebble and it rolled beneath his foot. The boy and all went tumbling down in the darkness. It was not his fault, effendi."

His companion scowled and shielded his eyes against the late afternoon sun. The artifacts could be anywhere among the dried and wrinkled land. "Fool! The fault is yours. Hussein said he told you this misbegotten whelp was too clumsy to be trusted with such a task."

The youth in question wrapped his gray robe closer and bowed his head, trying to make himself invisible. Yusef had already gotten one beating from his uncle for dropping the precious load he'd been carrying last evening. It didn't take intuition to know another was probably in the offing.

"I gave him nothing of value to carry, effendi," the headman lied, thinking of the lovely alabaster canopic jar bearing the face of a long-dead queen. Ah well, there were still three of four intact. He gave a shrug. "Necklaces of wire and glass beads, amulets of faience, and such."

"I want every last bead and scrap found," "Mr. Smith" said furiously. "All we need is for word to get out that a new tomb discovery has been made!"

His uncle prodded him sharply in the ribs. The boy

lifted his thickly lashed eyes. "I shall recover them all, effendi. It is a matter of honor."

"Mr. Smith" sent him a look of utter contempt. "The honor of a thief? Bah!"

The boy scurried down the steep and treacherous slope, his pale gray robe and dark hair blending with the bleached rock and deep shadows. He was filled with resentment at the Foreign buyer, but more so at his uncle. If he had not said anything about the mishap, who would have known?

Yusef clambered down and disappeared from view, determined to find every single item that he had lost. He would scour the rocks, to find every tiny gold bead, and place it all in his uncle's hands, thus redeeming his honor.

As he scrambled down, the boy remembered his first trip to the valley by night, when the ceiling of the other tomb had caved in, leaving it smothered beneath tons of rock. He thought of the mirror that had fallen from his belt near this very spot. He had meant to find the mirror as a surprise for his uncle. Now he would keep it for himself.

Was he not the one who had found it and saved it from the rockfall? But that was not Yusef's primary motivation: after it was discovered that the tomb was buried under tons of rubble, the others had turned on him in anger. He had been beaten and shamed, cursed and called a lowly dog— and he would have his own revenge for that.

4

"**You're giving a real ball!**" **Minnie said, waltzing** around Tess's boudoir. While she had no interest in attending one herself, she found the idea fascinating. "Will you wear a tiara tonight? Do you feel like a princess?"

Tess laughed. "Yes, I shall wear a tiara. And no, I do not. I feel like a very harried hostess thrust in the midst of a whirlwind."

Beneath its outward serenity, Claybourne House was all a-bustle behind the scenes. Deliveries from Fortnum and Mason had been made earlier in the week and, at the moment, the men from Picard and Sons were busy transforming the ballroom at the back of the house into a floral bower. This evening Tess would play hostess to the *ton* at the grand affair. She bit her lip. It would be her first real test.

"Today all is chaos, but I suppose everything will turn out well."

Minnie twirled like a ballerina. "I am sure that it will be quite splendid. Like a scene from a play."

"Yes," Judith said aggrievedly, "and we are condemned to watch from behind the scenes, peeking through curtains like nursery children."

Tess sent her a look that spoke volumes. "We will not cover that ground again, if you please!"

Judith started to protest but Tess held up a hand for silence. "You think me hard-hearted, no doubt. May I remind you of the myriad things you must learn before making your debut in the highest circles of society? You were not born to it, like your fine friends at Hazeldean."

Judith blushed and her head drooped like a flower on a graceful stem. It gave Tess a pang to see that vulnerable white nape, but she forced herself to continue.

"While you are a gentlewoman by birth and breeding, you must learn the intricacies of society that they are taught from the nursery. And you have been raised to know that a lady does not whine, nor does she ruin the good times of others by sulking or making a scene in front of them!"

Deep mortification colored Judith's face and throat. "I am sorry, Tess," she said in a lowered tone. "I truly do believe that you have my best interests at heart. I shall, of course, comport myself like a lady. I give you my word."

"I have no doubt of that," Tess said more gently. "You have never given me the slightest cause to think otherwise."

Minnie took a discreet step back, lest she be included in Judith's promise. Claybourne House was like a vast fairyland to her, beautiful and yet somehow not entirely real. She remembered how merry they had all been together in Swanfield, before Tess had gone to be companion to their great-aunt. From the way her two older sisters had become so *very* serious, Minnie had deduced that comporting oneself like a lady was not particularly amusing. And being a "great lady," like Tess, was even worse!

Tess crossed over the floral carpet to Judith and put her hand on her sister's heated cheek. "I shall tell you something that will lift your spirits. Leland and Alicia have persuaded me against my better judgment: you shall make your come-out when we return to London before Easter."

Judith jumped up and flung her arms around her sister. "Dear, *dear,* Tess!" Her features, already lovely, were transformed with inner radiance. "I cannot believe it!"

"Neither can I."

In fact, Tess had been surprised when Leland broached the subject. They had been sitting over the tea tray with Alicia last evening when he'd brought it up:

"I predict that Judith will be a sensation when she is launched in society," Alicia had remarked. "She bids fair to being a diamond of the first water."

Leland had been staring into his cup for several minutes, and finally spoke. "Next year there will be quite a few beauties launched, all with birth, breeding, and large fortunes. None of the young ladies this Season, however, can hope to hold a candle to Judith."

Tess set down her empty cup and looked at her husband. Leland smiled across the tea table. "I know you think her young—indeed, that air of refreshing innocence only adds to her charm. I believe it is in her best interest to let Judith make her come-out this next Season, when we return from the country."

Put that way, how could she have any objection? By the time they went up to bed it had all been decided.

"I had planned to tell you after we returned from our drive in the park," she told Judith. "Leland will take a subscription to one of the assembly rooms while we are still at Claybourne Castle," Tess said, "so that you may practice your dancing before we return to London. I predict that you shall be enormously successful, and make a splendid match!"

With her beauty and Leland's patronage, she will be able to marry wherever she chooses, Tess thought. *And,* she added like a prayer, *if she is fortunate, find a loving husband who wins her affections, as well as her hand.* Her sisters would be free to follow their hearts. The knowledge was bittersweet.

Minnie made a face. "I hope you have no such plans for me," she announced. "I have decided that a husband, no matter how doting, is an encumbrance. I shall be a spinster, like Lady Alicia, and do anything I please."

Although only a few months shy of her sixteenth birthday, Minnie was a bit behind her peers in discovering the opposite sex. She was much more interested in poking about Leland's fossils and antiquities than in discussing the latest fashions in the pattern books, or in wondering how to wear her hair to best advantage.

Tess smiled. "Another few months and you will change your mind. Trust me on this."

"Did you?"

"Of course." Tess turned hastily away and unlocked her jewel case. At the same age, she had already fallen in love with Roman. Her fingers trembled as she fumbled with the catch. *Oh, Roman, why did you ever have to come to England—come here, of all places on earth, and remind me of what might have been!*

Minnie mulled over her sister's comment. "It must have been in London, then. Why, there was nobody in Swanfield, except Roman and Mr. Burleigh, and they were both too old."

There was no reply from Tess, who pretended to be checking the clasp on her diamond choker. Glancing up, she saw Judith staring at her, eyes round. She half expected her to ask about Roman. Judith—suddenly self-conscious—glanced hastily away.

Tess was rattled. *Oh, dear, she is putting two and two together. But after my lecture on acting like a young lady, she will surely know better than to ask directly.* She had no such confidence in Minnie's discretion. Fortunately her youngest sister wasn't aware enough of the world to have made the connection.

Locking the jewel case again, she handed the key into her dresser's keeping. "We are going out for a drive, Celeste. Please put this away in the jewel closet."

The maid dropped a curtsy. She was so excited about dressing madame for the ball that she could hardly keep from dancing like the young mademoiselle.

Later, as the three sisters were driving in the park, Judith was uncharacteristically quiet. Minnie didn't notice. "When will Roman be back from Salisbury? Do you think he will arrive in time for your ball tonight?"

"I hope . . ." *Most sincerely not!* Tess cleared her throat. "I imagine he might, although he said it could be nearer the end of the week before he'd finish his research."

"He was very excited about the scrolls his friend at Shakleford Priory had purchased!"

Tess didn't respond. She wondered if there even *was* a friend named Phineas Blane and a place called Shakleford Priory outside Salisbury—or indeed, if Roman had even gone into the country. For all she knew he might be holed up in London in a hotel somewhere, avoiding another meeting with her.

There was no doubt at all in her mind that the reason he'd left was the scene that had occurred between them in the parlor. Taking himself out of the reach of temptation was the proper, the gentlemanly, thing to do. And perversely, she resented him for it.

She'd lain awake all that night, wishing he would go away, and come down late in the morning to discover he'd already left. Relief had mingled with fear that she might never see him again. Every day the conflict of feelings grew. It left her low and out of sorts.

Tess realized she'd clasped her hands so tightly that her

wedding ring was biting into the side of her finger. *I must get my emotions under control!*

While Judith made ecstatic plans for her debut (and Minnie imitated her with remarkable accuracy), Tess was forming plans of her own. Perhaps she could talk Leland into going to his country seat earlier. There was no reason they couldn't remove themselves to Claybourne Castle by the middle of next week.

Then Roman would go back to Egypt, and the door to their past would be firmly closed, once and for all.

At the British Museum, Roman busied himself examining the texts and transcribing notes. His dark head was bent over the table and his wide shoulders were hunched with tension. He'd arrived back in London well before noon, and in a state of great excitement. Phineas Blane's collection had held an important clue in the memoirs of a Greek traveler, Philos of Athens. The memoirs had referred to a certain papyrus—a portion of which lay on the table now before him.

Roman touched the artifact as little as possible. It was extremely brittle and fragile. The edges had flaked away in places, and some of the remaining symbols on the section of scroll were faded. Others were completely missing, where the papyrus had been carelessly handled in its long journey from a looted rock tomb to a Turkish marketplace, and eventually to the heart of London. The damage to the precious manuscript would ordinarily have filled him with anger, but Roman only felt an overwhelming awe.

Each hieroglyph was meticulously rendered, yet with a certain grace of line that spoke of a master. The scrap that Phineas Blane owned was in even worse condition, yet Roman was certain the same hand had written each of them. The question was, were they part of the same scroll? It was intensely frustrating.

He took the last of the carefully preserved specimens and placed it on the table before him. His heart gave a sudden leap: there was the top half of a cartouche, with the titles of the goddess Isis . . . and he'd just seen the bottom half of it in the roughly triangular piece that Phineas had showed him. He opened his journal to the appropriate page and placed his careful drawing beside the small section of papyrus.

A match, by God!

Roman's hands shook a little as a surge of adrenaline shot through his veins. Next to it were the words he'd found inscribed on the ancient stone not far from the Valley of the Kings. He knew the phrases by heart:

> "Beautiful Isis, who resurrected Osiris, her beloved brother and husband, and caused this temple to be raised in praise. Isis, whose path is paved with gold and who guards the ancient knowledge . . . the wisdom of the gods, and who stands with her dainty feet upon the jeweled pillars of . . .

It was torn there, quite jaggedly. At the moment Roman would have sold his soul to Old Nick, for the missing portion.

Carefully, reverently, he unrolled the final segment of papyrus. Unlike the others, it was remarkably well preserved, soft and supple except at the very edges. The first part was illegible, and his disappointment keen. He worked cautiously but methodically for several hours, translating the faded hieroglyphs.

Then Roman came to the phrase that made his breath stop and set his heart beating like a kettledrum: ". . . caused to be made by the priest Amunoseh, who safeguards the temple of Isis at the entrance to the valley. Beautiful Isis, golden Isis . . . who protects the secret knowledge of the gods, who stands forever upon the jeweled pillars of Imhotep, illuminated by the . . . sun.''

The surge of adrenaline made him almost sick with excitement. The papyrus referred to the temple and its location before the section ended in a torn edge. It was the final clue to confirm what he already suspected. The temple of Isis would be found just where he had believed it to be, near the tomb of Amunoseh and buried beneath the rubble of a later burial.

Roman's eyes glowed with satisfaction and anticipation. He had found the information he sought. It was an archaeologist's dream—the project of his choice, searching for precious knowledge. All he needed now was the backing of an interested and informed patron with deep pockets.

He'd leave England for Egypt as soon as he could. With the Mediterranean separating him from Tess, the pain of seeing her again—as another man's wife—would eventually fade away. He turned back to the papyrus and his eyes lingered like a lover's on the graceful hieroglyphs drawn so long ago.

''Beautiful Isis, golden Isis, who guards the secret knowledge of the gods,'' he breathed, almost like a prayer.

But in his mind it was Tess's face he saw.

While Tess dressed to play her part as hostess, Minnie lounged on the chaise with a book in her sister's boudoir, occasionally reading excerpts aloud.

Judith perched on the settee, trying very hard not to look wistful. It was clear that she wished she were joining the dancers tonight, instead of being relegated to the status of schoolgirl. It was very hard for her to have to watch the preparations without taking part. *Soon I shall be dressing for my first ball! I cannot wait. Oh, if only Tess and Leland had come to their senses sooner!*

This particular ball had come all too soon for Tess. She was glad they were giving it in the "little Season" before Christmas, and not in the spring, when London society would be in full swing. She felt almost as ill-prepared to greet the glittering guests as she was to face Roman again. He'd returned an hour ago, and Minnie had hurried to announce his return, sure that Tess would be pleased to hear the news.

It had been difficult to hide her consternation. Tess could not ignore the fact that Roman was beneath the same roof. She was grateful for one thing: he wouldn't ask her to stand up with him. She knew him too well to expect him to show her the courtesy due his reluctant hostess.

Celeste stepped away to fetch the tiara, leaving Tess to confront the elegant stranger in her mirror. She could scarcely recognize herself in the fine gown of gauzy gold tissue from the House of Worth. The skirt was pulled back to reveal an underdress shot through with silver threads, the low bodice sewn with hundreds of pearls interspersed with minuscule gold, silver, and crystal beads in a pattern of stars. With every rise and fall of her breasts the gown shimmered and gleamed.

For a moment her image shifted, became that of a complete stranger, one born to wear splendid jewels and costly gowns. *So, this is Tess, Lady Claybourne,* she thought in wonder.

No. She shook her head in a gesture of dismissal, and the woman in the mirror did the same. The illusion shattered. *It is only myself, Tess Mallory, playing dress-up just as I used to in my mother's old dressing gown!*

Celeste had dressed her mistress's hair simply in a Grecian style, entwined with gold and silver ribbons and strings of matched pearls. Deftly slipping the low sunburst tiara of pearls and diamonds into the coiffure, she wisped a few curls at Tess's temples and stepped back to admire her handiwork.

"Ah, my lady, you look like a statue of Venus come to life."

She was delighted to have so young and beautiful a mistress. Dressing Lady Alicia to look her best was a challenge; preparing Lady Claybourne for a ball was a great pleasure. How the other ladies' maids envied her!

Giving her mistress the hand mirror, Celeste unlocked the jewel case. "The diamond suite, my lady, or the pearl rope with the diamond brooch?"

The maid held them up, great sparkling gems that caught the light and threw it back a hundredfold, and a rajah's ransom in pearls, that could loop around Tess's throat several times and still hang down to her waist.

The wealth of jewels made Tess's mind reel. Any one of those glittering creations would buy and sell the entire village where she'd spent her early years, including Squire Martin's Heath Hall.

She felt herself disappearing beneath the weight of her responsibilities and her title. Suddenly Tess desperately needed something to remind her of who she really was, before she got lost in the false glamour. In the last six months she had come so far, so fast, she was afraid she might go rocketing off the face of the earth without something solid and real to tether her to it. She needed something of the past to hold on to tonight. She remembered her mother's simple ornaments.

"There are a pair of pearl-drop earrings in the white leather case. I shall wear them with the small gold and pearl necklace you will find with them."

"But my lady!" The maid was horrified. "My lord will surely expect you to wear one of the heirloom sets!"

"They are heirlooms from my mother's family," Tess said crisply. "I shall wear them tonight."

The maid opened the case and took out the necklace. "Oh, the string is broken, my lady! What of this oval locket?"

Tess froze. Roman had given her the locket set with a single pearl on their last Christmas together in Swanfield, when he'd pledged his love to her. How long ago that was! That young, idealistic Roman had nothing to do with the dangerous, cynical man who was now a guest beneath her roof.

Despite the heated kiss in the parlor, she knew that *this* Roman despised her—or at least despised what he thought she had become.

Perhaps the locket would help him see the truth: that beneath the jewels and elegant finery she was still the same.

Although disappointed at first, Celeste changed her mind when she fixed the earrings to her mistress's earlobes and clasped the simple locket about her neck. Instead of the chain, Tess had asked her to thread the gold oval on twisted ribbons of silver and gold, to match those in her hair.

"Oh, my lady! You were quite right!"

The starburst engraved around the central pearl echoed that of the tiara, and the total effect was enchanting. Celeste was gratified. The simplicity showed Lady Claybourne to be a true beauty, one who need not be draped with a fortune in gems to hide her defects.

"Exquisite, my lady! You will set a new style."

Leland entered from the dressing room with his gentle smile. "Yes, one that will have every other woman—not to mention the jewelers' guild—up in arms. And, my dear, every man worshiping at your feet."

Tess thanked him prettily, and he leaned down and placed a light kiss on her cheek. "You will outshine every woman in the room. My dear, you do me proud!"

She pinked with pleasure. It was the first time he'd ever said that to her. "I shall do my best."

Alicia entered, dressed in her new gown, with her brown velvet cape draped over her arm. Her toilette was not a success. The fawn and cream striped silk was a poor choice for her skin and hair tones, turning them muddy, and the profusion of ruffles, bows, and fringe overwhelmed her slight figure. Her features, which were quite pleasant, receded into the background.

To make matters worse, all her own dresser's gentle attempts at persuasion had been in vain. Nothing had kept Lady Alicia from piling on a heavy suite of necklace, brooch, bracelets, and rings, of massive topazes and yellow diamonds set in gold.

The maid had tried not to cringe. Mon Dieu, *it appears she has no neck! Poor thing, she has no style, no élan.*

Alicia linked arms with Tess and turned for Judith and Minnie to admire. "What do you think? Do not spare us."

Minnie's jaw dropped. "How elegant you both are!"

Judith nodded. "You shall be the most distinguished ladies at the ball."

Leland beamed at them both. "And the most lovely. I am indeed a lucky man to squire two such beautiful women this evening."

Tess realized that he meant it. The warmth between brother and sister was wonderful to see, and she felt herself enveloped in it tonight. Too often she had felt like a stranger, who had fallen by chance into a party of intimate friends.

Not that they ever did anything to make her feel excluded. Both, in fact, made a point to include her and not to discuss acquaintances she hadn't met as yet in front of her. If that couldn't be avoided, Alicia always included a little anecdote about the member of the *ton* in question, so that Tess learned as she went along.

No, it was her own sense of loneliness, of being out of her element, like a minnow swimming in a salmon stream. At least, so far, she had committed no horrid, public gaffes. She noticed Alicia staring at her simple locket, but her sister-in-law had no intention of criticizing.

"How charming you look. I predict your new style will become all the rage!"

Judith looked so wistful that Alicia put her arm around the girl's waist. "Shall I tell you a secret? That stained-glass panel in the yellow sitting room gives a full view of the entrance hall. If you turn down the lamps and look through the clear panes of the window, you can watch all the guests arrive. I used to do that myself as a child."

Judith was torn between delight and mortification. "While I am no longer a child, Lady Alicia, I shall enjoy watching the guests arrive very much. And I'm sure that Minnie will, too."

Leland escorted them down the staircase. The butler was in the formal entrance hall when they reached the ground floor.

"Where is Mr. McKendrick? Has he come down yet?"

"At your service, Lord Claybourne." Roman stepped out of the drawing room, looking splendid in evening clothes.

His appearance after being gone for over a week was a shock to Tess. In his absence, she'd tried to tell herself he no longer had the old power to make her legs weak or her heart pound. It had been a lie. She felt the color drain from her face, then rush back until her cheeks burned.

Roman came forward and made an elegant bow. Despite the civilized attire, he brought with him an aura of the wild and untamed. *An eagle in dove's feathers,* Tess thought.

She could tell that Alicia was surprised at the fashionable figure he cut, and the way the tight-fitting coat showed off his superb shoulders. A tinge of jealousy curled through the pit of her stomach.

Instantly she dismissed the emotion as unworthy. Alicia was a wonderful woman, quiet yet warm, soft-spoken but highly intelligent. And as the unmarried sister of a wealthy peer of the realm, she would make an excellent catch for a man like Roman. *Just as I made a brilliant match in marrying Leland.*

The comparison gave her no comfort.

While Tess would love to see Alicia happily settled, she would miss her greatly. As to Roman, the thought of seeing him in the role of her husband's brother-in-law didn't bear considering. It would be agonizing.

And yet she could not begrudge either one of them the happiness that had eluded her.

Tess was aware of Roman glancing at her and then away, and wondered if he'd noticed the necklace. She hoped he had, although he gave no sign as they went into the drawing room. She never could read his face these days, except when he was angry. Then it was impossible for him to hide his emotions, they came boiling out so suddenly and completely. It was like watching granite turn molten, a force of nature both fearsome and awe-inspiring.

She took a place beside Alicia, while the men went to the side table where whisky and soda awaited them. Roman looked so handsome he took her breath away.

What kind of lover would he be? Controlled and masterful, or wildly passionate?

The thought came unbidden, flustering Tess. Then she realized it had not come from her own mind, but from Alicia whispering in her ear.

She looked at her sister-in-law in startlement. It wasn't the kind of question she would have expected to hear from a gentlewoman, and certainly not from one as meek as Alicia.

Glancing across to make sure the men had not heard, Tess lowered her own voice. "I have not considered the matter. Nor do I intend to."

"Ah, now I have shocked you! I must confess," Alicia said, looking contrite. "I have been reading naughty stories."

"I cannot believe it of you. In fact," Tess said, noticing the dimple at the corner of Alicia's mouth, "I think you are pulling my leg."

Her sister-in-law laughed softly. "Only in a manner of speaking. I recently viewed a splendid painting of David and Beersheba at Lady Norton's town house, and looked up the story in the Bible. King David saw Beersheba and lusted after her, and he had her husband placed in the front lines of battle, so he would be killed, and then seduced the man's widow. Is that not strange to find in the Holy Scripture?"

"I suppose that since the world began, men have committed every sin there is, to possess the women they desired."

Alicia laughed. "Without our civilizing influence, they would be living in withy huts and dashing one another's brains out with clubs."

It was time to take their places in the receiving line, and they went out to await their guests.

Lady Lowell Clarkendale greeted Tess with her warm smile. "My dear, you cannot believe the carriages lined up in the streets to disgorge their elegant passengers. I predict this affair will be a mad crush, and that you shall be all the rage!"

Turbaned dowagers, hopeful mamas of debutante daughters, lords and ladies, and all the highest ranks of society had turned out in force. After half an hour the faces and names became a blur to Tess as guests streamed past.

It was an eternity she was able to make her way to the ballroom with Leland and Alicia.

The chamber was one of the largest and certainly the most beautiful in all of London. The plaster ceiling was molded with medallions, all gilded and intricately painted. The lusters of the great chandeliers twinkled like stars in the light of hundreds of candles. *And I am hostess here,* Tess thought wonderingly.

Masses of flowers transformed the room into an exotic indoor garden. A card room had been set up in the parlor through the far doors and another pair of doors led to the room where supper would be served later. Gilt chairs with rose satin seats were lined up in precision before the tall windows.

On the opposite side there were six curtained alcoves, separated by mirrors, where ladies not wishing to dance or observe the sets, could sit and converse. The draperies were looped back with cloth-of-gold ties, and several formidable matrons had already commandeered one alcove for their own.

When the band struck up the first dance, Leland led out the Duchess of Warfield, the highest-ranked lady present, and the duke presented Tess a sweeping bow. "I believe this is my dance, Lady Claybourne."

As they wove through the opening steps, Tess was startled to see Alicia partnered by Roman. How he had arranged that, when there were so many highly ranked gentlemen, was beyond her. *Or,* a little voice whispered, *perhaps it was Alicia who had arranged it.*

They certainly seemed to have much to say to one another as the patterns of the dance brought them together time and again. Tess was so engrossed in what they were doing that she trod on her partner's toes.

"I am so sorry," she apologized breathlessly. "I don't know why I am so clumsy tonight."

"You are grace personified," the duke replied sardonically. "It was sheer bad luck that my foot was in the wrong place at the wrong moment."

When the set ended he escorted her to the side and went to fetch her a glass of champagne. A fashionable man in his mid-forties had joined the ball in progress. The cut of his evening dress was impeccable and his dark blond hair was cut in a flattering style, although he wore far too many rings than was the current style. Making his way through the crowd, he favored Tess with an elegant bow, and took the seat beside her. She was a little flustered; he was obviously of the first rank, but she had no idea of his identity.

"Pardon my informality, Lady Claybourne, in not waiting for your husband or Lady Alicia to introduce us first." He smiled at her surprise. "We are by way of being relatives, you might say. I am Audley, your husband's cousin."

So this was young Lord Brocklehurst's father—and Leland's heir.

"Oh!" she exclaimed in surprise. "I had imagined that you were—"

"Too well-bred to show up tonight?" He tipped back his head and laughed.

"Traveling abroad," she corrected him. "At least, that is what the note with your felicitations on our marriage claimed."

His smile was amused. "You are being polite. It's true there is no love lost between this branch of the family and my own. A pity—there was a time when we were much closer. Leland always sends me an invitation through his secretary—people would talk, you know, if he did not— and I usually manage to be out of the country. I have not availed myself of his hospitality in many years."

Tess eyed him levelly. "Why have you come now,

then? Out of curiosity to see if the new bride is up to snuff?''

He looked taken aback, then laughed aloud. "Impertinent! Perhaps, my dear Lady Claybourne, I have merely stopped by to see how well he is managing my inheritance.''

"Perhaps you presume too much," she suggested coolly. "Should our marriage produce an heir, you will find yourself quite out in the cold!"

"So, you would dash all my expectations?"

Although he was charming on the surface, there was a subtle sting beneath his words. Tess did not think she liked him. "From what I have heard, my lord, it would be not be the slightest inconvenience to you. They say you are rich as Croesus."

"Ah, beautiful, loyal, and incredibly blunt!" The Duke of Audley lifted her hand to his lips and kissed it. "Yes, it is true. Claybourne House, Claybourne Castle, and all their accouterments are mere bagatelles to me. There. I have been equally blunt. I hope you do not despise me for it?''

Tess had the grace to blush. "How could I fault you for it without condemning myself?"

Relinquishing her hand, he rose and made a graceful bow. "I like you, indeed I do. Do not curb your tongue one bit on my account. It is quite refreshing. And you are certainly no fortune hunter."

She felt hot color stain her cheeks. "Is that what they say of me?"

"Only the fools. And I shall make it my business to disabuse them of the notion." Leland joined them, bringing Tess a glass of champagne punch. The duke smiled suavely. "I congratulate you on your charming wife, Claybourne. You are the most fortunate of men."

With another bow, he left them. Leland looked down at

Tess. "Well, now you have met Audley. What do you think of him, my dear?"

Tess plied her fan to cool her cheeks. "He seems a very curious sort of fellow."

"Oh, he is clever with his tongue, and likes to say the most outrageous things." Leland glanced after his cousin, who was working his way to the door. "I believe he came here merely to give you his blessing. Although Alicia holds him in great dislike, he has stood the friend to me in the past. Perhaps it is time to mend our fences."

Tess wasn't at all convinced.

There was no time for more as the next set was forming, and her new partner came to claim her. The dance took her around and around the floor. When the set ended she stood face-to-face with Roman.

Tess's heart hammered. The moment she had both longed for and feared was at hand. Her courage failed her.

"I am quite danced out at the moment, Roman. You will have to seek another partner."

"I don't wish to dance with you," he said darkly, eyeing the locket he'd given her. "I'd like to throttle you!"

"I *beg* your pardon!"

"Yes, you certainly should—but I doubt that you would be sincere. How could you, Tess!"

She flicked her fan open sharply. "I have no idea what you mean."

"The locket! The one I gave you and that hangs from your pretty little throat tonight, mocking me and my memories of the past. Do you think I am not aware of the great gulf between us? I don't need to be reminded that you have coffers filled with jewels which you might have worn this evening, instead of that worthless little trinket!"

She recoiled as if he had slapped her. Her eyes were suddenly overbright with unshed tears.

"I do not think it worthless, Roman," she said in a tight little voice, and walked away.

Roman stood staring after Tess. He'd been seething since the moment he'd come into the drawing room and seen the locket against the white curve of her breasts, sure that Tess was throwing his poverty in his face. But the hurt he'd just seen in hers convinced him that he was wrong.

Cursing beneath his breath, he tried to make his way through the throng to her side. *Too late, damn it!*

The music struck up for the next dance, and he saw her take her place opposite Mr. Burdock. Supper would be served after this set, and her dance card was full. There'd be no getting her alone for the rest of the evening.

Tess curtsied to her new partner. Mr. Burdock's eyes narrowed in concern. "You look quite pale, Lady Claybourne. Would you rather sit this set out?"

"I am quite well, I assure you. It is only the heat and excitment of the ball."

Tess carried it off lightly and managed to keep time to the music and watch her steps. It was difficult to do, when she wished only to vanish into one of the alcoves and weep her heart out in sorrow and rage. No matter what she did or said, Roman was determined to misunderstand her motives. *Nothing will ever change!*

As she went down the line in the last set, people were already beginning to leave the ballroom in small groups on their way to supper. One man went in the opposite direction. Tess was surprised: Alicia had overseen the guest list, and Tess hadn't even realized that Brocklehurst had been invited.

She saw him thread his way through the thinning crowd and slip into one of the curtained alcoves. There was no doubt in her mind that he was waiting for some woman to join him for a little amorous dalliance—and he was audacious enough not to care if anyone noticed!

As she turned away she saw movement up in the gallery. The carved wooden screen opened a few inches and a pale face peeked out. Tess stopped in her tracks.

Minnie! What on earth is she up to now?

Her sister was making odd faces and gesticulating. Tess started toward the door to the opposite corridor, meaning to go up and give her sister a proper talking-to, when realization dawned: Minnie was trying to tell her that Judith was in the alcove where Brocklehurst had just gone.

Appalled, she turned on her heel and moved through the crowd as fast as a good hostess could, smiling and bowing and answering comments, but all the time making her way to the alcove as quickly as possible.

If Judith were found with Brocklehurst it would cause a great scandal. Leland was a powerful lord, but Judith was still considered a schoolroom miss. A young woman's reputation could be ruined by far less.

Tess threaded her way through the last group near the sidelines and slipped behind the curtain with fire in her eye. After the glitter of the ballroom, it was so dark inside that she was temporarily blinded. There was no sign of Judith after all.

"Well, well, well," a suave voice murmured in Tess's ear. Before she had time to think, she was caught up in strong, wiry arms into a close embrace. She writhed and tried to pull away, and her captor succeeded in kissing only her ear.

"What, a sudden attack of shyness?" he murmured, pressing his mouth against the corner of hers.

Tess was aghast. *This is ridiculous,* she thought in a panic. *My own home, and people not ten feet away and I dare not call out for fear of calling disgrace down upon myself!*

"Let me go!" she said in a low voice, and aimed a kick

at the unseen shins with the toe of her dancing shoe. At the same time she elbowed his ribs.

"Ow! You little . . ."

He didn't have time to say more. The curtain parted enough for her to verify that it was Lord Brocklehurst who had forced his attentions upon her—and to see Roman's silhouette blocking the entrance.

He sprang like a tiger and had the young man by the throat. Brocklehurst could not have cried out had he tried. He was being shaken like a rat by a terrier. As Tess's eye finally adjusted to the dimness she saw a grim scene: Brocklehurst with his eyes bulging, and Roman's face a mask of rage that distorted his features.

"Enough!" she said hoarsely. "You'll choke him to death."

"That is my intention," Roman growled. "Insolent cur!"

Tess hung on his arm. "You must not. Please, Roman, for the love of God!"

He gave Brocklehurst another shake that rattled the young lord's teeth, and then flung him away. He hit the wall and crashed into one of the gilt chairs, overturning it. Brocklehurst was livid.

"You'll pay for this, sir!"

"Will I?" Roman stepped toward him and his opponent shrunk back. "I'll see you at dawn, my lord. Name your seconds."

Brocklehurst rose to his feet. Even in the gloom Tess could see a thin trickle of blood at the corner of his mouth. He came at Roman menacingly. Tess had to give him points for courage. Most men would have slunk away before Roman's wrath.

"Why wait for dawn, McKendrick, when we can settle this matter now? Pistols or swords, it makes no difference to me!"

"Very well."

"No!" She stepped between them. "Are you both insane? Dueling is outlawed—and if you think I relish the notoriety of two unmarried men fighting over my honor, think again! You will be the ruin of my reputation. And yours."

At first she thought she hadn't gotten through to them. Then Roman lowered his fists. "Get out of here, you insolent pup, before I change my mind and thrash you to within an inch of your life."

Brocklehurst struggled between relief and indignation. Tess intervened. "Please, my lord. Leave now. And quietly."

"I believe," a small voice said from the corner behind a potted palm, "we had best all leave together."

"Judith!"

She came out of her hiding place. "I am so sorry, Tess," she said in a small voice. "I only meant to watch the dancing from a closer vantage point."

Tess rounded on Brocklehurst. "And you followed her in!"

"Can you blame me?" he asked, dabbing at his lip with a corner of his linen handkerchief. "I saw a beauty—one unknown to me—go into the alcove. I thought she was perhaps an upper servant in search of a little adventure."

Judith bowed her head. "Thank you, my lord. You have made my mortification complete!"

"Well, we had best join the others before someone comments." Tess took Judith by the arm. "Roman, if you will shield us, we shall slip away toward the gallery stairs. And you, Lord Brocklehurst, shall remain in here until the ballroom is emptied."

"Very well," he said. "My apologies to you, Lady Claybourne, and to your lovely young friend."

No one bothered to point out that Judith was her sister.

With Roman leading the way, Tess and Judith went a short way along the now almost empty ballroom, until they reached the velvet curtain over the gallery stairs.

After Judith went through the door, Tess looked up at Roman. "Thank you for coming to our rescue."

His jaw worked and she guessed he was fighting to hold back words. "Did you think I was meeting someone when I went into the alcove?"

Roman let out a gust of breath. "No. I was coming to apologize. Again."

She lowered her lashes. "After what happened following your last apology, I believe it would be better if you put them into writing!"

Turning, she went through the curtain and up the stairs. Roman stared after her. Then he tipped back his head and laughed.

Tess entered the gallery. Judith was waiting meekly at the top. "Where is Minnie?"

"Gone off to bed, I hope! Come, I will see *you* to *your* chamber."

As they went along the upper corridor, Tess continued her stern lecture. By the time they reached Judith's chamber she had covered everything her imagination could dredge up. "Remember, your reputation must be spotless if you mean to make your debut. And being discovered in a dark alcove with Brocklehurst! Why, your folly could have ruined your chances of being received at court."

Tess was highly doubtful that her sister had heard a single word of she said. Her sister hung her head, but Tess was not deceived. "Are you listening to me, Judith? I hope you have learned something of value this evening."

Judith turned to her, and there were stars in her eyes. "Oh, Tess! He called me beautiful!"

"We'll talk again in the morning," Tess said sternly.

As she went back down to join her guests, she sighed.

It seemed that Judith was going to be far more of a handful than Minnie.

After supper the dancers drifted back to the ballroom, but there was no sign of Tess. Roman was glad of it. She confused him, twisted his thoughts into knots. He was making his way toward Alicia when Tess finally entered. He only saw her from the corner of his eye, but he was acutely aware of her presence.

He went out onto the balcony to escape. It was cold and his breath made little puffs of frosty air before him, but he didn't feel it. His blood was on fire. When he'd seen Tess being manhandled by Brocklehurst he'd wanted to kill the young fool, then and there. It wasn't disinterested chivalry that had made him come to the rescue. It had been jealousy. The urge to tear the cur limb from limb.

Roman's heart contracted. *He* had wanted to be the one holding her. Kissing her. Making love to her.

At times he thought that she was not indifferent to him. And from what he had seen of her with her husband, it was no love match. Lord Claybourne seemed to show Tess no warmer affection than he showed his sister. It hadn't taken much observation on his part to see that she was isolated and lonely.

Removed from her friends and acquaintances to a completely new life among strangers, Tess was very vulnerable. If he were a complete cad he could use that loneliness and vulnerability against her. Draw her back into his life. Into his arms.

God knew, he wanted her!

Roman was a man of lusty passions, but he lived by a strict code: seducing a married woman—no matter how desperately he desired her—was not part of it. Yet he knew if it was inevitable. *I must leave as soon as possible. If I stay I will only cause harm.*

Egypt called to him. The harsh conditions and physical exertion were a good analgesic for what ailed him. Time and distance would be the only cure.

He would thank Lord Claybourne for letting him have the use of his library, and repay his kindness by finishing the translation of the ancient scrolls—and then he would book his passage to Egypt on the first ship out.

Thank the Good Lord that Claybourne never made good on his hints of wanting to sponsor my work when I first arrived. Roman knew that if the opportunity was offered now, he would have no choice but to turn it down, and live with the consequences. *At least there's enough to eke out one more season, although it will be on a shoestring.*

He leaned on the cold limestone rail, wishing it were instead warm with the molten sun of Egypt. *I am homesick for a land that is not my own. For an era that is not my own.*

The sooner he went back the happier he would be. Surely he would find someone else to fund his excavations, even after the season got under way. The *firman* for the Valley of the Kings—official permission to excavate the royal tombs—had been given to someone else, making it more difficult to find a backer. But all it took was one golden find to send wealthy men clamoring to back him, in hopes of uncovering treasures.

Roman had hoped to find a sponsor more interested in knowledge than gold. *Claybourne would be the perfect sponsor—if he weren't married to Tess.*

He made a decision. He'd finish the translation tonight.

First thing tomorrow, he would pack his belongings and book passage on the next ship bound for Egypt. The decision firmly set, Roman felt suddenly at peace with himself.

The door to the ballroom opened behind him. Someone strolled over to stand near him on the balcony. ''A cold night. Join me in a cigar to chase away the chill.''

Roman turned to find the Duke of Audley beside him. He accepted the cigar and they lit up, watching the blue smoke rise like veils and drift across the wintry gardens. It was several minutes before the duke spoke again.

"I hear you have come to England looking for an interested party to fund your work in Egypt."

"That is one of the reasons for my visit; however, since word got out that I am searching for knowledge, rather than precious gems and gold, no offers have been forthcoming."

Audley regarded him for a moment. "You are looking for the Temple of Isis, or so I've heard. You believe there are records there that will shed light on the very distant past."

"You're exceedingly well informed, sir."

"I have spent some time in Egypt. I find her history fascinating. And," he added, watching Roman carefully, "I am almost embarrassed to say that I have amassed more wealth than I could possibly spend in several highly extravagant lifetimes."

Roman didn't know what to make of the man. "My felicitations," he said dryly. "Life must be very pleasant for a gentleman of your means."

"Yes. But often boring. There are only so many horses to race, carriages to order, balls to throw—and women to seduce. Although you may hold quite another opinion on the latter."

"I doubt you would care to hear it."

"Exactly so. You are a man of great observation." Audley's cigar tip glowed like a red eye in the darkness. "Brocklehurst is my son. I understand you drew his cork tonight."

"Yes, by God." Roman bristled. "The young pup had

it coming. I'll tell you to your head that I'll do it again if I deem it necessary!''

"Excellent! We are in complete agreement, then."

"You take the role of fatherhood rather lightly, my lord."

"Not in the least!"

While Roman was digesting Audley's comment, the duke eyed him intently, taking his measure. He nodded suddenly after coming to a decision. "Come round and see me tomorrow at noon, and we'll work out an agreement. I shall outfit you with whatever you need in the way of equipment and supplies. Everything of the best. Further, I shall fund your excavations for a period of three years. Longer, should you find anything of interest."

Roman's eyes glittered in the darkness. The sudden offer, instead of making him relieved, aroused his deepest suspicions. "May I ask why?"

"I like your style, McKendrick. Let us just say that I am a man who is easily bored, and leave it at that. Although I may have one minor stipulation."

Roman had been waiting for the hook hidden in the bait. He had no intention of smuggling out antiquities, if that was the duke's plan. "If it doesn't break any laws, my lord, I should have no objections."

"Only the laws of paternal fondness, I imagine."

The duke tossed the end of his cigar into the withered flower bed below. "If you are not averse, I shall send my son along with you. Use him hard, McKendrick. See if the rigors of a season in Egypt can turn a pampered young dilettante into the man I believe he can become!"

"You drive a hard bargain, sir. I fear I might be forced to draw his cork again!"

"Ah, you may do so with my blessings, McKendrick." Audley smiled, then turned and went inside, leaving Roman alone in the night.

Roman no longer felt the cold. The problem of young Brocklehurst was something he could handle. *Outfitted with whatever I need, and funding for three years! I'd take a half-dozen young scalawags along for half the chance!*

Excitement coursed through him, and the stars that had seemed dim a moment earlier now shone diamond-bright with promise. His prayers had been answered, and by a most unlikely source!

Inside, Audley moved through the ballroom until he found Isabel Johnston, his latest mistress. He looked down at her with a bemused expression. "A lovely ball, don't you think? I find the new countess charming. I shall do all in my power to see that she is accepted in society."

The pretty young matron with a most accommodating husband looked up at him from beneath her thick brown lashes. "I know that smile, Anthony. What deviltry are you up to?"

"Nothing you need worry yourself about, my dear." His glance raked the room until it found Tess. His smile widened. "Merely amusing myself."

"Ah. And at whose expense?"

He tipped his head to one side. "That, my dearest Bella, only time will tell."

EGYPT

The sun was a blaze of white against the lapis-blue sky. The boy Yusef walked hurriedly through the busy souk, past the sellers of hot food, and live chickens and ducks, past the traders in silks and fine woolens, the purveyors of spices and medicines, the makers of jewelry, and reached the area given to metalworking. The noise was astonishing: the babble of voices in different tongues, bargaining, arguing, cajoling; the squawk of birds; the clang of hammer on copper.

At last he wound his way through the colorful bazaar to a certain buyer and seller of fine wares, in the street of the metalworkers. Brass braziers, jugs and cups; copper platters; teapots and goblets of silver alloy, beautifully wrought and chased with intricate designs. Ibrahim, the owner, was elderly and almost completely blind. It was his sons who made the wonderful pieces now—but it was Ibrahim himself who ran their stall, and to whom certain enterprising citizens of Gurneh brought in secret the artifacts of the ancient ones.

Yusef went past the laden tables beneath the outdoor canopy and passed inside, to the tiny cubicle where Ibrahim sat nursing his fragrant mint tea. He listened intently a moment. "You are alone today, young Yusef."

The boy was so startled he almost dropped the prize hidden beneath his robes. He hadn't expected Ibrahim to recognize his footsteps. "You are mistaken, effendi. My name is Ahmed," he said in a falsetto tone.

The old man smiled. "Come then, Ahmed, and tell me of how you came to my shop." He rose and motioned the boy to follow him into the back, beyond the striped curtain.

Yusef was awed. He had never been allowed in the back before. The room was small and dark, the surfaces covered with patterned rugs that muted the noise of the bazaar.

The old man offered him tea in a small glass cup with a handle of silver roses. He smelled the boy's nervousness as distinctly as if it were a perfume. An eager one. "I do not know a boy named Ahmed of your age. You are new to this place?"

"A visitor only. I have come here to your stall on business."

"Have you come to sell, or to buy?"

"To sell, effendi."

The old man chuckled beneath his breath. The boy was too young and ignorant to know that business was never the first topic of conversation. Indeed, it was often an hour or more before the subject of his visitor's business was even hinted at.

So, then. The rheumy eyes seemed to stare into Yusef's. "What have you stolen," he said smoothly, "and from whom?"

"Nothing! I swear it!" He was frightened now and started to rise. A bony hand shot out and caught Yusef's wrist. He was surprised at such strength in so elderly and seemingly frail a man. Ibrahim's grasp tightened.

"I found it," Yusef cried out. "In the val . . . in the desert. The abandoned oasis where the three wells went dry. It . . . caught the toe of my sandal."

"Sit. I will examine it now." Ibrahim waited, knowing the boy would not leave now. There was too much excitement in his voice for that. Too much greed.

Slowly Yusef drew the mirror from under his robes, where he had tucked it in the sash of his tunic. He handed it to the vendor without speaking.

With great care the old man accepted the mirror of unknown alloy. His gnarled hands moved delicately along the twined leaves that formed the handle, touched the smooth reflective surface, the ornate scrollwork on the back, the lotus blossoms on either side.

His face showed nothing of his thoughts, but his keen mind was working quickly. The workmanship of the mirror was marvelous, the size and shape balanced to perfection. The polished disc like satin. He didn't need the vision of his younger days to tell him this was like nothing he had ever seen before.

"You say you found this in the desert sands, not in a tomb?"

"No, effendi! I have not been inside a tomb in my life." Yusef was frightened now, his heart pounding in time to the sound of a metalsmith's hammer from the next booth.

"It is old, but not particularly so. Nor is it remarkable in any way, young Yusef . . . pardon me, young *Ahmed*," Ibrahim said. "You sound very like the nephew of an old acquaintance, you see." He smiled. "A dozen or more like this pass through my hands every year. But I like an enterprising youth such as yourself." He named a sum.

"So little!" The boy was sick, trapped in his lie—and the old man held the mirror's handle in a death grip. Even if he tried to snatch it and run away, Ibrahim would say something to Yusef's uncle and it would all be for naught. As he wavered, the vendor spoke again.

"If that is not what you expected, I am sure it is more money than you have ever had in your life. And where you found this object, you will find more. Of course, you will bring what you find to me. We shall have a pact."

Yusef was torn between anger and want. The old man had bested him this time—but there were more treasures to be found in the valley. For instance, the bead necklace and the carnelian scarab he'd hidden in his sleeping rug at home.

"It is agreed."

He took the coins and slipped away, while Ibrahim held the mirror and ran his fingers over the surface. It was ancient, he had no doubt of it. But he did not know this metal. It was not gold or silver or electrum or anything that had ever come his way. He would show it to his sons when they returned from the tavern where they had gone to fetch their dinner. He had a feeling that this mirror was something very special.

Suddenly he shivered. The day was warm but he'd been cold since sunrise. Putting the mirror inside a brass vessel for safekeeping, he lay down upon his pallet and pulled a warm rug up over him, well pleased with the afternoon's work. He had a new—and cheap—source of artifacts for sale. The mirror would likely fetch a good price, from the right person. Ibrahim ran the list of potential buyers through his mind, trying to decide which one to approach first.

In the dark well of the ornate vessel, the surface of the mirror shimmered like the surface of the sun. It sprang to life with shifting visions, mixing centuries without order or pattern, showing both the humble and the proud:

Great obelisks rose into a hot blue sky, temples were built and then fell into ruin as centuries passed in the wink of an eye. A Nubian princess bathed in a lotus-strewn pool. Hittite warriors invaded. Village women gossiped and hung their wash out to dry. Pharaoh rode across the sands in his war chariot; a steamship from England docked at the mouth of the Nile.

Somewhere—impossible to fix an era to the timeless scene—an old man lay down on a pallet in the back of his shop for an afternoon nap. Dust storms arose in the desert, obliterating temples and abandoned cities. A boy rode his harnessed water buffalo around in circles, drawing water from far below to the surface of the parched land. A train of camels was silhouetted against a darkening sky.

Date palms spread their spiky shadows on moonlit mud-brick walls. A young queen examined her face in a mirror of polished metal, her kohl- and malachite-rimmed eyes wide with alarm. Behind shuttered windows, a handsome Englishman made love to a beautiful, green-eyed woman.

In a dim, quiet room the same woman looked up from her dressing table in fright, spilling a container of face powder across the floor—and a knife flashed, its long, thin blade suddenly red as rubies with the fresh spill of blood.

In the street of metalworkers, in its hiding place in the brass vessel, the ancient mirror clouded and went blank.

Ibrahim, purveyor of fine metal objects, buyer and seller of treasures looted from ancient tombs, pulled his robe about his skinny shanks to warm his old bones and fell into a pleasant dream.

It was less than an hour later that Ibrahim's sons returned from a tavern and found their father curled up on his pallet with a smile on his seamed face. They thought he was sleeping until they saw that his rheumy eyes were wide open, still filled with echoes of glorious visions of eternity.

5

Tess sat at the foot of the long dining table used for high occasions. Branches of candelabra and matching epergnes of gilded bronze separated her from Roman at the far end where her husband should have sat. Instead Leland was alone on the right side of the table, directly across from Alicia.

Suddenly the table stretched and stretched, until the opposite end was almost out of sight. It was, Tess thought, like looking down the wrong end of a telescope. The room was poorly lit, despite the many candles, and the faces of the other diners wavered and changed. No one spoke to her, but she sensed they were all talking about her.

The footmen brought the courses out so rapidly there was no time to eat from one dish before it was whisked away for the next. "Shocking!" Mrs. Drake said, to her husband. "Absolutely shocking!"

Tess surveyed the room and found nothing unusual. The diners' knives and forks flashed in the candlelight, creating a cool breeze. She looked down and saw she was naked. Not a stitch on, except for swaying ear bobs that hung to her shoulders, the heavy coronet pressing down upon her head, and the massive emeralds of the Claybourne necklace glowing against her bare breasts.

How had she forgotten her garments? She prayed that

no one would notice. Then one of the footmen went around the sides of the chamber, lighting the tapers in the sconces and the tall standing candelabrum. She was suddenly aware that everyone in the room knew of her terrible gaffe, but all were pretending not to have observed it. Unable to flee the room, she sat there, utterly mortified, while the footmen sent her sidelong glances, and Alicia chattered brightly.

Tess took up her glass of wine and drank from it. Her hand trembled. A drop of red fell from the rim and ran down her breast, then splashed on her thigh. Roman was suddenly there beside her. He leaned forward and clasped one of her white breasts in his firm, bronzed hand. His thumb grazed the rosy tip and she felt her nipples contract and grow hard. The lights in the room blazed high, every taper in every sconce and candelabrum burning like the sun. And every pair of eyes in the room was fixed upon Tess, staring at her in all her nakedness.

Especially Roman. His eyes were dark, his smile filled with contempt. She was dimly aware of the gasp from her guests, and of Alicia's urgent attempt to draw her into the conversation.

"Don't you agree, dearest Tess?" Alicia called down the table.

Tess was confused. "Agree with what?"

But it was Roman who answered: "Why, Tess, with what all London is saying: that you are, at heart, nothing but a high-class harlot."

Tess awakened in her bed with her mouth dry and heart bounding. She knew that was what Roman thought her. He imagined she had simply sold herself to the highest bidder. That was unfair; while she had made an advantageous marriage, it was not a coldhearted choice based solely on Leland's wealth and high position.

But the Roman of her dream was right in one way: she

was indeed a harlot in her sleep. Since he'd come to Claybourne House, she had betrayed her husband a dozen times in her dreams. Had let the Roman who haunted her dreams kiss and touch and fondle her until she was aflame with need, frantic with hunger for him.

That she had no intention of following through on her body's urges while awake made her feel no better.

A tap on her door roused her, and a moment later Minnie swept in like a gust of fresh air. Tess groaned. She had forgotten how much energy young girls had.

"What a slugabed!" her sister said, sitting on the side of the bed. "Why, it's almost half past twelve."

Tess groaned and rolled over. "Do you forget we held a ball here last night? I didn't seek my bed until well past three!"

"All the more reason to take a lovely drive and put some color back in your cheeks. You're pale as milk."

Celeste heard her mistress and came in bearing a tray with her morning chocolate and toast. Tess waved the tray away. "I couldn't eat a bite this morning. Just some tea, if you please."

The maid hurried away to hide her smile. *Ah, perhaps Madame finds herself in an interesting condition.* Celeste's sister had always been the same way at the start when she was with child.

Within the hour the rumor that started with Celeste had circulated through the servants' hall.

Roman swore beneath his breath. "Look again, man! There must be something.

The ticket clerk checked his schedules one more time, then shook his head. "I am sorry, sir. I have nothing else at the moment."

"Very well."

He paid his passage on the earliest ship out, then walked

away from the steamship line's offices cursing in fluent Arabic. There wasn't a ship available on which he could book passage to Egypt for a sennight. The only two leaving before then took leisurely detours to other ports, and he was better off waiting the week.

Only one more week near Tess. It would test his mettle, but he would manage it. He might work it so that they only saw one another at table, and there were surely plans for them to dine out once or twice. Only one more week.

He felt less guilty staying at Claybourne House, now that Audley had offered financial backing. It would have offended his stern inner code to be beholden in any way to a man whose wife he coveted for himself. Too many nights Roman had lain awake, tortured by knowing Tess slept beneath the same roof, yet was as forever unreachable as the farthest star.

As for Lord Claybourne himself, Roman felt he had repaid him by finding the two references that confirmed the third in Claybourne's newly purchased papyrus. The chance to study the man's extensive collection had been well worth Roman's trip to England: he knew where to begin his excavations now.

On his way back from the docks, Roman gave the driver a change of plan. "Harley Street," he said, and gave him the direction. On his first trip to Egypt, he'd learned the importance of having a well-stocked medical kit at hand. He'd stop by and see his old friend Laurence Whitman, and order replacements.

First on his list was another large jar of the physician's special remedy: "Dr. Whitman's Sovereign Potion" was a strong purgative for deworming, and Roman had learned to dose any malingerers among his crew with it. He grinned. One bout with it was all it took to keep the laziest man hard at work, for fear of being given another dose.

Then there were Whitman's healing concoctions, the

green salve with which Roman treated his men's infected cuts; mullein leaf for desert catarrh; oil of peppermint for dyspepsia and oil of cloves for toothache; laudanum for severe pain; and willow bark extract for fever.

As they went along Harley Street he saw another hackney pull away from another physician's offices. It turned at the corner, and he was startled to see Lord Claybourne's distinctive profile. A woman in a dark hooded cape leaned against his shoulder, and Claybourne's arm was around her.

"Slow down," Roman called to the driver. As they went along the row he scanned the numbers. There was only one physician in the town house on the corner: D. F. Foster, obstetrician to some of the highest ladies in the land.

They passed his address and Roman felt as if he'd been hit in the pit of his stomach. *Tess, with child. Claybourne's child.*

It rocked his world. Anger, jealousy, despair, coursed through him like tidal waves, overwhelming thought and reason. He was well past his destination when it ebbed away, leaving him stunned and heartsick.

He felt like a fool for not anticipating her pregnancy. It had been inevitable that it would happen in time. His feelings for her were such a tangled web of regret, desire, anger, and loss he couldn't sort them out.

Why in the name of Christ did I have to come down Harley Street now! Why couldn't I have sailed away for Egypt next week in happy ignorance?

He fought the urge to have the driver let him down in the first park they passed, where he could walk and be alone with his thoughts. *Wallow in misery is more like it!* No, he wouldn't give in to such mooncalf behavior. It was time to get on with his life.

And he had a meeting with the Duke of Audley shortly

that would change it radically for the better. Roman gave the hackney driver the duke's direction.

"Can't make up yer mind where yer want to go, guv'nor?"

"What the devil do you care, as long as I can pay?" Roman snapped.

"Right you are, guv'nor." The driver didn't relish riding around London all day with a madman in his cab. He plied his whip with more effort than skill, and the vehicle moved through traffic at a spanking pace.

Roman reached into his inside pocket and took out the list of supplies a first-rate expedition required, which he'd written out for Audley. He didn't notice the speed of the hansome, or hear the bellow of outrage from the pedestrian who jumped out of the vehicle's way.

For several minutes Roman stared at the list blankly, as if it were written in Hindi. It was no use. It was impossible to concentrate on anything. All he could think of was Tess, carrying another man's child.

He cursed and leaned his head back against the seat. The next seven days were going to be unendurable.

As the Claybourne town carriage came to a stop before the foundling hospital, Tess glanced up at the church tower across the way. It was a little past three. Shopping had barely made a good dent in the day. Only five hours before she had to sit down at table and endure making polite small talk to Roman, as if they had no history between them.

Alicia noticed her check the time. "We shall not be much above a quarter hour. Perhaps Judith and Minerva would care to wait in the carriage? A foundling hospital is not likely to prove a pleasant experience for two delicately reared young ladies."

Judith looked relieved. A quick look at the gray building, and the whey-faced people on the streets, had told her this was not her milieu.

Minnie had her own ideas. "What, wait in the carriage and give up such a splendid adventure? I should be disappointed if we are left behind, as if we were still children. I would much rather visit the foundlings than kick my heels with only Judith for company."

Judith merely lifted her chin, as if Minnie's unthinking disdain had no power to hurt her. Tess looked from one to the other. It was Judith's reluctance more than Minnie's enthusiasm that made her waver. If ladies of their station did not help those in sorry circumstances, who would set the example? Great wealth was a great responsibility, and charity was an important part of it.

"Perhaps it would be better if you did wait outside," she said reluctantly. "I would not wish have you come along against your wills if it would upset you."

"Pooh," Minnie responded. "It won't upset me in the least. I intend to be a missionary and nurse lepers in the Sandwich Islands, you know. I cannot imagine that seeing infants of the poor can be any more disagreeable than visiting with people whose noses have fallen off."

"I thought," Judith said in a strangled voice, "you were going to be a poetess."

"Well, I was, but they always seem to come to a sorry end. If they don't die of consumption, they swallow drops, or leap from bridges. Very poor-spirited, I must say!"

"You have no sensibility!" her sister said primly.

Tess made up her mind. "If your heart is set upon it I shan't make you wait out here, Minnie. As for you, Judith, I believe that a girl old enough to make her come-out is old enough to see what life is like for the unfortunates among us. It would behoove you to take Lady Alicia as your model."

Her sister-in-law laughed and shook her head. "Polishing my halo, again? You give me too much credit, my dear.''

"I cannot give you credit enough.''

Alicia let the groom hand her down. "If you think of nominating me for sainthood,'' she said lightly, "remember that some give aid to the poor out of goodness of heart, while others may merely be atoning for their sins.''

Even Judith laughed at that. They went inside together in high good humor. As they entered, a woman in a billowing dark cloak with a veiled hat hovered in the shadows. The veil obscured her features slightly, but she seemed very young—and very frightened.

She came forward softly as Tess stopped and inclined her head.

"Lady Claybourne?''

"Yes?'' Tess sensed the woman's nervousness and offered an encouraging smile.

The stranger hesitated. "Lady *Alicia* Claybourne?''

Instantly Alicia put her hand on Tess's sleeve and drew her back. She addressed the young woman. "I believe it is I to whom you wish to speak. I am Lady Alicia Evershot. My brother is the Earl of Claybourne.''

"Oh! Yes . . .''

She seemed to shrink from the gazes of the others in their party. Alicia exchanged a knowing look with Tess. "I believe it would be best if I speak to this young person, while you take your sisters on to Matron's office. I shall meet up with you later.''

"Yes, thank you. Come, Judith, Minnie.''

Tess shooed her sisters along the hall with as much haste as was seemly. The dark cloak had done little to hide the fact—at least from the two older women—that its wearer was with child. It was obvious from her demeanor that the poor creature was of the middle class, and had gotten herself "in trouble.'' Tess imagined that the young woman meant to inquire whether the hospital would accept a child born of such circumstances.

As they turned the corner she saw Alicia escorting the woman into one of the side rooms. "How very odd," Judith announced, "for you to be accosted by a perfect stranger. And her outfit. So unfashionable."

"Don't be such an idiot," Minnie said, giving her sister a poke in the ribs. "The poor thing is having a baby and is not married and means to give it away. Isn't that so, Tess?"

"Really, Minnie! You must not speak so forthrightly in public where you might be overheard," Tess replied coolly. She invented a story on the spot. "I believe that to be a young woman who is seeking employment here at the foundling hospital. It was arranged for her to meet with Alicia today."

"Then she should be interviewed by Matron," Minnie rebutted. Her fertile imagination had filled in the details. "Perhaps she is an upper servant seduced by her employer's son, and thrust out into the cold quite penniless. No, her voice was too genteel! I believe that she was engaged to be married and anticipated her vows, only to have her beloved killed in a dreadful accident. Now her cold-hearted father has cast her off. And so close to Christmas too, the cad!"

"You are letting your imagination run away with you," Tess said rather sharply. "And later you will explain to me where you have been obtaining the novels that have given you such vulgar notions!"

"Now," Judith said victoriously, "you see why Minnie has been such a trial to me at school. She is forever thinking up stories to entertain her friends. I shudder at the thought of having to return to Hazeldean where I must endure more of the same!"

"That is quite enough from both of you," Tess announced. "Ah, I see Matron ahead in the nursery."

It was much later than the ladies had anticipated before the carriage returned them to Claybourne House. It had been a mortifying experience for Judith. She leaned her head on Tess's shoulder. "I am so sorry. You were all so brave. Minnie especially. I believe that she *could* nurse lepers without turning a hair. I did *so* try not to be sick, but . . ."

"No more of this nonsense," Tess said gently. "You were very good with the other children."

"I wish we could have taken them all home with us," Minnie said as they entered the foyer. "Think how lovely it would be to have dozens of sweet little babies at Claybourne House."

Roman had just crossed the hall, and overheard the last part of Minnie's speech. He went straight on to the library, where he buried himself among books and maps and papyrus fragments for the rest of the afternoon.

The last week of Roman's visit passed quickly. The Duke of Audley came by with his son in tow to pay his respects, and Tess took her sisters shopping almost every day. There were so many things to be ordered now, if Judith was to make her come-out when they returned from the country. Best of all, it provided her with an excuse to avoid Roman during the day.

At last it was Roman's final evening in England. Tess dreaded the moment he drove away for good, yet couldn't wait for him to be gone. Then she could return to the calm, benumbed state she had lived in for so long before his sudden appearance. She would busy herself with her sisters and her charity work, with her husband and sister-in-law, and lose herself in the gaiety of balls and routs and visits to the theater. There were a hundred ways to fill her days, she told herself.

If only there were some way to fill the hole in her heart.

They had dined unfashionably early, with Roman as their only guest, since Leland had announced a surprise. The men cut short their brandy and cigars to join the ladies in the drawing room soon afterward.

As the servants opened the doors for them, Roman was struck by the picture the ladies formed. Alicia had taken a chair and was busy at her embroidery frame. Tess was arranged on a settee with Minnie at her feet and Judith leaning over the back. Her gown of sapphire velvet was simply but exquisitely cut. No ruching and folderol were needed to highlight her classic beauty.

In that moment, seeing her laughing with her sisters, he knew she'd made the right decision. For her, and for them. *This is the life she was born for,* he thought. He realized then that his anger had been a defense, to hold his feelings at bay: if he pretended to despise her it would keep him from the full knowledge of how deeply he still cared for her.

I am the selfish one, not Tess. I must make my amends, and part with her on good terms.

He paused for just a moment, memorizing the pretty scene. It was all he would have of her to take back with him.

Lord Claybourne clapped him on the shoulder. "By Jove, I should have a portrait painted of the three of them, just as they are now!"

"Why bother with a mere painting," Roman said fervently, "when you have the real thing. No artist could do them justice."

Claybourne reverted to the topic of Roman's planned excavations. "I understand your meeting with Audley went well?"

"Yes. He is prepared to fund my work most gener- ously." Roman grimaced. "With one 'minor' stipulation. I am to take his son, young Lord Brocklehurst, with me, as a member of my party."

Minnie overheard and looked up as they entered the room. "I think that the duke has the better part of the deal. I dislike Lord Brocklehurst intensely. He is a horrid little toad!"

"What a terrible thing to say," Judith chided. "He is not little at all, but quite tall." She flushed a little. "I, for one. . . . I believe he is generally thought to be quite hand- some."

"You are only saying that because you know he ad- mires you."

"And you are only calling him a toad because he said you were a tedious girl and should be locked in the school- room until you learn your manners!"

Rising, Tess drew them both aside. "If," she said with quiet authority, "either of you believe this to be a proper discussion, I will myself lock *both* of you in the school- room—at Hazeldean!"

Judith blanched. "Oh! You would not! You *could* not be so cruel."

Tess softened. "No, I won't go back on my word. But I expect in future you will both conduct yourselves like ladies, in company."

Both sisters chastened, they went off arm in arm like the best of friends, to look at stereopticon pictures Alicia had purchased, showing exotic Egyptian pyramids and temples.

A commotion behind them made them turn around. Two footmen entered as Desmond opened the door. They were grinning and carrying a large wooden crate. Leland ges- tured to a corner of the drawing room where a small table had been removed.

"Set it there."

"Is this our surprise?" Alicia asked. "Whatever could it be?"

"An early Christmas gift. In a moment you will see for yourself."

He nodded and the footmen removed the carton front, which had already been loosened. Inside was a rectangular box of highly polished walnut, inlaid with book-matched burled elm. The rim around the top of the box was banded with brass stamped in a bird-and-flower motif. Lord Claybourne beamed.

"What do you think, my dears?"

"It is exquisite . . ." Tess began.

"Yes, but *what* is it?" Minnie interjected.

"Oh!" Alicia clapped her hands. "It is a disc music box, isn't it?"

Instead of answering, he raised the hinged lid. It stayed up as he bent to remove a flat disc the size of a large dinner plate, which he placed inside the top. A few winds of the crank in back, and the music box began to play. Unlike the tinkly music boxes they were all familiar with, the music that issued forth had a full, rich sound that delighted its listeners. It was entirely unlike anything any of them had heard before.

"It is like a choir of angels playing their harps in harmony," Tess said in amazement. They all gathered round.

"There are ten discs, each with fifteen songs upon it. Now, if we have a small party of young people over, you will not be forced to stay at the pianoforte, playing waltzes while the others dance."

"Oh, Tess!" Judith exclaimed. "You may teach us to waltz!"

"Leave that for the private dancing master Leland will engage for you," Alicia said.

Judith was over the moon. *A dancing master!* She had

never dreamed in her wildest moments that she would ever be taught by a private dancing master. Since Tess had become Lady Claybourne their lives had changed tremendously.

Looking from one sister's ecstatic face to the other's woeful expression, Tess burst out laughing. "Were there ever two young ladies so united by blood and so dissimilar in nature?"

They tried out the different discs until Alicia declared her head was spinning. "You must settle on either waltzes, polkas, ballads, or opera."

"Waltzes, then," her brother decided. "Mr. McKendrick, you are an excellent dancer—far better than I. Perhaps you would be so good as to take my wife around the floor a time or two, and show the young ladies how it is done properly."

There was no gracious way that Roman could refuse his host. He looked to Tess, hoping she would plead a headache or some such excuse. His eyes met hers across the room for a heartbeat. She lowered her lashes. "I would be happy to demonstrate the waltz for them."

While Leland pored over the selections, Desmond directed the footmen to roll up the long rug for the dancing. Tess chattered brightly with Alicia and her sisters. Her hands were folded tightly in her lap. *I must hold on a little longer. Just until the dance is through.*

She dared not look at Roman.

He leaned against the mantel, his arm stretched out along it, resigned to the exquisite torture of holding her in his arms again.

I am weak, Tess thought, wishing too late that she had refused. But the chance to be close to Roman one final time, to be in his arms once more, had overwhelmed her better judgment. A word from Alicia, and Desmond lowered the lamps before retiring. Judith watched with shining eyes, and even Minnie settled down to watch. The music began, the stirring notes of a Strauss waltz swirling through the room.

Roman crossed to Tess and bowed low over her hand. "I believe this is my dance, Lady Claybourne."

She gave him her hand, willing it not to tremble in his warm grip. As she rose she turned her head and smiled coolly. *You needn't have reminded me I am a married woman,* her gaze said as clearly as words.

For a moment his eyes were the storm-tossed blue she remembered, heavy with meaning: *I was not reminding you, Tess. I was reminding myself!*

Roman inhaled her scent, felt her supple body swaying imperceptibly toward him, and thought that he had never been so close to heaven—nor yet so close to hell.

They moved out into the center of the room, away from the brighter light. There was so much he wanted to say to her that he couldn't. Instead an apology would have to suffice. He lowered his voice so the others wouldn't hear.

"My dear, I am the worst beast in nature, to have so abused you when I first arrived at Claybourne House."

"It was a shock to both of us."

"Indeed! When I saw you so unexpectedly, as the wife of my benefactor, the shock must have unhinged my brain—I cannot otherwise account for my behavior. I was convinced that you had somehow instigated my invitation here. I was terribly wrong, Tess. I wish with all my heart I could take it back."

She looked up at him finally. "There is no need for apology. Let us forget the past, and start anew."

And cope with the present as best we can.

She placed her hand on his shoulder, knowing this would be the last time. Memorizing the texture of his coat, the ripple of muscle beneath it, the strength and power he radiated. It was as real to her as the fire burning in the hearth.

And then he led her into the dance. A shiver ran through her. Tess realized, despite her fine words, that the past was still very much alive. Memories thrummed in the air between them, sensations pierced her body like fine silver wires. She could not imagine any more exquisite torture.

The instant Roman's arm encircled her waist, the world faded away. Around and around the room they went, her blue skirts whirling out like bellflowers around her slim ankles. They had never danced together before. Not once. Yet, instinctively, they moved in unison, flowing perfectly with the bright river of music. It was as if they had never parted, but spent their lives together, anticipating and responding to each other's slightest change of mood.

Hands tightly clasped, intoxicated with each other's nearness, they forgot everything else. Everyone else. The slightest pressure of his fingers had her turning at his command, their bodies in tune to the rhythm, and to each other.

She was intensely aware of his every breath, the slightest pressure of his fingers. The velvet gown, the lace and corseting beneath, were no barrier to the warmth of his hand on her back. Her blood heated until it sang, and pleasure melted through her.

The drawing room whirled around her with every turn of the dance. The candle flames in the wall sconces blurred and merged until Tess's head seemed filled with stars. Like the girl in Anderson's "Red Shoes," she could have danced on and on forever, in his arms.

Roman wished he could pull her tightly against him and cover her face with kisses. Wished he could roll back time and change the paths they had each taken. The dance went on, like a wonderful dream. Her fragrance enveloped him, a subtle combination of French scent, milled soap, and the elusive something that was Tess, and no other. And for a few, incredibly sweet minutes, she belonged to him. Just to him.

He dreaded the dance's end, when he must relinquish her to the life she had chosen. Roman's eyes blazed with passion and the words he didn't dare speak.

Tess imprinted every detail in her memory, from the strong line of his tanned throat, the heartbreaking blue of his eyes, to the tiny place where he had nicked his chin shaving. She wanted to reach up and touch it, but contented herself with a smile.

When the music finally ended they were at the far end of the room, in the dimmer shadows. They needed no words to say all that was in their hearts. Tears sparkled in her eyes and one spilled over her thick lashes. Roman's back was to the others, blocking her from their view. Ever so gently he reached up and brushed the tear from her cheek, catching it on his finger. Then he raised it to his lips.

Her breath caught in her throat. Their glances locked and their spirits touched, fusing together like strands of molten glass. It was a most wonderful and unexpected gift. She smiled at him tremulously. For a few precious minutes, on this one night, she knew what it was to be young again, in the arms of the man she had never stopped loving.

It would have to last her the rest of her life.

EGYPT

The street of metalworkers in the souk was a hive of activity. Wealthy tourists from abroad came to winter in Cairo, and sought souvenirs of their travels. The scents of lavender water and bay rum mingled with cumin and coriander, sandalwood and sweat.

In the back room of the shop where Ibrahim had gone

to the bosom of his fathers, a young wife finished sorting through a tray of amulets and hollow silver beads. If she had been born a man, this is the trade she would have followed—crafting beauty from the shining metal. She admired each one as she polished it. Some were plain, others deeply incised, and still more molded into various designs.

There was one in particular that caught her fancy. No larger than a chickpea, it was fashioned like the Hand of Fatima. *So perfect, so exquisitely wrought! If I could keep only one for myself,* Suliya thought, *I would choose this.*

"What is that you have there?"

The girl looked up with a start. Yasmin, Akhmed's chief wife, stood over her. "Only an amulet I am polishing."

"Give it to me." Yasmin examined the Hand of Fatima. "I will keep this one for my own. After all, I have spent all day cleaning this shop."

All day sipping tea while I do the chores! Suliya thought. But she did not dare so say aloud. As first wife, Yasmin could do as she liked. Suliya prayed that one day she would have a boy child to raise her status, as did Yasmin.

The older wife resented Suliya's youth and beauty. "When you are done with the beads, sort the brass jars and vases on the floor from best to worst, and place those of the highest quality along that shelf. My husband shall sell only the finest wares in this shop."

Suliya finished the beads and moved on to the brasswork. Many were nested one within the other, and there were far more than it had appeared at first. She began with the smallest, selecting the best. The rest she set to one side.

The larger vessels were quite heavy, but she finished that task in good time. There was one urn too heavy for her to lift. Suliya tried to shift it and something thunked. The girl reached inside.

It was a mirror of highly polished metal, like nothing

she had ever seen before. She touched it wonderingly, running her fingertips along the lotus blossoms that framed the wide reflective surface. Ibrahim would have appreciated its fine workmanship. There was not a hammer mark, a single seam to show.

Light flashed from it. For an instant Suliya saw her own image looking back at her. But it was an older version of herself. Two other images wavered in the background, sturdy boys with their father's features and her own brown eyes.

"Now what have you found? Give it to me!"

She jumped as Yasmin reached out for the mirror. The images blurred and became nothing but the light bouncing off the brass vessels on the shelf at her back. She blinked. Perhaps she had fallen asleep for a moment.

The older woman took the mirror and checked her reflection. She was generally considered a handsome woman, if no beauty, but her image was harsh and lined, her eyes shadowed with brown circles as if she were ill. It frightened her.

"Pah, it is nothing!" Yasmin said. "Too plain. Perhaps it can be melted down for the metal."

Handing the mirror back to the girl, she went out and promptly forgot about it. The moment she was gone Suliya turned and tucked the mirror out of sight, inside the big urn.

Oddly enough, she also promptly forgot about the mirror.

It was only several years later—watching her two sturdy sons at play on a warm summer evening—that Suliya even remembered it at all.

6

The household retired early and Tess imagined she'd be awake all night. Instead, exhausted by the emotions her dance with Roman had roused, she fell into a deep and dreamless sleep.

It was just past dawn when she awakened. A sunbeam slanted through a gap in the curtain, bright and pure as hammered gold. Rising silently, she went to her window. *How can the sky be so rosy and golden, the world so lovely, on such a devastating day?*

Although Roman's ship didn't leave until the following morning, he would spend the day seeing his supplies safely stowed and spend the night at a hotel. Years ago, when she'd made her decision that she must be strong, and let him go to seek his fortune, she'd been sure it was the right decision. Last night it had seemed the worst mistake she could imagine. In the morning light she reconsidered. She was looking back knowing what had already happened.

If Roman had given up his aspirations of being an archaeologist, in order to marry her, he would have spent his life tutoring reluctant young boys in Swanfield. Eventually he would have come to resent her. Their love, so fresh and vibrant, would have been slowly strangled by recrimination and regret.

Better to have warm memories than cold reality.

As difficult as this day was for her, knowing that Roman still returned her love, it had all been for the best. *And,* she decided, *he must know it, too!* He deserved to find a new love and rebuild his life, solid and whole.

Once she had set him free to find his dream. Now she must free him to follow his heart.

When Tess came down at half past ten, Roman was in the drawing room, saying his good-byes to her husband. His trunk and valises were neatly stacked by the door, ready to be loaded. Just as Tess joined them, the quiet of the square outside was broken by the clatter of many hooves.

"By Jove," Leland said, going to the front window, "it sounds as if a parade were going past."

Roman looked past his shoulder. An elegant vehicle drawn by matched bays was reining in at the front door, followed by an old-fashioned coach packed to the roof with various travel gear. A sour-looking manservant was the only occupant of the second vehicle: Lord Brocklehurst was driving the first.

Within a few minutes he entered the drawing room and hurriedly exchanged greetings. "I don't wish to rush you, McKendrick," he announced, "but I have a devilish lot of gear to be put aboard."

"Do you, by God?" Roman said brusquely. "I told you to pack only essentials!"

Brocklehurst tried to stare him down and failed. Mentally he cursed his father for sending him off with McKendrick. He squirmed mentally, just thinking of that horrible interview with his parent.

"I have saved you from your foolish escapades for the last time, my lad," the duke had told his only son. "Now there will be an end to it! I am sending a spoiled and spendthrift boy away. I expect you to return a man."

Well, he would not be treated like a schoolboy by

McKendrick, too. He would set *that* straight from the beginning. "My father has always said that a *gentleman* travels in the style befitting his station."

"Ah, I see." Roman fixed the young man with a glance that combined exasperation with amusement. "And what exactly do you feel that entails?"

Brocklehurst colored. McKendrick had the same air of unchallengeable authority as his father. This was not going to be as easy as he'd imagined. Under Roman's stern scrutiny, he began reciting the items, feeling like a schoolboy called on the carpet.

"My favorite carriage, of course."

"Of course," Roman murmured.

"My valet. Several trunks of clothing, suitable for the hotter climes. My pillows and featherbed. A bed and folding screen. Several bolts of mosquito netting. My tableware and serving pieces. A portable desk and folding chairs. A bathing tub. A case of books, several cases of brandy. Wine . . . tinned fruit and hams . . ."

The list went on for several minutes, while the others listened in silence. Tess felt sorry for the boy.

Roman waited until Brocklehurst finally paused for breath. "We are not going to circumnavigate the world, we are merely going to Egypt!"

Since this last coincided with a view of Minnie, paused just outside the drawing room doors, the young peer bristled with indignation. "What," he asked more calmly than he felt, "would you suggest I leave out?"

"Almost everything," Roman replied. "The carriage will be of no use to you, the wine will not travel, you will be fortunate to find enough water to bathe where I propose to set up camp—and all your fine furnishings will offer is a wonderful hiding place for scorpions."

Brocklehurst paled, and Roman took pity on him.

"Take your valet, if you like. By the time he realizes

how stark our living quarters are, he will be too far from home to give his notice. As for your wardrobe, evening dress is, unfortunately, necessary at times. Other than that, rough wear will do. There is little time for socializing.''

That wasn't strictly true, but Roman avoided it whenever he could. Fortunately, he hadn't achieved the stature of some of his fellows, and was less in demand as a guest. All the more time for his work.

"Is that all?'' Brocklehurst said in strangled tones.

"Bring the tinned goods, books, netting, and brandy. The portable desk, chair, and camp bed too. Send all the rest back!''

It was a terrible struggle, but Brocklehurst swallowed hard, and nodded. "Very well. I bow to your experience in these matters, McKendrick.''

Roman knew how difficult it was for the young man to acknowledge that though he might be an earl, he was not the expedition's leader. Grinning, he clapped him on the shoulder.

"You learn quickly. I believe you'll do well, after all.''

Brocklehurst's face pinked under his approval, and he went off to give orders to his servants. As he left, Minnie's voice followed him out into the hall.

"Well!'' she said tartly. "Who would have thought you had such good sense?''

He sent her a withering glance but didn't deign to answer. Once he was out the door it was another matter.

"Infuriating girl!'' he muttered beneath his breath as he went down the steps. "Her sister may indeed make a brilliant marriage, but I predict that her barbed tongue will send any suitors fleeing. *She* will end up living with a meek companion, and a dozen pampered cats!''

Minnie watched him ride off. "Hateful creature!''

Her acute hearing had caught his departing words. They did nothing to enhance her opinion of him. But, Minnie realized, a good part of her heightened dislike of him was caused by a severe case of envy.

"Why are you scowling so?" Judith asked as she came back toward the drawing room.

"I think it most unfair that Lord Brocklehurst had no desire to go to Egypt, yet is haring off with Roman on a grand adventure while I . . . I would give *anything* for such an opportunity."

She burst into tears and ran up the stairs to her room.

It was time for Roman to go. Earlier Alicia had presented him with a handsome leather-bound journal. Judith, who had fond memories of him from their days at Swanfield Manor, had embroidered a handkerchief with his monogram. He was touched.

"I shall think of you whenever I look upon it," he told her.

Minnie belatedly wished she'd thought to make him something, as Roman turned to his host. "As for the opportunity to use your library, Lord Claybourne, I am greatly in your debt."

"You've repaid me many times over," Lord Claybourne said, pumping his hand. "Your translation of the Isis papyrus is worth more to me than all the gold in South Africa."

"And for me. The opportunity to see them was a rare privilege."

After his farewells to the others, it was time to say good-bye to Tess. All night long he had lain awake, remembering every minute, reliving every second of their waltz together: her small hand in his, the light in her eyes as she looked up at him. The warmth of her back through her velvet bodice as he guided her around the drawing room. Yet he could not resist one last, long look at her.

Tess had said far too many farewells in her lifetime.

She offered her hand and he took it in his strong clasp. Although she maintained her outward composure, her heart was breaking all over again.

"Good-bye, Roman. Godspeed."

Her fingers were so small, so delicate! Something pressed into his palm, warm from the heat of hers. Was it a miniature of her? His heart beat a little faster.

He relinquished her hand and descended the stairs to the waiting carriage. As it rolled away he turned back for one final glance. They were all still there, just as he'd left them.

The Claybourne groom snapped his whip high over the horses' heads, and they went past the park in the center of the square, quickly picking up speed. Roman waited until he was well away from the house before he looked at the object she'd slipped into his hand. He sighed as he uncurled his fingers. It was small and lightweight, yet it weighed like a cold heavy stone in his hand:

It was a simple oval gold locket, set with a single pearl.

"Have you never been to Egypt, Leland?" Judith asked when they went back into the foyer.

"I have not journeyed beyond the Continent. Travel does not agree with Alicia's constitution." Leland smiled contentedly as he escorted his wife and his sister up the stairs. "Let the Roman McKendricks of the world wander the globe in search of adventure. I have all that I need here."

They had reached the wide landing dominated by a huge portrait of Leland and Alicia. Tess had passed it hundreds of times, but today, in the strong sunlight, the painted children seemed almost alive.

It was an excellent rendering, and she was struck by how well the artist had captured their budding personalities. Tess was astonished. "Do you know, I have never noticed so many subtle details in this portrait before. It is as if the artist could see into the future and know how you both would grow to be."

Her sister-in-law examined the portrait pensively. "That is said to be Mr. Tallent's genius. I was sixteen at the time, Leland approaching his fourteenth birthday, and we had not seen each other in several months before we came to London and the portrait was done."

"You were at boarding school then?"

Alicia sighed. "Yes. It was painful. Leland could not bear to think that I was alone and distraught. He wrote me a promise that he would have us back together to Claybourne Castle, and that we would never be separated again. In six months we were back home, together."

"It must have taken a great deal of determination on his part to succeed."

Alicia gave a little laugh, remembering that long-ago battle. "In the end the trustees had no choice: a great earl, even a young one, demands careful handling! And you know the family motto: 'I Defend My Own.'"

The artist had rendered Leland's protectiveness toward his sister in the sheltering curve of his arm, the softness of his expression, the shy smile. A stack of books on the floor beside him hinted at his scholarly inclinations. It was only the line of his mouth that hinted at his determination. The artist had truly captured the indefinable air of a young man who was very much aware of the power he wielded.

The firm mouth of Alicia's portrait radiated a smiling confidence beyond her years. Her necklace and dress were those of a woman, not a young girl, both gems and gown a deep, rich forest-green. Tess looked closer and realized it was the famous Claybourne emeralds she wore about her throat. Most unusual. She wondered how they managed to shake those priceless gems loose from the trustees for the sitting.

"Really, you should have an evening gown made up in that color, Alicia. Why, I have never seen you in anything so flattering to your hair and eyes! The green makes you stand out."

"I do not care to stand out," the other woman responded. "And I stopped wearing any shade of green long ago." Her face looked wistful. "It has always seemed to bring me ill fortune."

Leland and Judith had gone on ahead to the drawing room. Tess paused. "I believe I shall go up to my room. I'm . . . I did not sleep well last night."

At once Alicia was all solicitous. "I'll see you to your chamber."

There was no way to shake her off without being rude. Tess planned to get rid of her as soon as politeness allowed, and have a good, long cry. Alicia was not so easily discouraged.

"Shall I ring for your maid? Would you like me to prepare one of Dr. Stowe's restorative powders for you?"

"No, I thank you. It is nothing serious. Merely a complaint common to the female condition. I'll rest until I feel a bit better."

"My dear! Can it be . . . ? Am I to be made an aunt?" Alicia went to her side, beaming. "Oh, how happy that would make me!"

"Oh! No!" Tess flushed, and shook her head. "You misunderstand me. It is only my monthlies. They ended just this morning."

Alicia's face showed her dismay. "Forgive me. I meant no intrusion."

"You could never intrude." Tess kissed her sister-in-law's cheek. "I know how fond you are of children—your work with the foundling home is exemplary! But I appreciate your longing for nieces or nephews to pamper and spoil."

"You know me well, dear Tess. Judith and Minnie add such life to the house! Only think what it would be like to have children at the castle, running about the meadows, learning to ride and fish and hunt!"

"Ah, I see it is little boys that you are wishing for."

Her sister-in-law gazed at her earnestly. "Daughters are well and good—I wish you dozens if you like—but oh, Tess. You *must* have a son!"

Her vehemence startled Tess. *Poor Alicia. Unless matters change radically, all her fine hopes are doomed to disappointment.* "I hope I may one day produce one," she said soothingly. "I understand that you dislike Audley and his son, and do not want them to inherit the earldom."

"It is more than that. We must talk. I suppose there is no better time. We are so rarely alone these days."

Alicia took a seat on the silk settee. Tess saw that her hopes of a quiet hour were fast vanishing.

"There were many papers that you signed with the marriage contracts, Tess. Tell me, did you read them all through? Do you remember them?"

"Why, yes. The solicitors went over how my expenses would be handled, what spending money I would receive each quarter, which jewels were heirlooms to be handed down in the family and which my own. My will had been drawn up, and I signed that along with the settlement papers."

"Was that all?"

Alicia's intensity had Tess confused. It was terribly unlike her usual good manners and innate reserve to inquire into something so private.

"Also there were the provisions that Judith and Minnie would be treated as sisters, with all the perquisites that entails. And Leland has more than kept his promises! They are outfitted with the very best, sent to the finest finishing school, and will both make their debuts with presentations at court. He could not have been more generous.''

"But you do not have any idea of the disposition of the estate, should Leland die before you?''

"Why, no! It was not discussed at all. I don't see the need for it. Surely that is up to Leland and his solicitors?''

"Think!'' Leaning forward, Alicia placed her hand over Tess's. "My brother is the last male in the Claybourne line. If anything happened to him and you had a son, we should all go on exactly as before. But if you do not produce a male child . . . I shudder to think of it.''

Tess stared at her. "I hope you mean to explain. I am completely bewildered now.''

"Men!'' Alicia exclaimed. "They think they will live forever.''

She knotted her hands in agitation. "It is all my grandfather's fault, for the way Leland's personal estates are entailed. Tess, you and I are essentially pampered paupers, living on my brother's largesse. I have nothing of my own, and when you married, nothing was settled upon you outright, in your own name. The title and estate—everything but your personal jewelry and clothing—will pass on to Audley! You and your sisters would have the dower house at Leland's country seat to live in, but your circumstances would be greatly reduced—and their chances of making brilliant marriages hopelessly dashed.''

"But my allowance—'' Tess began.

"Comes from the estate,'' Alicia finished. "It could be terminated at the whim of Leland's heir. I would not put it past Audley, or his son—and they would be well within their legal rights. As to myself, I have nothing of my own but a few bits of jewelry that were my mother's. My father expected that I would marry and that a settlement would be worked out at such time.''

Tess was too flabbergasted to speak. Alicia lifted her head and eyed Tess bleakly. "You will think me spoiled and proud. I have moved in the highest circles all my life. Rather than throw myself on Audley's mercy, I would sooner seek employment as a paid companion or governess.''

"You would regret it heartily, Alicia—and I speak from experience.''

Tess had already suffered once under the whim of someone who had the power to do her good or ill. "I was more housemaid and body slave than companion to my elderly great-aunt, and I don't relish ever being put into such circumstances again!''

"Then you agree that there must be an heir!''

"My dear, I certainly do.'' But how she was going to accomplish that with the state of her marriage was beyond Tess's comprehension.

Her maid was brushing out Tess's shining straight hair when Leland entered her bedchamber. ''Well, it was a quiet evening with our houseguest gone away. I hope your sisters were not bored?''

"Not at all! We had a delightful evening, I assure you.''

"Ah. I am very glad of that.'' He leaned down toward her.

Tess stiffened. *Not tonight. Not yet, while I am still grieving for what might have been!*

Leland gave her a light peck on the cheek and straightened. She fought to hide her relief. At the same time she was ashamed: after all, he asked so very little of her! He was her husband, and she must accommodate herself to his wishes.

She smiled up at him. Leland frowned slightly. And then he leaned down and kissed her cheek again.

Tess lay in bed as straight and still as a statue, listening to Leland's muffled sobs and curses. This was the first time he had come to her bed since Roman's departure. As every time before, it had ended in failure. God knew they had both tried. She had done everything he'd asked, to no avail. He could not be comforted—nor, for that matter, could she.

If he could not give her the solace of his body, neither could she offer him whatever it was that she lacked.

His mistress, she knew had a son of tender years. He had given Fannie Bonham a child—why was it that Leland could not bring himself to make love to *her?* Even if he still kept up the relationship with Mrs. Bonham, she doubted loyalty to the woman was the problem. The Claybournes were a proud family: his loyalty, his duty to his line, would always come first. The fault, then, had to be in her.

The mantel clock chimed three. Neither moved. Tess grew chilled in her thin lawn gown. Her breasts ached beneath the damp fabric, and she despised herself, for it was Roman's hot mouth she had imagined tugging at them. His hands she had imagined touching her. In her mind she had committed adultery, and she blamed herself for her husband's failure. But they were only married a short while. There was time yet . . .

It was another quarter hour before her husband finally stirred. He sat up on the bed and slipped into his robe. Then he spoke to her in the darkness. His voice was flat and eerily calm.

"Henceforth you may seek your bed at night knowing you will not be disturbed. I shall not come to you again."

Without turning to face her, he went to the connecting door and shut it behind him. She heard the distinct click of the lock being turned. Tess stared into the dim overhead shadows in shock. She had failed her husband and Alicia both. If Leland truly meant what he had said, their marriage, except in name, was over.

There would be no bright and secure future: no children for her, no heirs for Leland, no nieces and nephews for Alicia to pet and spoil. And no secure futures for any of the women beneath this roof. Despair settled over her like a weight of stone.

Tess sighed and rolled away. There was the other aspect to consider, besides this deeply personal domestic tragedy. Upon Leland's eventual demise, his title and estates would accrue to the Duke of Audley, and be absorbed among his myriad holdings. It would mean the cessation of a noble line.

The end of the house of Claybourne.

When Leland returned to his room, Alicia was waiting for him again. This time she had slipped beneath the monogrammed covers, and was half asleep. The moment she heard his voice calling her name, however, she was wide awake and eyeing him anxiously.

He shook his head. "It is no use."

"Is Tess very upset?"

"Yes, I believe so." He touched her hair. "Dear Alicia, always concerned for the welfare of others. But it is no use."

His sister was very thoughtful for several minutes. "Her background was thoroughly examined. Innocent, unworldly, yet a gentlewoman at ease in society. She seemed so perfect in every way! Oh, Leland, do you think we made a mistake in selecting Tess for your wife? Perhaps someone from among our own kind . . . ?"

"No . . . The fault is not hers. She is beautiful and kind and intelligent. Another bride would not have made any difference to me. And she is such a good companion to you that I cannot regret it."

He ran his fingers through his fair hair, a sign of deepest agitation in him. "You have dedicated your entire life to helping me, Alicia . . . sacrificed your happiness for my benefit. There is not a waking moment that I am not aware of it.''

His sister sat up and leaned her head against his shoulder. ''My life is good, Leland. Do not ever think otherwise!''

He could not be comforted. ''Every time it is worse. The humiliation of each failure piles upon the next, crushing me beneath their accumulated weight. I cannot go on any longer.''

''You *cannot* give up, Leland. Not yet!''

''The humiliation . . .'' He shuddered.

''You haven't finished the bottle of tonic the doctor gave you. And there are still the medicinal powders to try if the tonic proves insufficient. You must promise me you will not concede defeat. Not yet.''

''You are right, I suppose,'' he said dully. ''But if the medicines do not help . . .''

He sat down beside her and Alicia took his face between her hands. ''We will find a way. We always have. You must believe that!''

He noticed the gooseflesh on her arms. ''Poor thing, why, you're shivering.''

''The air in the passageway proved to be too cold for my lightweight robe. I am chilled to the bone.''

Her brother put his arm around her shoulders in concern. The room seemed intolerably warm to him. ''You are not coming down with a head cold, I hope? Perhaps you should stay here tonight, all snug and warm, instead of braving the passage.''

''No. You need your sleep.''

''Very well. In the morning we shall consider what to do. Matters always look less daunting by daylight.''

Alicia didn't answer. Her brow was puckered with concentration and she nibbled on her finger. Then she smiled. *Of course!* It was so simple.

"I have an idea. In fact, I have two. Either one will serve our purpose." She was looking into the shadows, almost talking to herself. "Yes, I am sure it will work out in the end. The natural course is best, but if that fails we may fall back upon the second."

He caught her hand in his. "Tell me!"

She turned her head and smiled at him. "I believe a change of scene will do us all good."

"Yes, but I do not think going home to Claybourne Castle will solve my particular problems." He sighed and leaned back against the massive headboard.

"I was thinking," she said, as if he hadn't spoken, "that it might do us all good to go abroad for the winter months. Away from all the shadows and unhappy memories. Somewhere warm and exotic . . . romantic!"

That caught his interest. "We could go to my Jamaican estates. We've never been. I believe you should enjoy that if you could tolerate the sea voyage."

"I was thinking of traveling east, not west."

He turned to face her. "I recognize that tone. What do you have in mind?" Leland looked long and hard at his sister. "You once said you could never abide to be so far from home."

"I am older now—and wiser, I hope." She took his hand in hers. "And I imagine Tess would find it . . . *romantic!*"

He stared at her, then a slow smile spread over his face. Taking her hand, he lifted it to his lips. "Most dear and most clever Alicia! What would I ever do without you?"

The steamship *Exeter* plowed through the choppy waters of the Mediterranean. A storm was brewing. On his previous journey to Egypt, Roman had stood at the bow, look-

ing forward, toward his new life. Determined to forget
Tess and leave his unhappy memories behind. This time
he found himself looking back.

Roman leaned against the stern rail, watching the ship's
white wake vanish into the distance. Three days out of
England, and with every passing hour, his sense of unease
grew. It was the last emotion he'd expected. Relief, regret,
pain—any and all of them would have been normal under
the circumstances. Especially pain.

Instead he had a deep-seated conviction that he had
made a terrible mistake in leaving. That he had failed Tess,
and failed her badly.

That didn't make sense. He turned and walked back
along the deck, lost in thought. There was something
wrong at Claybourne House, although he couldn't quite
put his finger on it. On the surface everything seemed fine,
but underneath strange and hidden currents swirled.

She had all the material advantages of rank and fortune.
Lord Claybourne and his sister seemed genuinely fond of
Tess and her sisters. Roman stopped in his tracks. *Damn
it all!* Perhaps that was it. *Fond.* Such a tame word. He
couldn't imagine living with Tess as husband and wife and
evoking nothing stronger than *fondness.*

*Claybourne could have looked as high as he chose for
a wife. If he is not in love with Tess, why did he choose
her?*

Lightning forked the sky and the blue waters turned
gray as slate. Hands gripping the rail once more, Roman
stared out over the tossing sea. His disquiet grew.

7

Egypt's sun was molten copper leaking across the western sky when Roman made his way through the still crowded souk, en route to the street of metalworkers. He had dined the previous evening with an American collector of antiquities. One of the artifacts he'd been shown was very ancient, and unlike anything he'd seen before: it was evident that thieves who worked by night had located a new, untouched tomb.

The din among the maze of shops and streets and open-air storefronts with colorful awnings was incredible. Visitors from abroad thronged the jewelry quarter, along with buyers and sellers of precious stones and raw materials.

Suddenly a small figure in a striped robe popped up near one of the shops. The air, scented with exotic spices and sweat, could not freshen the cloud of garlic that exuded from the tousle-headed boy.

"Come with me, I will be your guide, effendi," he said in heavily accented English.

Roman looked down at the shabby child. "The devil you will, you unsavory young guttersnipe. I know my way through the souk better than you do. Run along!"

The boy was determined. He touched Roman's sleeve and sidled closer. "It is said, effendi, that anything a man could think of or wish for can be purchased in the maze of streets—for a price.''

''All I wish for is peace of mind, you little scapegrace.'' He grabbed the boy's arm in an iron fist. ''Now. Relinquish my wallet, which you purloined from my inner pocket, or I'll haul you in to the authorities!''

The boy gave a start. His olive skin paled. ''An accident, effendi. It fell from your pocket into my hand.''

''With a little help from you! You're too young to be plying the pickpocket trade—and not nearly skillful enough.'' He eyed the boy. His clothes were clean and neatly mended. This was no street urchin. In fact . . . Roman tipped up the lad's chin. ''I've seen you before!''

''Never, I swear it!''

''Yes, and fairly recently.'' Ah, yes. He'd got him now. Roman's grin, not wholly pleasant, widened, showing his strong white teeth. ''You have the look of my old friend Akhmed, son of Ibrahim from the souk of metalworkers.''

His deduction was rewarded by a slight widening of the boy's eyes and a tiny inrush of breath. The boy struggled to get away. ''You scrawny fool! Does your father know you're out thieving in the marketplace, instead of learning your trade?''

''You are mistaken, effendi. I do not know the man of whom you speak.''

''Is that so?'' Roman grinned. ''I happened to be on my way to visit Akhmed when you accosted me. It shall be my great pleasure to take you there and introduce you to him!''

His captive changed his tune. ''Please, do not make me go with you! My father does not know I am here. He will beat me!''

''Is that so? Well, if it cures you of thieving, it will be a very good thing. The penalty is harsh. You wouldn't make much of a metalworker if you lost your hand to the sword, now would you? Come along. I've not got time to waste.''

The lad knew it was no use, and went along with Roman through the winding maze where tables of scarabs—both genuine and false—were sold along with the ornate jewelry of the region. From time to time he tested whether he could get away or not, without success. *The Englishman's grasp is surely like that of the crocodile.*

The booths were crowded with English tourists attempting to bargain with the tradesmen, and paying five or six times the going rate.

In the street of metalworkers Roman turned into an establishment more substantial than most. The tables outside were filled with brass braziers, vases, and salvers worked in intricate inlays of contrasting metals or mosaics of lapis and malachite. The better pieces, including the silver, were inside the tiny shop.

Akhmed looked up in startlement from his mint tea, as Roman thrust his son into the place ahead of him. ''The boy was lost. I found him wandering about in the souk of the goldsmiths and silversmiths, almost trampled by tourists. Fortunately for me, he found my wallet, which had somehow come out of my jacket.''

The metal artisan frowned heavily and exchanged glances with the Englishman. Roman had managed to convey exactly what mischief the boy had been up to, while saving face for both father and son.

''I thank you, Effendi McKendrick, for returning my worthless son to me with his skin whole.''

The boy's father gave his son a look that spoke volumes. ''Go into the back and polish the wares. Do not stop until they gleam like the sun.''

The boy sighed, shot Roman a disgusted glance, and went through the curtains at the back of the shop.

''I am in your debt,'' Akhmed said. ''The boy will not

seek adventure in those quarters again. Come, join me in a glass of tea.''

Now began the slow process for which Roman had come. It could not be hurried, and he resigned himself to half an hour of polite chitchat until Akhmed was ready to be told the reason for his visit.

From the man's nervousness, Roman suspected that he already knew: the artisan was from Gurneh, where the main occupation for generations had been finding and stealing artifacts from ancient tombs to sell on the black market. Egypt's heritage, like that of Greece, was fast disappearing into the vaults of private collectors around the world.

Finally it was time. ''There are new artifacts emerging in private sales this past week, my old friend. The authorities are as yet unaware.''

The other man looked around sharply for potential eavesdroppers. ''I have heard certain rumors, effendi. Inquiries have been set in motion. I shall have information for you soon.''

The Duke of Audley's backing had given Roman an open hand in negotiating. ''Excellent. Let the word go out that I am willing to buy anything they have found, at the going rate. They will not lose any profits. But I want the location of that tomb!''

Akhmed bowed his head. ''It must be done carefully. But it shall be done as you say.''

''It is the only way we can preserve the inheritance of your ancestors, old friend. At the same time we can keep the authorities from coming down on the thieves.''

''I should like to present you with a gift,'' Akhmed said, ''for returning my miserable fool of a son to me unharmed. Choose anything you like from among my wares.''

Before Roman could reply there came a resounding crash of metal and wood from the back storeroom, followed by ominous silence. Both men rushed through the curtain to see what catastrophe had occurred.

There were bowls and vases and platters everywhere. It took a moment to locate the boy in all the welter. Akhmed's son sat sprawled on the floor where he'd been knocked by a falling shelf.

"Owwww! I tried to reach the top row, and they all came down on my poor head."

"You should have used the ladder," his father scolded. "So much damage! Look at that brazier, all dented!"

Roman knew Akhmed was as concerned for his son as for his wares. He hovered over them while Roman checked the lad for broken bones. He seemed unharmed except for swelling near his right eye, where the corner of the shelf had caught him, and his index finger, which appeared broken. With the skill he'd learned in the field, Roman had the injured finger splinted and wrapped with strips of cloth. He wouldn't be trying to snatch wallets now.

"Leave the splint on for two weeks. You'll have a black eye. A cool compress and some mint tea will have you back to normal in short order."

Akhmed bowed. "Once again I am in your debt, effendi McKendrick. Please to select a gift of thanks from among my humble wares."

To refuse would be impolite. Roman cast his gaze over the jumble. Amid the heavily chased and ornamented designs, he saw a shape of marvelous purity and elegant line hidden beneath an overturned bench.

It appeared to have spilled out of one of the large brass vessels that had been stored beneath the bench. It was a metal mirror, obviously not of great value to its makers, or it would have been put up more carefully. It would be useful for reflecting light inside the tomb shafts where candles or lamps were too hazardous, or their smoke might ruin wall paintings.

"I will accept this mirror with deep gratitude," he said.

His host held up his hands. He didn't even remember how such an object had gotten into his shop. "Such a plain piece? Take it, and more, with my blessings."

"This will suit me perfectly," Roman said, and eventually convinced Akhmed that it was more than enough for the little he had done.

The man retrieved the mirror and wrapped it in colorful cloth which he bound with twine for carrying. "With my humble thanks," he said, giving Roman the parcel.

The moment the wrapped mirror exchanged hands Roman felt a jolt go through his hand and up along his arm, as if he'd touched a galvanic device.

His head felt light, and filled with warm effervescence, like tiny wheeling sparks. Then it was gone as quickly as it had come.

Too much heat and too little sleep, he thought, tucking the wrapped mirror under his arm, and making his way back out from the dim shop into the brilliant light.

"I cannot wait to see the fir tree!" Minnie perched on the window seat in the rose silk sitting room that separated her bedchamber from Judith's. Her eyes shone with stars.

Even the weather had conspired to make the holiday perfect. Outside the tall windows of Claybourne House, the blue dusk was thick with swirling snow. Inside, a clean evergreen scent pervaded the house. The grand staircase, mantels, windows, and mirrors were draped in fresh garlands, and Leland, Alicia, and Tess had been closeted behind closed doors in the drawing room all afternoon, preparing the tree.

"Do you think there will be lighted candles on the branches?" she asked.

"I am almost certain of it. Oh, this is the most exciting

Christmas Eve ever!'' Judith exclaimed, catching her sister's excitement.

It had been a long time since they'd all been together. Longer still since they'd received anything more than new hair ribbons or warm mittens. Both Tess and Alicia had been dropping intriguing hints all week.

A tap on the door announced the maid sent to summon them to the drawing room, and they went down eagerly, arm in arm. Desmond stood outside the drawing room, a faint smile hovering on his lips. When Judith saw him she tried to slow their pace to something more dignified, but Minnie didn't care. She trotted on down, compelling her older sister to hurry along, or trip down the staircase.

''Oh, Desmond! Have you seen the fir tree? Is it *very* beautiful?''

''You must see for yourself, Miss Minerva.''

At his signal the footmen threw the wide doors open. Both girls entered and gasped in delight.

The lamps had been extinguished and the drawing room was filled with the flicker and glow of firelight and candlelight. They'd expected to see a small tree atop a table, as in the illustrations of their ladies' magazine. The reality was far more impressive. The tree sent down from Claybourne Castle was a noble specimen, at least twelve feet tall.

Dozens of white candles in brass holders were clipped to the branches, illuminating the tree from top to bottom. It was garlanded with strings of silvered-glass beads and hung with faceted crystal lusters, reflecting the light in twinkling, winking rainbows. There were stars cut from embossed silver paper, bunches of gilded walnuts and pinecones tied together with sprigs of scarlet berries, and foil cones nestled here and there, filled with sugared almonds and other sweetmeats.

"Well, what do you think?" Leland asked. "Does it pass muster?"

For once, Tess's younger sisters were both rendered speechless. They stared at it, openmouthed, until Alicia clapped her hands in delight. Leland went forward to lead them into the room.

They looked up in wonderment, and for a moment Tess could see the two young girls she remembered from happier times. It was a storybook scene with a happy ending, and Tess felt her heart fill. She must never regret her decision again. How kind and good her husband and sister-in-law were! She must find a way to repay them. To enable Leland to be a husband to her in more than name, and give them all the heir they wanted so desperately.

I will be a good wife, she vowed silently. *I will find a way!*

After her sisters found their voices, they oohed and aahed over every bit of decoration. Alicia pointed out something they had missed—the small packages tied inside here and there amid the branches. The velvet boxes were tied with satin cords.

"Look, this one in gold paper is for Judith. Yes, and this one also! Oh, and here is one for Minnie and one for Tess. Shall we wait until after services tomorrow, or should we open them tonight?"

"Tonight, if you please," Minnie said. "Otherwise I shall die of curiosity during the night!" They all laughed at that.

"I have left Tess's gift from me in my room," Leland said. "I'll hang it with the others." He took himself off to fetch it.

Before he returned, Desmond announced a visitor: "His Grace, the Duke of Audley."

No one had heard his arrival. Minnie looked up in interest, Judith with studied nonchalance (she had never met a duke before—should she look pleased or indifferent?), and Tess with pleasure. Despite Alicia's dislike of the man, he had been kind and friendly to Tess whenever their paths crossed. She felt kindly disposed toward him for sponsoring Roman's work, and she found his witty conversations and caustic remarks entertaining. Most people, even those not in awe of his title, were rather afraid of his tongue.

Recently she had teased him on having little good to say about anyone. "My dear Countess," he'd replied suavely, "I have always made a sincere effort to be factual and accurate. Surely you cannot fault me for the fact that barefaced truth is often so very unattractive!"

As he entered the room now, his dark eyes scanned the candlelit tree and the family group around it. "Charming!"

Alicia gave him an icy smile that would have frozen a lesser man in his tracks. "Were we expecting you, Anthony?"

It glanced off him like a tinsel-paper spear. "Dear, dear. So hostile even on Christmas Eve, my sweet cousin? Fear not, I haven't come to count the silverplate!"

Her face flamed. "If you had, you might be sure it is all in order, down to the last teaspoon and punch cup."

"I would not expect less from you, my dear. You are a notable housekeeper."

His compliment only made Alicia angrier. Minnie and Judith exchanged glances with Tess, who gave an infinitesimal nod. This situation and stinging repartee was far beyond the abilities of untried schoolgirls.

Making their excuses, they withdrew as soon as the introductions were finished. Audley waited until the doors closed behind them. "Very pretty girls, Lady Claybourne, and very prettily behaved. I congratulate you."

Reaching into his coat pocket, he removed two parcels. "I have come bearing gifts. A peace offering, Alicia, if you will."

He handed one to Tess and the other to Alicia, who accepted it reluctantly. "If you please, I should like to see you open them now. Very selfish of me, but I cannot deny myself the pleasure of seeing if my little trinkets give you joy."

Alicia opened hers without expression. Inside was an elegant journal bound in pale blue leather. She thanked him stiffly. He bowed. "Every woman needs a diary in which to write down her adventures," he said. Alicia glared at him.

Tess removed the ribbons on her package. It contained the latest edition, in a finely tooled binding, of *A Traveler's History of Egypt*.

She wondered why he had chosen the gift, but thanked him. "I shall enjoy curling up with it during the cold, dark months ahead."

The duke leaned an arm along the mantelpiece. "It may be winter, but the climate in Egypt is sunny and exceedingly warm. I thought you might care to familiarize yourself with the famous sites and monuments you will surely visit during your stay there."

Tess was astonished. "You are under a misapprehension, my lord. We have no plans to visit Egypt."

"Really?" Audley arched an eyebrow. "That is very strange, Lady Claybourne—since the *Rose of Sharon* sets sail for Alexandria in two weeks' time—and both your names are on the passenger list."

In the silence that followed his announcement Tess could hear her own heartbeat. Her glance fell on Alicia, standing as if turned to stone. Leland cleared his throat and stepped back into the drawing room. He'd arrived in time to overhear the exchange.

"You have spoiled my little surprise, Anthony."

Tess swallowed. "Is it true, then? We are going to Egypt?"

Her husband crossed the room to her side. "It has always been an ambition of mine to see the great marvels of that ancient civilization. It was something I put off, even though Egypt is a very fashionable winter destination these days. But since Mr. McKendrick's translations, I have a great desire to view the sites mentioned in my new papyrus."

He looked down at her. "It is unfortunate that you had to learn of it in this manner. I hope you are pleased, my dear?"

She stared down at her hands. Egypt was the last place on earth she wished to visit. Fate seemed determined to throw her together with Roman again.

"But . . . so far away! My sisters . . . the foundling hospital. Oh! And there is so much to do in preparation for Judith's come-out." Her dismay was so patent that Alicia rushed in to smooth things over.

"You needn't be concerned. We shall hire a secretary to manage the details."

Tess was stunned, and didn't reply. Leland came to sit beside her and took her hand. "Perhaps I should have discussed the matter with you, my dear. I thought you would be pleased to go abroad. There is more to the world than London and Swanfield, Tess."

"Yes. I am very aware of it. I have always hoped to see something of other countries—but the timing of it, the short notice!"

"Do not worry your pretty little head. Minnie will be at school, and you know that Judith has been invited to stay with my godmother in the country. She can attend the local balls and assemblies in preparation for her come-out. Why, there will be little for you to do but decide which gowns and jewels to take with you."

"And Leland is going to hire a private boat—a *dahabeeyah* it is called—so that we might cruise the Nile and visit all the famous sites with every comfort imaginable. Think of the wonderful adventures we shall have!''

Tess bit her lip. So many detailed plans, and she had not been a part of any of it.

Alicia saw that she wasn't eliciting the proper response. ''It will be a splendid opportunity to visit Mr. McKendrick and view his excavations in progress,'' she added encouragingly. ''You should like that, I know.''

No, you do not! Tess wanted to shout. *It is the last thing I wish to do, and Egypt is the last place I wish to be.*

Although she was shaking inside, she schooled her features. ''Have the servants been told of this proposed voyage?''

''Why, of course, I have informed Desmond and the upper servants,'' her husband answered. ''There is a good deal of planning to be done on their part.''

''And yet no one saw fit to inform me.'' Tess withdrew her hand and rose abruptly.

''It is true I am new to this family,'' she said heatedly, ''but I would have expected that, as your wife, Leland, I would have the same courtesy extended to me as to your servants!''

With her head high, she swept past Audley and Alicia, and left the drawing room.

As she passed through the doors, she heard her sister-in-law's cutting comment to the duke. ''I hope you are happy with tonight's work, Anthony!''

''My dear cousin,'' Audley pointed out smoothly, ''you cannot blame me for thinking that Lady Claybourne was aware of your travel plans.''

''Go to her, Leland,'' Alicia urged.

Tess closed the door, shutting out their voices. She resisted the childish but satisfying urge to slam it behind her.

Instead of going up to her room, where someone might come seeking her, she went down the hall and turned into one of the state chambers. She found herself in the Blue Parlor, where Roman had kissed her so passionately. Sitting alone in the dimness, she fought to control her fury and humiliation.

Not for the first time, she brooded that nothing had changed at Claybourne House since her coming as the earl's new bride. She had no real part to play in the important decisions of the household. Or their marriage. She had as little say in matters that directly affected her as one of the antique trinkets in the glass-fronted cabinets.

The door opened quietly, and Alicia entered. "Tess?"

"Please. I wish to be alone!"

Her sister-in-law came to her side, moving through the darkened room with the ease of habit. "My dear, please forgive me . . . forgive *us*! Leland meant it for the best. He meant to tell you tomorrow, and thought you would be well pleased."

"How can I be, when such an important decision is made without so much as a word to me? I am not a child."

"No. No, you are not."

They sat awhile in silence. Finally Alicia spoke again, her voice low and hesitant. "No doubt you think it odd that such plans were made in haste. When you understand the reason . . . Oh dear, I didn't mean to discuss the matter in this awkward way."

Something in her tone alarmed Tess. "What is it? Please, let us have no more secrets between us."

"It is about Leland."

Tess's heart fell. Had he even shared the most intimate details of their married life with his sister?

"He has always had a delicate constitution," Alicia said. She spoke slowly, as if choosing her words with great care. "You will recall that he was slightly ill just prior to your wedding."

"Yes, of course. An minor inflammation of the chest," he said."

"Indeed—a chronic recurrence of his bronchial problems. He had never shaken the aftereffects, and his health has suffered. He didn't wish to upset you. It is nothing of a very serious nature, of course; however, his physician has recommended that Leland go abroad to a warm, dry climate to improve his health. The doctor is sure that it will do the trick. Leland wished to spare you any anxiety, by presenting the travel plans as a surprise Christmas announcement. Egypt was the logical choice."

Tess was shocked and concerned. "Poor Leland! And I received the news so badly." She put her hands to her cheeks. "Oh, I feel so ashamed of my dreadful behavior!"

"Nonsense. I can understand your hurt, fully. It was stupid of us not to discuss the trip with you beforehand. So easy to see in retrospect. But . . . you are not angry with us still?"

"How could I be angry under the circumstances? Dear Alicia, Leland's health must come before every other consideration!" She took her sister-in-law's hand. "You have both always treated me with consideration and kindness. I am the worst beast in nature. I should have known there was something more behind this!"

"Then you will come?"

"Yes, willingly."

"Darling Tess!"

"I should go to Leland immediately and make amends."

"He is resting. I told him that I would explain. He was afraid you would be angry that he hadn't taken you into his confidence about his bronchial problems on top of this fiasco. It is mortifying for a man to admit any weakness to a woman, you know. Especially to his new, young bride."

"Yes." Tess grasped the full implications of the situation. "I see that it must be so."

"I am so very glad we had this talk. I promise you shall enjoy the experience—and once in the warmth of Egypt, you will see the difference. Leland will be a new man!"

Much later, when Tess was in her own chamber for the night, she went over everything Alicia had told her. It all made sense now.

I should have realized he was not as strong as when we first met. Looking back, she realized that he had become quieter, more distracted, and that his cheeks had grown more hollow over the past few months, his face more lined, his step less brisk. And all the time he was bravely trying to put up a front so as not to alarm her, or appear less than manly in her eyes.

While her maid brushed her mistress's dark hair into a shining cloud, Tess mulled over all the consequences of her husband's bronchial troubles. *It is no wonder he has been unable to perform his marital duties,* she thought. *The problem is not that I have failed him in some unknown way, but that he is ill.*

There was real hope, then, to salvage a good relationship from their marriage. Hope that there might still be children. A child would change everything for the better.

Just as time in the warm, dry Egyptian air would improve Leland's weak chest and restore him to health. *I must focus on that,* she told herself sternly. Not on the mingled dismay and joy that overwhelmed her at the thought of seeing Roman again.

Or on the nagging feeling that this expedition abroad would somehow end in disaster.

As Roman returned to his hotel from the souk, he shifted with the package containing the mirror beneath his arm. It had felt light at first, yet seemed to grow heavier with every step.

He was starting up the wide steps, when he was hailed by a familiar voice. Turning, he recognized Captain Dupont, an influential man with high connections among the French officials who ran the Department of Antiquities. The sort of someone with whom a prudent Egyptologist would wish to keep on good terms.

"Well met, McKendrick. I heard you were back in Cairo. Come dine with me at my hotel and I will tell you all the latest news."

Roman looked forward to a casual evening, perhaps looking up his old friend Sheik Hussein Al-Rashid. Al-Rashid was a noted scholar and poet, a man as at home in the modern world as he was in that into which he'd been born.

The other man saw his hesitation. "You have new lines in your face since I saw you last. You English have a saying, McKendrick: 'All work and no play make Jack a dull boy.' I promise you good food, fine wine, excellent conversation—and the company of a beautiful and young American widow, sojourning in Cairo. What do you say to that?"

"Generous of you!" Roman laughed. "Very well, Dupont. I accept your kind invitation. I hope you will not regret inviting me to meet this beauty."

"Ah, but she will not be the only woman present— there will be twelve to dine. I should tell you that the *très soignée* Mrs. Miller has seen you in passing, and made inquiries of her friends. So you may have something more than a memory to take away with you tonight."

He gave Roman directions and went on his way. Cursing cheerfully, Roman went up to his room. Perhaps it was true, he was getting dull. Since returning to Egypt he'd thrown himself into his work with a vengeance. Anything to forget Tess.

As if that were possible!

He pushed her image away as he had a thousand times since leaving England. Mahomet, his dragoman, had noticed his abstraction and the dark circles of exhaustion beneath his eyes. His prescription had been much like Captain Dupont's:

"Find yourself a woman, Effendi McKendrick. One who can make you forget your troubles and ease you in mind and in body."

Unwrapping the mirror, Roman decided to take their advice. There were other pleasures in life—even if there was no one like Tess. But he must put her and the past behind him for good.

Whistling as he took the mirror out, he decided that perhaps DuPont's beautiful young American widow would share the same outlook.

At last the old cloth slipped free and Roman gasped in astonishment. How had he thought the mirror plain? The back of it was incised with elegant scrollwork that almost resembled hieratic script. Or—no—were those hiero-glyphs? He blinked.

The design seemed to shift as he tried to focus upon it. What had appeared to be a detail of a royal cartouche resolved itself into an intricate pattern of curves and whorls and spiraling lines. It made his head whirl. Turning it over, he examined the opposite surface. It was smooth and un-blemished and polished to a high luster.

"Neither bronze nor copper, but some alloy," he said aloud. The mirror was beyond his ken. He had never seen such curious workmanship. Nor, for that matter, could he fix it in a particular era or place.

He felt a fleeting vertigo, and set the mirror on the bed. It was stifling in the room and beads of sweat formed along his brow. Roman rose to throw back the carved wooden shutters. The sun had passed to the other side of the building, and the open window might catch a passing breeze.

As he turned back, a flare of light from the bed temporarily blinded him. If not for the chair back he used to steady himself, he might have pitched forward over the small table. Roman averted his head, then picked the mirror up, intending to move it into the deeper shadows of the small sitting area.

The handle, with its smooth and sinuously shaped lotus-blossom motif, seemed warm and yielding to his touch. Almost like the seductive softness of a woman's skin. That startled him, but it was the image reflected in the mirror's surface that froze him to the spot.

Instead of his own sunburnt features, Tess's lovely face looked out at him. She seemed to be looking right through him and beyond. He caught his breath in mingled surprise and longing.

Then, while he watched in silent horror, Tess's head was jerked back violently. Her eyes went wide with shock and fear, her mouth opened as if to cry out. Too late! A thin dagger blade caught the light like a line of fire, as the honed edge bit deep into her white throat. A great gout of crimson blood splashed across the image, blotting it out completely.

With a cry, Roman flung the mirror away.

It struck the corner of the bureau with a musical chime and glanced off, coming to rest in the shadows against the far corner of the wall. The bureau's veneer was chipped, but the mirror was unblemished, blank and innocent once more.

Roman heaved a few breaths, as if he'd been running for miles, then went to the basin and poured the pitcher of water over his head. *Heatstroke.* That was it. He'd been careless out in the sun, neglected to take in sufficient water, and was suffering the belated consequences. The entire episode was just a figment of a heated brain. A mirage born of heat and exhaustion.

Either that, or he'd gone completely mad.

A woman like Tess could do that to a man. Why, of all the women on the face of the earth, did she have to be the one he loved so passionately?

Roman sat on the edge of the bed, his bronzed hands trembling with reaction. The mirror was still lying where he had flung it. He watched it for several minutes, warily. Nothing happened.

Dupont is right. I need to forget about my work for a few hours. Forget about Tess. She is so much in my thoughts and dreams that I imagined it all.

But as he dressed for his dinner engagement, Roman knew that the terrible vision would haunt him as long as he lived.

PART TWO

EGYPT

8

A sense of excitement filled Claybourne House. First, the wedding of the earl to Her Grace in the spring, then the young ladies down for the holidays, and now the master and mistress jaunting off to Egypt with Lady Alicia! There had not been such a happy bustle since the present earl's father had gone off on a tour of the world.

Desmond watched over the disposition of the boxes and valises as if they held the treasures of the ages, rather than hats and gloves and shawls. The crested traveling carriage for the family was drawn up before the front door, with a second one behind it for the servants who were to accompany them.

"Easy there, mind you!" he called out as two footmen loaded the last of the smaller trunks in the second traveling carriage. The larger trunks and wardrobes had been sent ahead and Lady Alicia's maid, the earl's valet, and the countess's superior French dresser took their places inside it. Celeste carried Tess's small fitted jewel case in her own hands.

"Well, my dears," Leland announced, "we are ready to set off on our grand adventure." Although his voice was jaunty, there were shadows beneath his eyes. She felt a pang of concern.

By day nothing had changed. By night she slept alone

and undisturbed, just as he had promised. The connecting door between their rooms stayed locked from his side.

Tess smiled to hide her inner turmoil. Cairo was too far from Judith and Minnie—and far too close to Roman. Among the tightly knit society of English expatriates in Egypt, they were sure to run into him. It would be a sweet agony. She prayed that she would be able to endure it.

Alicia, meanwhile, was as thrilled as a child with a new pony. She had actually let Tess oversee her wardrobe for the trip, and looked amazingly pretty in a traveling costume of wine and black striped faille. Tess's own outfit was a more subdued navy faced in sapphire velvet, with cased-glass cylinder buttons in the same vivid hue.

As the last of their things went out of the house, Alicia laughed aloud. "Do you remember how stern your Mr. McKendrick was with Lord Brocklehurst over all his baggage? I shudder to think of what he would say, could he see ours."

Since Alicia spoke of Roman frequently, Tess couldn't help wondering if Alicia had let her choose her new clothing with an eye to attracting him. The stab of jealousy made her feel ignoble and mean.

If Roman and Alicia should make a match of it, she told herself sternly, *I could not withhold my good wishes for their happiness.*

She sighed. *I am not a very good liar, if I cannot even convince myself.* Hoping she would not be put to the test, she said her good-byes to the household staff and went out into the watery January sunshine.

It was difficult leaving England, leaving her sisters behind for almost three months, but of the two only Minnie had protested—and that had been about her own return to Hazeldean, not Tess's journey.

Everything had been taken care of properly despite the short notice Leland had given. Judith was happily settled with her friends outside London and Minnie, despite her strong protests, was back at Hazeldean. Tess had memorized the last paragraphs of her most recent letter:

Dearest Tess,

It is very hard to be left behind in this horrid, stuffy school while you are gone abroad. My only consolation is that I am not plagued by Judith's airs and graces and lectures on proper behavior.

I have viewed the antiquities in the local museum, and now have decided to become a lady Egyptologist, if there is such a thing. If not, I shall make one! My wish for you is to have a safe voyage and a pleasant sojourn in the land of the pharaohs.''

This nobly expressed thought was ruined by the lurid conclusion of Minnie's letter:

Do not concern yourself with my welfare. I shall manage while you are away. I only hope I may not be carried off by an infectious disease in your absence, leaving you to mourn in guilt the rest of your days. I remain as always
Your Loving Sister,
Minerva

Tess laughed and shook her head. It was really too bad that Minnie could not accompany them.

Judith had not even complained once. It had been decided that she would go to the assemblies with Lady Hammersmith's two daughters, and make her come-out with them after Easter Week. That was when the Season would begin in earnest, and fresh new faces were liable to catch the jaded attention of some eligible young suitor.

Celeste was already waiting in the second carriage with Alicia's maid and Leland's valet. In her schoolgirl years, she had never envisioned herself traveling in such style, like a fine lady. Her smart outfit of brown twill with gold braiding drew stares of approval from her companions. They were all agog over their venture to exotic shores. She clasped the precious jewel case tightly.

As her mistress was about to mount the first carriage, a small vehicle, piled precariously with an odd assortment of luggage, came dashing up the street. All eyes were fixed on the small determined figure that descended when it stopped. She was dressed in a warm dark amber cloak with matching bonnet that belonged to Judith. Only it was not, of course, Judith.

Tess started toward her younger sister. Alarmed, she still had time to notice that the girl had dressed her hair in a becoming style that made her seem older than her years.

"Minnie! What on earth . . . ?"

The girl folded her hands in their warmly-lined leather gloves—also belonging to Judith—and lifted her head. "I am coming to Egypt with you."

"You cannot."

"Then I shall have to sit here on the doorstep until you return, for lack of a chaperone. Hazeldean is closed for the term! An epidemic of the measles. With you setting out today, I had no choice but to come on directly."

"How fortunate that the academy is less than two hours away!" Alicia cried. "Another half hour and it might have been too late. We would have been on our way to the ship."

"Yes," Tess said, eyeing her sister suspiciously.

There was no way the school could have been emptied so quickly—why, just the matter of hiring carriages and notifying families would have made it logistically impossible!

She saw that the trunks from Hazeldean were clearly marked as to which contained heavy cold-weather clothes, and which the lighter spring fashions. Why, one valise was even carefully marked "Books to take"!

She sent Minnie a darkling glance. "And how fortunate that your things are all packed and ready to put aboard. Your timing could not have been more precise, had you planned it!"

Minnie smiled innocently.

The *Rose of Sharon*, while luxurious, was not a large ship. On the voyage out, the first-class passengers soon got to know each other. While the others played at cards or visited among themselves, Minnie devoured the book that the Duke of Audley had given to Tess. She could not believe that soon she would be seeing the very same places illustrated in the book on Egypt!

"My gift from the duke seems to have found great favor," Tess remarked.

"Really, the Duke of Audley is so much nicer than his son! What a very odd thing heredity is."

As it turned out, Audley was sailing on the same ship to visit his son. "Quite the little family reunion," he had drawled when they met at the captain's table for dinner the first night out.

Thus far his presence had been a plus, as far as Tess was concerned. She was only mildly astonished at the friendship that had sprung up between her younger sister and the tart-tongued lord. She enjoyed being treated as an adult and loved to hear of his adventures in foreign lands. For Audley's part, he seemed to be amused by Minnie's frankness and enthusiasm.

Heaven knows, there is nothing of the die-away airs, so en vogue *now, about Minnie!*

"Do you dislike Lord Brocklehurst so much?" Alicia asked.

"He is odious! My feelings for him are of the same

degree as those you hold for his father,'' Minnie said.

Alicia stared at her gravely, then shook her head. ''I wish I could believe that.''

''Why do you dislike Lord Audley?'' Minnie asked baldly. ''He seems to bear you no ill will. In fact, he speaks quite kindly of you.''

Less so regarding Leland, however. She kept that last to herself.

''There is apparently no accounting for tastes,'' Alicia said crisply, and changed the subject.

Among the acquaintances that Tess and Minnie made was an elegant spinster who had traveled around the world accompanied only by her maid. Her anecdotes were intriguing: Miss Riley-Burnside had published several books of her adventures under a masculine pseudonym, and they had proved to be quite successful.

Minnie was delighted. ''Then *you* are T. Riley-Burnside? I have one of your books with me. It was a Christmas gift to my sister from the Duke of Audley. I am reading it now!''

The spinster gave her a wry smile. ''If you like it, then you may tell me so. Indeed, you may gush most profusely; however, if you do *not,* I'd much prefer that you keep your opinion private.''

Minnie laughed. ''I shall swear an oath upon it.''

Meanwhile, she was quite curious about Mrs. Reed, a pale young Englishwoman. ''I saw her briefly one evening on the afterdeck.'' Her brow puckered. ''She looked quite familiar.''

''I suspect she has one of those faces,'' Alicia replied. ''There are certain sets of features that appear with some regularity in the general population.''

Minnie wasn't convinced. She had little opportunity to pursue the subject. Mrs. Reed kept to her stateroom, reportedly suffering from seasickness. She seemed to come out only after dusk, heavily swathed against the cool sea air, and quite obviously in the late stages of pregnancy.

While none of the other passengers paid any heed, Minnie was intrigued and wove fantastical stories about Mrs. Reed. "Perhaps she is really a spy. Or a princess, traveling incognito. Or," Minnie said, warming to the topic, "she may be horribly disfigured from some tragic accident, which would account for her veils and scarves."

"Perhaps," Tess said sharply, "she is only a woman of delicate constitution, traveling out to join her husband, who is assigned to the diplomatic service."

"Pooh. Is that what the purser says?" Minnie pursed her lips. "No, that is far too prosaic. Really, Tess, you have no romance in your soul!"

Her sister looked quickly away. *Ah, if only you knew.*

On their last evening out, Tess ran into Mrs. Reed standing at the rail, as she took a stroll about the deck. The stars were incredibly bright out on the open water and she had taken to watching them before retiring for the night. For once neither of them was accompanied.

"Good evening."

The young mother-to-be gave a start. "Oh! I . . . I did not hear you come along. So . . . so good to get a breath of air!"

"Yes, is it not? I imagine you will be glad to set foot ashore tomorrow."

"I . . . we . . . that is, yes. I . . . I am a poor sailor. How I dread the return voyage!"

"No doubt it will be much easier," Tess remarked, in reference to the woman's condition. *Poor thing, she is but a child herself. How hard it would be to give birth in a foreign land, without one's friends and family.*

The woman shivered and huddled into herself in a bundle of misery. Tess impulsively put her hand on the young woman's arm.

"You are Mrs. Reed, I know. I understand your husband is in the diplomatic service and that you have no acquaintance in Egypt. We shall be in Cairo for the winter. Should you require the assistance of a fellow Englishwoman . . ."

"I . . . so good of you, Lady Claybourne! Thank you . . ."

Without another word, Mrs. Reed bolted clumsily away and vanished into her stateroom. The woman's behavior was so odd that Tess hoped that she wouldn't come to regret her impetuous offer.

She went along the deck to her own stateroom suite. The door to the second bedroom was closed, as it had been every night of the voyage. She wondered if the same would be true when they arrived at their accommodations in Cairo.

Leland had made the acquaintance of two Americans and a Dane, and the four formed a group to while away the journey with cigars and endless playing at cards. It seemed to have improved his spirits. At the beginning of their trip he had been irritable and prone to sudden outbursts of anger.

"I have never seen him so jumpy," Alicia had commented to Tess. "I think he has placed so much hope upon this visit improving his health that he is all raw nerves."

As the skies cleared and the air warmed, Leland's spirits had quickly improved. If his health progressed as rapidly, the door to his bedchamber might not stay closed much longer.

Minnie popped in to kiss her sister good-night. Tess was surprised. "You should have been in your bed hours ago. We make port in Alexandria in the morning, and after a night there, we'll be on a small packet, steaming up the Nile. It will not be nearly as comfortable as this ship, I assure you."

"I don't care how beastly the Nile packet might be," Minnie said, hugging Tess, "for it will be then that the real adventure begins!"

Sun streamed through the carved wooden lattices covering the window, rousing Roman from his exhausted sleep. He became aware of his surroundings gradually. A fountain plashed softly in the near distance. Soft sheets, perfumed with a faint hint of rose petals, and the satin curve of a woman's breast beneath his outflung hand.

Then he remembered. *Tess.* He'd made love to her all through the night, showing her pleasures she had never imagined. Guiding her to the summit, then retreating until she begged for him to drive her over the edge.

And he had. Time and again as he drove into her she had cried out, urging him on. In all his dreams he had never imagined her so responsive to his slightest breath and touch.

His hand closed on her breast, his work-hardened thumb running over the textured tip. He would never get enough of her.

"You're insatiable," a husky voice murmured in his ear.

His eyes flew open. He was lying naked in an unfamiliar bed. An unfamiliar room. The long hair of the woman beside him spread like a silken veil across the pillow. Long, curling, blond.

He sat up and it felt as if a sword had cleft his brain. "Christ!"

"Too much champagne, darling?" Closing his eyes, Roman lowered himself back against the mattress. He had no recollection of the previous night. That had never happened to him before. He opened his eyes cautiously and surveyed the honey-brown eyes looking back at him, the sensuous mouth in an attractive, slightly predatory face. At least they were familiar.

He recognized the dashing American divorcée who was wintering in Cairo with friends. Her name floated up out of the depths of his consciousness.

"Ah. Mrs. Miller."

"So formal by sunlight, Roman?" Her voice was low and velvety. "Last night you called me Sally."

"Sally, then." He cleared his throat. This was incredibly awkward.

She sat up and stretched like a cat. Warm light gilded her body and his own responded—as she knew it would. He was magnificent!

She leaned over him, her long curls and the tips of her breasts brushing the dark hairs of his chest. Sally Miller knew exactly what was going through his mind. After all, she'd plied him with enough wine to bring it about. Roman McKendrick was said to be a man married .to his work. The challenge had been irresistible, and she'd set about seducing him. He hadn't needed much coercion on her part.

And he'd proved to her—time and again—that he was no monk! She could not remember ever having a more daring or experienced lover.

He'd taught her things none of the others had. Her body was replete but she wanted more. Her mouth hovered over his. "Shall I ring for coffee?" Those ripe lips curved in a smile. "Or . . . ?"

"Or!" he said, snaring her in his arms and rolling so their positions were reversed.

Her body was lush and welcoming beneath him. As she shifted her legs apart he felt her engorged nipples rub against his muscular chest. In the arms of the willing widow, he could assuage his needs, if not his deep loneliness. Roman sighed without realizing it. Life went on, and he would be a great fool not to take what was offered so eagerly.

Winding his strong brown fingers through her golden hair, Roman crushed her mouth beneath his. If the old adage that "happiness is where you find it" was true, he didn't have far to seek.

In the corner of the room a worn leather case lay in shadow. Inside, the ancient mirror awakened. Images rippled across the surface once more, shifting as rapidly as light dancing off water. Colors blended: Nile-green and the leached sands of the Valley of the Kings; silk and satin gowns in rainbow hues, the shine of diamonds and eyes as green as emeralds; the darkness of a deep tomb shaft, and the fierce Egyptian sun glinting from a bloodstained blade.

The light from the mirror grew in brightness until it leaked through the edges of the leather case. The couple on the bed, if they noticed at all, mistook it for sunbeams slanting through the shutters.

The Claybourne party was at the ship's rail, enjoying their first glimpse of Alexandria. The sun beat down with surprising vigor for the early hour. Behind them the Mediterranean waters sparkled blue-green and clear in the distance, as the gangway of the steamship was lowered and secured. Here, where constant wavelets lapped the pilings, they were oily and rubbish filled.

Gulls, sounding no different than English gulls to Minnie's ears, shrieked and wheeled overhead. One darted down and snatched up a floating tidbit, flapping so close she felt the wind of its wings.

Although they had the best cabins aboard the ship, Tess and her party were glad to disembark. The voyage had been rough, and the buffeting winds the first half of the trip had kept them inside.

Ships' officers had changed to tropical uniform, and took their places at the head and foot of the gangway. With the baggage unloaded on the dock, the passengers began to disembark. For some this was the final destination. For others, like the Claybourne party, this was the transfer point to the boat that would carry them south, up the Nile to Cairo.

Tess spied young Mrs. Reed standing by the rail, heavily veiled against the sun, looking lost and unsure and very pregnant. Her "happy event" was almost three months away, and Tess wondered how Mrs. Reed would manage through the heat until then. She had been looking especially pale since they'd arrived.

"Are you sure we cannot take you up with us? There is room in the carriage."

"Thank you, Lady Claybourne," she said softly, "but I am being met."

"Very well, if you are sure."

"Dry land, at last!" Alicia said, as she stepped off the gangway. She had discovered that she was not a good sailor. "I may decide to stay here rather than brave the voyage back!"

Minnie's excitement was marvelous to behold. Her hazel eyes were wide and shining, like a child at a pantomime. Only the other ships and the mounds of baggage were familiar. Everything else was wonderfully, exotically foreign. "Oh, I cannot believe that we are actually in Egypt!"

"Leland says the pyramids are visible from our hotel balconies in Cairo, and that we shall visit them! Shall we actually ride on camels, do you think?"

"I sincerely hope not," Tess said dryly.

"I do wish Judith were here to see it with us."

"Yes," Tess agreed, "but she will be far happier at

Lady Hammersmith's with her young friends until we return."

"Look! There is a man with a great white bird on his shoulder. Oh! And the sky. So incredibly blue!"

"Mind your step instead of the sky," Tess said, taking her sister's arm, "or you'll be seeing stars instead."

Only Leland's quick action and an unintended jig step on her part kept Minnie from tripping over a coiled length of rope. Tess was surprised at his strength. The fresh sea air had already wrought an improvement.

"Be careful," he admonished her. "You might injure yourself."

The porters came past, carrying Alicia's monogrammed trunks and valises tot heir baggage carriage. Suddenly one of the men slipped and a green leather case went flying into the street, where it was crushed by a passing vehicle. Bottles of headache powders, physics, and herbal remedies smashed beneath flashing hooves.

In the twinkling of an eye Leland rounded on the man, cursing and shouting. "Clumsy fool! See what you have done?"

Taking the porter by the shoulders, he shook him like a terrier with a hapless ferret gripped in its teeth. The poor man was used to being abused by the wealthy visitors, but this tall, furious Englishman terrified him.

Alicia cried out and ran to her brother's side. "Leland! Stop! Stop it at once!"

"Your case," he shouted. "Look at it! Smashed to flinders, everything gone! The imbecile has ruined it."

"Leland, hush! You are creating a scene."

He flung the man away from him in disgust, sending him sprawling into a piling. His sister put her hand upon his arm. "It is all right," she said firmly. "There was nothing in it that cannot be replaced in the bazaar!"

Leland flushed when he saw Tess and Minnie staring at

him in alarm. "The case was our mother's," Alicia said, wringing her hands in distress. "A wedding gift to her from the Maharani of Birandoor. Such a lovely thing! All the stoppered bottles and vials fitted into velvet nests, and were etched with her crest and monogram."

"I understand," Tess said soothingly. "It is too bad to lose a valued heirloom to such a careless mishap."

"Yes. And there were several rare herbal preparations in it, such as snakebite and scorpion sting remedies." Alicia bit her lip. "Not to mention the laudanum and other poppy extracts. Oh, I should not have left it with the rest of the baggage."

"The fault was not yours," Leland said abruptly as he joined them. "It sits squarely on the shoulders of the shipping line's porter—who is no longer employed by them as of twenty seconds ago."

The entire episode had upset everyone. By the time Leland had calmed down, they were glad to find a carriage waiting for them, and left the area with relief. Soon they were on their way through the streets of Alexandrea. Unlike the gulls, Minnie thought, the people and trees and smells were so very different from England!

Then they turned up a wide boulevard that, except for the heat and the date palms, the men and women in their native robes, might have been a resort in her own country. Large European-style hotels lined both sides, and their occupants were promenading along the terraces or driving along in their carriages as if they were on their way up Bond Street or the Champs Elysée.

Why, already Tess and Alicia have exchanged nods with several acquaintances, and Leland tips his hat with the regularity of an automaton! What is the good of going to a foreign land, if we are going to live exactly as we do at home?

She struggled anew with her disappointment. She had

hoped for latticed windows, mosaic tiles, and tiny wooden balconies high above the streets. Leland had hired a house belonging to a wealthy American widow just outside of town. At least, to Minnie's way of thinking, that was slightly better than one of the hotels.

"Mrs. Miller is an acquaintance of Lady Tottingham's. She is staying with friends, and was willing to let us have it as long as we like. The house is still too full of memories for her. She and her late husband wintered in Egypt for many years, until his recent death in Luxor."

"Poor woman," Tess exclaimed. "To be in a foreign country at such a time must have been an ordeal."

"I know little about her; however, perhaps we should invite her to luncheon," Alicia said. "If she proves to be presentable, we may very well ask her to a dinner party."

Minnie thought it was very strange: if Mrs. Miller was good enough to let her house to them, then it seemed only natural that she would be invited to dine in her own home! *Oh, how much simpler life was before Tess married. But then,* she thought contritely, *we should not all be so happily settled.*

The house was some distance past the outskirts of the city, as it turned out, along a dusty road. The green strip of the Nile and its irrigated banks wound past small clusters of houses, people working the land as they had since before biblical times, and small boys riding water buffalo tied to water screws. Round and round they went, like figures atop a souvenir music box.

Tess enjoyed the exotic scenery, but most of all the sense of timelessness that covered the land like a huge crystal dome. If not for the modern carriages, they could be anywhere in Egypt's history and nothing would change.

Her own life was changeless in a completely different way. It was like a piece of cut crystal. It could be picked up and moved from one continent to another, yet it remained curiously the same, flaws and all.

The only difference was that with every drum of the horses' hooves she was coming closer and closer to Roman. She dreaded the inevitable meeting with him. If she could see him without him seeing her, watch him talk and laugh and move unobserved, she thought she would be entirely content.

Liar! a little voice in her head argued. *You would not be content until you were near him. And then you would want to reach out and touch his hand, his hair, the strong line of his jaw.*

And then, fool that you are, you would want more!

It was true. Tess couldn't bear to think of it. She turned to her companions and chattered brightly until their hotel came into view.

Three days later they were in Cairo. They found the house they'd hired sitting in a private oasis filled with palm trees, spiky ground plants, and its own wells. The outer wall was plain and blank, except for the studded entry doors and a few intricately pierced shutters on the upper story. Inside it was paradise.

There were green plants like giant pincushions, topped with colorful exotic blooms. Mosaic tiles covered the walls of the cobbled entry court and fountains jetted up and fell back like diamond sprays, in the latticed shade of palms. Both Tess and Minnie were awed to silence.

A manservant in long robes and a turban came out and bowed in welcome. Leland looked surprised, and Alicia stunned. "This is not at all what we had been given to expect," she said indignantly. "I expected something a good deal more . . . *English.*"

"But it is beautiful," Minnie breathed. "The *Arabian Nights* come to life!"

Tess turned to her with raised eyebrows. While the tales were entertaining and magical, their erotic nature was not suitable reading for schoolgirls. "And what would you know of them?"

Minnie blushed. She'd made extensive use of the libraries at Claybourne House over the Christmas holiday. She hadn't meant to give her illicit late-night reading habits away.

"It is just a saying."

The servant and driver exchanged words, followed by shrugs and much gesticulating. Another bow, and the servant went back inside. "What did he say?" Leland asked sharply.

"Effendi, you were not expected for yet another two days. The house is still occupied."

"What the devil does that mean?" Leland rounded on their driver, his face white. "I understood that Mrs. Miller is staying with friends in Luxor! We have not traveled across the Mediterranean only to be turned away on the very doorstep!"

A second servant in flowing robes hurried out, and bowed low. "A thousand pardons, my lord," he said in French-accented English. "That worthless fool of a boy did not understand. You are to enter and make yourselves at ease. All is in readiness for you within."

The anger ebbed from Leland's face. "Very good."

The serving man led them into a room fashioned in typical Egyptian style, with the traditional cushioned bench built into the wall on three sides of the room. A wide border of colored mosiac and mirrored bits lined the walls, fine rugs covered the cool tiles of the floor.

Juxtaposed with the exotic setting was a very stuffy set of English parlor furnishings looking stiff and disapproving of their exotic surroundings, like affronted spinsters who had suddenly found themselves in a seraglio.

The salon was off to one side of the room and Alicia sighed with relief when they entered it. Except for the plain plastered walls and the opening to a small, private courtyard, it might have been a salon in any English country manor: portraits, horsey prints, comfortable furnishings, tables covered with Battenberg-lace cloths, and collections of brass boxes, candy dishes, and glass paperweights.

They were interrupted by the arrival of their hostess. A servant came trailing behind her with a large, masculine-looking valise. Mrs. Miller was pretty in a candy-box way, all blond curls and deep dimples. She was dressed in half-mourning, and the lavender-gray traveling suit flattered her pink and white complexion. Tess noticed that Mrs. Miller carried a small but expensive leather jewel case over her arm.

"My dear Lady Claybourne, welcome to Cairo! How fortunate I stopped by to fetch this. In my haste to vacate I left several household items and all my jewelry behind! Luckily I had hidden the jewels, or I doubt they would have still been here upon my return. The people are very poor, and the temptation might have proved overwhelming."

Tess could tell by the set of the servant's jaw that he had heard and understood. She tried to smooth the moment over before Minnie blurted out something impolite. "We are so pleased to have a chance to meet you, Mrs. Miller, and thank you in person for your hospitality."

"Oh, you will meet me everywhere in Cairo! Or anywhere along the Nile, for that matter. You will find the Europeans and Americans form a very small and tightly knit society. We shall be thrown together constantly, Lady Claybourne. As you will soon see."

After a flurry of introductions and greetings, Mrs. Miller prepared to set off to a covered carriage. The servant carried battered valise past, Tess and she noticed the initials burned into the side in large block letters: "R. McK."

No, it couldn't be. There had to be more than one battered valise in Egypt, and more than one man with those initials. Hadn't there?

Tess brushed the matter aside and went to check out the rest of the house.

After seeing to Minnie's arrangements, she went to examine her own. She found her chamber spacious, with a sitting area, a large bed swathed and canopied in veils of mosquito netting, and a separate dressing area beyond. It was obviously Mrs. Miller's own chamber, and had been arranged to suit Western tastes, although the lush reclining couches, numerous tassled pillows, and voluptuous fabrics seemed to have come straight from a harem.

The bed had just been freshly made up, and a young woman let the mosquito netting fall back into place before giving a slight bow and departing.

Celeste had already laid out her mistress's combs and brushes on the low vanity. "Oh, Madame has lost a button," she said, leaning down to pick up something from the floor.

The maid turned the oval of gold and onyx over in her hand. "No, it is a man's cuff link." She set it down on the dressing table.

As the maid unpacked, Tess looked about. Open dishes of dried rose-petal potpourri filled the room with fragrance. Two marvelous lanterns of brass were strategically placed. Their tops and sides were pierced. At night, when the candles inside were lit, they would create dancing stars on the ceiling and walls. *It seems Mrs. Miller is quite the romantic.*

A curtain of tone-on-tone rose silk hid a wooden door in one wall. The tour of the mazelike house, on top of her excitement and tiredness, had made Tess lose her bearings. She opened the door cautiously, wondering if it led to Minnie's chamber, or perhaps to that of Celeste.

It was only an empty anteroom, with a door leading to a pleasant courtyard, cooled by trellised vines and fountains. She stepped out and looked around. The low wooden benches placed beneath the vines would be a lovely place to sit and read on a quiet afternoon.

Returning to her chamber, she shut the door in relief. That emotion was immediately followed by one of shame: she had secretly feared that it connected with Leland's room.

Tess leaned her head against the carved wood. She knew that she would not have felt the same sense of initial panic, if she'd thought it had been Roman's room on the other side. The coming months in Cairo would be a trial. She hoped she would be able to avoid him as much as possible.

Tess went to the dressing table. Her hair needed a good brush-out after the grit of the drive. As she pulled the pins from her chignon, her gaze fell on the cuff link beside her comb. It was the kind of plain and masculine jewelry that Roman favored. In fact she thought she had seen him wearing something almost identical.

Picking it up, she rolled it over in her palm. There was no engraving on the back, and she laughed in relief.

9

The morning after their arrival, Leland escorted Tess and Alicia to the souk. He rejected their houseman's suggestion of hiring a guide. They found the souk fascinating. The marketplace was ablaze with color, the pathways through the awninged, open-air booths and tiny shops appeared to be crammed with people from the earth's four corners.

"What a shame that Minnie is missing this!"

"She wanted to explore the gardens—no doubt hoping to find buried antiquities poking up among the fountains."

"Perhaps she is wiser," Alicia said. "The heat is already unbearable. Shall we turn back?"

"It will be equally hot every day," Leland said sharply. "You must acclimate yourself to the weather. And you know that you wish to replace your ruined vials and philters."

"I suppose you are right," Alicia said. Her face was quite red with the exertion of their walking.

Passing by the cajoling vendors of carved wood, and gold jewelry and carpets, they went straight to the quarter housing the purveyors of spices and herbs. Alicia was in no mood to dawdle. While Tess looked at bottles of perfumed oils, she set about trying to replace some of the items she'd lost when her mother's traveling apothecary's chest was run over.

The open-air stands and small shops were filled with opaque jars and colored glass bottles filled with mysterious unguents and potions. Tess wandered inside after Alicia, and picked up a small flask of deep Mediterranean blue buried behind the others.

"What is this, if you please?"

The man behind the tiny counter muttered and took it out of her hand, then growled something toward the back of the shop. A woman came to a gap in the curtain and gestured. Tess obeyed the summons. Try as she might, she couldn't follow the woman's gestures and shrugs. She poked her head through the curtain and called to Alicia to join her. They left Leland behind, restlessly picking up and setting down small vials of scent and jars of perfumed unguents.

It was cooler inside the thick walls at the back, although food was cooking on a small brazier. A beautiful baby with thick, curly hair dozed on a nearby cushion. Tess fought the urge to snatch up the child and run away with it. If the small pot tipped or was grabbed by tiny hands, the infant would be painfully and hideously scarred.

The woman gestured her to a small stool. Although she was probably not more than ten years Alicia's senior, her body was stooped, her face lined and worn. Only her dark eyes seemed alive.

Her eyes, Tess thought with a shiver, *are ancient.*

She looked away, scanning the shelves along the wall. There were very few herbs she recognized. She wondered if Alicia would be able to restock her traveling pharmacy as easily as they'd hoped.

"So," the woman said suddenly, in heavily accented English, "you have come for female medicine."

"I have come for many medicines," Alicia corrected.

The woman nodded. "Of course." She stirred the food on the brazier. "And among them, you wish to obtain the potion in the blue vial."

"Why, yes, it is a very pretty vial."

"Ah." The woman knew this game. She reached into a covered basket and pulled out several tiny bottles. Except for color, they were almost identical: one red, one dark green, one blue. "You know how they are used?"

Alicia's irritation showed. "It would be best if you tell me. I would not wish to make a mistake."

"The blue is for the beginning. It will bring on the flow almost immediately. The green for the middle time." She held up the red vial. "This, only for the most dire of circumstances. It is very potent. If it is given too late . . ."

Her foreign visitor was staring at her most peculiarly. She stirred uneasily. Perhaps she had made a mistake. "You do understand me?"

"Oh, yes. I am afraid that I understand you all too well. You are under a severe misapprehension. It is not potions of that sort which I seek. At the moment, I am sorely in need of a headache powder."

"Ah, yes." The woman backtracked hastily. "It is also good for deworming, in small doses."

Sorting through the narrow shelves, she brought out a selection of her wares. "This for the stomach, the other for the head. Especially good for fevers."

While they talked over packets of dried herbs and clay pots of unguents, Tess played with the baby. A fat, healthy-looking child, but whether boy or girl she couldn't tell. When the infant fell asleep, she went back out looking for Leland.

Alicia was very decisive, and in no time at all they were finished. She handed the woman coins in the amount she had asked for, and received a neatly bundled package in return. This she put into the wicker basket the woman provided for another coin.

When she came out into the noise and heat, Leland had made several purchases himself. His coat pocket was stuffed with little bundles. He took the basket from his sister. "Did you find everything you required?"

Alicia nodded. "Everything and more. Powders for ringworm and tapeworm and all sorts of disgusting things, as well as potions to protect fair skin from the harsh sun, and relieve the bite of scorpions."

She gave her brother a pointed look. "There are several herbs to make women conceive and for men to sire strong sons."

His smile was quick and warm. "Why, I believe you are right, my dear. It *is* possible to find anything in the world in the souk."

Roman had only one more day in Cairo before setting out for Luxor. He hurried down the stairs of his hotel. He'd dressed in haste and been unable to find one of his cuff links. Three messages had come within minutes of each other: the first to meet Ahkmed at his shop in the street of metalworkers, the second bidding him to dinner with the fair Sally Miller. If not able to cure him of his problems, she at least had a pleasant way of making him forget them for a while.

The third, and most thrilling, was from his dragoman on the excavation site. They'd uncovered a bit of pavement and a limestone block with faint marking upon it only this morning. It seemed his luck was on the mend.

Tess had wandered off to one side to examine a lovely length of silk. It was gauzy white, with subtle designs woven into the fabric, and looked faintly iridescent along the inner folds. *It would make a beautiful gown for Judith's coming-out ball. If only I knew the price of it!*

She turned around to point it out to Alicia, and found herself suddenly cut off from the others. Her apprehension melted away in a few seconds. Nothing could possibly happen to her with so many people around.

"They are likely back the way I came."

Making her way down one side of the street, she was suddenly besieged by children asking for *baksheesh,* and merchants trying to sell her items. Others merely watched her from the corner of their eyes. Her skin prickled.

She stepped beneath a striped awning that fronted a small shop. A wealth of bright brass and copper vessels were cleverly arranged, not tumbled haphazardly as in the shops she'd passed. It made it easier to see the fine quality of the wares.

A boy sat in the shade, buffing the metal, and a man hovered in the doorway of the shop: *A fine English lady. She will buy many bowls and trays and goblets. I will bring out my best for her.* There were many fine items he'd obtained when his aged father, Ibrahim, had died and his shop in Luxor closed.

One by one he set out his special wares for her delectation. None of them caught her eye. It was an older urn that lured her nearer. The metal had a different feel and intriguing silvery sheen. She tried to ask its price, but could not overcome the language barrier. She wished that they had hired a guide after all.

Tess tried again, opening her reticule and taking out a handful of coins. The boy's eyes grew large. Suddenly a shadow fell over her.

"It is unwise to display the amount of money you are carrying on your person, madame. You put yourself at the mercy of thieves and pickpockets."

She whirled around. "Roman!"

His stopped in his tracks as if he'd hit an invisible wall.

Then he blanched beneath his tan, and uttered a savage oath. "Tess! What in God's name are you doing in Cairo?"

It was difficult to speak around the sudden constriction in her throat. "We . . . we will be wintering here."

Words seemed inadequate as she struggled with the shock of coming face-to-face with him. Her palms were damp, her mouth dry, and her head whirling. She'd been dreading the moment, but hadn't expected it to come without warning. Roman certainly didn't look pleased. His blue eyes sparked with anger.

"Audley has come out also, to see his son," she said hurriedly. "He had invited us to view your excavation site. I . . . I hope you do not mind."

"Mind? Christ, I mind like hell!"

He'd found his voice now, and it came out like a crack of thunder. They were beginning to attract even more attention, but he was oblivious. "Goddamn it, Tess, what diabolical new torture is this? I came back to Egypt to get away from you!"

Her back stiffened. "I am sorry if my presence disturbs you. You may be sure that I shall not accompany the duke when he pays his call upon you!"

Her voice was so low he could scarcely hear her, and despite her brave façade, her lower lip trembled slightly. Roman felt as if he'd been hit in the stomach. His face softened. "Oh, Tess . . ."

There was only so much pain and temptation a red-blooded man could endure. He knew in that moment, that if they were thrown together again, they would become lovers. It was as inevitable as the rising of the sun. Good intentions and high principles be damned. He wanted her. The need was overwhelming.

Tension shimmered between them. She was beginning to tremble. Tears were not far from the surface. *Dear God,*

*only let me get safely away without making an utter fool
of myself.*

"Good day, Mr. McKendrick," she said formally. "I
will do my utmost to see that our paths cross as infre-
quently as possible."

Without further ado, she turned to dart away into the
crowd. Roman moved quickly. His hand clamped around
her arm. "Don't act like a simpleton. You cannot go wandering about on your own," he said sharply. "It isn't
safe."

"Ridiculous! There are people milling about everywhere! And, I might add, watching our every move."

"I have seen crowds go deaf and blind when it suited
them. So unless you want to end up in a harem, or raped
and dead in some dirty alleyway, you will stay with me
until we find the rest of your party!"

She was so angry she could hardly speak.

Ahkmed's son saw the potential for a profitable sale
vanishing like a mirage. He addressed Roman in rapid Arabic. "The lovely English lady, she says that she will buy
this so beautiful urn."

Roman eyed him wryly. "Then you have better ears
than I, my wily friend. How much?"

He looked down at Tess and named the price. "There
is a saying that only a fool or a tourist gives what is asked
in the beginning. Half is about right, and you'll both be
happy. It may take an hour of bargaining, however."

"I don't wish to spend an hour arguing with this man!
Nor do I want to spend another moment in your company." She had worked herself up into a fury. "In fact, I
do not want the urn any longer. I wish to return to the
house!"

"Only with my escort, unless we find the others."

Tess was upset. She tried to remove his strong hand
from her arm, and noticed the bit of white shirt extending

beyond the cuff of his coat. She went very still as she glanced at the other. The cuff link there was quite familiar—a perfect match for the one Celeste had found on the floor of the bedchamber.

"You have lost your cuff link," she said coldly.

"What?" The swift change in her demeanor, from heat to ice, caught him off balance. Roman frowned down at his sleeve. "Oh, that. I must have dropped it at the hotel this morning."

Her face was white and set. "No, you did not. You lost it in Mrs. Miller's bedroom. Of course, you are the one who told us how 'tightly-knit' your 'little community' was in Cairo! I am glad you had the decency not to let us know all your polite phrase entailed, in front of Judith and Minnie."

"Damn it, Tess . . . !"

"It is terribly hot. I wish to go back to the house for some shade and a cool drink."

That, he thought glumly, *makes two of us.*

He handed Ahkmed's son a few coins from his own pocket and tucked the urn in the crook of one arm. "We'll look for your party, first. They must be frantic with worry."

He escorted her from the street of metalworkers, back to where she had last seen the others. It was some time before they found Leland and Alicia: they were happily haggling with a merchant over a fine Kirman rug.

Alicia spotted them first. "Why, it is Mr. McKendrick!"

"Your servant, Lady Alicia." He bowed to her but had only a curt nod for Leland. "You should take better care of your wife, Lord Claybourne. The souk is no place for a woman of her class to wander alone!"

Tess's husband scowled. "I do not need you to tell me my business, McKendrick!"

"Think again! She was alone and flashing a purseful of gold and silver. It is a wonder she wasn't attacked and robbed before I ran into her."

Alicia intervened to smooth things over. She placed a hand on her brother's arm. "Leland, Mr. McKendrick meant no criticism. He is merely informing us of the situation. It is true that we are quite ignorant of the local customs."

"Yes, of course." Leland smiled. "This heat has brought on a damnable headache. I thank you for proving the good Samaritan. I shall see that she is always escorted."

"I can see to it myself," Tess said sharply. "I am not a child!"

Her outburst embarrassed everyone—including Tess. "Forgive me. The heat has made me irritable."

"We are unused to it as yet," Leland said. "We shall go back to the house now. McKendrick, perhaps you would care to dine with us this evening. Audley may join us, as well."

Roman hesitated. The last thing he wanted was to spend another evening observing the Claybournes' domestic bliss. Unfortunately for him, the last thing he could do was turn down the chance to feast his eyes on Tess's face once more.

Ah, well. If we are to be thrown into one another's company constantly for the next few months, I had better get used to it. The pavement will keep until tomorrow.

"I shall look forward to dining with you." *Like a man going to the gallows.*

Tess couldn't know Roman's train of thought, but she intuitively shared his sentiments.

Alicia went into Leland's room. The shutters were drawn against the afternoon heat, and the thick walls spared them the worst of it. Leland leaned back against his pillow in the blue dimness, with a cool compress upon his brow.

"How is your head?" Alicia asked.

"Much better. Your potion worked quickly. What was it?"

She held up a brown glass bottle containing an amber liquid. "I found some interesting things in the souk. This has not come my way before, but it is thought of quite highly here."

"I prefer it to the awful stuff you used to force down me."

He noticed several more colorful bottles strapped to the lidded wicker basket she had also purchased, in the souk of basket weavers. "Those are quite lovely. Whatever are they for?"

"Elegant bottles for not-so-elegant problems. This brown one is for dysentery. The blue is a purgative, used for food poisoning and deworming if given in small amounts." She paused. "Evidently the entire bottle could be taken by a woman who wished to avoid carrying a child to term."

"Forgive me. I should not have inquired."

"You needn't apologize." Alicia gave a short little laugh. "We have no secrets from one another. None at all."

Her brother closed his eyes.

In a few moments she heard the sound of his soft breathing. Packing up her chest of medicines, Alicia tiptoed away.

Dinner was a strained affair. They dined informally, and Tess and Roman studiously avoided exchanging more than polite comments. Alicia managed to ignore the Duke of Audley, while giving the illusion of carrying on a conversation.

Fortunately Minnie was allowed to join them, and her pleasure and bright conversation filled the awkward silences that arose. She had always treated Roman like an older brother or uncle, and pumped him with questions about his work.

"You will see it all for yourself when you visit the site," he laughed. "We're excavating the remains of a very old temple, whose existence had been completely forgotten. It was silted up during a very ancient flooding of the Nile, when the river changed its course. I found one of the references that helped me locate it while I was a guest at Claybourne House."

"The Temple of Isis," Leland breathed. "Where Imhotep placed his mystical sphere. 'Round as the moon, and more glorious than the sun.' "

Audley had not heard the story. "And what is this mysterious object?"

"It is a globe or disc," Roman said, "that supposedly reveals the past and predicts the future, according to the earliest references. There is an obscure legend that it has the power to cure disease and even convey eternal life to its owner."

"Pure poppycock!" the duke exclaimed.

Leland looked up sharply. "Why do you say that? You know nothing about it."

"My dear fellow," Audley drawled, "it is self-evident. Otherwise Cairo would be overrun with this Imhotep and an entire cohort of ancient Egyptians!"

"But what of the pavement you have uncovered?" Minnie asked ingenuously. She sensed that Leland was on the verge of losing his temper in a spectacular way, and had jumped in to avert a crisis.

In the past month or two, she'd begun to be more aware of the social currents that had previously flowed invisibly around her. There were things simmering beneath the surface: Tess's life was not the fairy tale that Judith imagined it to be, nor was Leland as quiet beneath his easy charm as she had always thought, and Alicia's calm façade was exactly that. *And I thought that becoming an adult would mean the end of all my little problems,* she thought now. *It seems that life is much more complicated than I knew.*

Roman was already answering. "I haven't seen it as yet. In fact, it was Lord Brocklehurst who discovered it." He looked in Audley's direction. "The lad has a good eye, and has taken to excavating as if born to it. I think he has found his niche."

The duke looked pleased. "I see my investment is already paying dividends."

With the dessert course removed, Tess seized upon the moment to rise, and put an end to the meal. "I hope you will not linger too long over your whisky and cigars, gentlemen. We are eager to hear more of Mr. McKendrick's discoveries."

Taking her cue, the men joined the ladies in the courtyard sooner than was usual. The air was still warm, and stars pricked the soft night sky, undimmed by the glow of lanterns. The fountain plashed softly, hundreds of shimmering globules of precious water spangling the air.

It seemed impossible to Tess that the beauties of the oasis existed in the midst of the sun-seared landscape. "I could sit out here all night," she announced. *Anything to keep from having to go to my room.* The knowledge that Roman had made love to Mrs. Miller there in the bed was like a knife to her heart. To her maid's astonishment, she had elected to sleep on one of the divans instead.

Alicia nodded at the flat leather case Roman had brought with him upon his arrival. "Have you found another rare papyrus, Mr. McKendrick?"

"Unfortunately, no. It is a puzzling artifact I obtained in the souk several weeks ago. Earlier this evening I took it to Professor Warring, in hopes that he might put an approximate date to it, or shed some light on its history. He was as baffled as I.''

"May we see it?" Minnie asked.

"It would be my pleasure." Setting his drink down upon the brass table beside him, he picked up the leather case and opened it. The mirror gleamed against the dark cloth in the muted light—almost, Tess thought in wonder, as if it had its own internal source of illumination. It was fascinating.

"It is old," Roman told them. "But exactly how old, or where it might have been made, is a complete mystery. It is utterly unique to my knowledge.''

He handed around the mirror, and its smooth surface reflected the light with a lovely silvery sheen. "It is exquisite," Tess said. "No, it is absolutely breathtaking!"

It was curiously light, despite its width and length. No heavier than her own silver hairbrush. She examined it eagerly. The metal surface was so highly burnished that it might as well have been a looking glass. The silvery gold metal gave her complexion a warm glow, but otherwise its reflection was true. How had it stayed so bright and un-marred?

She caressed the smooth handle, looking into the mirror and thinking of the others who had seen their own images reflected in it. Wanting to feel her connection with them. It was a magical moment.

After a moment she turned it over to examine the back. "Oh, look, here is something on the back. Swirls and interlocking curves forming the outline of a woman. How curious.''

Roman held his hand out imperiously. "May I?"

It was more command than request, and she gave it back to him. Yes, in the half-light, it did indeed look like a woman. More precisely, like the goddess Isis. He couldn't believe he hadn't worked it out before. Perhaps it was only visible on dim conditions.

Leland rose and came to stand over his shoulder. "Whatever its history, it obviously belonged to someone of rank. The director of antiquities is calling upon me tomorrow, with a visiting expert from Berlin in tow. Perhaps you will allow me to let them see it?"

"Of course." He gave it back to his host with reluctance.

Leland ran his long fingers over the metal. "A pretty thing. But not Egyptian, I think."

Roman didn't refute his opinion, and in time the discussion moved on. Minnie was half asleep in her chair, with a striped cat curled up on her lap. Tess had noticed several padding quietly about throughout the evening: they seemed to have come with the house.

Alicia listened to the men contentedly. Only Tess seemed restless. It was too early to retire and too dark to read. She picked up the mirror again. Imagining that she was a noblewoman of ancient Egypt, preparing for a banquet like the ones she'd seen illustrated in her book. A serving girl would be adorning her hair with jeweled combs and beads and fragrant flowers . . .

A wave of dizziness washed over Tess as she looked into the mirror. An iridescent sheen rippled across the surface. Instead of her own countenance, another face looked back: a woman clothed in sheer white linen, with a collar of gold and inlaid turquoise. Her features were not Egyptian, but she wore the royal uraeus crown upon her braided wig. As Tess stared at her, the woman looked at Tess in astonishment, her smooth jaw dropping and her eyes opening wide.

Suddenly the mirror's view changed. Quick, flashing images of a peristyled hall, a tranquil lotus pool, and then a dizzy, tumbling whirl toward a rapidly approaching mosaic floor. Then nothing.

Tess rose and gave a little cry. Her face was the color of unbleached cotton, her lips almost bloodless.

The world was spinning, and she was badly frightened. As she swayed, she was scarcely aware of the shouts, the sound of footsteps running toward her.

Both men started up but Roman reached her side first. "What is wrong? Have you been stung by a scorpion?"

Tess shook her head. Her vision was oddly distorted and she couldn't speak for fright. In the lamplight her eyes showed too much white.

Roman caught her as her knees crumpled, and swept her up into his arms. "Take her to her room," Alicia said breathlessly. "I will show you the way."

He carried her with her head cradled against his chest and her long skirts trailing over his arm. He laid her carefully on the bed where earlier he had made love to Sally Miller. It seemed almost profane.

Kneeling beside the bed, he took her hands and chafed them between his. "Tess!" She didn't respond. "Tess, can you hear me?"

She turned her head just a little. "Roman," she whispered hoarsely. "She saw me. She looked back and she *saw* me."

"Who did?"

"She is delirious!" Alicia exclaimed.

Jesus Christ in Heaven! Roman was terrified. Her eyes were open but unfocused. There was nothing in his experience that could strike someone down so suddenly, but there were dozens of tropical diseases to which she had no immunity.

"Send for a physician," Leland barked to one of the goggling maids.

"No," Tess protested. "No doctor."

Her hands clutched at Roman's fingers. "I am not delirious. I know what I saw. The woman . . ."

"What woman, my dear?"

Tess's eyes were large, her voice tight with strain and fear. "The woman in the mirror. She looked into it and saw *me* looking back—and *she dropped the mirror*."

Then she fainted dead away.

Tess awakened in the morning to find Alicia sitting beside her bed. She vaguely remembered being awakened and dosed with some foul concoction—then nothing until morning. There seemed to be a large gap in her memory, as well.

"What has happened? My head feels the size and weight of a boulder."

"Fatigue and heatstroke. You must guard yourself in this clime, Tess. I fear it does not agree with you."

"No, I remember now. It wasn't the heat," she said slowly, struggling to sit up. "I was looking at Roman's mirror." It all seemed like a strange dream.

"Yes," her sister-in-law said dryly. "Then you went white as a lily, your eyes rolled up in your head, and you fainted dead away! If it was caused by looking into a mirror and seeing your reflection, then we shall have to cover every looking glass in the house."

She held up a thin porcelain cup. "Sip this tea and rest awhile, and I'll have a tray brought in to you."

"I am not thirsty."

Alicia smoothed a cool hand over Tess's brow. "You are feverish and the tea will help to cool you. We would not want you to endanger your health."

Tess did as she was told. When the tea was finished, she found it was hard to keep her eyes open: *Alicia has dosed me with something in the tea!* By the time Celeste arrived with broth and toast, she was sound asleep again.

It was night when she awakened once more. The shutters were half open, letting in cool air and bright starshine. She felt completely alert and pleasantly refreshed.

I should go and see Minnie, she thought. *She may be awake and fretting.*

She lit a candle from the low lamp Celeste had left burning, and went out. Minnie's room was deep in shadow and her form still beneath its swath of mosquito netting. Seeing that her sister—and apparently the rest of the household—were fast asleep, Tess went down to the parlor.

The ormolu clock on the table ticked steadily. It must be nearly dawn, but the air was still cool, and deep indigo beyond the windows. She wandered around the room with her small taper, picking up Mrs. Miller's *objets d'art* with morbid curiosity. They were expensive but fussy, heavily carved or encrusted with gold. Tess thought them rather vulgar.

"More money than taste," she murmured to the cat that rubbed against her bare ankles, purring. There were quite a few within the compound, but this one seemed especially friendly.

She spied Roman's case on the desk, atop the blotter. *Careless of Leland to leave it out!* It was very unlike him to treat an artifact so cavalierly. Perhaps in the excitement caused by her faint, he'd forgotten about it. Obviously he didn't place the same importance upon the mirror and its age as Roman did.

She hesitated. Convincing herself she was taking it for safekeeping, she picked up the case and tiptoed back to her room. The urge to take out the mirror again proved so strong that Tess couldn't resist another peek. She threw the bolt on the door softly, then went to the divan.

The episode with the woman in the mirror had seemed

so real! Was it possible for heat and exhaustion to create
such a fantastic mirage?

She had to know. Steeling her nerves, Tess took the
mirror up. Her hands were shaking. Where the smooth handle had felt cool before, now it seemed to radiate a com-
forting warmth. With a slow, deep sigh, she turned the
reflective side toward her. It showed nothing but her own
face, filled with curiosity and apprehension.

She laughed softly. So, it had all been a mirage, a trick
of the light with excitement, exhaustion, and heat all com-
bining to affect her brain. *What a fool I am!*

Unable to sleep, she went out into the courtyard and sat
on the wide edge of one of the fountains, trailing her fingers in the water of the mosaic basin. The sky began to
lighten in the east faintly. At Claybourne House the servants would already be up at this hour, moving through
the silent house to open the draperies, light the fires laid
the night before, and begin breakfast preparations. Here all
was still. She found it a most pleasant way to start the
morning.

"Tess."

She heard Roman softly calling her name, and looked
up. He stood across the courtyard, dressed in riding
clothes. His handsome face, partially screened by a tangle
of thick, woody vines, looked haggard in the pale dawn
light.

"Whatever are you doing here?"

She was wearing a nightdress and robe of fine lawn.
She looked like a woman of ancient times in one of their
almost transparent dresses of pleated linen. He could see
the shape of her limbs beneath the gauzy fabric, the outline
of her soft, rosy-tipped breasts. It stole his breath and
brought the heat raging through his veins.

"I came to inquire about your health before I set out
for the excavation site. Rather than rousing the household,

I thought I'd slip in and ask your maid how you fared."

"You seem to know your way around Mrs. Miller's house quite well," she said scathingly.

"I know my way around Mrs. Miller," he said. He couldn't resist seeing that light of jealousy flare in her eye. *Oh, Tess, you little wretch! Will you never set me free of you?*

She looked so miserable, he relented. "After all," he went on, "she has let me use the house in her absence."

"Of course." Tess managed to load all sorts of meaning in those two words. She had no doubt that he and the widow were lovers.

"I didn't come to argue with you. I merely wanted to assure myself that you are all right after yesterday's episode."

Tess forgot her pique. "Roman, it so very peculiar! When I looked into the mirror yesterday, it was no longer a mirror. It seemed to become a window!"

She described the strange vision she'd had of the young woman with the royal cobra crown upon her braided wig. "I would have sworn that I was seeing her—and that she was seeing me, as well. Alicia and Leland treat it all as a figment of my imagination."

His eyes sparked blue in the increasing light. "This is important. Tell me how she looked. Every detail you recall."

By the time she had finished, he was very thoughtful. Her description of the room, the woman's garments, and her jewelry were all accurate and fit a narrow time period.

The previous evening's discussion came to mind. He recalled the description of Imhotep's wondrous creation which he'd read in Claybourne's papyrus fragment. *"Round as the moon, and more glorious than the sun."* Could it be that the object was not a globe at all, but the disc that formed the mirror?

Not that he believed in the existence of a magical artifact which could actually show the past or the future. That belonged to the illusionary realm of mythology.

But how to explain what Tess described? There must be something in the crafting of the polished surface that distorted images and twisted light, creating false visions. Yes, and that, coupled with the illustrations Tess had seen in books and the collection of artifacts at Claybourne House, had supplied the rest. There was no other rational explanation. Still . . .

"I should like to examine it more carefully when I return at week's end. Will you keep it safe for me till then?"

"Of course."

"Can you put your hand to it now?"

"It's in my bedchamber."

He ran a hand along his jaw. "If you have somewhere you can hide it—a place where even your maid will not come across it—I would be grateful. Tell anyone who inquires that I came by and took it away with me."

"Very well. I'll put it in the bottom of my traveling desk. No one else opens it, and there is a false bottom. You may take your case back. There isn't room for it in the hiding place."

Roman hesitated. "Perhaps I *should* take it with me. I am coming to believe that it may be very old, and exceedingly valuable. If so, there are men who would do almost anything to possess it. I don't wish to put you in any danger."

"Now you are being ridiculous beyond permission. It will be safe till you return on Sunday."

He smiled sardonically. "Never underestimate the ruthlessness of certain wealthy collectors, my dear. England and the Continent are full of unrecorded treasures, smuggled out of Egypt."

"If it is so old and valuable a treasure, it belongs here."

Roman smiled. "That's my Tess!" For a moment it seemed that he was going to gather her into his arms and hug her.

Shaking her head, she backed up. "Not yours, Roman. You must not speak so carelessly. People will begin to think that there is something more than mere friendship between us."

For a moment his face shone with naked hunger. "I wish to God there were!"

Faint sounds came from within the house. "Go now," she told him. "I'll have the case sent round to your hotel later. But please hurry before a servant comes upon us! It would look very bad for us to be found in such a compromising situation. And you may be sure that the mirror will be safe with me."

"Very well." He could not resist taking her hand in his. "Be careful, Tess. Do not show it to anyone else," he said with quiet force, "or let anyone know it is in your possession."

"You seem obsessed with imaginary dangers."

His face was grave as he looked down at her. Raising her hand, he pressed his lips to it. Her heart skipped a beat at the light that shone in his eyes.

"It is only that you are so very precious to me, Tess. More precious than my own life!"

He wrenched himself away from her side, and left Tess standing alone in the vine-shaded court. She was still there long after he'd gone out through the wooden gate hidden behind the twisting stems. Holding his words close to her. Wrapping them around her bruised heart as if they were an embrace.

When she reentered her chamber, Tess felt that something was wrong. She had picked up the cat out in the courtyard and tucked it in her arms. The creature seemed content enough until she went through the door to her bedroom. Suddenly the kitten hissed and spat, then launched itself out of her arms. A long red scratch beaded with blood appeared along her arm, and her cheek stung.

Looking in Roman's mirror, she examined her face. There was no blood on it. No long red scratch on her reflected hand, although she could see it. Tess turned her head—and then realized that the face in the mirror had not moved at all. Holding her breath, she looked squarely at her image. It was static. Frozen.

The surprise on her face was not reflected in the mirror, either.

The brightly polished surface shimmered. Clouds of light and darkness chased one another over the surface. While Tess stared, the reflected image of herself turned away and walked toward an unfamiliar bed, becoming smaller and smaller.

Two lighted tapers flickered in crystal holders. As Tess looked to the side of the mirror, the image slid along as if she were turning slowly. Now she could see into the corner of the chamber. Her heart pounded and the hand that held the mirror trembled: she watched the Tess in the mirror sit before a vanity and begin to brush out her long hair. With every stroke her silver brush glinted in the soft light.

Another face appeared. *Roman!*

She turned quickly but there was no one else in the room. Tess glanced in the mirror and saw Roman again, as if he stood behind her, looking over her shoulder.

But she was still totally alone in the room.

"Impossible!"

Her knees felt watery. Sitting abruptly on the edge of her bed, Tess held the sinuous handle and felt it warm within her hand. Images floated and formed, and the touch of the metal against her palm and fingers became her only anchor in reality.

She saw visions moving as quickly as clouds across a wind-ravaged sky. A dark, cavelike place of half-dressed limestone, and Roman pressed up against her, his arm protectively around her shoulders.

She wanted Roman. Now. Wanted him to make love to her as she would never know, except in dreams. Her spirit was starving to be touched, and held . . . and thoroughly loved. By Roman.

Only by Roman.

Rising, she went to the side table and placed the mirror in the false bottom of her travel desk. She had no desire to let her vivid imagination frighten her half to death again. Sliding the secret compartment shut, she clicked the hidden latch that locked it safely away.

Tess only wished she could lock away her feelings for Roman in the fastness of her heart. She almost envied Alicia, who had managed to get through life thus far with her affections intact.

Her own affections ran deep, and were too passionate. She had always managed to control them fairly well; but now they were volatile and bubbling up too near the surface. Tess threw herself down on Sally Miller's silk-hung bed, and wept her heart out.

Nothing but heartache had ever come of loving Roman.

Or ever would.

The mirror dreamed in its new hiding place. Possibilities drifted like smoke over the burnished metal: things that were, or had been, or were yet to be. Land rose from the sea in smoke and fire. Armies marched on foot, on camel and horse, in chariots and treaded machines of khaki-green. Meteors fell from the skies, and machines flew through the heavens on fragile wings of canvas stretched over wooden frames.

Empires rose and fell with the breathing of the universe.

Waves rose from the sea, higher than the ziggurats of Ur and the lighted stone towers of sprawling cities. Infants were born in ice-bound caves, in marble palaces, in a circle of horses on the wild steppes of the Caucasus; in rooms of gleaming white tile and cold metal, and in snug brick houses with painted shutters and fanlight doors.

Lovers met, kissed, and made love. Others kissed and parted. Tears fell upon lace-edged pillowcases. And a knife blade flashed, wet and red with blood.

10

The elegantly appointed *dahabeeyah* that Leland had hired for his party was anchored along the banks of the Nile. They were taking a leisurely cruise, two weeks on the water, visiting famous sites in the utmost comfort.

It was, Alicia had declared, the only civilized way to travel. Minnie had already announced her intention of living in Egypt aboard her own *dahabeeyah* one day. "When I am an Egyptologist, like Roman," she'd said. Evidently this was one enthusiasm that showed some longevity.

She liked the informality of the life, as well. In Cairo they had exchanged their steel-boned corsets for lighter ones of stiffened muslin. Now that they were heading out into the desert, even Alicia, who was proper with a capital *P*, had decided they could forgo them for the day.

The salon in the stern was large enough to hold several sofas, chairs, and tables, elegant dining appointments able to accommodate a number of invited guests, and even a grand piano draped in a heavy silk scarf. Tess sat sideways on the bench, idly running one hand up and down the keys.

"Whatever can be delaying Leland?" she said for the third time.

"I cannot think why he is not yet back," Alicia agreed, twisting her fingers together.

He had gone off to examine some primitive ruins early

in the morning, and had not returned. The *reis,* the boat's captain, was lounging at ease on the riverbank with his men, playing some sort of board game. The ladies were waiting for Leland to join their party, before setting out to visit Roman and Lord Brocklehurst at the temple excavation site. Not that she was anxious to spend time confined in the carriage with him.

His attitude toward her had undergone a sea change since their arrival. The kinder and more understanding Tess tried to be with him, the more he withdrew. He seemed to avoid her whenever possible, and was increasingly cold when they were thrown together alone. *His health seems to have improved, and yet he has kept his word: he has not been to my bed once.* She suspected that he blamed her for the humiliation of his past failures.

Recently his aloofness seemed to be tinged with something more. Her feeling of growing discomfort and unease in his company was so nebulous, that Tess could neither define nor explain it.

"It is not like him to be late for an engagement. Perhaps he has been taken ill," Alicia said worriedly. "We should send someone after him."

"That would be a good idea—*if* he had left any word of exactly where this ruin is located. I spoke to the *reis. He* has no notion of any important ruins in the area."

"And indeed, why should he?" Alicia said tartly. "If there is no gold or treasure, he would not be interested!"

They had made plans to drive out to Roman's excavation site. An elegant picnic luncheon had been prepared and a commodious carriage waited to convey them there. Tess checked the watch pinned to the bodice of her dress once more. They were already over an hour behind schedule, and if they waited much longer they would have to brave the heat of the day on their return.

"Perhaps he has mistaken the hour."

Her husband had been in a fever pitch to see the foundations of the temple and avenue that Roman had uncovered. His vigor seemed to have improved since their arrival in Egypt; lately, though, he had grown increasingly preoccupied and forgetful. His absentmindedness seemed to grow worse almost daily.

Just then a dusty carriage came along the road that wound beside the river. Minnie pointed. "There he is now!"

Everyone was relieved. The trip to Roman's excavation site had been put off for almost two weeks: a rockslide had buried it deep, and it had taken longer than expected to clear it away.

Meanwhile, Tess and the others had been as far as the first cataract. They had viewed the Valley of the Kings, toured Karnak and Luxor, and visited Hatshepsut's mortuary temple at Dier-el-Bahri. Now they were anchored at Luxor once more.

The carriage pulled up to disgorge a lone passenger. "Why, it is Miss Riley-Burnside," Alicia exclaimed.

The world-circling writer had been covering much the same area as the Claybourne party, in an effort to update her works. Their paths had necessarily crossed several times. They went to meet her as she crossed the gangplank.

"Miss Riley-Burnside, what a lovely surprise! We thought you had already left Egypt on the next leg of your journey!"

"I decided to wait and see what your Mr. McKendrick has uncovered. Alas, I am the bearer of bad tidings."

"What is it?" Alicia cried. Her face was white and suddenly haggard. "My brother . . . ?

"Lord Claybourne?" The spinster looked confused. "No, I have come from Cairo." She glanced at Minnie. "Perhaps what I have to relate is not appropriate for tender ears."

"Pooh," Minnie said. "I have seen half-starved found-lings in London and beggars in Egypt with flies covering their eyes."

"Minnie," Tess said briskly, "please inform the *reis* that we will be remaining aboard this afternoon."

Her sister shot her an annoyed glance, but went off to do as she was bid. Alicia led their guest to a chair beneath the shade of a canopy. "Please, tell us what has occurred to overset you."

"I scarcely know how to begin." She composed herself and took the glass of cold tea that a servant brought out to her. "Do you recall Mrs. Reed? The lady who kept to her cabin for most of the voyage out?"

Alicia went very pink. "Yes. I have thought of her often. Have you had contact with her?"

"Not in a manner of speaking. This morning a woman came to my hotel in Luxor, and urged me to come with her. She would not be gainsayed, nor would she tell me anything except that Mrs. Reed was at a village near the hills, and in dire need of my assistance. Of course I went to her immediately. And now my dear Lady Claybourne, Lady Alicia, I have come to you for advice. I know not where to turn!"

"Is she in childbirth?" Alicia inquired hastily. "If there is not a midwife available, I have some skill with medi-cines."

The spinster looked grave. "I'm afraid the matter is beyond your skills."

"Oh, dear!" Tess exclaimed. "Has she lost the child?"

"My dear Countess, it is *she* who is lost. Figuratively, and now literally. You'll recall that she was reportedly traveling out to be with her husband. Instead she took a house in a small village not a half hour's brisk walk from here. Not, I might add, the kind of village that one of *our* kind would choose to inhabit. It is quite low and primitive."

"I don't understand," Tess said, frowning. "Why is she not with her husband? Has he been detained?"

The spinster shook her head. "The story grows more convoluted. 'Mrs. Reed'—that is surely not her name—gave birth prematurely yesterday, attended only by a local midwife. She had evidently dismissed her maid upon arrival.

"I gathered that she was quite hysterical. But by the time I reached the place, Mrs. Reed was gone."

"Gone! But . . ." Alicia seemed dumbfounded. "Perhaps there is some confusion and her husband arrived and removed her to a hotel or hired house?"

"Yes," Tess agreed. "That seems a likely answer."

Miss Riley-Burnside lobbed a bombshell: "And leave the newborn infant behind, in care of a wet nurse?"

A shocked silence followed her announcement.

The spinster tipped her glass of tea and swallowed it with a most unladylike gulp. She wished it were stronger stuff. "Have you any whisky or brandy? I need to calm my nerves. This has been a most unsettling morning!"

Tess brought the brandy decanter herself and filled a glass for the lady. "You may wish to partake of some, as well," Mrs. Riley-Burnside remarked. "My tale is not a pretty one."

Alicia fetched two more glasses and poured out a drink for Tess and one for herself. They sipped in silence a moment. The voice of the men on the shore carried on the light breeze.

Minnie tried not to pout as she drank her lemonade. It seemed decidedly insipid and schoolgirlish, watching the others drink amber liquid from cut-crystal glasses.

Miss Riley-Burnside finished her brandy and sighed. "Thank you. I feel much restored. If only my faith in human nature could be restored so easily. I was very mistaken in my notion of Mrs. Reed's character.''

"But . . . why would she do such a thing? There must be some explanation. I cannot believe that she would abandon her child,'' Tess said at last.

Alicia grew increasingly agitated. "Where is the infant now? Who is caring for him, poor, neglected little creature!''

"That is why I have come to you, Lady Alicia. You have experience with orphans and foundlings, and will know what to do. The family from whom she hired the house has no idea what to do under the circumstances. They do not wish to notify the authorities for fear of being involved in trouble.''

"But Mrs. Reed's husband . . . !''

"My dear Lady Claybourne, there *is* no husband. There never was. The girl was evidently unmarried, and came to Egypt to hide her disgrace.''

"Where is the child?'' Alicia repeated urgently.

"He is still installed at the house she hired, with the wet nurse to care for him—I didn't know what else to do. But now, with all due apologies, I must throw this affair into your laps. I have no experience of infants myself— and I am on my way to Jerusalem at week's end.''

"There must be an explanation,'' Tess said slowly. "She will return for her child and explain everything.''

"I am afraid that is unlikely. I found this on the bureau in her bedchamber. It appears to be the last part of a letter to the cad responsible for her condition.''

Miss Riley-Burnside opened her reticule and withdrew a piece of folded of paper. She handed it to them wordlessly.

Tess and Alicia read it in silence:

. . . and I pray—I know—that you will not abandon me now, despite your cruel words. If you will not help me,

what am I to do, where am I to go? The weight of my
great shame is unbearable. I do not know how I can
bear to live with it!

It was unsigned. Tess looked up in shock. "Oh, poor
creature! I do not like the sound of this. Do you . . . do you
think that she means to do away with herself?"

Miss Riley-Burnside reached for the decanter herself,
poured out another tot of brandy, and swallowed it in a
gulp. "I believe that she already has. I have since learned
that the police pulled the body of a young European
woman from the Nile not an hour ago. The description is
a match."

Alicia gave a sound of distress. She looked faint, and
Tess hurriedly poured her sister-in-law another drink. Minnie clutched her empty lemonade glass as if it were a life
preserver. This was a side of life she had never seen before. It seemed that such drama was not nearly so glam-
orous in reality as it was in her favorite novels.

Some time later Tess and Alicia arrived at the village
where Mrs. Reed had been living since her arrival. Miss
Riley-Burnside had stayed behind to chaperone Minnie,
over the girl's protests. She wanted to see the baby.

"Poor little thing! Only hours old, and already burdened
with tragedy. Do let me come, Tess. I could hold him in
the carriage!"

Tess gave her a sharp look and a little shake of her
head. "We will discuss it later, after we determine more."

Alicia hurried out on deck. She had hastily lined a basket with soft blankets to create a makeshift bassinet, and
carried a tapestry bag filled with whatever items she had
deemed necessary, and they'd set off almost immediately.

The carriage came to a stop before one of only six
houses. It was set off a little from the others by its larger

size, and the date palms in its small garden. Obviously it belonged to the headman of the village.

An older woman came to the door the moment the carriage pulled up. She held the side of her veil across her face, but her eyes and forehead were creased with concern. Tess tried to make introductions. The woman spoke no English, but communicated well with gestures, and led them inside. Safely indoors again, she let her veil drop.

The main room was built in typical style, with a built-in bench of the same construction as the house around three sides. It was covered with a multitude of carpets and cushions. Everything was exceptionally clean and the quality of the decorative items displayed the family's status. Tess was relieved to know the child was in good hands.

A younger woman lounged on the bench, with a toddler playing at her feet. She was trying to feed the newborn. Her breasts were full with milk, but the baby wouldn't nurse. He fussed with a thin, mewling cry.

Tess's heart contracted. "Oh, he is so tiny! All head and belly and spindly limbs."

She was surprised that they hadn't swaddled him, as was common with other infants she'd seen. Alicia snatched the newborn up from the wet nurse, and wrapped him in the clean shawl she'd brought with her. It was striped cotton, as warm and soft as a blanket. Holding him tightly, she rocked him in her arms. The tiny eyelids fluttered closed.

"Is there a physician in the village? Send for him at once," Alicia cried. "No, wait! We shall take the child to him!"

Tess put her hand on her sister-in-law's arm. "He is only sleeping! See how his chest moves?"

Alicia laughed shakily. "Of course. I was frightened."

"It would be far better to bring the physician here," Tess said. "In fact, it would be better to leave the child here until we know what we should do. We are not equipped to care for him aboard the *dahabeeyah*—nor," she added pointedly, "are we capable of feeding him. He is too young for goat's milk. He needs mother's milk, and must stay with the wet-nurse while we make arrangements."

"She can come with us! I will pay her well."

"And bring her own child, whom she is nursing also, with her? Once aboard, in whose stateroom shall we install them?" Tess pointed out gently. "We must think this through."

Alicia wavered. "What you say makes a deal of sense."

While Alicia continued to rock the baby, Tess withdrew a small pamphlet of useful Arabic phrases from her pocket, and tried to patch together a semicoherent explanation of what they wanted from the two village women.

It was late in the afternoon when they finally headed back. The physician had come and pronounced the baby healthy enough for all his early arrival into the hostile world. The wet nurse had agreed to care for him and Tess had left money for his keep.

"I hate to leave him behind," Alicia said anxiously.

"There is nothing we can do at the moment to resolve the situation. Never fear, we shall come up with a plan that will serve. We'll not abandon him."

Alicia smiled. "Dear, kindhearted Tess. I knew I could count on you."

She had been handling the ribbons of the carriage herself. Pulling it over into the shade of a cluster of palms, she reined in. "Tess, there is something I must ask you. It is rather awkward."

"You may ask me anything," Tess answered. *Except about Roman McKendrick.*

Alicia turned to Tess and covered her gloved hand with her own. "My dear, I know that for some time you have been worried about conceiving an heir. No doubt you will think this idea of mine is harebrained . . . but . . . if you do not conceive, perhaps you and Leland will consider adopting a child.''

Tess was confused. "I would. But it would not alter the fact of the estate being entailed, if that is what you mean.''

Her sister-in-law flushed. "There might be a way of getting around it.''

A horrible conviction was creeping over Tess. "Do not spare me! Say what you mean outright, if you please.''

"My heart bleeds for the poor baby we have just left behind.'' Alicia stopped, cleared her throat, and then went on as if giving a well-rehearsed speech. "You no doubt wish to secure your place in the world, and to see your sisters creditably established. It is only a thought: however, we are far from home. We could extend our travels, and in time . . . several months at the least . . . you and Leland could return home to England with an heir. It would be a good deed of the highest level, and would solve everyone's problems quite neatly.''

Tess was incredulous. "You are asking me, if I hear you correctly, if I would be willing to pass Mrs. Reed's child off as my own? To proclaim to the world that the bastard child is actually your brother's son and heir, in order to defraud the Duke of Audley of his rights?''

"You need not put it so baldly!''

"There is no other way to address it. Alicia, are you going mad?''

To her astonishment, her sister-in-law—calm, sensible, practical Alicia—burst into frantic tears. "I think perhaps I already have!''

They returned to the *dahabeeyah* in silence, having agreed that the matter would not be broached again between them.

Alicia broke her promise only once, just before they left the carriage. "You will not reconsider?"

"No, my dear. I cannot."

"Even . . . even to give that . . . that poor woman's child a home?"

"We shall find him a good home, Alicia. But not with us."

When they returned Leland was in the salon, waiting for them impatiently. "We must be off before it grows too hot, or we shall have to wait until tomorrow."

"If you had returned as scheduled, we would be there even now," Tess said. She was irked with his attitude. Minnie and Miss Riley-Burnside had explained the situation to him. She felt he should have been understanding, rather than irritable.

"Fortunately," Alicia intervened, "it worked out for the best. We were able to see to that poor, abandoned baby."

"Yes. Well. Let us be off!"

Miss Riley-Burnside declined to accompany them. "I have had enough excitement today, thank you!" She took her leave. Leland was in such haste that everyone became nervous, and there were several trips back to their rooms for forgotten items, such as shawls and hat and parasols, only adding to his peevishness. He even snapped at Alicia, something Tess had never witnessed before. Then he rounded on her.

"Can you not get your household together for a simple carriage ride, madame! Is that too much to expect?"

"No more so than simple courtesy," Tess replied, her cheeks aflame.

"Do you wish to visit your Mr. McKendrick, or not?"

"I was under the impression that we were *all* visiting him—and Lord Brocklehurst, as well. And the answer to your question is no! What I would really like to do is to retire to my room with a headache powder!''

A scene of epic proportions threatened, but it was Minnie who saved the day. ''Indeed, my head is sore. Alicia, perhaps you have something in your pharmacy chest that would make us all feel more the thing.''

Her suggestion was a good one. Alicia gathered her scattered wits and went to her room, returning with various herbal remedies which she dispensed liberally. By the time everyone calmed down it was too late to set out and the expedition was postponed until the following day.

Lord Brocklehurst arrived early and unexpectedly. He was dressed casually, and his hair was windblown beneath his hat, but he had put on a jacket in deference to the ladies.

''McKendrick was concerned that you might lose your way, and sent me to be your guide.''

''Excellent,'' Leland pronounced. ''Alicia, why don't you ride with me in the smaller carriage. Tess and Minnie may go with Brocklehurst, since they can fit three abreast in his vehicle.''

Tess felt a great relief. The thought of all of them jammed together, coupled with Leland's vagaries of temperament, had been fretting her. This promised to be far more enjoyable.

And she could hear news of Roman, without having to feign the slightest indifference. In fact, any questions that she had concerning him were sure to be broached by Minnie. ''Thank you, Lord Brocklehurst. We shall be pleased to drive out with you.''

''I promise to get you there and back in one piece,'' young Lord Brocklehurst said soothingly, as he handed the ladies up into the carriage.

Tess thought he had grown more mature and subdued since their last meeting. *Audley must have been proud to see the change in him.*

Minnie thought the young lord looked fit and very pleased with himself. The sun had bleached his hair and turned his fair skin bronze. The rigors of excavating had filled him out with hard muscle. Why that irritated her was something she chose not to explore.

She was almost sorry she hadn't remained behind; however, that would have been rude in the extreme. And she did *so* want to see Roman's temple!

Tess labored under similar feelings. The urge to see the excavation site was strong, the urge to see Roman again, even stronger. Each time she did it was like probing a savage wound. She tried to let her mind become as empty and featureless as the wasteland around them.

Leland and Alicia had fallen behind. Tess looked over her shoulder and her jaw dropped. They seemed to be having a violent argument. Leland was shouting something—she could hear it carrying vaguely on the breeze. "Pewling brat" and "not likely to survive the day" caught her ear. She saw that Alicia was weeping hysterically.

Tess hastily positioned her parasol to block the view, should Minnie look back. Luckily she was deep in conversation about Egyptian mythology with Lord Brocklehurst. Tess sighed. Apparently Alicia had broached the subject of passing off Mrs. Reed's child as his heir to Leland, as well. If so, it was even less of a success than it had been with herself.

They passed through the narrow strip of green, cultivatable land where palm trees raised a screen against the heat. Immediately the desert engulfed them. Despite their hats and parasols, the sun was already a scourge, the jolting of the carriage a penance.

The horse stumbled and Brocklehurst reined in hard, forcing the animal's head up. "Easy! Good girl!"

After gaining control, he glanced over at Minnie, but addressed his remark to Tess: "The footing is treacherous until we pass the rocks. Then it is fairly smooth until we near the temple site.''

The little party progressed past a small, mud-brick pyramid, its edges so rounded and worn it appeared to be melting back into the earth.

"How different it is from England," Minnie said. "Our kings and queens are buried beneath bronze and marble effigies, surrounded by altars and windows of stained glass like jewels. Here they are hidden away in the dead landscape, sealed in darkness along with their jeweled treasures.''

"If you studied their beliefs in the afterlife, as I have, it would make more sense," Brocklehurst replied. Minnie didn't deign to answer.

They passed out of the flatter area into a rock-strewn plateau. Cliffs rose in the distance, dry wadis branching out like the creases of a crumpled fan. "It looks as if someone had taken a flat piece of cloth and bunched it up into wrinkles," Minnie exclaimed.

Tess sucked in a tiny breath. Roman stood atop the highest point of the plateau, looking like a god in the sunlight. His shirt was open at the collar and his sleeves rolled up to bare his arms. She knew he'd been watching for her arrival. Her heart went into double time.

"We'll leave the carriage here in the shade of the rocks," Brocklehurst announced. "One of the laborers will look after the horses, while we go the rest of the way on foot.''

He gave Minnie a sly appraisal, wondering how she'd cajoled her way out of the schoolroom. *An enterprising girl, Miss Minerva Mallory.* He saw that her cheeks were already quite flushed.

"A hot exercise, I'm afraid. I hope you are up to it."

"Pooh," Minnie said. "I am not one of your simpering drawing-room misses. I am game for anything.''

"That," Tess said acerbically, "is something I can vouch for personally."

He didn't reply. When they reached Roman's site, the young man showed them a canvas lean-to set up against the rock. "You may rest here, if you like. Or there is an old tomb shaft where we keep our supplies cool. You might prefer that."

"I think *not* the latter," Tess said dryly.

"A tomb shaft? Can we go all the way inside it?" Minnie exclaimed simultaneously.

"Only if someone accompanies you," Brocklehurst warned. "It is black as pitch inside, and rubble-strewn. You mustn't go gallivanting off to explore on your own."

Minnie tossed her curls. "I may not be 'out' yet, Lord Brocklehurst, but I am not a child."

A surprising dimple appeared at the corner of his mouth. "No," he agreed. "You are certainly not."

As he walked away, Minnie stared. "What do you suppose he meant by that?"

A soft, rhythmic rattling interrupted them. Two men were sifting rubble through a wicker basket, shaking out the dirt through the widely woven spaces in order to find any artifacts among the debris. The process was repeated by two other men with a smaller basket shaker.

And nearby, Tess saw with chagrin, was Mrs. Miller with several of her friends, sipping lemonade and sorting bits of broken pottery vessels. She appeared totally absorbed in what she was doing; however, Tess saw the woman glancing at Roman from beneath her thick lashes. As Roman went toward her, she reached down into the folds of her dress, then held her hand up as if she had plucked something from the basket.

"A scarab!" she cried. "Oh, and here is another!"

Her thin white gloves were covered with limestone dust, but two small pieces of carnelian glowed in her palm as the sun struck them. Tess started forward eagerly, intent on examining the other woman's discovery, and collided with a young workman coming from the tomb.

The lad stumbled and fell sideways onto the path, and his basket fell heavily to the ground. The contents spilled out, scattering among the rock and debris already cleared away.

Roman realized, as Tess didn't, how close she had come to disaster. To her left, the makeshift path fell away thirty feet. "For God's sake, get out of the way before someone gets hurt!"

Humiliation flamed through Tess. Two weeks ago he had been the Roman of old. Today he treated her like a fool! She turned and stalked back along the path toward the tent.

While the workman retrieved his basket, Brocklehurst started toward Tess. She waved him away.

"Do not let me interrupt your work," she said brusquely. "It will only give Mr. McKendrick more reason to shout at me."

"He's in the devil of a temper. Something more must have gone wrong," Brocklehurst said hurriedly. "I know he has been anxious for you to visit us here."

"Yes," Tess murmured. "I can tell that by his kind words of welcome!"

Fighting her fury, she stalked off toward the canvas shelter that Brocklehurst had indicated. For two weeks she had been dreading and longing for this meeting. Wondering what would happen when they came face-to-face again.

Now she knew: he would shout and do his best to make her look like an utter imbecile.

When she reached the canvas awning, Leland and Alicia had arrived. The rocky plateau absorbed the sun's rays, and the heat was relentless.

"And this is the cooler season," Alicia said, fanning herself languidly. Where both she and Minnie looked ruddy, Leland was pale. "We must all drink plenty of water and stay as cool as possible. Should it get much hotter, we may have to consider returning to the *dahabeeyah*."

Roman came to meet them. Grayish dust clung to his hair. "I'm afraid I shall be a bad host to you. We've excavated an intact room along the western wall of the temple; however, there is imminent threat of another collapse. We'll have to shore it up. I may be tied up most of the day."

Tess thought that Leland's enthusiasm would lead him to volunteer his assistance. She was wrong. "We understand, of course," he said. "It would be better if we come back another day."

They ended up setting out their picnic luncheon just inside the entrance of the tomb shaft. It was definitely cooler, but the setting made Alicia nervous. "I cannot fully enjoy partaking of food in such a morbid place."

"But it is not!" Minnie protested. "These were not places of the dead, but dwelling houses for the spirits of the departed. Only look at the lovely paintings farther down the passageway!"

As she started toward them Tess held her back. "Remember what Lord Brocklehurst said." For a moment her sister looked mulish. "You would not want him to think you too young to visit a working excavation site," Tess added smoothly.

"I have no intention of doing anything rash," Minnie said, conveniently forgetting that, in fact, she had just been about to do something foolish.

A shout went up from the temple site, and Tess's heart stopped. Had the wall caved in? Without thinking, she found herself running across the broken landscape, with Minnie at her heels.

She arrived at the excavation area. Roman and Brocklehurst were clapping one another on the back, and the men were grinning happily: a cache of precious artifacts—collars and bracelets and little statues of Isis—had been found buried at the base of the wall that had been shored up. There would be bonuses all around. The golden treasures gleamed bright, sending arrows of light back toward the sun.

Leland clambered down to congratulate them. Roman started forward, but stopped in mid-stride and hunkered down. One of the toppled stones was partially turned on its side. Something had caught his eye.

Sometime in the more recent past, the block had been covered up with mud-brick. Most of that had fallen away completely. With the angle of light just right, Roman had made out incised lines beneath it.

Rubbing the now-brittle mud plaster gently with his bronzed fingers, Roman cleaned off the clinging remnants. Ancient hieroglyphs, lightly incised, covered one side of the block completely. The top surface appeared to have formed part of an altar. A section of the undecorated plaster fell away as he touched it, and Roman took in a sharp hissing breath.

"Brocklehurst! Look at this!"

"Good God, McKendrick!" The young man knelt beside him, thunderstruck.

The picture on the altar block was lovely. The goddess Isis stood on a dais, while at her feet a young man knelt in homage. From the tools thrust into the belt of his pleated linen kilt, it appeared that he was an architect or builder. But it was the gift he presented that had struck both Roman and his young assistant:

A round disc held between lotus buds, whose elegantly twisting stems formed the handle.

"It's your mirror, McKendrick!" Brocklehurst exclaimed.

"No," Leland said, standing over them. He looked almost sick with excitement. *"It is the Mirror of Imhotep!"*

Tess took a drink from her picnic canteen, then poured some on her handkerchief and wiped her face. The excitement of the find was beginning to pall as the temperature rose. The rock seemed to gather up the heat and hold it, like the inside of a blast furnace.

She'd been sitting beneath the rough canopy of the sorting area, in Mrs. Miller's place, since they'd dined. Alicia walked over to her. "Why, your gloves are quite ruined! I hope you have found something worth the loss of them."

"That depends upon the value you place on slivers of smashed pottery, three common faience beads, and what I am told is the broken rim of a stone beer bottle. Nothing nearly as fine as Mrs. Miller's scarabs."

"That is too bad. I thought the scarabs were quite lovely."

Tess made a face. "I believe she bought them in the bazaar and dropped them in her to basket impress Roman."

She raked through the basket again, shredding out the tips of her right glove and the skin on the end of two fingers. "If so, it is foolish of Mrs. Miller. Roman will be able to tell if they are authentic or carved a week ago by some enterprising carver, intent on selling them to travelers with more money than sense."

Alicia laughed and plied her fan. "Yes, Leland says the manufacturing of false 'antiquities' has been a vocation in Egypt since the time of Alexander."

"How is he feeling?" Her husband had been overly excited, almost overwrought, ever since the Isis Stone had been found.

"Much better, since I gave him a dose of my herbal remedy. Despite my entreaties, however, he intends to stay on the site until they finish work for the day. I believe he hopes that Mr. McKendrick will go back to excavating once they finish shoring up the temple wall."

"Do you think that is wise? I would not wish him to have a relapse," Tess said. "Although he has been out of sorts at times, I have noticed how much improved his color has become."

"I believe that he will be himself again, once he becomes more accustomed to the heat. Lord Brocklehurst advises us to move back into the cooler air of the tomb shaft until the worst heat of the day passes. You should join us."

"It is not so bad beneath this canopy, and I wish to work a bit longer. I'll join you if the heat becomes too intense."

"Very well. I wouldn't want you to become ill, as Minnie did."

When Alicia was gone, Tess rose and shielded her eyes. Minnie was on her way back to the *dahabeeyah,* despite her protests; but Tess had seen the signs of incipient heat prostration, and had overruled her.

Mrs. Miller had claimed that she'd had enough of the sun herself. "If you like, I shall take Miss Minerva back to the boat, and stay with her until your return," she'd volunteered.

Ignobly, Tess had wondered if the woman's offer had come from kindness of heart, or a wish to ingratiate herself into the Claybourne party. They had departed only minutes ago, and the carriage was clearly visible in the strangely transparent light of Egypt, which seemed to magnify distant objects with an almost magical clarity.

There was a shower of stones, and Lord Brocklehurst came down the slope, wiping his forehead with a handkerchief. His blond hair was dark with sweat. He stopped beside Tess and looked after the departing vehicle.

"I believe that, left to her own devices, your sister would have stayed on until she succumbed to sunstroke!"

"Yes. I love Minerva dearly, but she can be a little headstrong when her enthusiasm betrays her."

Brocklehurst didn't seem to hear her. "She's a capital girl!"

His admiration irritated Tess. *It must be the heat.*

Indeed, it had grown worse in the past few minutes. Brocklehurst left and Tess wondered what to do. Sweat trickled down her temple and she knew her gown was damp. It had to be much cooler in the shadowy tomb shaft, where Alicia and Leland were sitting on folding camp chairs.

Three things kept her from joining them: she didn't like confined spaces, and she wanted to avoid Leland, whose easygoing charm of earlier days seemed to have deserted him completely. Most of all, she wanted to prove to Roman that she was every bit as interested in his work as Mrs. Miller had shown herself to be.

I am as foolish as Minnie, she sighed. *No, more so, for at least Minnie let me override her with common sense. I am broiling!*

Glancing away from the bright, reflective rock, she spotted the small dark outline of another opening. An old, blind shaft, Brocklehurst had said—a tomb begun and then abandoned in the time of the pharaohs.

Tess considered her options. She could change her mind and join her husband and sister-in-law in the tomb shaft, and let her nerves be flayed by Leland's agitations. She quickly ruled that out. He always did better when he was left alone to Alicia's sisterly ministrations.

Well, then, she could try to find relief in the abandoned blind shaft, which was apparently not very deep and wasn't as likely to make her feel as if she were smothering . . . or she could sit where she was until she passed out and made an utter fool of herself.

Certainly not an appealing prospect! she thought bracingly.

As she was debating whether the promise of cooler air was worth the exertion of crossing the hot valley floor, she saw Roman come along the line of men handing baskets of debris from the work site. He scanned the area, and she sensed that he was looking for her. Her heart sped up.

She had to admit to herself that this was why she had stayed and why she braved the burning air, sorting the finer rubble for potsherds and the occasional broken faience bead. She wanted his approval—and she was desperate to see him. Speak to him. Touch him.

Roman started forward and she felt her insides trembling. The yearning to be near him had become more desperate with every passing day. During the long nights aboard the *dahabeeyah,* she lay awake listening to the gentle lapping of water, and envisioning his beloved face. In her dreams he came to her. Held her and loved her with all the repressed passion in their souls.

By morning light she lay awake long before her maid tapped on the door, alone and bereft. *Oh, Roman. What have I done to us both?*

She smiled hesitantly as he crossed the plateau toward her. He'd gone only a few yards when his dragoman hailed him. Roman turned and strode away, in the opposite direction to where Tess sat waiting.

Disappointment knifed through her. Anger followed.

She had waited all afternoon to see him and now he was gone off again somewhere! Rising, she deserted her task and went off toward the blind shaft.

The short walk filmed her face with sweat. "I would have been cooler had I stayed where I was!"

When she reached the opening, Tess realized that it was a good three feet off the ground. She glanced at her expensive dress, already covered in desert dust. A little more wouldn't matter. Using a fractured block as a stepping stone, Tess clambered up and into the entrance.

It was definitely cooler in the mouth of the shaft, although the difference was less one of sun and shade, than that between a griddle and an oven. The low ceiling was almost at head-cracking height, but widened considerably just beyond. She could feel the cooler air on her cheek.

If I close my eyes once I am there, I can pretend I am somewhere much, much larger!

Reluctantly, she stooped to crawl away from the entrance and go deeper. It went down at a steep angle, and she paused after a few feet, thinking of bats. And scorpions.

No, this was most definitely far enough.

Her canteen water was warm but she drank more, eagerly. She could always have it refilled. Leaning against the smooth rock wall, she was grateful for its coolness. It would be even cooler if she unbuttoned her bodice a little, and removed her boots and stockings. No one would ever know.

She took them off and folded them neatly, then opened her bodice as far as her waist. That was better. Thank God she had left her corset behind.

As she folded her stockings she noticed something incised into the limestone wall. Tess leaned forward. A round shape, with curving lines beneath it.

Could it be an engraved image of Roman's mirror?

It was very like it! Tess felt a surge of vindication. Mrs. Miller was not the only one who could make discoveries! Tess started to rise and almost bumped her head on the low ceiling. She'd forgotten how small this space really was. She closed her eyes and imagined herself, not in a shaft, but in a room. A very large room. A *ballroom*. Yes, that was better.

She gave a little cry when she heard something scuffling at the shaft entrance. Tess opened her eyes to discover a large form blocking the light. "What in bloody hell do you think you are doing, Tess?" Roman shouted.

She snatched the edges of her bodice together. "Cooling off. Go away!"

Instead he pulled himself into the shaft entrance. "I told you not to go wandering about on your own. I don't have time to play nursemaid to you, while you play the heedless explorer."

"You needn't bother yourself about my whereabouts," she said icily. "I am perfectly capable of entertaining myself."

"I'm not talking about entertainment, you little fool. The desert is unforgiving to the ignorant. And," he said bitingly, "you have certainly proved yourself to belong in that category!"

There was real fury in his voice, and as he came farther inside she found herself backing up inside the shaft. Roman's wide shoulders blocked most of the light. He stumbled over her boots. "What the hell . . ."

"I told you to go away," she said smugly.

"Not until I have you by the hand and lead you out with me."

"I am not going anywhere until I put my garments back on."

That announcement gave Roman pause. Delicious images danced in his mind, tempting him beyond endurance.

"Are you mad? Get dressed, at once."

"It is only my shoes and stockings," she said quickly, buttoning up her bodice crookedly.

"Well, I have made a discovery of my own," she announced with a tiny tremor to her voice. "Move to the

right. There, you see? By my foot.'' She lifted it, forgetting
that her shoes were still off.

Roman's mouth went dry. He fought the urge to take
that slender little foot in his hand, and caress it. Follow
the elegant curve of her ankle and calf and . . .

"The carving down by the floor,'' Tess said impatiently. "Surely you recognize it.''

She was so nervous she felt as if the floor were trembling beneath her. As she reached out to touch the oval
with her toe, Roman launched himself at her with a mighty
roar. As his shadow moved away from the carving, she
barely had time to see that it was not the mirror's outline
etched in stone as she had thought, but the familiar Eye
of Horus symbol. There was no time for more.

The floor of the shaft shuddered. Dust rose around her
in heavy bands, like the folds of a thick, gray veil. Time
was suspended for a long moment, and then everything
seemed to happen simultaneously. In a split second she
was flung into the whirling heart of chaos.

Roman's voice mingled with a terrible groan that
seemed to come from the tomb itself. Tess was frozen in
place, unable to move or think. The groan split into a
shriek of stone on stone, and then a deep, vibrating rumble,
as if the gates of hell were opening wide beneath them.
Then Roman landed on top of Tess, knocking the breath
from her body.

They slid together over the gritty floor of the shaft,
which seemed to dissolve into dust beneath them. Roman's
arms wound round her tightly. Even as the support beneath
them vanished, the air turned solid. Amid the thunderous
sound, it was suddenly impossible to breathe. Her eyes and
nose stung, her mouth was clogged with dust so that she
couldn't even scream. Then they were falling into darkness, plummeting down like Dante's lost souls.

*   *   *

Tess awoke to utter blackness. It closed around her, thick as velvet. There was no sound, no sensation. A heavy numbness suffused her limbs. She couldn't move or breathe.

I am dead, she thought in wonder.

She felt no fear, only a detached surprise: everything she had been taught, everything that she had believed in, was untrue. She was dead, and there was nothing at all. No pearly gates, no glorious songs of cherubim and seraphim. Only blackness and despair.

"Ah, then I am in hell," Tess whispered, and was startled by the muffled sound of her voice.

Then she heard subdued sounds overhead. Like voices shouting from afar. There was an ear-shattering screech of stone on stone, and a scattering of sharp, stinging bits struck her temple.

Memory came flooding back, and pain along with it. And after them came fear. She'd been in the blind shaft with Roman . . . touched something on the wall . . . yes, and then the floor had collapsed beneath them, and the walls above had caved in.

The thought of it made her dizzy. She felt as if all the air were sucked out of her body. Her lungs were on fire, the side of her arm burned terribly, and she felt black and blue from head to toe.

This was worse than hell. She and Roman were buried alive.

11

"**Dear God!**" **Her voice was weak and her heart** pounded. Her ears buzzed, and her chest ached. There was very little air—and no movement nearby. She was terrified.

More slivers of fractured limestone fell over her arm. It throbbed terribly. As her head cleared, Tess realized that she was lying facedown in the dark, with Roman beneath her. She felt the warmth of his chest against her cheek, the strength of his muscled thighs. Tears of relief stung behind her lids. She'd know his scent anywhere.

"Roman?"

He moaned softly. "You're alive!" She was so relieved she touched his hair, his face, his shoulders, reassuring herself that he had no obvious broken bones. "Roman? Roman, are you badly injured?"

Silence was the only answer.

"Roman, my love! Oh, please, please speak to me!" Her voice trailed off into a dust-choked cough.

She felt his chest rise slowly and fall again. "Oh, thank God!"

He was just beginning to come round when there was a muffled *whump* overhead. A shower of fist-sized rocks beat down upon them. Tess braced herself over Roman protectively. One of the falling missiles struck her a glancing blow on the temple. She felt no pain, only a bizarre numbness in the side of her head.

Roman shifted slightly beneath her.

"Tess? What the hell . . ." His voice was groggy.

"We're in the tomb shaft. The floor collapsed."

He remembered then. "The Eye of Horus . . . the mark of the thieves . . . to use caution. They knew it was rigged to collapse . . . must be . . . the undiscovered tomb they've been pillaging."

"I caused it when I touched the mark, didn't I?"

"No. It was . . . the shift of weight . . ."

She listened to his breath rasping. "Roman! You must tell me where you are hurt."

"Only a bump on the head, I think." His mind was clearing, but he realized the air was growing bad. He wondered if anyone knew where they were.

Tess's head was growing fuzzy from the poor air, but she knew what he was thinking. She felt a detached sadness, and an unnatural calm. "We're going to die, aren't we."

Cradling her head against his chest, he held her close. "I can't think of any way I'd rather die, Tess, than with you in my arms."

His words, the passion in his voice, moved her to tears. "I'm so sorry. So very sorry. You can't die because of my stupidity."

His fingers touched her mouth and stopped her from talking. "Hush, my love. There's still time. I don't intend for either of us to die unnecessarily. Be still a moment while I think."

As she lay with her head against his chest she could hear the rhythmic beating of his heart. His breath ruffled her hair. They were entwined in the darkness, in a grim parody of lovemaking. It was exactly what she'd thought she'd seen in the ancient mirror, but she had interpreted it in error at the time.

There was no escape and she knew it. Already she could feel the air becoming thicker. She didn't want to die; she could bear it as long as Roman held her, taking comfort from the warmth and strength of his body.

His thoughts marched along with hers. Sighing, he tangled his fingers in her tumbled hair. "This is how I used to think it would be, Tess. Egypt. You and I, together." His other hand splayed out across her back. "But not," he laughed, "in the belly of some unknown ancient's tomb."

"How much time do we have left?" she asked softly.

"Don't give up yet! I put my faith in Brocklehurst. The lad has a good head on his shoulders. If there's a way to get us out, intact, he'll discover it."

For the past few minutes he'd been craning his ears to try and make out the shouts and taps from above. Now he heard an ominous slithering of rock. If Brocklehurst didn't get them out by sundown, he might as well take his leisure in opening the shaft. It wouldn't matter to them any longer.

Above, Lord Brocklehurst directed the men in the rescue attempt. His skin was slick with sweat and he was sick inside. He didn't guess why McKendrick and Lady Claybourne had gone into the blind shaft. He didn't want to know. He wanted to get them out, alive.

Even now they might be dying—or dead. The men were frightened they would somehow be blamed for the accident, and looked to him for direction, as second in command. Brocklehurst knew it was up to him to get them out.

In a few short weeks working with Roman, he had grown wise enough to know how very little he really knew; the best method to decant wine or the latest fashion in sporting vehicles were of no import in the desert where survival was a daily challenge. But some of these village men had been excavating tombs since before he was born. They had a wealth of experience to tap.

"Mohammed, you will take charge of rigging up the rope-and-pulley system to remove that large piece of limestone. Omar, you and your men will shore up the side. Put your backs into it! The rest of you, dismantle the sides of that supply wagon. We will use the wood as levers."

Under his direction, the crew put a mighty effort into their labors. Despite what seemed like forever to Brocklehurst, they managed to get the broken chunks of the massive rock seal cleared away. Now there remained only the treacherous task of making an opening to where McKendrick and Lady Claybourne were trapped, without bringing tons of rock down upon them.

Inside the remains of the shaft Roman and Tess were pressed side by side against the rocky wall. The air was close and both were increasingly soporific.

Roman tried to breathe shallowly, afraid his larger body would hog the precious oxygen she needed to survive. There was a fine line between saving their air and breathing deep enough to keep his brain clear so he could help their rescuers.

He gave Tess a tiny shake. She lifted her head, then let it fall against his shoulder. He gave her another shake. "You must stay awake, Tess!" he commanded. "For the love of God, stay awake."

"Roman. I love you, too," she murmured drowsily into his shirt. "I always have. I always will . . ."

His embrace tightened. Her bones felt so small, as if the strength of his arms could crush them. Roman shuddered at the images of what might happen if the rock above them smashed down.

Time and again he cursed himself. Through hindsight, he saw how a series of minor missteps and faulty decisions had led to this disaster. He'd been so concerned about preserving his precious temple, and his fear someone being injured if the wall came down, that he'd let himself be sidetracked. Why had he spoken so sharply to her, and not apologized. Why hadn't he gone to her later, to explain? Tess would never have gone exploring on her own if he hadn't ignored her.

Her breathing was soft and shallow. How long could she hold out? How long would the blocks above them, so precariously positioned, keep from falling and crushing them?

Tess no longer responded to his voice or touch. Roman was getting groggier by the minute. Just as he despaired, there came a terrible grinding, like the gnashing of huge limestone teeth. It was followed by a rattle of loose rocks. He prayed while a rain of limestone bits dusted their huddled bodies. Miraculously, a chink of golden light pierced the darkness, illuminating the layer of gray dust that covered the shoulder of her dress.

"McKendrick? Lady Claybourne? Can you hear me?"

"We're alive, Brocklehurst, but barely!" He gulped in great breaths of air. "Only get us out of here before the rest collapses!"

In minutes the gallant workers had the opening widened. Brocklehurst hunkered down and studied the situation. The vertical shaft, where the great sliding stone had once lodged, was too deep to reach the unfortunate adventurers.

"Make a sling of rope," Brocklehurst ordered. "We'll use the block-and-tackle to pull them out."

It was done quickly, but to Roman it seemed agonizingly slow. Roman felt the warm beating of Tess's heart against his, the ruffle of her breath in his hair. "Wake up, my love. Tess, you can't let go now! We are saved!"

She was having the loveliest dream, and didn't want to awaken. His voice finally penetrated to her consciousness.

Waking, Tess stirred in his arms. "Roman?"

"Yes, love. I am here. Everything is all right now."

"I had such a wonderful dream . . . so real!"

Her hold on reality seemed so fragile, so tenuous, that he encouraged her to tell him more. "We were together," she said dreamily. "A chamber with rose-colored walls and carved wooden shutters. A bed covered with pillows . . . books and drawings spilling from a table onto the chair beside it . . . we were so happy, you and I!"

As she described it, he felt gooseflesh rising on his arms. She was describing his bedchamber at the villa Al-Rashid had lent him. How could she so accurately describe a room that she had never seen? As the men lowered the rope sling down to them, Roman cupped her face between his hands and looked down at her.

"You never should have left me, Tess. We belong together. God help me, we always will!"

His mouth hovered an inch above hers. He had to kiss her. Just one time, before they tried the treacherous ascent.

Their mouths touched. Her lips were soft beneath the powdery grit that covered them both. Such tenderness poured through him that his breath hitched in his chest. The only thing that mattered to him now was that she survive.

"Are you awake enough to hold on to the sides of the sling?" he asked her gently, as he wrapped it around her. She nodded. Roman gave a sharp tug on the rope sling and the men began the dangerous task of hauling her up and up, inch by inch past the massive limestone blocks wedged so precariously against the beams. And finally, blessedly, out of the ancient, dust-filled womb and back into the world of the living.

Yusef gaped at her and backed away. *"Afreet!"* he cried out and made signs to ward off evil. Several others followed his example.

"They are fools," Mohammed said in his smooth English. "You are covered with limestone dust, and they think you are an evil spirit risen from the tomb."

As he helped her from the sling her legs buckled beneath her bonelessly. She had no more strength than an infant in arms. Her skirt and shirtwaist and what she could see of her hands were all coated with a layer of grayish-white, like a sifting of loose plaster.

Brocklehurst saw that she was all right, and set the men to work hauling Roman up in their makeshift sling. They strained and pulled back on the rope, assisted by the foreman's shouts and curses. The blocks groaned and shifted. A huge puff of powdery dust obscured the opening. Tess held her breath.

After an eternity, the top of Roman's head cleared the opening, liberally covered with dust. Another heave on the rope, and he came out of the jagged hole all at once, like a djinn popping out from a broken bottle. Tess's heart gave a leap of relief. Then she started laughing. He was so coated with dust that his hair, skin, and clothing were the same color. He looked as if he'd been turned to stone. Little wonder she'd startled the men.

He looked around, said something to Ahkmed, then came straight to Tess's side. She was still laughing. In fact, she couldn't seem to stop. Or possibly she was weeping now. She couldn't tell.

Roman knelt down before her and took her by the arms, shaking her hard. "Stop it, Tess! Now!"

But she seemed unable to control herself. The laughter came, mingled with hiccups, although her face was wet with tears. Roman lifted his hand and slapped her cheek sharply. The shock of his action was worse than the sting of the blow. Tess cradled her cheek, stunned to immobility.

She looked so small and vulnerable he wanted to pull her into his arms and comfort her as he had when they were young. It pained him that he could not. He touched her cheek where the red flag of his handprint burned. "You were hysterical. I had no choice."

Tess only nodded, still speechless. Roman turned around. "Where are Lord Claybourne and his sister?" he asked in the local tongue.

Yusef looked decidedly uncomfortable. "They are gone, effendi. The great lord, he was taken ill, and they left."

Now it was Roman's turn to curse. "We'll take her to my quarters. Mohammed, send someone for a physician immediately."

"I shall go myself, effendi, at once."

Now that they were safe, reaction rocked through them. Tess's eyes fluttered closed. She was dehydrated and in shock, he was sure. But she was safe.

And she had said that she loved him.

The physician, a soft-spoken Egyptian with gentle hands, came out of Roman's bedchamber where Tess lay beneath a light cover. He clapped his hands and a girl appeared as if conjured up by magic.

"Fetch me an empty bottle or jug. I will mix up an elixir to restore her health."

The girl looked in a cupboard but could not find an empty container. She went to her mother, who looked after the house. "The doctor requires a bottle for an elixir he is preparing."

After a moment's hesitation, her mother rummaged in a chest and pulled out a small blue bottle. It was empty, but the bitter odor lingered on the stopper. "This should do. Rinse it well, first."

While she cleaned out the bottle, Roman was getting a briefing on Tess's condition from Dr. Peltier.

"She is bruised about the arms and hands, but there are

no broken bones. Her pulse is strong and steady. Her pupils are normal, and I can find no bumps or lacerations except for the one on her scalp. I believe it is dehydration and shock, which will heal with rest.''

''Thank God!''

''Is it possible she could be with child?''

Roman blanked. Tess, carrying her husband's child. He'd seen them in Harley Street only a few months earlier and had thought so then, although nothing seemed to have come of it.

''I do not know. I suppose anything is possible,'' he said thickly.

''There could be internal injuries, of course. This is why I ask so delicate a question.''

Roman's bronze skin turned pale and gray as tin. ''There must be some way you can tell!''

''I would suggest an internal examination of your wife's womb, with your permission.''

''She is not my wife,'' Roman blurted before realizing it.

''But I was given to understand . . .'' The doctor was shocked. He turned his hands up in a typical Gallic gesture. ''Then we have the difficulty. I cannot examine her, monsieur. If she is not conscious to give her own permission, then I must have her husband's permission.''

''Damn it, man, I have no idea where he might be at the moment. If her life may be in danger, time is of the essence.'' He advanced ominously on the little man until the physician backed up against the wall. ''You will examine her or I shall throttle you on the spot!''

''You do not understand! I am half Egyptian. This makes my position most awkward where Europeans are concerned.''

''Yes, I understand there are idiotic prejudices in the world, even if the reason for them is nonexistent. But I do not understand letting a young woman die because of them. So, Dr. Peltier . . .''

Rolling up his sleeves, Roman continued his advance.

The doctor brightened. ''I will send for the midwife Miriam. She is Coptic like myself, and has studied herbs and other healing. There can be no objection to her.''

''Very well. But quickly, man!''

Roman took a chair beside his bed where Tess lay with her eyes closed. It had been almost two hours since they'd brought her back to his hired house and she had scarcely stirred in all that time. He'd sent Brocklehurst to bring word to Lady Alicia and Minnie.

He heard sounds of activity from outside the house as the doctor went off to fetch Miriam in his own carriage. A quarter hour passed. It was the longest fifteen minutes of Roman's life, except for those when they had been trapped together in the tomb.

He took her hand in his. So small and delicate, so perfectly formed—her nails like translucent shells. The orange-red stone in her wedding band reminded him that she was not his, nor would she ever be.

How had two young people from Swanfield ended up like this in far-off Egypt, with their lives so intricately entangled, yet so inescapably separate?

The midwife arrived, a thin, competent-looking woman with a lined face and wise eyes. Roman felt better the moment he saw her. She bowed her head in greeting and dismissal.

''I will wait in the study,'' Roman said.

The room was a small one adjoining the bedchamber. Plain wooden shelves held books, papers, and stacks of correspondence. A decanter stood on the table beside the blotter and inkstand, and Roman poured himself out a stiff drink. Nothing to do but wait. It was like a parody of a father pacing the floor while his wife gave birth.

Roman had never envied any man before, but he envied Lord Claybourne. If Tess was with child, he wished desperately that it could have been his own.

There were no sounds from the bedroom at first. Then, voices were raised, first the midwife's, then Monsieur Peltier's, like actors running their lines. Fear and hope coursed through his body. Hearing his name called, he went back into the bedchamber.

"No bleeding," the doctor told him. "Everything appears in order."

The woman was talking again, and Roman's worst fears were activated.

The doctor looked stunned.

Roman asked the question he'd been dreading. "She has not lost the child?"

"I do not understand, monsieur."

"For the love of God, man, is Lady Claybourne pregnant or not?"

The doctor looked at Roman as if he and all the world had run mad. "How can she be, effendi? She is still a virgin."

Roman's reaction was swift. "Don't be a fool!"

"I assure you, Monsieur McKendrick, the lady is *virgo intacta*. The midwife has the task of certifying young maidens prior to the brokering of a marriage. She is certain of it."

Roman rubbed a hand over his jaw. None of it made sense. "How is she otherwise?"

"No worse for wear, except for some bruising. Her general health is good, and she is young and therefore resilient. I have given her a light sleeping draught. She will sleep until evening, and awaken perfectly restored! However, I would recommend that she not be moved for a few days."

"Thank you. I shall arrange for her sister and Lady Alicia to come to her."

They shook hands and Dr. Peltier left.

As he drove away from Sheik Al-Rashid's villa, the doctor was thoughtful. He had been as surprised as Monsieur McKendrick by the lady's condition. More so by his own parting advice. It was not exactly a betrayal of his oath. It would certainly do Lady Claybourne good to rest. That, however, was not the reason for his recommendation that she not be removed from the house as yet.

He had given in to the quixotic notion that he was fostering an already rooted romantic attraction. The physician in him did not approve; the romantic in him could not have done otherwise. After all, he reminded himself, he *was* half French.

Tess gradually swam up to consciousness. She had been having the most wonderful dreams! Her eyes opened.

She was in a room that was vaguely familiar. Pierced brass braziers warmed the room against the desert night and made patterns on the ceiling. The walls were colored a deep rose shade, the windows covered with carved lattices—and Roman sprawled in the chair beside the bed with his head tipped back and eyes shut.

"I know this dream," she murmured, stretching. "This is the dream where we make love."

His eyes flew open. "Tess!"

She held out her arms to him and he thought that he was the one dreaming. "Thank God! You have been in a deep sleep for hours!"

She shook her head. "No. I was in a dream. Roman, you would not believe the things I saw! It was just like when I went into the mirror." Her eyes were dark emeralds in the dim light, her voice soft. "It started out so badly! I was aboard the ship, ready to leave for England. I had waited and waited for you to come and say good-bye, as you had promised.''

She struggled up and the sheet slipped, revealing her thin chemise. ''But you never came! It was so terrible, Roman.''

''Hush, darling. You need to rest.'' He sat down on the edge of the mattress and pushed her back against the pillows. He thought she was confused.

Roman poured some of the tonic into the cup on the bedside table, and held it to her lips. ''Here. The doctor mixed you up a decoction to take when you awakened.''

''I don't want to wake up,'' she said. ''I want to stay in this dream forever, with you.''

''It's not a dream, Tess.''

She smiled at him oddly. ''Everything is a dream. Put that cup down.''

''You have to drink this. I promised the doctor.''

Tess peered up at him through her thick lashes. ''If I do, what will you promise me?''

''Anything you like. I give you my word on it.''

Taking the cup, she downed the sweet draught in one long swallow. ''There. And now you must keep your promise.''

Roman laughed in relief. She didn't act like someone who'd been trapped in a tomb and received a knot on the head—she acted like a woman who had just finished her one too many glasses of champagne. He crossed his arms and bowed like a djinn.

''Name it, beautiful lady, and your wish is my command.''

She sat up so the thin sheet fell to her waist. Her figure was slender and full breasted, her face suddenly dark with desire. This dream would end properly. She lifted her arms to him and wound them around his neck. Her breasts brushed against him, filling his body with heat.

"Make love to me, Roman!"

He caught at her hands. All the laughter was gone from his face now. "You're another man's wife, Tess. And you're still a virgin . . ."

"I was born a virgin, and I will die one, unless you make love to me." Looking into his eyes, she saw all the longing and thwarted passion that she herself felt, reflected in them.

"Leland does not desire me. He cannot force himself to . . ." The seductive light died in her eyes. She dropped her arms from Roman's neck, and covered her face with her hands.

"At first he would come to me and attempt . . ." Her voice broke on a muffled sob. "You cannot know what it is like. The humiliation . . . oh, Roman, what is wrong with me that my husband refuses to even seek my bed? Why will no one love me?"

"Christ, Tess! You cannot blame yourself."

"But even you will not love me!"

"Not for lack of desire! Do not torture me, Tess."

She faced him again, her skin flushed with longing. "I am so lonely. So alone. Give me tonight, Roman. Give me something to warm me when I am all alone in my cold bed."

He was only flesh and blood. Roman pulled her across his lap and into his arms. His kiss was hard and punishing as his fingers wound through her long tresses. His other hand smoothed over her back, along the lush curve of her hips and thighs.

This was insanity. It was late, and any moment might bring the others down on them. The danger of it only added to the urgency of his need. If this one time was all he would ever have of her, he would make the most of it for both their sakes.

Still holding her in his lap, he slid the straps of her

chemise over her shoulders. It fell down, catching on the tips of her breasts. He lowered his head and nuzzled it free, then took one tender bud into his mouth and suckled it. Her body arched with pleasure. She offered him the other, cupping it in her hand. Her wanton innocence was a drug in his blood. Stretching her back across his arm, he nibbled at the breast she offered, tugging at it until she shuddered with delight.

"I never knew . . ." she whispered. "I never imagined . . ."

"Shhh. This is only the beginning, my love." Holding her tightly with one strong arm, he held her on his lap while he explored the satin texture of her legs, the smooth roundness of her thighs. Her chemise pushed up and his hand moved higher until it dipped beneath the hem. She was ripe and liquid, and it was all he could do to force himself to be gentle. God in Heaven, but he wanted her with every atom of his body!

Tess purred with pleasure as he stroked between her legs. His thumb brushed the silky folds of skin and she gasped against his mouth. He retreated, then touched her again, moving his thumb in tantalizing circles. She opened her legs to him, and her sultry female scent mingled with the night air and the heat of the braziers. He parted the soft petals and slid a finger inside. She went rigid for just a moment. Her mouth curved in a smile of bliss.

This was no dream, Tess realized. This was Roman, and this was real. She moved against his questing fingers, pleasing them both. There was no false coyness about her. Her trust in him was utter and complete. For one brief moment she would learn what it was to truly be a woman, and she would learn it in Roman's arms.

He withdrew and she protested. A second later he touched her again, deeper and harder. "Oh, yes!" She braced herself, lifting her hips, and his warm hand cupped her. "More," she said greedily, and his fingers worked their magic, sending bursts of fire and lightning deep into her core.

He did something to his clothing, then sat her upright on his lap, so that her breasts cupped his face. He caught them between his hands, nursing one tip and then the other until she felt as if she would die from the joy of it. She wriggled against him, not knowing what she wanted, only knowing she needed more. He lifted her hips off his lap then, and she felt him hard against her inner thighs.

There was no easy way to do this, he knew. Better to make it one sharp move to pierce her, and then fill her with sensation upon sensation until she forgot the brief pang. Gently he slid a little way into her, listening to her tiny hisses of pleasure. This wasn't the way he'd ever pictured it between them. He'd imagined soft, romantic scenes, an easy coupling—not this fierce ardor that had come over them like a spell.

He kept her lifted and felt the warm honey of her against his skin, and knew she was ready. Her hands caught the chair back behind his shoulders as he shifted her hips higher and positioned her. Then he brought her down smoothly, impaling her on his shaft.

She gave out a little cry, and he pressed his face against her throat as her head tipped back, covering it with kisses. He caught one pebbled summit between his teeth and worked it until she jerked against him. Oh, she was a passionate little thing, his Tess! Hadn't he always known it? Hadn't he always guessed that they were two of a kind? A dark exultation flowed through his veins and he rocked her hard against his thighs.

Tess was incapable of thought. The sudden jolt of pain as her hymen was breached, was followed by one of pleasure so intense she felt as if she would pass out from it. Then he took her hips and rocked her gently on his lap, moving her more vigorously with every thrust. Her body arched, spasmed, and she cried out sharply. He wanted to take her then, but he held himself back. He would wring every drop of pleasure out of this for her.

Still holding her, he rose and she wrapped her legs around him. It was wonderfully wicked that he was still almost fully clothed, while she had nothing but the thin chemise in a band about her waist. He lowered her to the bed and covered her with his body, pushing her knees apart. He pressed kisses against her ear, her jaw, the delicate curve of her throat. Then he began moving against her, slow and steady, while she urged him on and begged for more.

At the crucial moment he forced himself to withdraw, and fought to hold on to his control. Not yet, not yet.

"Roman! Don't stop."

"My darling, we have hardly begun!"

He kissed her breasts, suckled at their soft peaks until they were swollen and tender. His mouth moved lower, down across her abdomen and down between her thighs. The probing of his tongue was exquisite, the touch of his mouth, ecstatic. Then he parted her and found the tiny bud that was the seat of her pleasure. He flicked his tongue over it until she writhed and moaned, then tugged at it gently.

Pleasure exploded through her body in waves of sensation. Her hips bucked and she almost threw herself off the bed in the intensity of it. Only Roman's strong arms kept her from falling. When it was over her body was slick with sweat, and the secret place between her legs throbbed. She wanted more.

Roman slid back on the bed and lifted her hips, then plunged into her. He filled her as she took him in, satisfying some deep, primal need. He stretched over her so that the rough hairs of his chest would brush her nipples, heightening the sensation for her. He meant to take his time, start slow and work his way up to speed. She wouldn't let him. *"Now, now, now!"*

Time and again he plunged into her, possessing her utterly. Making her his. In the beginning he had thought that this would be their only time, that he would make every second of it count. Now he knew that he could never, ever let her go. Whatever it took in sacrifice or force of action, by God he would make her *his*!

Tess was buffeted by emotion and the strong thrust of his hips, driving him deeper and deeper into her. She lost all consciousness of the world. It had narrowed to herself and Roman and their wild, sweet dance of love. With every thrust of his muscular body, she lifted her hips to take him deep.

Again and again in a rhythm that mounted, that took them higher and higher until the earth was a tiny sphere whirling below, and they were flying through a shower of stars. Then, one last thrust and she felt his seed burst hot inside her, and the joy of it sent her plummeting from the heavens. Her body shook with pleasure, with passion, with the knowledge that she had given him the same.

Another shudder, stronger than before, shattered every conscious thought into a million bright splinters of heat and light. Then she was safe on earth again, locked tightly, fiercely, possessively in her lover's arms.

12

"It is not safe, mademoiselle," one of the servants protested.

Minnie was ready to set out from the *dahabeeyah* for the sheik's villa where Tess was resting.

She had recovered from the heat about the same time that Alicia and Leland had returned. Alicia was dreadfully ill with some sort of sick headache and Leland was closeted in his room with a bottle of brandy. When Lord Brocklehurst had come pounding up on a lathered horse, with news of Tess's accident, Minnie had taken charge at once.

Celeste was nervous. The silvery moonlight brought out the stark and ancient beauty of the countryside. It also brought out thugs and thieves. A brigands' moon: enough light to see by, yet slight enough to provide cover for robbers and murderers among the indigo shadows.

"Perhaps we should wait until morning, mademoiselle," she whispered. "It would be better to travel in daylight."

"It would take more than brigands to keep me from my sister's side! We have the escort of Lord Brocklehurst and one of our men. We shall set out now, without delay. If you feel unequal to the task, I shall go without you."

"Well said," Brocklehurst commended her. "Rest assured that I will bring you safely to Lady Claybourne's side.''

''I do not doubt it. Roman's note said they would be dead if not for you.''

Brocklehurst colored and guided the carriage over the bumpy track. ''I did nothing anyone in the same circumstances would not have done.''

Minnie eyed him gravely. ''I have known Roman McKendrick since I was a child. He is not given to exaggeration. If he says that you saved their lives, I have no reason on earth to discount it.''

They rode in silence a while through the silver light. He was amazed by the way she had refused to give in to hysteria. She had briskly marshaled her resources, informed the others of her intentions, and set off for Roman's compound, all in less than a quarter hour.

''I am impressed with your efficiency,'' he told Minnie. ''My own sister would have needed three days to accomplish it all, moaning and weeping the entire time. There are times when I wonder how we can possibly be related.''

That made Minnie laugh at his jest, just as he'd intended. ''Judith and I are very different on the surface. But I believe she would have come up to scratch in a crisis as well as I.''

''You are generous,'' he said, and returned his attention to the drive. He had seriously misjudged his companion. She was a remarkable girl!

He tooled the carriage along the river past the sleeping villages. If he gave the whip a bit more of an elegant flourish, it had nothing to do with the presence of anyone else in the carriage.

Certainly not that of Miss Minerva Malloy.

Tess leaned back against the pillows. She had been at the villa four days now, prolonging her stay far longer than was wise. Alicia had sent a note explaining her absence, along with several items Tess had requested, but she had not visited. Nor had Leland.

Tess was glad. Meanwhile, she and Roman took every advantage of their time together. It was easy enough to send Celeste out into the gardens, under the pretense of chaperoning Minnie in a house of men. Roman had taught her how to take every stolen minute for a kiss, a caress. And every night, while the others slept, he came to her room.

Her body seemed to have changed. It felt softer, fuller, and more feminine. And she was as eager and passionate as he. They had made love in the bed and in the moonlit garden. Even on the brocade divan in the sheik's library one afternoon, while Brocklehurst and Minnie drove out to visit the excavation site. It was rash and reckless, and only added to the bittersweet wonder of their love.

But now it all came to an end. Tess's things had all been packed up. If only she could neatly fold away her emotions and box up her pain. Alicia had recovered, and she and Leland were coming to take Tess and Minnie back to the *dahabeeyah*. Tess didn't tell Roman that they were scheduled to return to Cairo by week's end. And to England, shortly after.

Roman had proclaimed her love for her a thousand times, but said nothing of the future. Both knew it was out of the question. They could remain lovers in theory, meeting when Roman came to England after the heat ended the excavating season, or if Tess ever returned to Egypt. They could never be anything more.

If she left Leland, Roman would be ruined, and Minnie and Judith with him. He would have no profession and no way of supporting them. The situation was as damnable as the first time they had parted years ago.

As to herself, she didn't care a fig for her own reputation. Tess would have thrown it away willingly, if it hadn't meant bringing the others to ruin with her. She sighed. To know Roman loved her, to snatch a few moments of joy in illicit meetings would be the most for which she dared to hope.

Sounds of carriages heralded the guests' arrival. Tess looked around the rose-colored chamber, where she had known such great happiness, and tried to fix every detail in her memory. Already it was fading, like a dream.

A knock at the door called her back to the present. She opened it, still in her dressing gown, and was startled to see Roman. "They're here."

"I know."

The simple words said it all. It was over. Then he stepped inside the room with a smothered oath, and shut the door behind him. Gathering her up in his arms, he kissed her hungrily, ruthlessly. He pressed her against the wall and molded her body to him in one last passionate embrace.

Her robe fell open to him and his hands were on her flesh, his mouth upon her breasts. She gasped and went liquid beneath his questing hands. The need was too overpowering: *"Take me, Roman. Take me now! Quickly!"*

He couldn't resist her. Her eyes were dark with passion, her lips soft and blurred from his kisses. He thrust inside her, hard and urgent with need. Tess flung her head back and he covered her throat with kisses. *"Now!"* she said. *"Now!"*

He took her with consummate skill, up and over the crest of passion, until she clutched at his arms and cried out softly against his chest. Then he arched his back and shuddered, spilling all his longing and love into her. When he finally wrenched away, his face was dark with desire and his eyes blazed. "It won't do, Tess! I can't let you go to him! I'll tell him everything. You needn't face him."

"No, Roman . . ."

"Stay with me, goddamnit!" His strong hands dug into her shoulders. "Divorce him and marry me. We'll go away somewhere together . . ."

She gathered her resolve and pushed him gently away. "It can't be, love. In time you would grow to hate me."

"Never!"

"Please, Roman," she gasped as he kissed her again. "Don't make it any more difficult than it is."

"For the love of God, Tess!"

"Yes," she said. "And for the love you have for me."

There was no way he could argue against that. But someday he'd be established and Judith and Minnie would be married off. Then, respectability be damned! To him it was far worse a sin to deny their love for one another.

He sighed and kissed her. Tess was adamant. For now. By God, he'd manage to persuade her somehow!

Her eyes were brimming over with tears. He wiped them away with his thumb. "I won't press you now. But perhaps someday I shall ride up, throw you over my saddlebow, and carry you off into the night, like a fairy tale."

"This is real," she told him gravely. "I took a vow . . ."

He interrupted her by placing his fingers over her mouth. "Yes, you did. You vowed to be a good wife. But, God in Heaven, he has been no husband to you, Tess! He broke the vows first, and he must have known he would, when you exchanged them in church. It was a cruel thing to do to you."

A sudden thought came to him like a spear of light. "My God, you have grounds for an annulment at the least."

They heard Minnie's voice out in the courtyard and he pulled away. "Think of it. Promise me. I'll come to you tonight, love. I swear it!" Then he was gone.

Tess leaned against the wall, trembling. This mustn't continue! Roman didn't understand. Life was simpler for men. Their instincts were bold and more basically defined: they took what they wanted, and the devil take the rest.

For a woman life was not so black and white, but an entire rainbow of conflicting needs and obligations. She wasn't able to separate her own good from the welfare of others who depended upon her.

Oh! If only her sisters were safely settled. Then it would be different. Giving up her title and privilege would be no hardship. Tess would be very sad to lose Alicia's friendship, but she could survive the loss of it; what she could not survive was exposing Leland and Alicia to ridicule, knowing that she had ruined her sisters' chances of happiness, and dashed forever Roman's chances of advancement in his chosen field.

She roused herself and poured water into the intricately enameled washbasin. If there was any hope of ending her marriage honorably, word of an affair with Roman would do it. She knew, in her heart, she was too weak, too much in love, to want it to ever end. She wanted him so desperately that she ached. They were treading a dark path, but she couldn't turn aside from it any more than she could stay the sun in the sky.

There was barely time to bathe hastily and throw her garments on. She didn't ring for Celeste. The room still smelled of passion. Of Roman. Locking the door from the inside, she went to the long shutters at the window that led to the courtyard and out to face the rest of her life.

Roman had only left her once to visit his excavation: his find. Once the rubble of the collapsed block had been cleared away, an exciting discovery had been made: the blind entrance was a trick. The shaft led to an unplundered tomb.

"I knew it the minute I saw the thieves' mark that Tess pointed out to me," Roman told the others. "It was recent. A mark may be placed to warn of traps or signify a find— but in my experience, it is never placed inside a blind shaft leading nowhere. That, and the care that had been taken with the pit trap, told me there was a burial of note inside."

Indeed it was: the burial of a high priestess of Isis. It was an early tomb, without the rich gold and expensive funerary displays of the later eras. For Roman it had something more valuable: paintings and descriptions of the temple site he was excavating—a papyrus covered with strange symbols, in no language he had ever seen before. And a rendering in red and black ink, of the legendary enchanted mirror.

It was an exact picture of the one he'd been given in the souk, and which lay, at the moment, hidden in a document box in a locked cupboard at his villa. He would have to retrieve it from her.

Someday, somehow, he would find the key to it and unlock its secrets. His reputation, at least on a scholarly level, would be made. Then he'd convince Tess to leave her husband and marry him.

They went out together to tour Roman's find. Tess found the courage to go back into the tomb shaft, but it was very difficult for her to endure. "It is shored up and the traps all circumvented," she assured the others.

Alicia, while pretending to examine a lovely mural of pleasure boating on a lake, had been watching her sister-in-law intently. She moved over to where her brother stood, looking at another painting.

"They are lovers," she whispered without meeting his eyes. *"I am sure of it."* Leland looked away.

In his role of host, Roman gave them a tour of the

anteroom, explaining the significance of the depictions of gods and goddesses, and the joys of everyday life. The wall paintings were exquisite and perfectly preserved. There were depictions of the high priestess Menept lounging before a lotus-filled pool while other women sipped wine and female musicians played their lyres and flutes.

In another, the high priestess made offerings at a flower-garlanded altar. Tess went back to the first and stared. An oval disk with a twined handle of lotus leaves was held in the priestess's hand. "By God, McKendrick!" Leland exclaimed. "It is the mirror you brought to show us."

"Yes, or its twin." Roman hoped it wasn't the same one, for that would mean the inner sanctum had been breached by the tomb robbers of the area some time in the past. The disappointment would be crushing.

"Do you recall the legend I told you in London?" he said. "Of the magical object that was 'round as the moon and more glorious than the sun'? It is all there, in the inscription. The very legend I discovered in your papyrus."

"The Mirror of Imhotep! Where is it?" Leland almost shouted. "I must see it, at once!"

Tess stared at him in surprise. It was the first animation she'd seen in him.

"I have it at the villa I hired will show it to you when you visit," Roman promised.

Leland's agitation continued. "These hieroglyphs—have you done a translation? Do they say anything about the mirror? About its magical powers?"

"The translation is not finished. I believe it does speak of foretelling the future, but to my knowledge there is nothing of any other powers."

Long after the others worked their way to the far side of the antechamber, Leland stood looking up at the painted depiction of the mirror.

After the luncheon, they returned to the villa, and the men went into the library while the ladies took a leisurely turn about the garden. Lord Brocklehurst addressed his cousin. "What of the baby that Lady Claybourne and Alicia took under their wing?"

"He has been given over to the authorities for placement," Leland said brusquely. "I do not think we should discuss this where the ladies might overhear."

The young peer accepted the rebuke. "As you say. Such matters are not a fit subject for gentlewomen."

Minnie, who was in the courtyard nearby and whose sharp ears *had* overheard, was rather indignant. She popped her head around the open library doors.

"How very odd," she told Brocklehurst astringently. "Men feel that we are fully capable of handling the details of caring for the child born of scandal, and yet nothing of it must sully our ears in public discussion."

Brocklehurst tipped back his head and laughed. "So, we men are not only peculiar as a species, we are hypocritical as well!"

Minnie flushed. "I do not include you in that company, Lord Brocklehurst. You seem to have more good sense."

He smiled warmly and offered her his arm. "Come, take a turn about the garden with me. "Do you know, Miss Mallory . . . Minerva . . . I have a great desire to hear my name on your lips, rather than my title. I wonder if you will do me the honor of calling me by my Christian name?"

"My lord! I . . . that is, Edward . . ."

She didn't finish the sentence. Her brain was reeling at the sudden leap forward their relationship had taken. An exchange of Christian names was almost tantamount to an engagement.

"Yes?"

Minnie blushed. She was reading more into his request

than it warranted. "I . . . I see that you have adopted the informal style of Mr. McKendrick."

Brocklehurst came to a dead halt and caught her hand. She stopped and tipped up her chin. Despite the smile on his lips, his blue eyes looked perfectly serious. "Is that what you really think, my dear?"

His dear! "Yes. No. No, *Edgar.*"

To Minnie's astonishment, his smile widened to a white grin in his tanned face. Then he pulled her behind a trellis and kissed her soundly.

To his great gratification, she kissed him back.

Tess watched the way Minnie and Brocklehurst were making calves' eyes at each other with mingled amusement and consternation. Her little sister was growing up before her eyes. Was it possible there would be a love match coming out of this fiasco? That would salvage something.

But, she thought suddenly, *Judith will be mad as fire!*

She realized that Roman was speaking to her. "I suppose it is time to show him the mirror." Claybourne had asked about it several times.

"I'll fetch it," Minnie said. Roman had shown it to her earlier, in his study. She was hoping that Edgar might break away from Leland, perhaps to steal another kiss from her.

Roman nodded. He wanted a minute with Tess alone. "Thank you, Minnie. It is in the locked cupboard." He gave her the key and Minnie went off to get the mirror, trying to attract Edgar's notice.

She went across the courtyard, through the library, and then into a second courtyard that housed the main sleeping chambers. Minnie smiled. She was fairly sure she heard footsteps following along behind.

Slipping into the room that Roman used as his study, she went straight to the cupboard. It was only the work of a moment to open it and find the mirror hidden inside a box of documents.

Minnie picked it up as a shadow fell over her shoulder. "It is a beautiful thing, is it not?" she asked breathlessly.

There was no answer. She was turning around, when something struck her temple, and sent her toppling to the ground.

"The young lady will be fine," Dr. Peltier announced after examining Minnie. "It is merely a contusion. The skull and brain are unharmed."

"Thank God," Roman exclaimed. He was raddled with guilt.

"Fortunate also that Lord Brocklehurst was almost on the scene and frightened the thief before he could carry off the mirror," Leland said, taking a swallow of his whisky. A stunned silence followed his words.

Dr. Peltier looked stern. "Egypt does not seem to agree with the ladies of your family, Lord Claybourne. Perhaps you should cut your visit short and return home."

Tess looked at Leland. She couldn't help comparing him with the man he'd been when they'd married. Nor could she avoid comparing him with Roman. They were so vastly different in every way! "Perhaps Dr. Peltier is right," she said, and turned on her heel and left.

Later, Tess returned to the bechamber to find Minnie sleeping quietly. She stayed with her all night, not because there was any danger, but because she wanted to think. And she didn't want to be alone with Roman. Not yet.

The next morning, Alicia arrived to take them back to the *dahabeeyah*. "Come into the garden with me, Tess. There is something I must say to you. I know how upset you were with Leland last evening."

"How could I not be? So unfeeling!"

"And I must be equally so."

"Can this not wait until we are back on the boat?"

"There is no good time to hear what I have to say, but it cannot wait any longer. We must talk *now*."

"As you wish." Tess felt increasingly apprehensive. "What is it that requires such urgency?"

"We must not return to England yet. Not until you conceive Roman McKendrick's child."

"What?" Tess felt the blood drain from her head.

Alicia's voice was high with tension. "I know that you are his mistress. And I know that Leland cannot father a child on you, because he does not lie with you!"

"What new madness is this, Alicia?"

"Why do you think we came here to Egypt, all but pushing you, ourselves, into Roman McKendrick's arms?"

Tess's heart hammered. She couldn't credit what she was hearing. "And what reason did you have to make you think that I would fall into his arms?"

"Do you think an earl would marry a commoner, without first investigating her past?"

"I see. And that is why Roman was invited to Claybourne House!"

"Not at all. His translations are said to be exceptional. But when Leland made the connection that the rising young Egyptologist had been your childhood sweetheart, it seemed like an omen!

"Of course," Alicia added, "by the time we were aware of the relationship, matters had deteriorated. The attraction between the two of you was obvious. We hoped that you would become lovers in London. If only you had conceived his child then, our difficulties would be over. Instead we had to follow him back to Egypt."

Tess was in shock. "I thought we came for Leland's health," she said dully. "What an utter fool you must have thought me!"

"No!"

Tess jerked her hands away. "I have tried to be a wife in all ways to Leland. Endured humiliation and terrible loneliness. I fought my attraction to Roman at every turn, and have suffered agonies of conscience!"

She gave a mirthless laugh. "You were my friend, as dear to me as a sister. And all the time, from the very beginning, I was a pawn in your plans. No, a *brood mare*, brought blindly to stud."

"No! My . . . our affection for you is real, Tess. You must not think otherwise. This is not about you . . ."

Tess's intuition took a giant leap. "This is about Leland, isn't it?"

Blind, blind, blind! As her sister-in-law spoke, things were clicking in her brain, like pieces of a difficult puzzle coming together. She *knew*! There was no kind or diplomatic way to say it.

"It all becomes clear to me. Lately Leland has seemed detached from everything. He is forgetful. He rambles. Or mumbles. And his eyes last night! They looked so odd and blank!"

She paced the walled garden-court. "Why did I not see it earlier? I have read that such symptoms are the result of ingesting morphia or opium. *That* is why he is unable to be a husband to me. He is in thrall to the drugs."

The words hung heavy in the air. Alicia looked away. In the extended silence that followed, Tess could hear her own heart beating. She started to turn away, and the other woman's hand snagged her arm like a claw.

"It's true," Alicia said after a long pause. "My brother is indeed taking a form of the drugs. But it is not what you think. Leland is not an addict, nor is he merely indulging himself in the pleasures of poppy juice."

Her face was bleak, her own eyes opaque as stones. "He is dying."

*   *   *

Alicia was in the garden, and Brocklehurst was reading aloud to Minnie while she lay on a divan in the salon. They had decided not to brave the long ride back until the heat of the day had passed.

Roman caught up with Tess as she left the salon. Slipping his arm around her waist, he pulled her into a nook. "Everyone is occupied. I think we should follow their example." He nibbled on her ear.

"Roman . . ."

He was too busy kissing the nape of her neck to pay any heed. She pulled away sharply. "We must talk. Quite seriously."

"I am very serious," he told her. "Come, love."

Tess put him gently away. "We must end this. Now. Oh, God! This is so difficult!"

He was stunned by the finality in her voice. "What are you saying?"

She struggled to find the words. Leland and Alicia had betrayed her loyalty, and yet she could not abandon them in their terrible need for so many reasons. There still remained some tatters of her former affection for them. They had used her badly, yet they had done her some good as well. And it had begun honestly enough.

"His fondness for you—like mine—is very real," Alicia had told her. "But you see, we had no idea how desperately ill he was, when you were wed. Our London physician said that the disease might progress slowly, that he might live out a fairly normal lifespan. It was only when he returned from the Continent that we learned the sad truth."

All the time Tess had thought Leland had been shooting in Scotland, he had been at a clinic in Austria, receiving treatments. The doctors there had given him six months to live. Perhaps less. However, they had also told him that some people with his condition had outlived their predictions by years.

Tess was shattered. She could not abandon Leland and Alicia—and she could not ask Roman to wait for her. He deserved better.

"I am going back to England. We sail for home in two weeks."

Roman felt as if he'd been hit in the stomach. He tried not to panic. He'd seen her in this mood before. The last time he hadn't recognized it for what it was, but this time he did: Tess had an overactive sense of duty.

It was Swanfield all over again.

It was utterly ridiculous—and so utterly Tess!

"Something has occurred. Will you tell me what it is?" She shook her head. "I cannot. Please don't press me."

He tried not to panic. He was sure he could cajole her out of it, given enough time. But two weeks!

"Don't say anything yet, except that you love me." His heart pounded with sudden fear. He could not bear to lose her! "Say that you love me, heart of my heart."

"I do, Roman, Oh! I do!",

He regarded her for a moment, then leaned down and kissed her forehead. "That is all I need to know."

He watched her walk away, wondering what had caused this sea change. It was nothing he couldn't work around. He would convince her to get an annulment. If Audley pulled out his backing from a sense of family loyalty, so be it. There were other places he could go.

By God! He would find a way, or make one.

After the women had departed he sent Brocklehurst off to the excavation site. He clapped the young lord on the shoulder. "Forget about the girl for a few hours, and pay some attention to your work for a change."

And I will try to do the same. Feeling restless, he went inside to the library and removed the mirror from the hiding place beneath the floor where the sheik kept his own valuables. He would take some rubbings of the mirror's incised tracings and see if any other shapes or images than the Isis one emerged. He had a theory that the lines were of varying depths, and that by going deeper with each rubbing, he could eventually make out the patterns they formed.

His finger traced the curves of the design on the back, as caressingly as it had touched her body. He still could not make out the hieroglyphs in the central cartouche. All he knew was that it had been added to the artifact much later.

Suddenly the designs seemed to shimmer and shift. Not designs, but lines of hieratic script. Names and honorifics of pharaohs and queens coalesced before his eyes. Roman uttered an oath.

The mirror twisted in his hand, the twined stems of the lotus flowers suddenly warm as melting wax. He was looking at the surface as it came alive. Then he was looking through it.

His jaw dropped. He was looking at a portrait, with movement. He saw Tess sitting at a desk with her back to the door. From the view of the Nile through the window, he realized she was aboard the *dahabeeyah*. She was writing swiftly in her journal, intent on the words. Something flashed into view from the right side of the mirror:

A dagger's blade, thin as misery, and sharper than regret.

Sunlight flashed as it plunged down. He saw Tess rise, trying to escape. A crystal paperweight flew past her head, shattering the looking glass above the desk into a glittering web. As Roman watched in horror, the scene played out.

The dagger's blade came across Tess's slender throat, bit deep. The mirror went blank as a gush of blood seemed to hit it from inside.

Roman cried out and dropped the mirror. When he picked it up, Tess and the room he'd seen her in were gone.

All that was left was the image of a fallen dagger, its long blade wet with bright, arterial blood.

He raced out of the villa, shouting for the fastest horse in the stables. They brought out a rearing black gelding. The animal snorted as it smelled Roman's fear. Cursing, he mounted, using only the rope bridle the groom had put on. He'd ridden the beast bareback before, and there was no time to stop for saddling.

Praying harder than he ever had in his life, he pounded off across the desert on a wild ride toward the Nile.

A strange hush had fallen over the *dahabeeyah*. Minnie realized she hadn't seen a servant in hours. Not even the *reis*. Perhaps it was a day of religious observance. She found Leland sitting in the drawing room in his dressing gown, with a glass of whisky in his hand and all the shutters closed. Minnie was suddenly chilled.

"Leland, what is going on? Alicia has been locked away in her chamber and Tess looks as if she has been weeping."

He rose unsteadily. "Do not be concerned, my dear. I will see to it. It would be best if you go to your room."

She watched in dismay as he lurched past her, imagining that he was drunk. Everything had gone wrong in the past day, and she didn't know quite how—or exactly *what*.

She went out to the rail and watched the river flowing smooth and green. A rectangle of sheer cotton was caught further down and it waved like a flag. No, a veil . . .

A sense of déjà vu came over her. It reminded her of Mrs. Reed the only night they'd spoken aboard the *Rose of Sharon*. And she knew why the woman had looked so familiar, swathed in her veils. She was the same woman who had come to the foundling hospital, veiled and seeking a private interview with Alicia. Could Alicia have arranged for her to come to Egypt to have her child?

And why? What was the link?

Minnie hugged herself. She wished that it were still last evening at the villa, before she'd gone to fetch the mirror, when the world was a shining, wonderful place. When she had sat in this very room, dreaming wonderful dreams of the future. Most of all, she wished that Edgar was here to hold her and comfort her, and kiss away her fears.

Their relationship was too new to presume upon, and yet . . .

Calling for a manservant to deliver a message, she hurried to the writing desk and dashed off a hasty note. Unlike her usual style, it was short and to the point:

> Dearest Edgar,
>   Please come to me at once.
>   I need you.
>
>   Minnie

*   *   *

Tess's head was aching. She cringed when Alicia tapped at her door. "For the love of God, Tess, let me in. We must talk."

"Enough was said last night. Everything is a lie!"

But she opened the door. The tattered remnants of her affection for Alicia and Leland still fluttered amid the chaos. They had done what they thought was necessary. That they had not considered her feelings, or her morals, was another point entirely. All their lives, Alicia and Leland had only thought of one another.

Her sister-in-law entered. She had aged greatly in the span of a few hours. "I have not spoken to Leland yet."

When she had gone to him the previous night, he was

curled up on his side in poppy dreams. He looked so like the young boy she had loved and cared for, that it had almost broken her heart. Alicia had spent the night curled up beside him, holding him in her arms.

"Please don't leave, Tess. We can work this out."

"We went over all this," Tess said wearily. "How sure you were that I would be unfaithful to my vows! All my guilt and agony were for nothing! But I cannot stay here as Roman's mistress, in hopes that I will bear his child. I would not rob him of his rights as a father! How could you *think* it of me?"

"There are women who would think it well worth it, in order to wear a coronet! And there is a greater ratio of other men's children foisted upon the nobility, I daresay, than among the middle classes."

"Ah, yes. And they inherit, while the children of poor young women like Mrs. Reed are condemned to foundling hospitals!"

Alicia blanched. "Do not speak of her, I beg you!"

"Why? What was she, insurance, in case I didn't conceive a child by Roman?" For a moment Tess thought Alicia would faint with fear. Her skin looked gray and lifeless, and her hands shook.

Something else became clear to Tess, like a dense fog lifting. "You befriended Mrs. Reed on board. Or, perhaps the friendship started even earlier?"

"Do not blame me for her death!" Alicia shook her head. "I meant nothing but good. She was a governess, and had been ill-used by the master of the house against her will. When he learned she was with child, he threw her into the streets without a penny. At first I meant only to help her through her delivery, and place her child in the foundling home. I swear it. You must believe me, dearest Tess."

"Do not call me that! I am nothing more to you than a

chess piece. And I cannot believe you if you say the sky is blue and the grass green. Lies spill from your mouth like water from a torrent.''

Alicia knelt beside Tess. ''No! I thought that I would help a young woman in need, and perhaps help our cause as well. If you conceived by your lover, Leland would have set her up here as a young widow. If you did not, it would be wise to have another plan in place.''

''Lady Alicia Evershot, the great organizer.'' Tess's voice dripped bitterness. ''Keeping half a dozen schemes up in the air, like a circus juggler. And to think I once admired your skills!''

''Forgive me. I misjudged your motives in marrying my brother. I thought that fear of losing everything if Leland . . . if Leland . . .''

She could not say the fatal word. ''If anything *untoward* happened . . . That fear would force you to agree to adopting her child as your own.''

Tess rubbed her temples. ''Last evening you told me that Leland had married me in good faith. *Was* that the truth?''

''You are young and beautiful,'' Alicia answered. ''Leland married you with every expectation of fulfilling his obligations toward you as a husband.''

''He had no reason to doubt he could do so?''

She looked at Tess, dull-eyed. ''None at all. I was sure . . . *we* were sure that Leland would be able to consummate his marriage with you. *I* knew, far better than anyone, that he had never had the slightest difficulty in the past!''

''How can I believe anything you tell me? There seems to be no end to the lies and wickedness.''

''Perhaps it is best that the Claybourne line end. There is something wrong with us. We cannot love like other people.'' Alicia took a deep breath. ''We can only love each other.''

Tess froze. Yes, she should have seen it. "I knew the attachment between you and Leland ran deep. I hadn't guessed that it was unnatural, as well."

"Do not look at me like that," Alicia said, weeping. "What could have been more natural? *We were children!* Thrown together by fear and loneliness." She lifted her chin. "And only later, by desire.

"At the time it had not seemed wrong to comfort one another by whatever means we could. Surely God will forgive us that—we are being punished enough in this lifetime."

Tess could think of nothing to say. Once, as a child, she had fallen from a tree and stunned herself. She felt like that now. The world had turned topsy-turvy, but she was completely numb.

Alicia rose. "No doubt you despise me."

Tess reached out and took the other woman's hand. "Was there no one to help you?" she said softly. "No one to whom you could turn?"

"Why would we need to?" Alicia shrugged. "We had each other. It was sufficient for both of us."

Shock made Tess frank. "And so you never married."

"How could I? Any man would know immediately that I was not a virgin."

It was mind-boggling. Tess could scarcely reel it all in. She understood Alicia's obsession with children. "It is fortunate that . . . that you never came to be with child."

Alicia's eyes went wide and dark. The truth was written all over her face. "We hid it from the world. He was born in the little airless passage between our bedchambers. We were terrified. So much pain! And blood! Leland has never forgiven himself. And from that horrible day, he has never been able to . . ."

She broke down in tears. Tess overcame her repulsion and went to her then, and took her sister-in-law's cold hands in hers. "Poor Alicia. How frightened you must have been! What . . . what happened to the child?"

"I have never asked. Leland sent for Audley. We didn't know where else to turn, and he had always been fond of us. He took the child away, and carried me off to his country seat to recuperate—from 'influenza' is what the world was told. That is why I cannot bear to look at him. He is the only person in the world, besides yourself and Leland, who knows my shame. His disgust lashes me anew every time I see him."

Tess saw more than Alicia realized. Still locked in an incestuous relationship with her brother begun in childhood, she had been well on her way to falling in love with her cousin. What a tragedy!

"I think you do him wrong. Audley has never spoken of you except with respect and concern."

"I need to think, Alicia. Give me time to gather my thoughts." And to talk to Roman. Everything had changed so drastically. A terrible knowledge had been growing on her with every passing moment. She remembered Leland's disappearance the morning of Mrs. Reed's death. The arguing between Alicia and Leland on their carriage ride out to the excavation site, and Alicia's tear-swollen eyes upon arrival.

"One more thing! I must ask it, I have no choice. Did Leland have anything to do with her death? Was it truly suicide, or had she threatened to tell me the truth?"

Alicia's face was white and immobile as stone. Her eyes were bleak and empty. "I will not answer that."

A frisson of fear ran along Tess's spine. *A wind from the grave*, her father had used to call that sensation. "There is nothing more for us to say, then. Please leave me, Alicia. I need to be alone with my thoughts."

"What do you intend to do?"

"I have no choice. I shall seek an annulment as soon as possible."

Alicia's color came flooding back. "Why not wait until Leland is dead?" she asked bitterly. "You will not have long to kick your heels before hurrying back to your *lover*."

She went out and closed the door.

Leland was standing in the dim corridor. Alicia faced him. "Tess knows all. Do not despair! You know that she is Roman's mistress. If we are lucky, she will still bear a child—a healthy child—to claim your title!"

Then she pushed past him and ran out along the deck.

Meanwhile, Tess hurried to her desk. She would write to Roman immediately. They had to get Minnie safely out of this house of secrets. He would think of something.

There was a commotion outside on the riverbank. Someone had just arrived, and Tess had no patience to deal with it. She rubbed the back of her neck. The headache that had nagged at the fringes of her mind was rapidly getting worse. Where was the bottle of tonic that Dr. Peltier had given her?

Rummaging through her reticule, she produced the small, ornate blue bottle. She didn't hear the door open behind her. As she tipped her head back and swallowed the bitter draught, she heard a cry of rage behind her.

Leland recognized that small blue bottle.

Someone seized her hair and jerked her head back with the howl of a beast. It turned her blood cold.

"Stop!" Leland cried. "You will not cheat me of an heir! You will not deprive Alicia of her due!"

It was too late. The bottle fell from Tess's hand and shattered. Empty.

From the corner of her eye, Tess saw the letter opener gleaming in his hand. She rose and tried to dodge the blade. The chair overturned. "How dare you!" he cried, yanking her hair until tears blinded her. She realized that she might not leave the room alive.

Something solid whizzed by her head and smashed into the looking glass above the desk. The sound was startlingly loud. Alicia had thrown a glass paperweight at her brother. "No, Leland. You must not kill her!"

"She drank the potion. The bitch drank the potion! There will be no child to save you, Alicia." His voice broke. "My Alicia!"

Tess wanted to scream but her throat was closed up tight. He held the dagger against her throat and she felt the sharp edge press against her flesh. In a moment it would be over. *Oh, Roman!*

Minnie ran into the room, howling like a banshee. "Don't touch her! Leave Tess alone!"

There was a sudden, hard blow . . . a sharp jerk . . . a liquid gurgle. Then Leland sagged away from her, and the dagger fell from his hand. He crumpled to the floor, and lay unmoving. Roman stood in the doorway. The heavy hunting knife he'd thrown protruded from Leland's throat. It had passed clear through, like a knife in cheese.

The tip of the blade lay against the carpet, wet and red with blood.

Tess couldn't quite take it in. It had all happened so quickly. A mere split second to change the outcome of so many lives, forever.

Alicia began to scream. Her grief was heart-rending. "No! Leland, my darling! My precious love!"

Falling on her knees beside his bloodstained body, she pressed him close to her heart and keened. It was the most horrible sound Tess had ever heard, filled with anguish and drained of all human hope.

Tess felt the blood drain from her head. Her knees buckled, but Roman was there instantly, to hold her up in his encircling arms. She leaned into the hard strength of him.

"It's over," she murmured. "It's *over!*"

"No, my dearest darling, my heart of hearts," Roman whispered as he rocked her gently. "It is just beginning."

Epilogue

Midnight, in a room painted the color of roses.

"Roman! I love you so much."

He laughed down into Tess's eyes. "I love you more."

"Impossible!"

"Then let us say I love you to infinity."

As he worshiped her with his body, to prove it, light reflected from the plain gold band upon her finger, inset with a square emerald. After ten years and four children, she was still as beautiful as the first day he saw her. And as desirable.

Tess ran her mouth across his chest, bringing his nipples erect. Felt him grow and swell as she arched to welcome him. Later, she snuggled in Roman's arms and looked back along the path of time.

Ten years ago, she had thought her life as a woman was over. She chuckled against his hard shoulder. She had been as wrong about that as she was regarding Lord Brocklehurst's parentage. He was Audley's son, and despite Minnie's mellowing influence, grew more like his father every day. Which was not, Tess thought, a bad thing at all.

"Why are you laughing?" Roman said, caressing her back with his strong hands. "Share the joke with me."

"I have something better to share with you." Tess

arched her breasts against him and welcomed him once more.

Roman grinned down at her. "I am certainly up to the task."

Tess matched him kiss for kiss, stroke for stroke, urging him to love her completely. Later—much later—she would tell him that there would be a fifth child in the spring. A girl, this time. A magical child, born of their love and passion.

She knew, because she had dreamed of her many times. And because, once upon a time, she had seen her laughing face in a certain mirror of polished bronze. The mirror had vanished from the sheik's villa, while Roman had been riding like a wildman to her rescue.

He nuzzled the nape of her neck. She always smelled like roses to him. "What are you thinking of, lying awake so quietly?"

Of Alicia, living alone and running her many charity works with efficiency and humility. People spoke of her as a saint. Tess did not dispute it. Of Audley, who watched her from a distance, yet was always there to help her if need be. *Like a wolf dog, guarding a lost sheep.* Of Judith, happily married to an American cattle rancher—and of course, of Minnie and Edward, who lived a stone's throw away with their delightfully eccentric brood of little scientists and would-be novelists.

Life was good.

"I was thinking of the mirror, and how everything seemed to start with it. And sometimes I wonder—why us? And other times I regret that it was lost because of me. That we will never know its history."

The mirror had not turned up since its disappearance, to their knowledge.

Roman smoothed her hair. "I have no regrets, love. I've

lived long enough to learn that some things are not meant to be.'' He kissed her shoulder. ''And some, like us, just are.''

Tess smiled. That was how she felt about the new child. She was *meant* to be.

They drifted off to sleep in each other's arms, while the desert moon rode high.

The mirror dreams. Not the weight of centuries nor the crush of rocks can harm it. The thief who stole it from Roman McKendrick's desk at the villa could not fathom its magic. It is the mirror that chooses to whom It will reveal itself.

Its reasons are its own.

It was the mirror's visions that so frightened a potential buyer, he flung it overboard, into the smooth green waters of the Nile.

While two lovers sleep in a room the color of rose, the mirror shimmers in the midnight blackness of the water, amid the muck and reeds.

Years pass, and still the mirror dreams. Machines, like mechanical insects, swoop through the skies bearing pleasure seekers toward the sun of tropical lands. Huge cities rise.

And fall.

Ice covers the earth with terrible cold. Humankind survives, but does not learn. From vanity and urge for power, a gigantic crystal cracks in the center of an island paradise. The land sinks and people scatter to the earth's four corners. The plains of Egypt absorb them, the jungles of a land bridge in the new world welcome them, and the jungles of the old world hide their histories in tangles of vine and stone. The mountains between what will someday become Spain and France offer shelter to still others.

And still the mirror dreams, backward and forward in

time. Time, which circles in upon itself like the oval rim of the mirror.

The burnished surface shivers and scintillates below the Nile's water.

A star falls all through the night. Out of the mists a man comes limping, with a smile on his face and all the knowledge of the stars in his head.

Pyramids rise amid the sands of Egypt. Generals fight mighty wars with horses, chariots, and carapaces of dull green metal. Man-made clouds rise up from the ground. Marble cities gleam bright in the night sky over Earth.

The mirror blooms with all the colors of the rainbow, but there is no one to see its magic or unlock the power at the heart of its mystery.

Yet.

Seasons and centuries pass. A young child awakens from a dream early one morning. While her parents and brothers sleep, she leaves their house and walks gracefully down to the river. It flows, green and eternal, bringing the gift of life to those who live along its banks. Today it has a special gift, for a very special child.

The girl plunges into the shallows of the Nile, parting the reeds that bend aside, almost bow to her touch. Diving deep, she reaches inside the blackness between the reeds, already knowing what she will find.

Her small hand closes firmly about the handle of twisted lotus stems as she pulls it to the surface. Sunlight bursts upon the surface of the mirror and reflects from the girl's stormy blue eyes. There is a smile on her face as she gazes into it, and a faint stirring of the knowledge of the stars in her heart. There is so much to learn. The mirror has chosen.

One lesson, she was born knowing: of the myriad things that humankind creates, evil always is vanquished. It is only love that endures.

Survey

TELL US WHAT YOU THINK AND YOU COULD WIN

A YEAR OF ROMANCE!
(That's 12 books!)

Fill out the survey below, send it back to us, and you'll be eligible to win a year's worth of romance novels. That's one book a month for a year—from St. Martin's Paperbacks.

Name _____

Street Address _____

City, State, Zip Code _____

Email address _____

1. How many romance books have you bought in the last year?
   (Check one.)
   __0-3
   __4-7
   __8-12
   __13-20
   __20 or more

2. Where do you MOST often buy books? *(limit to two choices)*
   __Independent bookstore
   __Chain stores *(Please specify)*
       __Barnes and Noble
       __B. Dalton
       __Books-a-Million
       __Borders
       __Crown
       __Lauriat's
       __Media Play
       __Waldenbooks
   __Supermarket
   __Department store *(Please specify)*
       __Caldor
       __Target
       __Kmart
       __Walmart
   __Pharmacy/Drug store
   __Warehouse Club
   __Airport

3. Which of the following promotions would MOST influence your decision to purchase a ROMANCE paperback? *(Check one.)*
       __Discount coupon

   __Free preview of the first chapter
   __Second book at half price
   __Contribution to charity
   __Sweepstakes or contest

4. Which promotions would LEAST influence your decision to purchase a ROMANCE book? (Check one.)
   __Discount coupon
   __Free preview of the first chapter
   __Second book at half price
   __Contribution to charity
   __Sweepstakes or contest

5. When a new ROMANCE paperback is released, what is MOST influential in your finding out about the book and in helping you to decide to buy the book? (Check one.)
   __TV advertisement
   __Radio advertisement
   __Print advertising in newspaper or magazine
   __Book review in newspaper or magazine
   __Author interview in newspaper or magazine
   __Author interview on radio
   __Author appearance on TV
   __Personal appearance by author at bookstore
   __In-store publicity (poster, flyer, floor display, etc.)
   __Online promotion (author feature, banner advertising, giveaway)
   __Word of Mouth
   __Other (please specify)_____

6. Have you ever purchased a book online?
   __Yes
   __No

7. Have you visited our website?
   __Yes
   __No

8. Would you visit our website in the future to find out about new releases or author interviews?
   __Yes
   __No

9. What publication do you read most?
   __Newspapers *(check one)*
     __*USA Today*
     __*New York Times*
     __Your local newspaper
   __Magazines *(check one)*

__People
　　__Entertainment Weekly
　　__Women's magazine (Please specify:_____)
　　__Romantic Times
　　__Romance newsletters

10. What type of TV program do you watch most? (Check one.)
　　__Morning News Programs (ie. "Today Show")
　　(Please specify:_____)
　　__Afternoon Talk Shows (ie. "Oprah")
　　(Please specify: _____)
　　__All news (such as CNN)
　　__Soap operas   (Please specify: _____)
　　__Lifetime cable station
　　__E! cable station
　　__Evening magazine programs (ie. "Entertainment Tonight")
　　(Please specify: _____)
　　__Your local news

11. What radio stations do you listen to most? (Check one.)
　　__Talk Radio
　　__Easy Listening/Classical
　　__Top 40
　　__Country
　　__Rock
　　__Lite rock/Adult contemporary
　　__CBS radio network
　　__National Public Radio
　　__WESTWOOD ONE radio network

12. What time of day do you listen to the radio MOST?
　　__6am-10am
　　__10am-noon
　　__Noon-4pm
　　__4pm-7pm
　　__7pm-10pm
　　__10pm-midnight
　　__Midnight-6am

13. Would you like to receive email announcing new releases and special promotions?
　　__Yes
　　__No

14. Would you like to receive postcards announcing new releases and special promotions?
　　__Yes
　　__No

15. Who is your favorite romance author? _____

WIN A YEAR OF ROMANCE FROM SMP
(That's 12 Books!)
No Purchase Necessary

OFFICIAL RULES

1. To Enter: Complete the Official Entry Form and Survey and mail it to: Win a Year of Romance from SMP Sweepstakes, c/o St. Martin's Paperbacks, 175 Fifth Avenue, Suite 1615, New York, NY 10010-7848, Attention JP. For a copy of the Official Entry Form and Survey, send a self-addressed, stamped envelope to: Entry Form/Survey, c/o St. Martin's Paperbacks at the address stated above. Entries with the completed surveys must be received by February 1, 2000 (February 22, 2000 for entry forms requested by mail). Limit one entry per person. No mechanically reproduced or illegible entries accepted. Not responsible for lost, misdirected, mutilated or late entries.

2. Random Drawing. Winner will be determined in a random drawing to be held on or about March 1, 2000 from all eligible entries received. Odds of winning depend on the number of eligible entries received. Potential winner will be notified by mail on or about March 22, 2000 and will be asked to execute and return an Affidavit of Eligibility/Release/Prize Acceptance Form within fourteen (14) days of attempted notification. Non-compliance within this time may result in disqualification and the selection of an alternate winner. Return of any prize/prize notification as undeliverable will result in disqualification and an alternate winner will be selected.

3. Prize and approximate Retail Value: Winner will receive a copy of a different romance novel each month from April 2000 through March 2001. Approximate retail value $84.00 (U.S. dollars).

4. Eligibility. Open to U.S. and Canadian residents (excluding residents of the province of Quebec) who are 18 at the time of entry. Employees of St. Martin's and its parent, affiliates and subsidiaries, its and their directors, officers and agents, and their immediate families or those living in the same household, are ineligible to enter. Potential Canadian winners will be required to correctly answer a time-limited arithmetic skill question by mail. Void in Puerto Rico and wherever else prohibited by law.

5. General Conditions: Winner is responsible for all federal, state and local taxes. No substitution or cash redemption of prize permitted by winner. Prize is not transferable. Acceptance of prize constitutes permission to use the winner's name, photograph and likeness for purposes of advertising and promotion without additional compensation or permission, unless prohibited by law.

6. All entries become the property of sponsor, and will not be returned. By participating in this sweepstakes, entrants agree to be bound by these official rules and the decision of the judges, which are final in all respects.

7. For the name of the winner, available after March 22, 2000, send by May 1, 2000 a stamped, self-addressed envelope to Winner's List, Win a Year of Romance from SMP Sweepstakes, St. Martin's Paperbacks, 175 Fifth Avenue, Suite 1615, New York, NY 10010-7848, Attention JP.